A Raven Bound with Lilies

Stories of the Wraeththu Mythos

Dedication

Ruby, this one's for you,
for how your inspired and visionary artwork
has brought my characters
and the world of Wraeththu to life,
since the early days, now, and into the future.
Thank you.

A Raven Bound with Lilies

Stories of the Wraeththu Mythos

Storm Constantine

IMMANION PRESS
Stafford England

A Raven Bound with Lilies: Stories of the Wraeththu Mythos
By Storm Constantine
© 2017

This is a work of fiction. All the characters and events portrayed in this book are fictitious, and any resemblance to real people, or events, is purely coincidental.

http://www.stormconstantine.co.uk

ISBN 978-1-907737-80-0

IP0131

Cover art by Ruby
Cover design and interior layout by Storm Constantine
Illustrations: Ruby, Wraeththu Mythos logo, pages 10, 35, 36, 165, 202, 226, 258, 262, 286; Storm Constantine, pages 82, 102 and raven glyph; Danielle Lainton page 166

Set in Book Antiqua

An Immanion Press Edition
http://www.immanion-press.com
info@immanion-press.com

Books by Storm Constantine

The Wraeththu Chronicles
The Enchantments of Flesh and Spirit
The Bewitchments of Love and Hate
The Fulfilments of Fate and Desire
The Wraeththu Chronicles (omnibus of trilogy)

The Wraeththu Histories
The Wraiths of Will and Pleasure
The Shades of Time and Memory
The Ghosts of Blood and Innocence

The Alba Sulh Sequence
The Hienama
Student of Kyme
The Moonshawl

Blood, the Phoenix and a Rose

The Artemis Cycle
The Monstrous Regiment
Aleph

The Grigori Books
Stalking Tender Prey
Scenting Hallowed Blood
Stealing Sacred Fire

The Magravandias Chronicles:
Sea Dragon Heir
Crown of Silence
The Way of Light

Hermetech
Burying the Shadow
Sign for the Sacred
*Calenture
Thin Air

*Silverheart (with Michael Moorcock)

All books listed are available as Immanion Press editions except for those marked with *

The Wraeththu

A Brief Definition of Their Origin

Humanity is in decline, ravaged by insanity, natural disasters, conflict, disease and infertility. A mysterious new race has risen from the ghettos and ruins of the decaying, dying cities. The young are evolving into a new species, which is stronger, sharper and more beautiful than their forerunners. Androgynous beings, they transcend gender and race. They possess keen psychic abilities and the means, through a process called inception, to transform humans into creatures like themselves. But they are wild in their rebirth, and must strive to overcome all that is human within them in order to create society anew. They are the Wraeththu...

A Word on Pronouns

Within the Wraeththu Mythos, hara are referred to as 'he', since back in the 1980s when I first started writing within the mythos, this pronoun seemed to me less gender specific than 'she'. A lot has changed in both culture and language since then, but to glue a new pronoun over all the stories would feel at best clunky and contrived. I ask readers to look beyond the loaded meaning of the male pronoun, and to read it as non-gender specific.

Storm Constantine

The Alchemical Hermaphrodite

Among the seven planets, I am called the Sun.
My pointed crown symbolises the process:
First, we become completely subtle and pure
And bind with Mercury.
Then the black raven grows.
It is buried in the grave,
Rising anew,
Adorned with lilies, and betrothed.
Then at last the Sun-Child appears,
Bedecked with purple on his throne.

...I'm neither male nor female.
Rather, I have both genders.
My flesh and blood prove it.
My blood is male, my flesh female.
The power of both is spiritual.
I have both male and female organs.
So people call me a hermaphrodite.
My treasure is the Earth Element,
where there are minerals, metals, and such.
Yet I'm nothing that you may suppose.
I am One Substance by my nature.

From *'Hermaphrodite Child of the Sun and the Moon'*
translated by Mike Brenner, 1997

O Turba of Philosophers and disciples,
now hast thou spoken about making into white,
but it yet remains to treat concerning the reddening!
Know, all ye seekers after this Art,
that unless ye whiten, ye cannot make red,
because the two natures are nothing other than red and white.
Whiten, therefore, the red, and redden the white!

From the seventeenth dictum
of the 12th century *Turba Philosophorum*

Contents

From Enchantments to a Raven

When I was writing the first Wraeththu novel, *The Enchantments of Flesh and Spirit*, I had no idea that, over thirty years on, I'd still be so immersed in that world, and writing novels and stories about it. Since 1985, when I first began working seriously on the Wraeththu Mythos, I've written nine Wraeththu novels, comprising three trilogies. (This is aside from the other fourteen novels I've written, six non-fiction titles, and dozens of short stories.) In addition, Immanion Press has published 'shared world' anthologies, edited by Wendy Darling and me, in which other writers contributed stories to the Wraeththu Mythos. There have been four of these anthologies to date, and we're currently working on compiling a fifth. These books are affectionately referred to as the 'Para' collections, since the first one was named for its title story 'Paragenesis', and the other three all had titles beginning with 'Para'. I contributed two stories each to these collections.

Last year, I also published three connected novellas, under the title *Blood, the Phoenix and a Rose*. But that mini-trilogy started life as something completely different. It was supposed to be the book you now have in your hands.

Initially, the idea was to collect all my published Wraeththu short stories in one volume. In addition to these, I had on my computer, (and also on old typed-up pages), half-written stories I'd never got around to finishing, several dating back nearly forty years. A few of them I'd already plundered for tales that appeared in the 'Para' anthologies, but there were still plenty to work on. My plan was to complete these stories and include them in the collection.

The first of these was 'Song of the Cannibals', of which I'd written only three pages, way back in 1988. Not long after I began work on the piece, 1 realised it wasn't simply a short story, because the characters showed me more of what was going on in the house of Sallow Gandaloi, where the tale is set. I was eager to uncover all the secrets with them. Once I'd finished writing it, I knew at once of two other stories connected with it that just had to be told. These were 'Half Sick of Shadows' and 'A Pyramid of

Lions'. They filled an entire book between them, so my story collection temporarily had to be put aside.

Now, nearly two years since I had the original idea, I've had time to compile this book. I'm glad about this delay, as it allows me to include two stories that would otherwise have been missed out, as they'd only just been written for *Para Animalia*. I feel it's appropriate now to include them in another book so that this volume includes all the Wraeththu tales I've so far completed.

As well as the published stories, I've included a few poems, dating back to 1977. The other material is four prose pieces that are, in two cases, juvenilia. The remaining two are simply curios – ideas I had and ran with a short way, but didn't pursue. I haven't tampered with any of these four pieces too much, except for tidying up sloppy grammar, or excising instances of excruciating purple prose here and there, nor have I extended them into full-length tales. They are fragments, one of them hefty, since I intended it to be a novel.

The earlier pieces hark back to the 1970s, before I'd even worked out what the Wraeththu *were* in any detail. 'The First Inception' must have been written as early as 1973, when I was still at art college.

When I went back to all this material a few years ago, after decades of it being stored in old folders – physically in a filing cabinet, and on my computer – it was a revelation, because I'd forgotten so much of it. I can remember writing Wraeththu poems and stories round about 1977, but had forgotten that my first forays into harish territory had begun far earlier. It's interesting that even in these early stories, I was playing with the idea of inception, that Wraeththu blood can 'turn' a human, even though I had yet to develop a proper structure for the procedure. Interesting too to be reminded that Lianvis, a relatively minor character in *The Enchantments of Flesh and Spirit*, was one of the first hara I created.

Jarad, Lianvis's companion in the story, is the same har who appears in 'Pro Lucror', which also appeared in the *Paragenesis* anthology, published in 2011. I recall I wrote quite a bit about this character at one time, but sadly most of it has been lost. Jarad eventually evolved into a salient figure in Wraeththu lore, but it was only a few years ago, while I was writing 'Pro Lucror' that I decided to give him that persona.

The second piece of juvenilia, 'The Ruins Walker', was my first attempt to write the book that become *The Enchantments of Flesh and Spirit*. This early prototype appeared in a less edited form in the UK edition of *Shades of Time and Memory*, but for this book I've tidied it up a bit more, as well as given it a title. Initially, I tried to write my first Wraeththu novel from a human girl's perspective, but I abandoned it after only twenty pages or so, because that viewpoint was limited in terms of the story, and prevented me from describing the Wraeththu fully. I needed a harish character's viewpoint, and I didn't begin work on this until around 1984. This was because I didn't know who the character would be, or what his voice was like. After I'd ditched the first attempt, I went back to the idea a year or so later, and began to write in this unknown har's voice. But I didn't gel with him, and although quite a few pages of that remain, I didn't take it any further. The elusive character who was meant to tell the tale didn't come to me properly for a long time. It was only when the first few paragraphs arrived in my head, in one fluid rush, and the character Pellaz made himself known to me, that I was ready to write that novel. Prior to that, I'd only written lots of fragments, as well as poems and unfinished stories.

I can't remember now what I intended to do with Cereia, the female protagonist of 'The Ruins Walker'. The opening paragraphs are very similar to those of *The Enchantments of Flesh and Spirit*. She sits upon a balcony in the city of Immanion to write her life story. It's implied she's no longer human, so perhaps I envisaged her becoming Kamagrian, although the term for this more feminine aspect of Wraeththu didn't emerge until I was writing the second book in *The Wraeththu Chronicles*. Unfortunately, I can't remember, and I didn't leave myself any notes! When I reread Cereia's story, her strong voice came through time. I was surprised at how well some of her story had been written by that very young and inexperienced writer all those years ago.

The other two pieces are more recent. The first of these, 'The Lion of Oomar', was written some time in the late 80s. Originally, it was going to be a short story, but then, when I was putting ideas together for novels to follow the *Wraeththu Chronicles*, I decided to adapt it to tell the tale of how the Maudrah tribe of

Jaddayoth was created. However, the patois-style voice I'd used originally for the short story was difficult to maintain, and I was daunted by the thought of trying to keep it consistent throughout a full-length work. I abandoned the piece, and then never got around to writing the novel with a different narrator. I've now given the story a conclusion of sorts – well, enough to have ended a chapter with – and have included it here as a curio.

The second piece was written not long after I finished work on *The Bewitchments of Love and Hate*. It comprises a few pages from the diary of Tyson har Parasiel, the son of Cal and Terzian, who were among the main characters in *Bewitchments*. I wondered how Tyson would be able to live with the legacy of his parents, how this might affect how others saw him. I scribbled a few pages of his diary as an experiment, almost as notes for a later story or book, but they never got used. For this collection, I finished off the fragment, by adding the last section in which Tyson talks on his birthday with his brother Swift.

As for the other stories, they all have a history and a reason for being, so I'll talk a little about each one. The tales are presented in in this book in chronological order – not of when they were written, but when they take place in Wraeththu history.

'Paragenesis' is the 'creation myth' of Wraeththu, concerning the first har of all. The story was originally written for the anthology *The Crow: Shattered Lives and Broken Dreams*, (edited by James O'Barr, published by Donald M Grant, 1998), even though it has nothing to do with The Crow mythos. The editor simply asked me to write something attached to the theme of being an outsider, or different, maybe in a ravaged world: it was so long ago, the memory of the specifics has gone! But I do recall I asked him if I could write a Wraeththu origins story, and he gave me permission to do so. It tells the story of Thiede growing up in the shattered remains of human civilisation – knowing he was different, and not sure what that difference meant. This, rather than the fragment I mentioned earlier, is the true 'first inception', when Thiede creates a companion to be like himself: Orien. The wise seer Orien became a very important figure in Wraeththu lore, and his tale ended tragically.

When Wendy and I published *Paragenesis* in 2011, this story provided both the title and the first tale of the book.

'Pro Lucror', as I've said, evolved from a fragment I had from years ago, involving the characters Jarad and Lianvis. I expanded the original idea greatly. The story involves the early years of the savage Uigenna tribe, when the leader Manticker the Seventy was challenged and defeated by Wraxilan, the Lion of Oomar. These events are mentioned briefly in the third Wraeththu novel, *The Fulfilments of Fate and Desire*, and more deeply in the sixth novel, *Ghosts of Blood and Innocence*, but I was keen to expand upon the story, as it's such an important part of Wraeththu history. Jarad, a bitter har, is a reluctant agent for Wraxilan. It's not that he doesn't agree with Wraxilan's vision for the tribe's future; he simply doesn't care, and would prefer to be left alone. But when a har as powerful as Wraxilan demands something from you, it would be folly to refuse. At the end of this story, it's revealed who Jarad eventually became.

When I reread this story, I could 'see the joins', in that the first section is the older material, polished up a bit, but this flows into the new writing, and I think you can tell when that happens. However, I've resisted tinkering with it, because in a way that shift of style is appropriate. Jarad moves from a dead life back into what he truly is. He wakes up, begins to heal, finds his own power.

As to the meaning of the title, it derives from my activities in the MMORPG *World of Warcraft*, and is rather an in-joke with my WoW friends. There's a saying in online gaming, which is ftw or 'for the win'. It means being the best, the greatest, the most cool, or sure to succeed, and there are other, more subtle meanings it's almost impossible to describe outside of the game. Years ago, a friend was creating a new guild in WoW, and he put 'for the win' into an English-Latin translation application. It came up with Pro Lucror. As Uigenna hara might very well have responded to the question 'why the hell are you following this unstable maniac Wraxilan?' with the words 'for the win', it seemed an appropriate title!

'By the River of If Only, In the Land of Might Have Been' was the first Wraeththu short story I actually finished. I wrote it for a fanzine that was produced by the creative collective 'Thirteenth Key', which formed to promote the Wraeththu Mythos in the late 80s. This magazine was the first publication to be given the name 'Paragenesis' and, in many ways, was the prototype for the later

'Para' anthologies, since other writers contributed stories to it. 'By the River of If Only' has a dreamlike, fairy-tale ambience, and features the Obliviata tribe, who were one of the originals, even if they've not had a great deal written about them since.

'Beneath My Skin, a Vein of You' is one of my favourites, which I loved writing. It appeared in *Para Animalia*, an anthology about Wraeththu's relationship with the natural world, which came out in 2016. The tale came to me fully-fledged, with a strong narrator and a powerful ambience. It's inspired by stories of people who simply disappear for no reason. They're never found, and no one knows if they're alive or dead. And maybe, if they do come back, they're not quite the same.

I've developed a fondness for exploring rural Wraeththu communities, who live close to the land and are attuned to it. I've written a lot about the savage beginnings of Wraeththu, and also about the political intrigues of its ruling tribes, but what interests me at the moment are ordinary hara, who cannot help but lead extraordinary lives, because of what they are.

'Clouds Like Hair' is a Wraeththu fairy-tale I wrote for *Para Animalia*, based very loosely on versions of the old folktale published by Hans Christian Anderson and The Brothers Grimm – 'The Wild Swans' and 'The Six Swans' respectively. My story concerns a very different community to the one I wrote about in 'Beneath my Skin…', but they also live close to the land. It's a cautionary tale, told by a hostling to his harling, and warns of the dangers of the forest, where magic and its denizens are strong.

'Without Weakness' appeared in *Para Kindred* in 2014. This was one of the stories I developed from an elderly fragment – literally a single page of writing. It features two fairly major characters from the first two trilogies – Ashmael Aldebaran, a high-ranking har in the Gelaming army, and Katarin, a Kamagrian 'parage'. Neither of these characters were in the original piece, which simply featured a group of humans waiting in terror for a brutal Wraeththu tribe that was fast approaching their enclave. All that remains of the original piece is the dread that was invoked in it. But, of course, the arrival of Wraeththu is far from the end for these people. There wouldn't be a story otherwise.

To accompany the release of *Para Kindred*, we organised a 'blog special', in which all the contributing authors wrote short 'sequels' to their tales that appeared online over a series of days. 'A Social Incident' is my sequel to 'Without Weakness'. To say anything about it would be a major spoiler.

'Painted Skin' was also written for *Para Kindred*, which was an anthology that explored how weird strains of hara might have developed in hidden corners of the world. The piece was new and didn't include any old material. It was inspired by figures from Scandinavian folklore, and what might happen if someone, or something, who wasn't human became incepted. Perhaps, once humanity had gone, these beings might emerge and hide within harish society – or perhaps that could be wishful thinking on behalf of a har seeking magic in his life. The city of Trisque and its harish inhabitants felt very real to me as I was writing the tale, as did the mysterious clock-maker who beguiles the protagonist. It remains one of my favourite mythos stories.

'The Elle Har', which follows this tale, is the blog sequel I wrote to help promote the book.

'Beyond a Veil of Stars' is another story developed from a very early piece. It was originally entitled 'The Claws of Wraeththu', and I began writing it after my first novel came out. I remember having to read some of it aloud for a radio interview, and my mother, who used to be an elocution teacher, taught me how to recite it properly, as an actor would. But again, I never finished the story. It sort of lost its way, and I wrote myself into a hole from which I couldn't escape.

In the early 2000s, I offered the incomplete story to a Wraeththu fan fiction group and light-heartedly challenged them to finish it, with several writers contributing a few pages each. Because it was a fun project among friends, it ended up a little silly, and it was only when I was looking through my old stories to find something to adapt for *Para Imminence* in 2012 that I hoiked out the original first half and knocked it into shape.

Para Imminence contained tales about the future of Wraeththu, and again it's difficult for me to say much about the story without giving spoilers. It involves a human community, and one of their members being afflicted by a mysterious illness so serious that the people turn to the unthinkable in search of a cure.

The final story, 'A Tour of the House' was inspired by a visit to a local stately home – Shugborough Hall, which had once been the seat of the earls of Lichfield. The last inhabitant was Patrick Lichfield, famous for his photography. After he died, his private apartments were opened to the public, and were kept pretty much as he left them. I felt it was an intrusion into his life. The walls were adorned with all the photos of his famous friends back in the 60s – musicians, actors and actresses, and so on. I wondered what wild tales the wall could tell, if only they could speak, and felt sad that all those pretty, wild young things were now either old and withered, or dead. From the feelings I took away with me, 'A Tour of the House' was born. It appeared in *Para Imminence*, and concerns a descendant of the Tigron Pellaz going to visit the house *We Dwell in Forever*, hundreds of years after the events of the first novels took place. I wanted to invoke those feelings I'd had, and found it very enjoyable to write, even if it is somewhat wistful in tone.

Storm Constantine
June 2017

Paragenesis

I have scars upon my left hand, but not upon my right. If I hold my hands up to the eternal sun, light shines through the flesh. But there is no flesh. I am idea, essence. I am the flash of sunlight off chrome. I am the seasons. I am the shadow beneath the eaves. I am a scrap of litter scratching across cracked asphalt. No, I am bones and blood. I am crude and heavy. I am what I am.

When I was sixteen, I ran away from my leaf-shrouded home in the enclave for the rich, about twelve miles from the city centre. Perhaps it began as a suicide bid. All I did was move my limbs, without conscious volition, toward the wilderness of stone and glass that circled the city itself like a plague. It was the hinterland of decay, spreading both outward and inward, threatening city core and enclave alike. People could lose themselves there, and I wanted to be lost.

I remember that day; she was standing at the kitchen sink with her back to me. She could always sense when I walked into the room. I'd see her spine tense beneath its dress of cotton, its caul of skin. How cruel had Mother Nature been to make her spawn a child she could only fear? Blessed was the day when she no longer had to touch me, when I could feed and bathe myself, tie my own laces, rub my own hurts. I could not despise her, for I shared her bewilderment, her bitterness. When I'd been born, no doubt she'd decided to make the best of it. I was a beautiful child, but for those hidden abnormalities. Later, she probably realised that even monsters could be beautiful. My father was a non-entity, consumed by work. We rarely saw him. Our home always seemed empty, when she and I were in it together. The spaces between us were too great, and as I grew older, they became gulfs.

On that final day, I could not bear to see that stiffening spine any longer. She had birthed me and raised me; now her responsibility was over. I turned around and walked away, out of the shady house into the sunlight, past the bike lying on the tarmac, where a few red leaves had drifted down, past the rope that hung from the old willow, still swinging and where I never played. The street was devoid of children; empty. Empty. This had never been my home.

On the horizon, a grey-green cloud hung above the city. It was a walk of about four hours to reach it along the main highway. Sometimes, a bus might come, rattling and armoured, but not very often. People with eyes like pebbles rode the bus; not coming from anywhere, going nowhere, just riding. Perhaps they thought time would stop for them in that way. I would not ride the buses, for I was afraid that if I did, I would be absorbed into that shadow community and never leave it. Another freak on the back seat.

It was mid-morning when I left the enclave, and already the sun was fierce in the late summer sky. At the high metal gates, the eyes of the guards were hidden behind black glass. They stood motionless, like automatons. I passed between them, showed my ID card, and the gates slid open. A minute later, someone else might come by, and the guards would come alive. They'd touch their helmets, grin to show their white teeth and utter a pleasantry. But not for me. After I'd gone, one would say, "That's the weird kid from Acacia," and the others would sneer.

I walked along the slip-road that led to the highway. It seemed hotter beyond the enclave, and the air shimmered about me. Vigilantes had strung someone from a pole. I could see the body dangling on the other side of the road, surrounded by trees. A cloud of flies danced around it. Beneath it, someone had left some artificial flowers. Perhaps the enclave guards, high up on the gates and watchtowers, had seen it happen.

I cannot remember feeling anything then. I just walked, kicking up dust that smelled of metal and age, buffeted by the searing wind of passing vehicles. After an hour, a truck stopped to offer me a lift. The back was filled with people, crammed together like pigs on the way to a slaughterhouse. They were probably just crop-pickers, returning to the city. My feet were aching, so I hopped up into the back. Certain people always picked up on my strangeness, and this occasion was no different. My fellow travellers were like frightened animals. I saw furtive shuffling and nervous eye movements. I didn't say anything. Eventually, one of the men offered me a cigarette and I smoked it, looking out through the truck canopy at the passing road. My mother will have missed me by now. Her relief will fill the silent house, washed by waves of shame. She will grip the edge of the sink and blink at the garden, where the sprinkler turns slowly on the lawn.

I did not resent being born different. The resentment came from other people's reactions. I was so ordinary in most respects. Dogs had never liked me; we could never keep one. Sometimes, things happened around me, over which I had no control. It wasn't my fault. It was the look in her eyes. I made the saucepans fly once, but not toward her. She just screamed, her hands pressed to her face, staring at the mess on the floor. Other kids didn't like me very much, despite my parents' efforts to find me friends. I didn't mind being alone. I'd tell my mother things she thought were her private thoughts, and then her mouth would compress into two white lines. Later, I'd hear her telling my father about it: "He must *listen* to us, for God's sake! Do something!" I didn't listen. I just knew. It was like she told me things herself without words.

It was the doctors I hated the most. There was nothing wrong with me; I wasn't ill. But my mother kept taking me back to that neat office that smelled of nothing, and let the white coats prod at me. I said, "just let me be", and they would smile tolerantly, spreading my legs on the table for another look. They must have taken a hundred photographs. "It isn't Froehlich's syndrome," I heard a doctor say to my mother, "because apart from the genital abnormalities, there are no other physical deformities."

Her reply: "Then what is it? Can you operate?"

"That is a decision your son will have to make for himself later on. We have counsellors..."

She thought I should have been twins: a boy and a girl. But it wasn't that.

I got out of the truck on the outskirts of the city, in an area called the Longhills. Once, it would have been a thriving neighbourhood; now a ruin and an ideal place to hide, to think, to do whatever would come next. Tall buildings with broken crowns reached towards the veil of evil cloud that always hangs above the city. I think it is the city's aura, an expression of its soul, soiled and poisonous. The people who live in that place are barely human, but then I had been taught to think that neither was I. Perhaps this was the place where I belonged. I wanted to cast off the trappings of affluence and live close the edge of survival. Discomfort did not bother me.

I walked as best I could along the sidewalks, avoiding debris, bundles of cloth that may have been corpses and the smouldering remains of fires. What did people burn here? Sometimes, it seemed they burned their own possessions. I saw fragments of books, jewellery and crockery blackened among the embers. The smoke was toxic. Someone had burned a wasps' nest. A substance like syrup leaked from its collapsed mass. I saw few people. They kept out of the sun during the day. They slept then. Welfare trucks occasionally slid across an intersection ahead of me. They might contain bodies or miscreants or supplies. Perhaps all three at once.

At three o'clock in the afternoon, when the sun was at its most vehement, I stood in the centre of a street and looked up at the sky. Buildings loomed over me, derelict and rotting. I wondered what the point of it all was. Why do we continue to live? What drives us to survive in an environment so hostile to life, an environment we have made for ourselves? Civilisation was a Leviathan whose limbs were too weak to support it. Now it sank to its knees, bones cracking beneath its weight. And all who rode the Leviathan were tumbling down, their screams thin like that of insects. My difference was just one more symptom of this fall. Our purity was mangled and dysfunctional. In those moments, I saw myself as the avatar of the world's destruction, a cruel joke in the distorted form of the primal human. I could do as I pleased, for it did not matter what would happen to me.

Soon, I began to feel hungry, but willed the pangs away. I could see no way to feed myself. It was cleansing to be able to step aside from human needs. I felt excoriated, but also renewed. For a while, I sat inside a broken building, where the walls were black. I listened for sounds: the faraway throb of rotor blades, the occasional human cry, cut off short, and once the distant bark of a dog. I watched the sun slide down behind the splintered towers, and thought how in the enclave, the day would be drawing to a close. Men would be emerging from the units in the nearby industrial park. They would climb into their sleek transporters, hail a manly good-night to the guards on the wall, and drive the short distance up the tower-studded avenue to the gates of the enclave. Here, wives who sought to enact the rituals of a past Golden Age would be waiting in kitchens that were devoid of stain. The women wore aprons and smiled at their children, keeping back the pain, the fear, the utter chaos that massed on the horizon of their fantasy world. None of it was real, but then I had never really conspired in my parents' dream. My very existence cracked its fragile shell.

At dusk, a gang of girls stole in through the windows of my sanctuary. They saw me crouching in the rubble, which I quickly realised was *their* rubble, and began to snarl at me and utter strange ululating cries, their bodies dipping and rising like snakes. Their leader rushed at me a couple of times, brandishing a knife near my body, but I sat as still as I could, looking at her face. Presently, she came to a decision and gestured for her minions to get on with their business. They unfolded loot from tattered sacks, and set about dividing it amongst themselves. The leader flicked glances at me occasionally. I recognised something within her that later I identified as the indomitable human spirit. Society no longer existed for her, yet she continued to thrive, albeit in a debased fashion. The girls ate and laughed together, handing round a plastic bottle of murky liquid. After an hour or so, their leader offered it to me. It was a vile, base alcohol that left a trail of fire in my throat and tasted only of chemicals. The girls asked me nothing about myself, even though they must have made judgements about my cleanliness, my neat clothes. They were separatist females who hated men. They could have killed me, perhaps, but it seemed they recognised something within me with which they felt comfortable and could accept. I ran with them for a week or so, raking over the ruins, pillaging the debris. They seemed to repel rival male gangs by the strength of their voices alone, using a repertoire of chilling screams and cries. Boys would lope away from them like chastened dogs. Often, the leader would climb to the highest, most precarious point around and stand there with arms outflung, uttering a world-filling shriek of anger. They did not know about despair. I envied them.

In the asphalt wilderness of Longhills, there were few adults. Perhaps they had wisely moved away, or else been killed. Sometimes, choppers would drone over the streets and emit a stinging spray, which the girls told me was supposed to kill disease. Why would the city authorities bother? I didn't believe it. The spray probably just killed fertility.

I felt more at one with the desperadoes of the wilderness than any of the people who hid within the enclave. It was because these outsiders expected nothing and gave little in return. They did not make demands upon one another. Co-existence, and therefore a certain amount of co-operation, were the only remaining aspects of community. Pleasure was without contrivance: a good find among the rubbish; a chance meeting with a group who had something to barter; a basement found untouched, like an unopened tomb full of treasure; an abandoned welfare truck still laden with vitamin-enriched gruel. We were grave-robbers, really, for most of humanity had already died in that place. But I liked the simplicity and honesty of their lives, the fact they did not judge me.

One day, one of the gang was shot by a sniper and the leader told us we would have to move area. A sixth sense told her this was the beginning of something bad. So, we gathered up what little we had and left Longhills behind, burrowing off through the darkness, and into another decayed sector called Coldwater Valley. It must have been an industrial complex at one time, and here the survivors were older and hostile to strangers. We prowled carefully between the arching metal structures that were now smothered with tendrils of quick-growing vines. Echoes were strangely muffled by the vegetation. Any human group we came across yelled and threw things to repel us; we were not welcome. Finally, one group, crazier than the rest, directed a fire cannon on us and killed all but five of us. Our leader was among the fallen; a blackened crisp in the road. How quickly life can be expunged. It seemed inconceivable that what was left of our companions had ever housed souls. We, the survivors, went back the way we had come, but it was the end of our group. We split up, and I went alone deeper into the madness of the ruined land that surrounded the desperate core of the shrinking metropolis. Its towers seemed to have huddled together, as if in fear.

There was much activity in the air nearer to the city core. Choppers roared through the skies, and once I saw one crash. People emerged from the jumbled ruins like cockroaches and swarmed all over the wreckage, picking it clean. I did not look like an enclave boy any longer. My head was thatched with lice-infested hair, my clothes were tatters, to which I was forever adding more layers, whatever I could find. I had learned to snarl in the way that meant, "stay away if you value your health." I also learned much about myself. Because the convenient utensils of life were no longer available, I was forced to live on my wits, and in this way discovered that the boundaries of my difference were much further than I had imagined. It began this way. I'd been going through the belongings of a dead man on the street, who had died of a sickness rather than murder. He had many treasures, which I was greedily transferring to my own pockets. Then a group of tearaways came slinking along the spiky walls around me, uttering low, hooting cries. Their message was for me to leave, to abandon my find. I don't think they would have attacked me if I'd simply obeyed this request. But there was too much for me to leave. I growled back. They must have thought I was mad; there were at least seven of them. Their leader dropped down from the wall and sauntered toward me, looking to either side all the time. I remained hunkered down beside the corpse, my hands dangling between my knees. I didn't feel afraid at all. It was as if there was someone else inside me, far wiser than I knew; someone fierce and confident. An arrow of indignation flew out of me, and somehow touched the crumbling substance of the wall behind the gang leader. There was an explosion, a gust of dust and rocky debris, and then my would-be attacker was on his hands and knees before me, his head hanging down. He shook his hair and drops of bright blood flew out. At once, I jumped to my feet and snarled. My eyes felt full of sparks that I could shoot like bullets from a gun. The gang just melted away, dragging their fallen leader with them. After this incident, I felt so much stronger, safer.

Perhaps I overestimated my strength.

Some days later, I found a hole for myself deep beneath an old department store. It had been cleaned out thoroughly years before, but some people must have lived there for a while, because I found a few mattresses, some of which had not been burned. Rags had been hung from metal beams in what remained of the ceiling. It was a musty labyrinth full of silent ghosts. I imagined it had once been home to a whole community, who had either been smoked out or died from some contagious infection. There were no bones about as evidence, but the wilderness scavengers are very thorough, so that meant little. In this place, I made myself a nest. I did not think about the future, but took simple pleasure in surviving from moment to moment. The wilderness was the garbage heap of the world, yet I learned to see beauty in it: the different colours of the sky at various times of day, and how they conjured sculptures from the rubble, shining through blown-out windows, making a cathedral of light of the starkest structure. The passing of civilisation in itself was a wondrous thing.

I would walk the cracked streets, marvelling at the way stringy vegetation was slowly reclaiming the land. Mother Earth had learned the saying that revenge is a meal best eaten cold. She was implacable, eternal, and the green tidal wave of her reclamation was evidence of humanity's frailty and insignificance. The people had regressed, but in their barbarity possessed a startling innocence. The complex rituals of life had been pared away, and if the people were dying, at least they would do so with swift dignity, rather than being hooked up to machines in a long coma of slow decay. Those who lived in the cities, the enclaves, were deluding themselves. They should give themselves up to the inevitable. I thought I too would soon die, and these were my last days. Each one dawned fresh and vital. I wanted to experience life through my senses to the full, and because of this, learned how my touch was death.

He was older than me, yet seemed younger. We met when he strayed into my lair, and after a few warning shots of snarls and aggressive gestures, realised we were not enemies at all. He was like me: a runaway from the theatre of luxury. His mother had been a pill-head, who sometimes had not even recognised him, while his father, a scientist, had hardly ever been at home. I tingled with empathy as he described his former sterile environment: the ceaseless hum of domestic appliances, and the automata who kept the place running, while his mother lolled on the couch, living in some better world. He explained to me the phenomenon of why people like us ran away. "We know it's over. Society is dead, but some of us know we can still exist beyond it. It's like a sinking ship. We have to jump overboard with faith and hope, otherwise we'll just be dragged down with the wreck and drowned. This is the age of the individual; the age of the hive has passed. We're all floating in the sea, clinging to our bits of wreckage, but eventually we'll become sea creatures ourselves and learn how to breathe its element."

How could I not love a person who spoke like that, with such passion and optimism? He didn't know about my difference - especially the physical aspect. I didn't want to tell him, because he was my first real friend. If he knew, it would change things. He might be disgusted or, worse, full of pity.

Some girl he knew gave him a flask of alcohol. We flavoured it with the remains of a bag of sugar substitute we'd found in our basement, and one night sat across from one another and drank it. It felt shamanic, the rhythmic passing of the flask from one to the other. We both knew we wanted to be drunk, for there was business between us that the barriers of a sober mind inhibited. I was acutely aware that before the night was over he would know about me. I felt nauseous with nerves, eager for the intoxication that would free my tongue and allow me to speak the words that must be spoken.

He began to talk about the future again, rambling on about some faraway utopia that could be constructed from hopes and dreams.

Something about his vision made me uncomfortable, and I said, "This is the end, not change. We are dying."

He crawled over to me then and put an arm around me. "No, no, you're wrong. This isn't death at all. You're living in the past. Look forward, not back. Don't let the past become your future."

I wanted to believe, and partly did, unaware of how he spoke the most ultimate of truths. He put his head against my hair and said, "I have to ask you something. Don't answer if you don't want to but... are you really a girl?"

I laughed a little, more out of embarrassment than amusement. What could I say? The answer was neither yes nor no. "What makes you think that?" I asked.

I could tell he wished he'd never spoken. "I don't know. The way you walk and talk. Just body language, I guess. I'm sorry. You must think this is just an excuse to..."

I touched his arm to silence him. "I am what you say."

He grinned in relief. "I knew it. You want people to think you're a boy, because people will leave you alone then." He paused. "I'm sorry. That sounded patronising."

I shook my head. "No, don't apologise. The thing is, I'm male too."

He frowned. "In your heart, your head?"

"No. In some ways, that would be simpler."

"Then what *do* you mean?" The puzzlement had swept back; the tide of delight and anticipation had receded.

"It would be easier to show you," I said and stood up.

The only light came in from outside, but then we of the wilderness rarely craved artificial light at night, other than a fire for protection. I peeled away all the layers of my tattered clothes, feeling as if each discarded item represented a year of my life. It was all being sloughed away. When finally I stood naked before him, he sat with his chin in his hands and said, "You look male to me."

I squatted before him and took one of his hands in mine, guiding him to the truth of the matter. He didn't say anything then, but kissed me. I felt his fingers digging into my shoulders like spikes. I could feel his heart racing. He'd wanted to do this for some time, and now felt he had been given sanction. I welcomed it too, but some part of me became annoyed that he looked upon me as a female and took it for granted that I must be dominated. Did women ever feel this way? It might sound like justification, but I feel that he was partly to blame for what happened to him. We should have come together as equals, but then I didn't know he was not equal to me. I was stronger than he was, and forced him into submission. It was only a game, I swear. I just wanted him to realise what we were, or could be.

It took him a day to die. I was helpless. I tried everything, but whatever mutant substance lived in me was poison to him. Not all the water in the world could wash away what I had done to him. My essence ate into him like acid, devoured his being. The only blessing was that he didn't realise what was happening to him. With my hands, I was able to stroke away most of the pain. With my thoughts, I willed his mind to a far place, that idyll he had spoken of, and there he died.

I set fire to our home and emerged from it into the night against a backdrop of flames. I had been right and he wrong. Humanity was dying and I was one of nature's weapons. I could never love, for to love me was to die. Could anything be crueller than that?

If only I had known the truth then. He could still be here now. The one who discovered that truth with me was but a pale spark to his radiant sun, but perhaps that was all part of it, the great lesson I had to learn.

For days, perhaps weeks, I roamed the wilderness, feeling more drunk than I had on that hideous night. I truly wanted to die, and sometimes climbed the high, broken towers to think about throwing myself over, but even in my grief I was too afraid of being broken, dying slowly. I kept seeing his face, hearing his laughter, and then an image of his death would come to me, the terrible writhing, the whimpers. I was more of a monster than even my mother had imagined.

I came to an area that had been inexpertly flattened; a plain of rubble, from which rusting spikes rose like the bones of dinosaurs. Here, I collapsed and stared up at the sky, watching the colours change and the stars reveal themselves. I could move no further. Here, it would end. I felt strangely at peace, and numb. I could not feel my body.

When I saw the stooped shadow gliding towards me over the stones, I barely raised my head. Death had come for me. It loomed over me, breathing heavily, and dark greasy hair brushed my face. I saw a glint of metal and heard muttered words. "Be still, my pretty. Don't be afraid. I shall come to you without pain."

I didn't know he meant to eat me. I just thought of sex and murder, but he opened a vein in my arm and began to drink, nibbling the flesh at the edge of the cut. He was a modern vampire, human and reeking, not at all the romantic vision I'd seen in old movies. As I lay there, feeling the pull as my blood pulsed into his diseased mouth, I wasn't sickened or afraid, but amused. It's not easy to find food in the wilderness, and some will do anything to live. If my death meant the life of a debased creature like this, then so be it. There was some justice in it, I thought.

But I did not die. I found myself awake with raw morning light falling down upon me. Beside me was a wretched creature who squirmed upon the ground, clutching his belly. His hair had come out in clumps and lay upon the stones. I felt weak, but also vital. As I looked at him, I laughed. Not only was my touch death, but it seemed I was also very difficult to kill. Part of my new role, I decided, was to stay with my victims until they found peace in death. I would do what I could to ease their agony.

Unlike my beloved, this one did not die after the first day. Sometimes, he was raving and hallucinating and became violent with a preterhuman strength. At other times, he wept and mumbled about his childhood, his fingers over his face. His body was hot and bloated. He must be strong. How long would it take him to die?

After two days, it began to rain, and I dragged him into a

ruined office block. The rain itself can be toxic. Here, I built a small fire, and then went foraging, killing four bedraggled pigeons. I came back with two birds, and some welfare rice I'd haggled for with a band of oldsters I'd come across. My attacker, my victim, could not eat, but I cooked the pigeons and watched him as I fed. There was no feeling within me, merely a faint sense of curiosity. His skin was peeling.

On the morning of the third day, I woke up and found myself alone. I thought my companion must have died in the night, and some scavenger had come in and taken the body. Then I heard the words, "what am I?" and turned to see an angel in the doorway. As his skin had peeled, so had all the filth. He stood before me, holding out his arms, looking at his smooth flesh. I could not give him answers. There were none. I felt that I had made him into something more and above me. He shared my difference. I had birthed a daughter-son.

I had thought him the most degenerate of beings, yet I quickly learned that he blazed with vitality and intelligence. Perhaps this was just another aspect of the change he had undergone. He asked me questions constantly and experimented with the force of his being. Unlike me, he was curious about the way he could affect reality; make inanimate objects move, heal pain, hear the whisper of others' thoughts. He was proud of what he'd become, and did not hide it, but the shadow community to which he'd once belonged were now afraid of him. They did not want his healing power, his radiance. They saw not an angel, but a freak.

Unperturbed, he became almost evangelistic about our condition. "We must make more like us," he said.

I was appalled and shook my head. "No. You're a fluke. It's not meant to be this way."

"How do you know?"

We were not easy companions, yet our similarities, and the fact that I had made him the way he was, kept us together. He had changed so much from the wretch he'd been. We lived in the office block where he'd undergone his transformation. One evening, he made me climb a nearby hydro-tower with him, where the rusting shell harboured clear water. He took off his clothes and dived in, summoning me to join him. "We're not part of the filth now." He sluiced my hair and rubbed the grime from my skin. "I want the grief to run from your body with this water.

You must be renewed, like I am."

I think the transformation had affected his mind. He needed a religion to run.

"How did you do it?" he asked. "Tell me. Tell me."

"I don't know. It just happened. You were trying to devour me."

The light in his eyes was like that of the stars; cold and distant. "Yes," he murmured. "Yes."

I should have known he'd act independently. One day, he took me to a building near our lair, and here revealed to me his twisting litter of children. I was horrified, yet also amazed. Twelve people, both male and female, shivered and whimpered at my feet; all of them infected with his blood. I had seen myself as an avatar of death, but remote and accidental. Here was someone who was an active instrument of it, only he did not realise the fact. He thought he was a god, with a god's powers. If I'd done something to end it then, what would the world have been like now?

Of the twelve, only four survived, and all of them male. We tried to soothe the agony of the others with the healing power in our hands, but the experience was harrowing. "I don't think this process can be conducted with females," my companion said, with scientific detachment. "But we must try it with others."

"No!" My protest went unheard.

I would not help him, other than to attend to his victims as they suffered. I didn't even think about killing him, or trying to stop it any other way. At the time, it simply didn't enter my mind, but now I think it was because part of me knew that what was happening was preordained. My companion saw it as a cleansing ritual for the world. He loved the creatures he made, marvelling at their beauty. I saw them as perverted homunculi; as lovely as the angels of hell. Yet, despite this, they were also part of me and I was part of them.

I under-estimated the regard my companion had for me. He did not set himself up as a leader of our developing clan of beautiful monsters. That privilege he reserved for me, even though I shunned it. "It's your responsibility," he told me. "You began this."

"Only because you were hungry," I reminded him.

"Can't you see the potential here?" he demanded. "This is the beginning of something. It's what comes next."

I could only look down at the corpses of those who had not survived. The cost of the selection process was too high. "This is murder," I said.

He nodded. "You're right. We should give people the choice." As an inducement, he now had seven successful transformations to parade before the eyes of the desperate.

I never became involved in his recruitment drives, and for many years no other human tasted my blood. I can't say I wasn't affected by my companion's enthusiasm, and grudgingly I had to accept the benefits of being part of a community, something I had never previously enjoyed, other than those few weeks of running with the girl-pack. This was different, though. With the girls, I had been a tolerated outsider. Now, I was part of a group of individuals who all shared the same attributes. It was both scary and exciting.

Although we could not effect the change in women, a few of them, through persistent entreaty, still joined us. In many ways, we had more in common with them than with men. From our sisters, we learned about the wildest excesses of adorning our bodies. We became tribal, and developed our own rituals connected with the inception of newcomers, or the simple celebration of our estate. Sex became sacred, yet less taboo. There was so much to explore, and so many delights concealed in the labyrinth of our dual gender.

One night, we undertook a rite to name ourselves, opening up our minds with the effects of narcotic fungi. My companion became Orien; a name he felt held power. As for me, I wandered the star-gleam avenues of my mind, until I came to a place where a white shrine glimmered against a backdrop of stars. It stood upon the primal mound of creation, guarded by two pillars, and surrounded by the waters of life. Here, I learned my true name, the person I was to become. I am Thiede. The first of all. And the name we took for ourselves as a group was Wraeththu; a word that held all the anger and mystery of the world. The visions told us the truth: we were no longer human and must forget all that we had been before.

We were close-knit, and did not merely co-operate with one another. Laughter was spontaneous, and in our wild nights of dancing, as new recruits struggled with the process of transformation, I learned about the fulfilment that close friendship brings. I was intrigued by the way the different personalities within the group interacted with one another; the partnerships that developed, the enmities. We weren't above petty squabbling, but if anything from outside threatened our group, the ranks would close and seal as tight as a steel door. We weren't afraid to kill to protect ourselves, and sometimes that was necessary. Various human clans and groups heard about us, and some were afraid, and thought we should be eradicated. We were seen as vampires, as predators, who stole people away in the night. In fact, that was not true. We hadn't resorted to such measures since the first days of my companion's explorations. We had to keep on the move, but even so, humans would often sniff us out and come pouring over the ruins, holding flaming brands aloft, intent on burning us alive. Then we would rise up, howling, our wild hair flying, our faces striped with the colours of the night.

We never lost a single brother in our skirmishes. In our unity, we were immensely strong.

Everything that begins in the world starts small, be it a mighty tree from a seed, or a deluge from a single drop of rain. A cell becomes a child, becomes a king or queen. The greatest concepts are based upon the most fleeting of ideas. Such it was with Wraeththu, the race I spawned from my fear, my pain, my ignorance.

I stand upon the pillars of the world, and look down to see the carnage perpetrated by the human race that had been its guardian. I'm amazed that humanity, with all its cruel selfishness, ever rose to prominence, and that the world itself allowed the situation to continue for so long. We are the exterminators, who will rid the palaces of the earth of all its vermin. We have no choice in this role; it had been decided for us. We are the true messengers of the gods. The howls of slaughtered innocents rise from the ruins, the whimpers of the bereaved, the snufflings of the betrayed. I stand as a colossus above it all, looking down.

There is a star in the sky that is the soul of my lost love, and my own soul has fragmented into a thousand parts, into each of my children. But I don't grow weak from it, only estranged. There is much to explore about myself, and for this I need a real wilderness, where all the devils of the earth and the angels of the air can come to tempt me and teach me. I can't make the inward journey here in the city debris.

Last night, Orien came to me, worried that some of our brethren had split off to form a separate group. I tried to assuage his fears. "This is the way it will go," I said. "We were the catalysts, nothing more. We mustn't interfere with the growth of our child."

He thought I was mad, or damaged, and spoke softly. "The time will come, soon, for us to move toward the city core."

I nodded. "I know," I said. "You will."

He touched my shoulder. "*We* will. You can't deny us, Thiede."

And I smiled at him to reassure him, knowing that already I had left them.

Pro Lucron

The creature of darkness slunk out into the night and glared at the vague moon, which was faintly visible through the smog that hung over the city. He cursed quietly, shook his tousled hair, and stepped into the street. He walked along the centre of the road, where litter blew. There were bloodstains, sometimes, to step over. This was the place of ruins, best avoided. This was the place of demons. The creature walked away from it, towards the weakening, shrinking heart of the city, where humans tried to cling to a normal life. Armoured cars purred past, their ghostly lamp eyes gleaming dully.

He knew what he sought: a huge building without windows. There it was: the mausoleum of hope. The creature sighed, his hollow eyes fixed upon the immense stones. He leaned against a lamp post across the street from the building and waited; a trim tiger.

After maybe an hour, an automatic elevator in the building opposite slid to ground level and opened its metal doors, spewing forth uniformed workers from the vast interior. A soft, female yet metallic voice crooned: "Home to bed everyone. Home now to bed. Wake up fresh tomorrow. Fresh. Work hard tomorrow."

Exhausted figures began to stumble away.

The creature stirred restlessly. His hands were numb from cold. He scanned the figures, seeking the one for whom he had come, but they all looked the same. It was impossible to discern individual features. The creature sighed again and slunk away down the street. He must take a further risk.

The streetlights were already dimming, and patrolling guards lurked in every darkest corner. The creature hurried: it screamed inwardly with frustration.

A voice echoed from the darkness: "You're out a bit late aren't you... er..."

The creature turned slowly, and saw a guard whose face was mostly hidden by a black glass visor. The creature did not speak, but smiled a little. It would be enough.

The guard cleared his throat, gestured with his black gun.

"Well... er... hurry along home. The streets are no place for young... for you to frequent after dark."

The creature inclined its head and walked away. He heard the buzz of static, then a faint metallic voice issue from the communication device in the guard's helmet.

Jarad entered silently into his apartment. He walked softly into the kitchen, so as not to awaken his neighbours, for the walls were thin. He turned the light onto dim and downed a swig of his week's ration of milk. Unsatisfied, he turned on the water tap, but the supply had already been disconnected for the night. He shrugged resignedly and made his way into the plush living room. At the threshold, he turned up the light a little.

The creature was curled up in a chair, waiting for him. He regarded Jarad stonily.

Jarad's entire body went hot, then cold. "Why are you here?" His voice was harsh.

The creature's beautiful face adopted a smile. "It's where you live," he said.

Jarad wiped his mouth with the back of one hand. He could still taste milk, and it was sour. "How did you get in?"

The creature smiled wistfully. "I learned where you hide your spare key. Wasn't that difficult. Your mind print was all over it."

"You must go," said Jarad.

The creature shook his head slowly.

"You must," Jarad urged. "You can't stay here. You shouldn't be here. Go!"

"I can't. You must know that. If you want me out, you must use physical force. But I doubt you'd do that either."

Jarad flared his nostrils. "If you're found here..." He shook his head. "You had no right to come, to invade my privacy." He hesitated. "What do you want?"

"Want?" The creature extended his legs, clad in soft leather, and rose from the chair. He advanced upon Jarad and touched him on the cheek with a long-fingered hand. "I think you know."

Jarad flinched away. "Get back to where you came from."

The creature laughed. "Remember, you came from there too, Jarad."

"I escaped," Jarad said. "My choice. I won't live that life. If you're here to persuade me otherwise, you're wasting your time."

"You're deluding yourself," said the creature. "You can't

survive here. Not for long. You can't hide. Eventually, all this will be gone, and then what?"

"If that happens, I'll deal with it. I live from day to day."

The creature slunk back to the chair and arranged himself gracefully. He crossed his legs and rested his elbows upon the chair arms, linking his long fingers beneath his chin.

Jarad felt as if the creature stared holes in him.

"It's just a sickness you have," said the creature. "This fear, this denial. It can be cured."

"Not your way."

"What happened was wrong," the creature said. "You're not the only one to think it. There are mistakes, because we're so young. It was a mistake. It can be undone."

"It can't," Jarad said. "*You* are the mistake – all of you."

"Jarad... some things *can't* be undone. You know that too. You are one of us."

"No," Jarad said. "I wasn't given a choice about that either. Now I make it."

"You can't ignore what you are."

Jarad laughed coldly. "I'm doing pretty well, thank you. Watch me. You can sit there as long as you like, say what you like. It won't change my mind."

"Sleep on it," said the creature. "I'll give you that time."

Jarad shook his head. "It'll make no difference."

With a final wordless sound, he loped to his bedroom and shut the door carefully behind him. As he undressed, he watched the door all the time and then lay in bed staring at it. He shouldn't sleep, but he was too tired to resist. He was always tired.

Jarad awoke when the radio in the wall chimed: "Awake! Awake! To work! To work hard! A good breakfast and off you go!"

Jarad winced. There were prices to pay for living in the 'decent' area of the city over which the Society Government had tenuous ruling. Jarad stretched in his bed, and then froze. He saw that the creature lay asleep beside him. *Typical*, thought Jarad. *Only you could sleep through such an alarm.* But he couldn't help smiling. The creature was naked beneath the quilt, which covered him from the chest down. His tawny skin was as smooth as fur. Jarad's hands felt hot and dry. It took all his strength not to reach out and touch. All his strength to confine that heat to his hands.

"I hate you, most beautiful of creatures," he said aloud.

The lovely eyes unveiled at once and blinked at him. "You talk in your sleep," the creature said. "You never used to do that."

"How would you know? We never slept together."

Jarad got out of bed and dressed himself quickly in his plain uniform clothes. "I'll have to get you out before the cleaners arrive," he said. "If you're seen..."

The creature laughed softly and pulled the quilt over his head.

"Get up!" Jarad snapped. "If you're seen, security will be alerted."

The creature sighed, and then threw back the quilt. Jarad stared for a moment, then averted his eyes.

The creature sat up. "Come home, Jarad. We want you back with us."

"Who sent you?" Jarad asked.

The creature pushed back his long honey-coloured hair that fell down over his chest, nearly to his waist. "Not anyone in particular," he said, "although your name has been mentioned often. You're a lost child, Jarad. We care for you."

Jarad laughed caustically. "Care? Is that what it is?"

"Yes. Listen, I'll be honest with you. Manticker is planning an assault on City Heart. It will be destroyed – you along with it, most likely. Get out now, while you can. I know for sure that if you return to us, Wraxilan will discipline those who wronged you."

"Why? Why should he care?"

"The Lion cares for his own. You're part of his phyle, part of Oomar."

"Yet you say he did not send you, nor did he bother to look for me himself. You're lying. He doesn't give a shit."

The creature raked his hands through his hair. "He didn't know what happened. None of us did. We only found out once you'd gone. You lost yourself pretty well. I only found out where you were because we took someone for inception who'd heard of you. That was a big coincidence. It was meant to be. Come home. Wraxilan will give you a blade. You can cut throats with it, if that's what you want."

"Why should I be so important?" Jarad asked. "Aren't numbers the important thing? There's only one of me. You can always find more, incept more."

"You're one of the best," the creature said. "We can't let you slip away like this."

"But look what I have here," Jarad said, making a sweeping gesture with one arm. "Would I have all this back there? Warmth, comfort, clean water?"

"You would have freedom," the creature said softly, "and me also, if you so desired."

Jarad made an angry sound. "Doesn't everyone have you?"

The creature shrugged. "That didn't used to bother you. I know you wanted me, Jarad, and I'm sorry I played with you. It was just a game, and I didn't know you'd simply disappear. I'm sorry I wasn't there for you when you needed me." He grinned mordantly. "Do you see what you've done? I just apologised and I never do that!"

"You'd give yourself to me, just to lure me back?" Jarad uttered a snort. "There's more to this than you say. I don't flatter myself I'm that desirable."

The creature stood up and dressed himself. "You are. That was the point of the game."

Jarad frowned. "I can't be like you anymore. Don't you understand? They took that from me, all desire."

The creature nodded. "I understand... really. But it can be changed."

Jarad put his hands over his face. The possibility was there, he knew that. He had run away to lick his wounds. Perhaps he had always wanted to be found.

"Did you never think of me?" the creature asked.

Jarad did not lower his hands. "Of course, until I made myself stop." He heard the creature draw nearer.

"We can heal you, you know that. The question is: Will you allow it?" He took hold of Jarad's hands and pulled them away from his face. The creature's scent filled his head; bittersweet musk. He exhaled over Jarad, his breath bringing brief visions of comfort and safety.

Jarad knew he should pull away. He must. "Call me by name, Jarad." The creature's arms were around his body, lips so close to his own.

"Lianvis," he said. "Don't do this."

"Come home."

Their lips touched and all physical sensation faded away. In the visions that followed, the city was dyed red in the light of a setting sun. There were no humans, no labour facilities, no cars, no pain. Birds wheeled among the broken towers and the green crept back over the land. Jarad was lost in that world, that beautiful lie. He saw himself with Lianvis, in a bower of roses that grew in the corner of a deserted parking lot. It was a dream he'd once had.

Lianvis pulled away, creature no more. "Will you come with me?" Long fingers caressed Jarad's face.

"Yes," Jarad said, weakly.

Jarad guessed that Lianvis had really expected him to put up more of a fight, and was therefore disorientated by his relatively easy victory. He took Jarad swiftly into the eastern, forbidden zone of the city, where their own kind could gather in daylight. The human security patrols did not venture there. The SG believed that if the undesirable element was contained within its own sector, the populace of City Heart was safe. It was a short-sighted view that would eventually mean the end of human occupation in the city.

A café called *Chains*, supplied with produce by the black market, provided breakfast for anyone awake at that hour. The sausages frying so temptingly in the filthy kitchen were made of dog meat.

While Lianvis bartered at the counter for black coffee and burnt toast, Jarad went to sit at a table outside. There were no other patrons.

Lianvis returned with food. "Here," he said. "Eat."

Jarad grimaced. "I don't think so. I think I should go home."

"Too late for that," Lianvis said. "Let's just say I've musked your apartment. The next human who enters there will almost certainly report the matter to the authorities, since they know that token, and they'll have bad dreams for three months."

"You're disgusting!"

"A scent through the pores, that's all. What do you take me for?"

"What you are." Jarad sipped the coffee.

Lianvis studied Jarad carefully. He wouldn't be able to see into his companion's mind. Whatever Jarad said about denying what he was, he still expertly shrouded his thoughts. Lianvis would know that Jarad had been attacked some months back, and that terrible things had been done to him, because the perpetrators would have bragged about it afterwards. They were hara, they were braggarts. It didn't take psychic ability to predict that. But none of them would have guessed Jarad would disappear for good.

"Wraxilan questioned those responsible for the assault on you," Lianvis said.

"Questioned..."

"They insisted it had only been 'a bit of fun'." Lianvis grimaced.

"Really. And the Lion accepted that?"

"Fun gets out of control sometimes. He knows that." Lianvis paused. "I know it wasn't that, Jarad. You always kindled jealousy very easily. It caused resentment."

"So much so, some trash tried to gut me. Yeah, that fun really got out of control." Jarad spat at the ground by his feet, but he couldn't spit out the bile in his heart.

"I'll take you to Wraxilan tonight," Lianvis said.

Jarad shrugged.

"Are you worried about facing those who attacked you?"

"No."

"You should talk about it. We all know pelki happens, but not among our own kind."

Jarad put his head to one side. "It was rape, Viss. Don't dress it up with a tame word."

"Pelki is not tame," Lianvis said. "That's why we use it."

Jarad laughed coldly. "I bled so much I thought I would heal up completely, that it would all just *go*. Perhaps it has. Perhaps I'm human again. Perhaps I'm male."

"That's not possible. If you've been injured you should see a healer."

"Sometimes, it aches."

"Jarad..." Lianvis reached out and laid a hand over one of Jarad's, which was curled around his coffee mug.

Jarad did not pull away from the contact. "They hated me. Why? I didn't ask to be made Wraeththu. I had no choice."

"I know."

"Did you... have a choice, I mean?"

Lianvis shook his head.

"It's wrong," Jarad said and took a big mouthful of the scalding coffee, pulling away from Lianvis' touch. "By staying with them, we condone it."

"I'm not sorry about it," Lianvis said. "I'm happy with what I am. We don't have to be like the others." He paused. "There's someone I want you to meet. He's a thinker. He talks sense."

"Really!"

"Yes. His name is Velisarius. He's also a healer. He'll help you."

Jarad grimaced. "I know of him. He's a freak. Seems to me he's into justifying his existence by getting into religion. That's no answer."

"You're wrong. It's not religion."

Again, Jarad laughed. "There's no room for hippy mystics in Wraeththu, Viss. I'm surprised your friend is still alive."

"It would do no harm to talk to him."

"Whatever. I was stupid enough to fall for the breath-sharing, lost my wits, lost my life, so here I am! Do what you like. I don't care."

"I don't believe you. I don't think you really liked that life you'd made for yourself. What the hell did you do in that squalid building?"

"Process data. It was mindless. I wanted that."

"Wraeththu are here to stay," Lianvis said. "You'd better get used to it. You *are* har."

"I'm not sure I am anymore."

Lianvis drained his coffee. "Come on, I'll take you to Velisarius. Before anything, we should get you checked over."

Velisarius lived, quite appropriately in Jarad's view, in an old church, which was squeezed between high abandoned buildings. Jarad and Lianvis had to clamber over rubble to reach the main entrance. A group of very young hara were playing a game with bones in the litter-strewn entrance hall. They must have been incepted recently. Jarad immediately felt old, and yet his own inception had only been two years before.

At Lianvis' request, one of the hara took them into the presence of Velisarius. Jarad expected the har to be meditating or chanting, but when they were conducted into the small room at the rear of the building where Velisarius lived, the self-styled mystic was making a table. The air smelled of freshly-cut wood. The symbolism of that was not lost on Jarad. He sneered inwardly.

Velisarius glanced up from his work. He looked younger than Jarad had expected. His long hair fell in a plait over one shoulder. "This is a surprise," he said to Lianvis. "You're not usually about so early."

"I've brought somehar to meet you," Lianvis said. "This is Jarad."

"Ah," said Velisarius, in a tone that indicated he knew who Jarad was.

"Will you look him over?" Lianvis asked. "What happened to him... it caused injuries."

Velisarius nodded. "I'll take a look, if he wishes it."

"You're not a doctor," Jarad said, unable to keep the venom from his voice.

"No," Velisarius agreed. "I was a second-year medical student."

Jarad grimaced. "Oh. OK."

Velisarius went to wash his hands at the sink at the back of the room. "What were you before?" he asked.

"Still at school," Jarad said. "We were raided. Only five of us survived inception."

"I was taken because I was stupid enough to walk around at night on my own," Velisarius said. "Still, it was what was meant to be. Will you undress and lie down on the bed? This won't take a moment. I can tell from looking at you that the damage wasn't too great." He smiled. "I mean, physically."

"You didn't study psychiatry, then?" Jarad said, unzipping the front of his uniform.

"Sadly, no," Velisarius said, "although there are many hara who need it. Lianvis, go and find somehar who can make us tea."

Lianvis, who still stood at the threshold, departed without a word.

Jarad lay down on the bed. "I'm not sure about this, but I guess I want to know as well. Can you really tell from looking at me how bad it is?"

Velisarius nodded. "I can tell a lot from a simple glance, yes. I read auras."

"Of course you do." Jarad raised his knees. He felt vulnerable, embarrassed.

Velisarius put a hand on Jarad's brow and a soothing cool wave of energy passed from his fingers. "Relax," Velisarius said, and then grinned. "I'm a healer."

"I can feel that," Jarad said. He felt drowsy, as if the other har's energy was anaesthetic. Velisarius's gentle touch was also cool.

"Hmm," Velisarius murmured.

"What?" Jarad raised his head to see Velisarius peering intently between his legs.

"This will require a minor operation. I can do it now, if you like."

"What's wrong?"

"You've healed all wrong."

"I knew it! I said to Viss I'd healed up."

"Well, not quite that bad," Velisarius said, "but I'll need to make an incision."

"Maybe you should just leave it."

Velisarius glanced up. "I'll pretend I didn't hear that."

"I mean it."

"I don't have to be a psychiatrist to tell you that a har denying half of his being is unhealthy," Velisarius said. "Don't move. I'll be right back."

Jarad led his head flop back and closed his eyes. He wasn't afraid of pain. He was afraid of what he was, all the feelings he didn't understand, that woman inside him.

Jarad rested in Velisarius' room for most of the day, lulled by the sound of a saw through wood, the hammering of nails. Lianvis sat on the floor beside him and read a book. Jarad dozed, drifting in and out of consciousness. One time he woke up weeping; it was as if some other personality was living in his body. Velisarius had packed the wound, and now Jarad's lower body throbbed in pain, as sensitive nerves protested at the intrusion. Lianvis said nothing but put his hands on Jarad's belly. Healing warmth flowed from his fingers.

"You see," Lianvis said softly. "We *can* be different. You'll heal quickly."

By evening, Jarad felt more or less normal. He ached slightly, but it wasn't too much to tolerate.

"Be thankful for your new physiology," Velisarius told him. "You'll be as good as new in a day or so."

"Lianvis said we should talk," Jarad said.

Velisarius smiled. "I hope we will. Come back any time."

He wasn't touting for converts, then.

Outside, night had come. The sky was clearer than it had been for a while. The moon was just past full. Lianvis and Jarad walked through the narrow backstreets, with high walls to either side.

They went to the area known as City Zoo, where abandoned warehouses had been turned into nightclubs. Loud music boomed from every open doorway, and the light within those places was red, turquoise, livid green. They were in search of Wraxilan, and Lianvis knew his favoured haunts.

This was the territory of the Uigenna, the largest and most powerful Wraeththu tribe, into which Jarad had been incepted. Exotic hara, clad in their strangest costumes, lined the streets, eyeing up the competition and the talent. The wind carried litter and sighs. Huge, scrawny alley cats lithed along the sidewalk, glancing from left to right for adversaries. Jarad could see that Lianvis was smiling: clearly, he savoured this environment. Jarad simply thought it shallow and crass. Whatever initial attractions the Uigenna way of life had had for him, he'd quickly grown to despise it. Most hara he'd met were stupid, posturing fools.

The smoke of dry ice billowed out from the clubs, pungent with the smell of sweat and incense. Lianvis turned into one of the open doorways, pausing only to make sure that Jarad was still following. Two tall hara, whose faces were tattooed with curling black patterns, stood aside to let them through, nodding a greeting to Lianvis as they did so.

The light inside was crimson, and it was difficult to see much through the smoky atmosphere. A long bar that ran down the side of the main room served lethal hooch that was brewed in the cellars below. This noxious liquor was flavoured with various fruits and caramel, and coloured with livid food dyes, which tended to stain the teeth. Heavy industrial dub pulsed from the immense sound system, and the entire space was one enormous dance floor, filled with gyrating bodies.

Jarad looked back; the street seemed very far away. He'd been here before. He'd met friends here often. Strange, he couldn't remember some of their faces now.

There was a mezzanine gallery above the dancers, and Lianvis gestured for Jarad to follow him to the metal stairs that led to it. Up there, hara were lounging on cushions, smoking marijuana in tall pipes.

Tiny spotlights picked out various revellers, and in the light of one of them sprawled Wraxilan, the Lion of Oomar, and leader of this phyle of the greater tribe of Uigenna. He was magnificent, like a dream of androgyny made flesh. His wild blond hair looked almost white. He lay on his nest of cushions, his head thrown back, eyes closed; a plume of smoke emanated from his pursed lips. His perfect arms were covered in tattooed serpents, some of which had the head of a lion. Wraxilan was neither shallow nor crass. He was, however, dangerous, brutal and merciless. He had the murderous impulses of a psychotic man and the cold, vindictive zeal of a paranoid woman. Jarad had always avoided him, kept his head down. There were privileges to being in Wraxilan's inner cabal, obviously, but he was quick to take offence, and those who fell out of favour sometimes disappeared.

Jarad hung back while Lianvis approached the phylarch. A group of twenty of so hara sat around him, and they now appraised Jarad with cool or suspicious gazes.

After Lianvis had spoken, Wraxilan sat up and stared directly at Jarad, who made a gesture of respect by touching his brow. It was impossible to converse over the music, so Wraxilan got to his feet and gestured they should go through a door behind him. Jarad's heart was beating fast. His mouth was dry and his wound began to throb once more, making his belly feel hot.

Beyond the doorway was a narrow, dimly-lit corridor. Wraxilan led his companions to another room. He opened a door to reveal three hara experimenting in dim light with some sort of drug: a pale green powder they were rubbing into each other's eyes.

"Out!" Wraxilan said and the room's occupants gathered up their equipment and hurried away.

There were cushions on the floor in here also, and Wraxilan sat down. He gestured for Lianvis and Jarad to do likewise. "So," he said, "the wanderer returns."

Jarad, lost for words, raised his hands briefly, then let them fall back into his lap.

"Drink?" Wraxilan asked. He pulled a flask from the pocket of his brushed leather shirt.

"Thanks." Jarad took it, swigged a mouthful of sweet fiery liquor. He handed the flask to Lianvis.

"It's good that Viss found you," Wraxilan said to Jarad. "You shouldn't have left us. After what happened, you should have come straight to me."

"At the time, I wasn't thinking straight," Jarad said carefully. "Also, you were out of the city, and I was in fear for my life."

Wraxilan nodded. "Understandable. I was watching you, Jarad, sizing you up. It annoyed me when you left."

"I had no idea."

"No." Wraxilan gestured emphatically. "Well, I'll get to the point. I need hara like you. There are too many fools. They're no use to me. They're the sheep. I want wolves."

"Hmm," murmured Jarad.

"It all bores you, doesn't it?" Wraxilan said. "I like that. The ones who attacked you didn't like it at all. They wanted to bring you down a bit, make you know your place. But you just walked away. I wasn't happy about that."

"What do you want me to do for you?" Jarad asked.

"Help me do what has to be done," Wraxilan replied. "Organise our phyle. See to training, organise raids, that sort of thing. We can't hide in the ruins forever. We have to take this city, and every other city. Humanity's time is done."

"Big plans," Jarad said. "Is this under Archon Manticker's direction?"

A flicker flashed across Wraxilan's eyes at the mention of the tribe leader. It was no secret Wraxilan coveted Manticker's power. Such was the way of the ambitious *protégé*. Manticker had incepted Wraxilan, and once they had been close. "We all do what's best for our tribe," Wraxilan answered.

Jarad nodded. "Of course. But what will your other hara think about my place in your scheme?"

Wraxilan gestured carelessly with one hand. "Don't worry about what hara think of you. They won't dare to touch you again."

"OK," Jarad said. Here was another thing he really had no choice over. "Whatever you want."

Wraxilan laughed, rather uncertainly. "You puzzle me. I expected you to haggle over terms."

"No," Jarad said. "Your terms are clear. Your protection will be useful. No doubt I still have enemies."

"I like you," Wraxilan said. "You talk straight. No bullshit. That's good." He paused. "What do you want me to do with your attackers now?"

Jarad paused for a moment. One thing he was sure of was that turning up again and causing trouble or drama amongst hara who most likely hated him was unwise. Best to keep a low profile. "What's done is done," he said eventually. "If they try anything again, it might be a different matter."

"I *am* prepared to punish them."

49

"I know. Perhaps that is enough."

"You know what I think?" Wraxilan said. "This experience has sharpened you, made you strong. You're a changed har, my friend. Use it to your advantage. Work well for me, and you'll keep a good position."

"I'll do my best," Jarad said.

"I heard you visited Velisarius today," Wraxilan said, in a tone that was just a shade too casual. "I hope he fixed you."

Jarad shrugged. "Just about. I'll be healed in a day or so."

"Good. I look forward to that."

Jarad inclined his head. The meaning was clear.

Wraxilan stood up. "Well, get Viss to find you a room around here somewhere. I'll see you later."

"Happy now?" Jarad asked, once he and Lianvis were alone.

"What?" Lianvis appeared to have been lost in thought.

"I did what you wanted. I'm back with a vengeance."

"Are you?"

Jarad stood up. "So, find me a room."

Lianvis hesitated. "Wraxilan's is not the only way, Jarad. It's good to be part of his phyle, but the heart doesn't have to go where the body goes."

"I'll talk to your healer friend if it's what you want," Jarad said. "But now, I'm just tired."

"Then let's go."

They found a disused room, or rather an abandoned room, because there were some bits of furniture in it: a bed, a chest of drawers, lots of clothes and rubbish lying around. Someone had left this room one day intending to return, but had never done so. Jarad took off his uniform. He'd never wear it again. He'd wear the clothes a dead har had left behind.

Lianvis appeared anxious about something. Jarad didn't know what. "I'm not going out into the club again tonight," he said. "Want to stay here with me?" He sat down on the bed, which was low to the floor, just two thin mattresses on top of one another, covered by a grimy quilt.

"OK." Lianvis sat down beside him. "You seem really distant, Jarad."

The balance of power had shifted. It had begun from the moment they'd set foot in the club.

"I'm here," Jarad said.

"How do you feel?"

"Fine." He put a hand on Lianvis" shoulder. "You made me an offer, remember?"

"Perhaps you should wait."

"What I'm planning won't hurt me."

Lianvis smiled uncertainly. "I see."

"I want to fuck you," Jarad said flatly. "So deep it hurts."

Lianvis moved away from him slightly. "Don't call it that. It's not that."

Jarad laughed coldly. "Well, I don't know what you'll be doing, but I'll be fucking."

Lianvis stood up, leaving Jarad to bite only at empty air where once Lianvis's neck had been. "That's not it. You say you despise the others? Now you sound like them."

Jarad leaned back on his elbows. His face was inscrutable.

"What we can do together transcends..." Lianvis's voice trailed off. He must see he didn't really have an audience.

"I know what it is," Jarad said. "I thought we had a deal."

"We did." Lianvis sat down again, raked his hands through his hair.

"What's the matter with you?" Jarad asked. "I bet you've laid all of Wraxilan's phyle and half of every other one in Carmine. What's so different now?" He grinned slowly. "No... don't tell me it's *that!*" He laughed aloud. "Do you think you're kelos over me, Viss? Is that it?"

"If you're not careful," Lianvis said, "your bitterness will be your undoing. A bad thing happened to you. But you are Wraeththu. Get over it."

"You didn't answer my question."

"No." Lianvis paused. "I'm not kelos over you, but I *am* learning new things. One of them is that sex isn't just for mindless gratification. For us, it can be different."

"How so?"

"It can be like a drug, a natural high. It can give us power, real power. I've seen it. If you go into it with an open mind, you can go anywhere." He laid a hand on one of Jarad's arms. "Let me show you."

Jarad's eyes were still cold, but he said, "OK. Whatever you want."

"Share breath with me."

They lay down together, and in their sharing it was clear that Lianvis was trying to project what was precious and divine about their potential union. When Jarad reached to undo Lianvis's trousers, Lianvis stayed his hand. Jarad pulled away from him. "Viss?"

"Wait," Lianvis said. "Share breath for longer."

Drawing out the memories was like pulling shards of glass from Jarad's flesh, but Lianvis made him do it. He relived those harrowing hours when the Uigenna had abused and violated him. They had done terrible things, far worse than Lianvis would have imagined. It was more than simple resentment or envy that drove them, much more. It was self-hatred too, and terror of what they had become.

When they broke the kiss, Jarad was shuddering, his face pressed into Lianvis's hair.

"You had to face it," Lianvis said. "Understand that."

Jarad raised his head. He felt very tired, weary of life itself. "Your foreplay sucks," he said.

A week later Jarad saw two of the hara who had changed his life to darkness. Given the close-knit nature of their community, he was surprised it hadn't happened sooner. The moment he saw them, he acknowledged this and realised he'd been waiting. They were with a third har he didn't know. They weren't slouching around looking menacing or slinking in a pack down some twilit alley; they were horsing about in the sunlight, unloading foodstuffs from a truck, throwing sacks to each other. *Laughing.*

A needle went through Jarad's heart. The carefree laughter pained him more than if they'd turned and recognised him, growled insults, spat in his face.

Lianvis was trying to educate him, Jarad knew. But Jarad was impatient with the carefully-worded sentiments about how hara could be great and good. All Jarad saw were monsters, made even more monstrous because they were beautiful. Talk of the world being gifted to a superior race was nonsense to him. Who were they kidding? Most of the time, the hara around him behaved like characters in a bad B-movie of a post holocaust world. Posturing, strutting, dressing up, learning how to sneer in the best possible way, and how to carry a weapon so that it looked cool. When Lianvis said things like, "think of our ultimate potential," Jarad wanted to say, "Yeah, yeah, by the way, your hair looks good."

He felt that the sarcasm of that would be lost on this new earnest Lianvis. Perhaps it was like religion – clutching at straws when the hurricane was going to blow them all away anyway.

And Lianvis was worried about Jarad – Jarad could feel it. He knew that Lianvis could sense him slipping away into a hinterland, present in body but not in mind and spirit. Jarad didn't care: he simply didn't know how to. And as he stared from the shadow of the porch of an abandoned store, fixing his eyes on the hara who had ruined him, he felt Lianvis touch his mind. He was like a stalker, ever vigilant, and now he melted through the sunlight, the sun behind him, hair lifted in the breeze of his own movement, tall and stately. He was dressed in close-fitting rags of burnt orange and gold. His arms were scored with tattoos. He was radiant. Like an advertisement for a better life a long time ago.

Don't Lianvis said through mind-touch. *Come away.*

He is just flesh, Jarad thought, *or a lovely moving image. None of it is real.* He projected to Lianvis: *What are you afraid I'll do?*

Nothing. It's what you're thinking that scares me.

Then get out of my mind. It's not your garden.

I'm going to see Velisarius. Come with me.

Jarad sighed. *I wish you'd stop trying, Viss. It's starting to annoy me.*

You don't want me to give up on you. Not really.

Lianvis was before him now, his back to the sun, so it was hard to see his face. Jarad noticed the hara at the truck had stopped what they were doing to look at Lianvis. They didn't even notice Jarad standing there. He was forgotten, although surely they must've heard the news he'd returned. Lianvis simply eclipsed him, he supposed.

Lianvis linked his arm through one of Jarad's and firmly dragged him away, back in the direction from which he'd come. "Wraxilan wants your anger," he said. "Why do you give in so easily and let him have it?"

"There's nothing *else* to do," Jarad said.

"You could try to stop feeling sorry for yourself," Lianvis said. "You want to hurt me by being like this. It doesn't hurt me, though."

Jarad was impatient with these conversations. They didn't interest him. He wondered whether in fact he actually liked Lianvis, further than the fleeting pleasures his body could afford. And even that seemed tawdry now, another big pose. *Our sex is better than humanity's – big deal. Doesn't make us any smarter.* He decided the next time he wanted to fuck Lianvis, he'd try to step back from the sensations and see whether the whole thing was really quite boring.

"I'm not trying to hurt you," Jarad said. "I just wish you'd wake up to the fact the world is a crock of shit."

Velisarius was surrounded by a troupe of adoring acolytes. He really fancied himself as some kind of harish messiah, Jarad thought. Yet another posturing idiot. He was no different from Wraxilan; he just read from a different script. The hara were preparing to meditate, hanging onto Velisarius' soft words as if they were scented apples thrown from the Tree of Life.

Jarad hoped that he wouldn't be asked directly to take part in what they were doing. The whole idea of it embarrassed him. Perhaps Velisarius and Lianvis picked up on this. Perhaps they conversed with each via mind touch to discuss how best to handle Jarad, make him malleable. Jarad stood at the back of the room, smoking a cigarette. The smoke made beautiful slow-moving patterns in a fan of sunlight falling through a narrow window. He forced himself not to look at them, refusing to see messages there.

When the group started to chant softly, Jarad went outside. He could still hear them, but once removed from the sight it didn't annoy him so much. He looked up at the sky. How empty it was. Not a chopper in sight. Things had changed in a short time. City Heart was a metallic glitter he could see across the river. From here, it was possible to believe life went on there just the same, as it always had. From here, in the sunlit afternoon, when most hara were asleep, it was possible to believe in some kind of future. The light was so mellow; it had always been this way. Certain sounds were archetypal and eternal. A dog barked in the distance, but there was no sound of children playing.

Wraxilan had given Jarad time to settle. The phylarch was not wrong in his assumptions. Already, Jarad was thinking that in two days' time, when the moon turned towards darkness, he would present himself at Wraxilan's side and say "I am here. What do you want of me now?" If it was raiding into the human-controlled zones, or subduing another harish phyle that Wraxilan considered might be problematical in the future, Jarad would do it. He made no distinction between human and har; neither species commanded his respect. In this, he knew, he would be very useful to Wraxilan, in the place of hara who might baulk at going against their own kind. Jarad looked down at his hands, which he held out in front of him, palms down. The skin looked tired.

He didn't hear Velisarius come up behind him and started when the har placed a hand on his shoulder. He didn't like being taken by surprise and, even though he knew from the first instant who it was, he was tempted to snarl, wheel round and throw a punch, just to make a point.

Velisarius laughed. "You would have found no target," he said.

Jarad shrugged, dropped the end of his cigarette to the floor, ground out its fire with his foot. He saw four cigarette butts lying in the dirt and realised he'd stood there longer than he'd thought. "Prayer meeting over?" he asked.

Velisarius stood beside him, gazing at the distant City Heart. "You want to know what's going to happen to Wraxilan?" he said.

"I think we all know," Jarad replied.

"He'll meet his match," Velisarius said. "He'll be broken in two, but not before he breaks our Archon in two. Wraxilan has his path, washed in blood, of course. He will be reviled and feared, and Manticker will be cast down and left for dead. He may well in fact die... in one way or another. But in the end, when history looks back, Wraxilan and Manticker will both be enshrined as hara of prominence."

"Supposing Wraeththu survive that long," Jarad said drily. "Foraging vermin will soon die if there is nothing left to forage upon."

Velisarius turned and gazed at Jarad with an unreadable expression.

"You must admit," Jarad said, "their chances are slim."

"You still regard yourself as apart," Velisarius said.

"Because I am."

"Yet you're still here, after a week. You could've left easily. I don't see anyone following you, stopping you. Wraxilan must know you better than you know yourself."

"I'm not interested in your talk," Jarad said, "or your prophecies. I'll do what Wraxilan wants for a while. When it all goes bad, maybe I'll travel." He grinned without humour. "See new lands, meet new people and kill them."

"You're not a natural killer, Jarad. Why try to pretend that you are?"

Jarad grimaced. "Is there a point to this conversation? If you have something to say, spit it out, I'll ignore it, then we can both get on with our day."

Velisarius paused before answering. He pursed his lips, sighed through his nose. Jarad guessed the har was thinking it was probably a waste of breath to say whatever was coming next. He wouldn't be wrong.

"Don't think I disagree with you entirely," Velisarius said. "Most of what you believe is right, and what disgusts you, disgusts me also. Uigenna can't continue in this way; they are sleepwalking. Wraxilan is right too, in certain respects. But he understands only how to rule through fear and that is weak. It is an armour with chinks."

"So, you choose the path of the prophet instead. It's bloodless, but no less controlling. You preach a different brand of fear."

Velisarius laughed softly. "You're wrong about me, Jarad. I'm not the sanctimonious, pious creature you believe me to be. I just can't walk in hot blood all the time. It makes me weary. Hot blood clouds the senses. You must know this."

Jarad shrugged.

"There are other ways," Velisarius continued, "and only a fool would think they are without pain, trial, cruelty and terror. That is our legacy; we can't avoid it. Our kind is fated to evolve from horror, and we might all have to do terrible things to plant seeds of growth."

"Do you know this off by heart? Do you have it written down?" Jarad snarled. "It'll make a great holy book some day."

"I know it off by heart," Velisarius replied drily. "But only because it's a universal truth." He paused again. "OK, enough talk. I'll get to the point. Wraxilan wants your talents because he thinks they'll help him. I want you for the same thing, but I think I can offer you more in return. Interested?"

Jarad laughed in a forced way. The question demanded that response. "You mean you're planning to overthrow Wraxilan?"

"No, I'm planning on taking the hara in whom he probably isn't interested anyway to create a new tribe. This will be a tribe who relearns the lessons we've lost in the debris of humanity's fall. We'll learn new lessons also. It's time for us to reach towards our potential. It is not here, grubbing in filth and squabbling like rabid dogs amongst ourselves. As part of the way to accomplish this, I realise we'll need hara like you, hara with that cold fire, but also with intelligence. I don't want mutton-heads."

"You mean like a body guard, or a militia?" Again, Jarad laughed. "You won't get away with it. Wraxilan might not be interested in the prayer-boys you have, but he won't look kindly on anyone hiving off. You know that. He'll pursue you, wipe you out. And, by the way, there's nothing you can offer me he can't."

"Well, there is, but you won't see it just yet."

"You're a fool to trust me. I'll go back and report all this. Wraxilan will be pleased with me. I'll earn points with him. Are you insane?"

"You won't tell him," Velisarius said quietly. "I'm not a fool. Give me a cigarette."

Jarad did so. He had to admit that, in spite of himself, he was intrigued. But he didn't want to believe that what Velisarius suggested was possible, because it would spoil his cynical view of Wraeththu.

"We'd have to go far from here," Velisarius said, accepting the light Jarad offered him. "We'll have to go the instant the young wolf goes for the throat of the old wolf. In that moment, we'll be ready and our departure won't be noticed. The phyles will rise up and the power struggle for Uigenna will begin."

"Manticker," Jarad murmured. He felt a clutch about his heart; he had to admit Velisarius was right. "Will it be soon?"

"You feel it," Velisarius said.

"Are you ready?"

"Mostly." Velisarius fixed Jarad with a stare. "I don't say the things I do to try and impress you. It's simply information you might find useful. Be prepared and alert. While the plans are in motion, the outcome is not yet decided. There are always hidden variables."

"I'm touched that you care."

Velisarius laughed without humour. "It's not care, Jarad. Like I said, you'd be useful to me too."

Wraxilan did not live, as Jarad had expected, in some harsh industrial space where the light was like metal. He lived in a ruin, yes, a shopping mall that had been turned to legend by wisteria. It had once grown in the central plaza; now it grew everywhere, nourished perhaps by corpses beneath the green. In places, there were carpets of a trailing vine with small leaves.

"So where do I start?" Jarad asked Wraxilan.

Wraxilan was like a great cat; when he wasn't stalking, he was sprawling. He liked heat. And like a cat, he had nests in various parts of the community; always soft cushions, curiously clean. Now he jabbed a finger in Jarad's direction. "What I like about you is the fact you don't care, not about anything. Yet I know you will do as I ask."

Jarad said nothing.

Wraxilan uncoiled from his cushions, began to pace. If he'd had a tail, it would be switching now. "I know this, because it's written all over you as if in black ink. It's the story of your life as it is now."

"Well, I'm ready to do as you ask."

Wraxilan studied him for a moment. Jarad knew what was on his mind, and didn't have to have psychic abilities to be aware of that. Now the phylarch's gaze became veiled. Perhaps untruths would follow. "You must admit that everything we've been through has affected some more than others, and I mean in a bad way."

"You could say that."

"And perhaps you could also say that extreme measures might be needed to make Uigenna what it should be. By that I mean cutting away the dead wood."

"There's no reason you can't break away," Jarad answered. "Most would follow you, and they would be the ones you want."

"I'm not thinking of breaking away. I'm thinking of... remodelling."

"I see. What do you want me to do?"

Wraxilan laughed. "I can see you really *would* do anything. We're both thinking the same thing, I know it. I'm touched you would go that far for me, even though I'm aware you wouldn't do it because you care, or because you're particularly loyal. It's just a job, isn't it?"

Jarad said nothing.

"I can fight my own battles," Wraxilan said. "What I want you for is the aftermath."

"There might be more than one battle," Jarad said. "Like I said, most would follow you, but not all." He paused. "Can we speak plainly?"

"Of course."

"This is about removing Manticker, isn't it?"

Wraxilan stared at Jarad for long, uncomfortable seconds with his tiger eyes. He was weighing up how much he trusted this har before him. Manticker was still powerful. "He's not who he was," Wraxilan said at last. "I'm not the only one who thinks that, for the good of all hara, he must stand down. He doesn't organise our phyles well; he just wants to go out crazily destroying everything in his path. He thinks he's invincible."

"He's not called Manticker the Seventy for nothing," Jarad said.

Wraxilan snickered. "Oh, I know that, but his vision is *not* acute. He can't see that we must consolidate our forces, train them properly. We mustn't be like humes, but we must stop being scattered. Every time I, or others like me, try to call a meeting of the phylarchs to discuss strategies, Manticker manages to disrupt or postpone it. He has his cronies, and they undermine me also. He's like a firecracker. Silent till he's lit. Then the fire comes upon him, and he summons all around him to go out on some crazy killing spree, often into territory where they don't have the advantage. Instead of planning and aiming for targets that are of strategic value, he mindlessly charges into... just anywhere. Hara die; it's a waste. Yes, he has been successful in this way for a couple of years, and that's why the more stupid among us follow him, but things are changing. I hope you agree with me on this."

Jarad thought for a moment. He supposed he should try to have an opinion. "Manticker won't go away quietly, but then we wouldn't be having this conversation if that was at all likely."

Wraxilan nodded his head briefly. "Yes, yes, but I need to know your exact thoughts on him. Do you agree with me?"

"I've already said I will do as you ask. Is that answer enough?"

"Not if you have any doubts."

"I have no doubts."

"Good. As you must know, there are others like you. For the time being, you won't meet them. But after tonight, you shall."

"Tonight? That soon?" Now a shiver of discomfort coursed up Jarad's spine. Did he want to get involved? No, not really. But he'd said he would.

"You'll be sent word," Wraxilan said. "Go to *The Animal Bar* about 8.30. I'll send someone to you there. You won't need his name, nor he yours."

"As you wish."

59

"That is all for now. It's best you don't know anything further until you're needed. Stay close."

It was a dismissal. Jarad inclined his head and walked away, scuffing through the tiny leaves; they released a stinging, green scent as he crushed them.

Jarad went directly to Velisarius; he wasn't sure himself why he did so. He had no intention of going with the har – or did he? Instinct guided his feet to the old church. He didn't question it.

Velisarius was, as usual, surrounded by other hara listening to him talk. He noticed Jarad in the doorway immediately and came to him, led him back to the porch. He didn't appear agitated, but Jarad sensed tension in him. "When?" Velisarius asked.

"Tonight," Jarad answered. "I can tell you no more than that, because that's all I know. But the plot is big. Wraxilan has planned it carefully, I imagine." He paused. "You didn't think it'd be this soon, did you? Are you ready?"

"I'm always ready," Velisarius answered. "I'm not sure you are, however." He looked Jarad in the eye. "Find me if you want to. You know the offer is there. I won't press you more than that. Just think about it carefully. Is Wraxilan's world the one you want to live in?"

Jarad glanced away. "I doubt I'll be able to get further word to you. Wraxilan has asked me to stay close. I don't want to compromise you. As it stands, he might know I've come now. Fortunately, you've been treating me. I have good reason to visit."

Velisarius twisted his mouth into a grim smile. "If what you say is true, he no doubt knows you were here earlier too."

"Come outside," Jarad said.

They went into the street, where there might be harish eyes watching from the rooftops. "There's always one good reason," Jarad said. He took Velisarius's face in his hands and kissed him. "That should be enough."

Velisarius appeared dazed. He hadn't expected that. "Be careful," he said, and went back into the church.

The Animal Bar was an area where Wraxilan's staff tended to congregate for relaxation, close to Wraxilan's residence. There was a yard out back, with benches and tables, dominated and greened with ancient fig trees. Moss grew over the walls and the tiles underfoot. Tame doves roosted among the fig leaves, filling the air with their purring song. The tables were spattered with their droppings. Jarad sat here alone, as he always did when visiting the place. He smoked cigarettes and drank the strong beer brewed on the premises, but not too much. His senses needed to be clear. Around him, conversation and laughter sounded like the cackle of hyenas. But there was no corpse for them to bicker over yet. It was as if he were invisible. Nobody paid him any attention. Perhaps they considered him jinxed.

Jarad watched the sun sink below the walls of the beer garden. He felt nervous, disorientated. Surely Manticker's hara must have suspicions of what was planned? He had strong adepts among his crew. Wraxilan was insane. This could not go well. *What the fuck am I doing?* Jarad wondered. He didn't feel in control of himself.

A har came out from the bar and began to light the lamps hanging from the trees. Shortly afterwards, a blond-haired har came into the garden and sauntered to where Jarad sat. He loomed over Jarad, helped himself to a cigarette from the packet that lay half empty on the table.

The har sat down. He looked younger than Jarad, smug with a false certainty he was splendid and superior. Jarad knew the aura well; he despised it.

"We'll leave here in five minutes," the har said. "In the meantime, look as if you're interested in my company."

Jarad uttered a short, choked laugh. "We are *not* in a movie," he said.

"You sure about that?" The har flicked back his hair, took a draw on the cigarette.

"Not really, no."

"Can I have some of that beer?"

Jarad pushed his glass across the table. "Polite of you to ask," he said.

The har took a swig. "Five minutes: we go."

The har offered no name and Jarad did not ask. As twilight came sifting through the streets, and the harish quarter came alive, they walked in silence. They were lightly armed, carrying only knives. Before they left the bar, the unnamed har mentioned, in response to a query from Jarad, that heavier arms would not be needed. Jarad voiced no further questions. His feet would lead him to his destiny, whatever that would be, one way or another.

Manticker's hara could be heard before they were seen. These were not remotely human noises, nor even animal, but something deeper, wilder, more profane. Jarad's skin prickled. *How could they not know what was coming?*

His companion signalled for them to stop walking, then led them into the shadow of a wall. Ahead, about two hundred yards away, was a hill; any building that had once covered it had been razed. Here a fire was burning; the flames leapt high, playfully, like the tail of a phoenix. Even from this distance, shadowy forms could be discerned moving around the fire. Were they simply celebrating their latest slaughtering foray, or was some kind of ritual taking place up there? Jarad could not tell. He closed his eyes, attempted to extend his senses. As far as he could feel, there were no sentries or lookouts posted. Could Manticker really be so lax about security?

"When the Lion comes, it'll be safe for us to move closer," Jarad's companion murmured.

Jarad opened his eyes, nodded. He wanted a cigarette badly, but any har with sharp senses might see the red spark in the darkness. He didn't want to take the risk and have that baying pack coming down to investigate.

"You can smoke," said the har, clearly picking up on Jarad's desire. "They're out of it, off their faces. They're not looking for trouble."

"Don't underestimate your enemies," Jarad replied, but he pulled his cigarettes from his jacket pocket, simply turning his back to light one.

"What's your name?" the har asked.

Jarad didn't want to say. He shrugged. "What's yours?"

"Terzian." The har suddenly became very still, his posture tense. "Wait..."

Jarad ground out his cigarette quickly.

"They're coming. Wraxilan is coming."

Jarad pulled on Terzian's arm. "Down!" He peered ahead as they crouched beneath the wall, trying to penetrate the shadows cast by the light of the fire on the hill. "What does he want of us? Did he tell you?"

Terzian shook his head. "We wait. We'll know."

"Fucking stupid strategy," Jarad muttered. "They're as bad as each other."

"Maybe so," Terzian replied. "But one will win. Who's *your* money on?"

Jarad could see Wraxilan's hara approaching now. He had to admit they were more organised than he'd thought. They were part of the shadows; ghosts gliding through patches of darkness, slinking along the tops of broken walls like cats, looking almost like cats. Unless you knew they were there, you wouldn't notice them.

"How many on the hill, you think?" Jarad asked.

Terzian drew in his breath. "Manticker's elite comprise about fifty hara, but he loses some of them regularly. Between thirty-five and fifty, I'd say."

"Do you sense any sentries?"

A pause. "No."

"It's too easy," Jarad said.

"There are others like us, pairs of hara closing in," Terzian said. "We don't know anything, so Manticker can't pick up too much from us."

"Our intention is enough," Jarad said dryly.

The shadows he'd perceived around them were now close to the hill.

"Let's move forward a short way," Jarad said.

Still crouching down, they edged along the wall, keeping close to it. As they drew nearer to the hill, Jarad could see a tall shape silhouetted against the flames, arms outspread. He paused, gestured for Terzian to do likewise. Sometime in the last few minutes, the power had shifted. Jarad was leader now.

A tingle went through him. He knew the tall figure was Manticker. What was going through that har's mind? He had survived countless battles. He had earned his epithet annihilating seventy armed humans in one raging spree. He had always won against desperate odds. Yet now he had let himself become vulnerable. Did he really believe he was so safe, in the heart of this merciless community he had created?

Jarad was overwhelmed with a feeling of futility. How was Manticker any worse than Wraxilan? None of it meant anything. He should turn now, leave, perhaps even seek out Velisarius and wait for the clamorous psychic cry that would mean either Wraxilan or Manticker was dead. Then he could make decisions.

But then there was a voice in his mind. *Oh, but you cannot go. Not you, Jarad.*

Jarad sucked in his breath; his body jerked.

"What?" Terzian hissed.

"Nothing."

"That wasn't nothing. You whole body just kind of... rippled. What is it?"

Jarad turned, looked the har in the eye. "Well, put it this way. *Someone* knows we're here. I got a message."

"What did it say?"

"That we can't leave."

"I wasn't thinking of doing that. Tell them."

Jarad sighed, suppressed a spasm of irritation.

The hill was surrounded now by Wraxilan's hara, and on the summit ahead of them all had become quiet, because Manticker's hara had become aware of the approach. Jarad moved forward again, more quickly.

He saw Wraxilan step onto the path of flattened dirt that led up the hill. It was flanked by torches. Wraxilan looked confident, commanding, a natural leader. In comparison, Manticker and his troupe stooped above him like addled witch doctors, bewitched by flame.

Jarad found himself halfway up the hill, Terzian close behind. It was as if they weren't actually there in body, but merely spirit witnesses.

Manticker was naked from the waist up, dressed only in some kind of shamanic garb; a kilt of rags, fur and feathers. His hair was a wild, matted tangle, dangling in ropes over his chest and down his back; his face was daubed with chalky lines of paint. The air smelled of blood around him.

They are the two selves of Wraeththu, Jarad thought. He wondered if some toxic fume from the fire ahead had affected his mind. Manticker was the wild primal feminine, the Dark Mother, crouched in shadows, goddess of entrails. Hers were the secrets of life and death, the essential secrets in the deepest part of every living thing. Wraxilan was the male principle of the sun; open, visible, radiant, swaggering. There were no secrets there. If Velisarius were here, he would surely say that this moment was a nexus point, and the only way forward was for these two forces to combine, to become bigger than the sum of their parts. But neither Manticker nor Wraxilan would see that. They didn't know they were avatars of greater forces.

Manticker uttered a hiss through his teeth. "What is it, cub?" he asked.

"Time for change," Wraxilan said, in a reasonable voice.

"That is every moment of every day," Manticker said. "You took long enough to get to this moment."

"Then you're prepared for it to be you and me?" Wraxilan gestured around him. "Leave these hara out of it?"

Manticker nodded, just once. "Why create waste?" He leapt into the air, spun around, and kicked Wraxilan in the face. Wraxilan fell backwards, but had scrambled away before Manticker could land another blow.

And so they fought their archetypal battle. Leaping shadows against the flames, a fatal dance. There were no weapons involved, other than their own sinew and bone. The hara around them were silent, perhaps not even daring to breathe. First the advantage went one way, then another. It was as if time had stopped, placing them in an arena of no-time.

Neither can win, Jarad thought. *Don't they know that?*

No, they don't....

Jarad shuddered. Was this Velisarius in his mind, or Lianvis? Were they watching from somewhere close? The touch did not feel familiar to him, though. It was distant, cold, a star of thought from some lightless reach.

There was blood upon the combatants now, claw marks down Wraxilan's chest, visible where his shirt had been torn away. A cut above Manticker's eye rained ichor down his face, onto his chest: it had filled his mouth. Maybe they would carry on fighting until they had torn each other utterly to pieces, and then still the battle would continue, in motes of harried air, in leaves and dust and ashes.

Jarad realised his hand was resting upon the hilt of the knife tucked into his belt. This body wasn't his. Even this mind wasn't his. He was riding a vehicle of flesh, an observer.

Time stopped. Then sped up.

Jarad reeled backwards against Terzian. He hadn't been aware of making any other movement, but heard Terzian breathe, "What the fuck?"

Terzian's hands were upon his arms, holding him up, gripping hard. Above them, the fight had paused.

Manticker was staring at his belly; a blade was sunk there

nearly to the hilt. The pause didn't last long. Wraxilan roared a lion's victory cry. And pounced. Gripped the knife, turned it. Turned it and gouged flesh for what seemed an eternity. Then he kicked Manticker away from him.

For a moment, stillness. And then a cacophony of snarls, shouts, growls. Both troupes of hara bayed at one another, their bodies rising and falling from crouched to upright postures. They looked like apes standing off against each other, rival tribes thrown into confusion because one leader had fallen. Wraxilan stalked around the fire, his arms held high, his head thrown back. Manticker lay on the ground, trying to rise, panting, as his lifeblood pooled about him from the ruin of his guts.

Wraxilan pointed at Manticker's hara. "Finish it!" he roared, and his own hara leapt forward with whoops and cries. So much for keeping other hara out of it. Manticker's hara ran and were pursued.

Only three remained by their leader, figures cloaked from head to foot, their faces almost invisible but for mouths painted black, and white chins.

The cries were dying away as Manticker's faithful scattered. Only now did Wraxilan lower his arm.

The three cloaked hara stooped down by Manticker, inspected him, but they must have known it was over. Jarad could feel Manticker fading away. The flames of his fire were not so fierce now; soon that too would die.

One of Wraxilan's aides had remained. Jarad did not know the har's name, because he was rarely around, and somewhat secretive, but he was older than most; an advisor. Now he glanced to where Jarad and Terzian stood upon the path. He beckoned them with a jerk of his head. "Did you see who threw that?" he demanded.

"No," Terzian said. "I didn't see it."

Jarad shook his head. Had he thrown the knife? He really didn't know. But there was no blade in his belt now. Wraxilan would not approve of this unasked-for assistance. He could fight his own battles. But Terzian must have seen. Why would he protect Jarad now? They didn't know one another.

One of the hara crouching by Manticker stood up, threw back the hood to his robe. He looked to be soume-prevalent, very feminine. His hair was dark, hanging to his waist. He pointed at Wraxilan. "You are cursed," he said, matter-of-factly. "You have my word for it."

Wraxilan uttered a snort, and gestured at Jarad and Terzian. "Kill them," he said. "We don't want his witches left alive."

Terzian moved forward at once, but Wraxilan's advisor said sharply, "No."

Wraxilan turned to him swiftly. "No?"

The advisor nodded once. "They are Sulh. Leave them be." In his words was the unspoken message: *Don't mess with them.* The Sulh were a foreign tribe, their hara often found close to phyle leaders and others of high rank. They were not feared exactly, but they were respected. No one knew who their leaders were. The advisor addressed the Sulh now. "Take these remains and be gone from this place. Our quarrel is not with you."

The Sulh set about lifting Manticker between them. Parts of him, it seemed, had become detached. Jarad turned away. He felt disorientated. Something huge was finishing in his life, something new beginning. The Sulh were moving away, melting into the darkness. But, Jarad was sure, they would not forget this night. He would not want to be cursed by a Sulh.

Feeling attention upon him, Jarad turned round again. Wraxilan was staring at him, his expression guarded. "Who threw the knife?" he asked. It was clear it had to be either Jarad or Terzian, since neither of them had joined the pursuit. That in itself was unusual behaviour.

Jarad simply stared back.

Wraxilan nodded, sucked in his cheeks. "Perhaps," he said, "it was the Aghama." Then he laughed, a little crazily.

"It saved time," Terzian said, "but the outcome would have been no different."

"Wouldn't it, now?" Wraxilan said.

Terzian placed a bunched fist upon his own chest. "You are Archon." He bowed his head.

"Yes." Wraxilan stared into the night, in the direction the hunt had taken, but nothing could be heard of it now. Embers popped in the fire, sounding like cracking bones. "We must celebrate," Wraxilan said. "The Archon and his faithful elite." He held out a hand and Terzian took it, kissed it. Jarad hung back.

Wraxilan looked past Terzian, directly at him. *And you?* His eyes seemed to say.

Jarad could barely function. He certainly couldn't speak. Everything had changed. These hara were no longer like mindless gang-boys playing at being hard and street-wise. They had become figures of history, and their words – every word – would be remembered. This night they had begun a new future, one that perhaps they might not have had before.

"It's as it's meant to be," Jarad managed to say. But he could not bring himself to bow his head, or to kiss Wraxilan's hand. He had played his part.

"Come with me," Wraxilan said quietly.

"I will be with you," Jarad replied, "but I need some time. I'll come to you."

"Squeamish, Jarad? Surely not."

At the mention of his name, Jarad heard Terzian draw in his breath. That name was known.

"Not that," Jarad said. "This is... overwhelming. More significant than... I need some time."

Wraxilan narrowed his eyes. "Very well. But don't take too long."

Velisarius and Lianvis were waiting in a doorway, in a narrow alley not far from the hill. Jarad wasn't looking for them, but of course they'd been looking for him. Lianvis uttered a sigh at the sight of him, embraced him. Jarad remained unyielding in his hold. He stared at Velisarius over Lianvis's shoulder. "Did you speak to me?" he asked. "In my mind?"

Velisarius shook his head. "No, but I heard... something. Not words, not even an idea, but... something."

"Who was it?"

Lianvis let go of Jarad, stepped back. His expression was bleak.

"Perhaps there's a wider interest than we thought in what happened tonight," Velisarius replied. He drew in his breath. "Our hara are ready to leave. Wraxilan's inner circle will be occupied this night. They won't notice us depart, and then we'll simply vanish into the landscape. Listen..." He put a hand upon Jarad's shoulder. "You hear that?"

There were sounds upon the night, not all of them audible with the physical ear. Songs of mourning, songs of victory, songs of yearning, the barking of dogs, the howl of cats, the clamour of metal breaking. "They know," Jarad said. "They all know."

"The writing of history," Velisarius said dryly. "It's interesting." He paused. "You won't come with us." It wasn't a question.

"This isn't my world," Jarad replied. "There is one, but it isn't here, nor with you."

Velisarius smiled. "I know. We will remain allies, though, Jarad. Don't forget that. One day, hara close to you will question it, but don't forget."

"Jarad," Lianvis said, so many feelings in the simple sound of his name.

"Be safe," Jarad said, reaching briefly to touch Lianvis's cheek.

"I will always know your name," Lianvis said. "Whatever it becomes."

"Go south," Velisarius said. "*If* you'll take advice from me. There are hara waiting for you. They don't know it yet, but they are. Uigenna are not the only way, and neither is mine."

Jarad laughed coldly. "Hara waiting for me? What am I to do with them?"

"You will know," Velisarius said. He addressed Lianvis. "Come, Viss, we have work to do. We cannot linger."

After Velisarius and Lianvis had gone, Jarad remained where he was, unable to move. What compunctions coursed through his flesh? He could barely tell. Something had touched him this night, *controlled* him... or had it simply been the actions of a part of himself that had become detached from his conscious being? He blinked up at the sky, so full of stars. The sky had come back to the earth as the lights of humanity winked out.

A sudden breeze came down the alley, scooping up litter and dust in its wake. Jarad would follow it, go where it led him. As he began to move, he felt as if the Jarad he'd been before was left standing behind him like a ghost. He'd stepped out of that shell. And the name came to him then: *You are Ponclast. You always have been. Own the name, and bring it to our history.*

The Resting Place

A pool, a silent grove:
These are the luxuries of my repose.
I fold my ebon wings,
On bloom-striated ground,
Lulled by the mellow sighs
Of the silver-eyed har who crept
From the lush, dark forest
And nervously came to my fire.
His eyes are copper now, in a flickering hail of flame,
Reflecting sadness that I cannot quench
Or even reach with my dull-grasping paws.

Dew flecks, dripping from my spreading plumes,
Spiralling, I rise, and morning comes,
Between the distant mountains and the sky,
Shy-peeping, with red, anointing rays.

Below me in the shrinking sward,
His hair is white and lovely on the green,
Trailing wild, eburneous and free:
A blaze of light
Against the carpet of young grass.

But still I leave;
To grasp the tenuous thread that leads me on,
A vagueness in the sky that screams
"I cannot stay!" And pulls again.

Higher, and the air is warmer.
My mane of darkness,
Heated by the sun:
My only warmth.
The distance, the promise
Sings the calling song.
I fly.

September 1977

By the River of If Only, in the Land of Might Have Been

There were no questions in the wilderness.

The debris of our camp was lit by a cold glow that came down from the sky. How? I don't know. We couldn't see the stars from there, and the sun and moon wore shrouds of impenetrable cloud, shining unseen above. We knew of these heavenly guardians, for they were in our legends and rituals. We spoke to them often, but we never looked into their faces. Our tribe was Obliviata, the Forgotten, aimlessly treading the Wheel of Life, around and around.

We were hardly ever cold in the wilderness, but never too warm either, never starving, never sated; existing in a tenuous state, between comfort and discomfort. To the East, the empty grey towers of a wasteland town poked at the sky; a place where lichens thrived. We gathered the lichens. Some could be used for healing, some for enabling the eyes to see beyond the edge of the world, some for poisons. The most toxic had the name of Sweetbreath, because its perfume made you weep with poignant joy before the dreams of death begin. It was said, among the hara of my tribe, that people craved death from the Sweetbreath, because the visions in its exhalations made our fragile lives seem too wearing and pointless an experience to endure. The victims of this candid fragrance gather handfuls of the lichen, filling their mouths and eyes and noses with its taste, its seductive aroma. Death might not come fast, but it is without pain, without regret; the dream becomes reality, becomes the final sinking that we all crave, all seek, becomes the numbing kiss that leaves only the lips sensitive to heat and pain. I have seen them, those people, as they died. They were all smiling.

To the South lie the plains, the canyons, where flames grow from the earth like flowers; red flowers. Gangarad the shaman told us that it was possible to pick those flowers, the sweet, hot fruit of fire. You could walk right in and take them in your arms. Somebody asked him, "But do they burn?" He smiled and said the caress of fire must necessarily always burn. "Then why do it?"

"Because, for a moment, you can be at one with that element. You can take it and taste it, the heat of it touches your soul. Though it will scorch your body black, you can pick the blossoms of fire, that are the tears of the Great Lion, the dew of the Rising Sun beyond the veil." These are the words of Gangarad, whose left hand was almost transparent from the scalding embrace of Fire. He was cautious. There are some that never came back from the South.

To the West lay the wide, sluggish river we called the Torrent of If Only. Perhaps this was because nobody ever followed it far enough to discover where it ended. "If only we could go with the river," hara would say as they sat on the sulphurous banks. It disappeared into a haze, sometimes with a gleam like gunmetal, sometimes green and slick as the undulating spine of a great serpent. If you drank the waters from the river of If Only you could live your dreams, but from a distance. I and my friend Omarel did so, just once. I saw the wilderness fade away. Around me, grass sprang like living wires from a fertile soil. Across the field, a slow figure moved towards me that had no face – for I faced the West, which is the direction of the twilight – but, all the same, I knew it to be myself; a self that was strong and free. I held out my arms for the uniting, the melding of flesh that could make me whole and spirit me away from the wilderness, but my body remained cold. I looked down. I stood in a circle of ash, where nothing grew, and I knew that wherever I trod that ash would be with me, binding me to reality. The figure glided past me; blind, wandering, searching. I roared with despair and found myself beside the Torrent of If Only once again, my chest constricted with a grief too great to be contained by flesh, that had to be screamed and screamed away.

The North was hidden from us. Nobody knew what lay that way. All we could see, far away, was a black wall that the shamans said was smooth as glass, and poisonous to the flesh. We were also told that the wilderness was so large, it could never have been traversed in one lifetime, on foot.

Sometimes, travellers came in from the east, because hara lived in the old cities there. They treated us with contempt, because they had Old Things the Men Had Left Behind which, they said, made life easier for them. We tolerated this behaviour, so that we could choose from the goods they brought for trade. Ananke, with the seeking eyes, once bargained for a silver net for me that I could wear around my neck. I wore it all the time for there were stars within it and stories of the past, where the wildernesses were but earth's own secrets and not a violent testimony bequeathed by humanity.

I had known for a while that Ananke liked me, and I liked him, although he had a reputation for eccentricity. When he gave me the silver, I lay in the dust and opened myself to him. Afterwards, I found I needed to do that again and again. Ananke did not seem to mind. He liked to speak about the stars to me, because they were important to him. I just wanted to inhale him, so that his scent was with me even when he wasn't there.

"I am a star," he said, "and at the end of each of my glowing points, there is a different feeling for you."

I didn't know whether I was supposed to laugh at that, but I did. We used to laugh a lot, but sometimes I felt it was only a superficial thing, like the gleam on water that hides the dark currents beneath. I wondered what it could be that was hidden within the laughter and whether I would like it. Ananke spoke to me with his eyes, trusting that I understood his silent language. I don't think I ever really did. And I never found out what lay within the laughter.

Then there was the time when Isatar went mad from the pull of the hidden moon and attacked me in the dark, by the river. I don't know why he chose me, but he tore my skin, and the silver net that Ananke had given me was lost in the dust forever. Poor Isatar. I had to hold him close for a whole day until he could see properly again.

Ananke went strange as a red eye. He no longer laughed and, soon afterwards, gave himself up for sacrifice at the Doon Tower in the east, so there were no more gifts for me. I gathered the special mushroom for him that weeps indigo blood and performed a ritual all by myself in his memory.

I wish that could have been a turn of the Wheel in my life, but it wasn't. Days came and went, as always. We gathered the lichens, charmed dew into our metal troughs, and fought those who came to steal our land. At night, I stared at the sky, as I always did, remembering the feel of Ananke's hands on my waist, his breath against my neck, his scent in my throat. I couldn't understand why I felt so strange, so sad, so empty, why all I could think about was him. Before he left, he'd said to me, "I'm going to Doon." It had surprised me. No-one went there unless they wanted to die, and Ananke was a respected figure in our tribe. As far as I could see, he had everything to live for.

"Why?" I'd asked, truly puzzled.

He'd sighed and looked around him and then at me. "Because I can remember."

"Remember what?"

"When things were pure. When I believed in the stars."

I couldn't understand him. It seemed nonsense. "And that makes you seek Doon? You won't be able to think about those things again after that!"

He'd given me an odd, almost fearful look, and had touched my shoulders with his long hands. "No," he'd said and put his lips against my mouth. So strange. He did not give me breath at all, just his touch. And then he left me.

Sometimes, I went to sing and dance in the ruins, behind the low-slung canopies and tents of the tribe. In my head, the sky was a different colour and the air full of rich scents. There, my confusing thoughts of Ananke could express themselves in movement, which I found more comfortable. Once, as I danced, a mad nomad came upon me and said, "You are lost! You are all lost!"

I asked him what he meant and he shook his head, muttering words I could not hear. I wanted to understand because I believe that all insane people must be incredibly wise, but he'd said all he wanted to say and only slapped at my hands when I tried to approach him.

After that, I walked alone to the foot of the Tower of Doon, expecting to see blood upon the stones outside, but there was nothing there. It was silent and lifeless, and I was too afraid to go inside, in case it thought I had come for death. I sat and leaned against its smooth side and thought of Ananke's hair and eyes for a while. Then a strange thing happened. I stood up and walked towards the east; just kept on going. There was no conscious thought that initiated this action, no decision that I could recognise. I just found myself walking.

"This is senseless!" I thought, because I had no water or food with me, and it would be very easy to get lost among the fallen towers and skeleton stones of the dead towns. There would be hostile creatures and hostile tribes living there too but, even knowing these things, I did not want to turn back. I *could* not turn back.

For a long time, I hardly saw a living creature, just the odd stray cur who whined and winced when it saw me, before darting away. Later, as the sun began to sink, a troupe of young harlings emerged from a grating at my feet, and pelted me with stinking mud and sharp stones. I ran, and they did not follow.

When the dark came, I happened across a palm-stroker sitting in the dirt by the side of an old road, in the shadow of a tumbled house. By that time, I was feeling hungry and thirsty. Corroding dust had shredded my sandals and had started work on my feet. I had kept walking for hours, my mind a fierce star of confusing light, leading me to only the gods know where. The palm-stroker, clearly taking pity on me, offered his hand out of the darkness, and told me he could change my future for the price of a pitcher of sweet juice. I looked around the desolate, empty landscape and replied that I would be hard-pressed to find somewhere to buy such a luxury, even if I could afford it. "You have seeking eyes," he told me. "Maybe for your breath I will change your future anyway."

I squatted down beside him. He had a small fire of twigs and moss, and I noticed a grey loaf of bread, half-eaten, protruding from a worn, leather bag at his feet. He caught the direction of my gaze. "Is it only Hunger's Haunt, then, that brings me your company, rather than a need for my art?"

I had to tell him. "I walked to the tower of Doon and it made me keep on walking. Perhaps that is my death. Perhaps I need your talents more than I realise, more than I need to quiet the beast gnawing my belly."

The palm-stroker laughed and offered me some of what he had. "Where do you come from, little seeker?" he asked as he watched me eat.

"From the west. I belong to a tribe that lives beside the Torrent of If Only."

"Ah, the Obliviata, the Forgotten Ones. You see, I have heard of you. Maybe, you are not as lost as you imagine. I know too that you sprang from the ruins of the tribe of Uigenna, from their blood upon the ground, in fact. You are far from the territory of your parent tribe here, you know, or perhaps I should say, the memory of your parent tribe."

"I didn't know we had a parent tribe." I was more interested in what was in my mouth than what my ancestry might be.

"Didn't your hostling, or your father, tell you the tales that are carried by mind, the Speaking tradition?"

"I never knew my father. He could be anyone. My hostling died from a toxic wound when the Grey-Limbs came and attacked us. I was very small then. I can only remember his hands – not his voice, his eyes or anything else."

The palm-stroker nodded, though I doubt if he was interested in details of my personal history. He was looking at my mouth and asked me to unbraid my hair, which I did. "So hidden from the sun and moon are we, yet they live on in the hair of our children," he said, stroking it. "Where will you walk to, little seeker? Will you walk until you die?"

"If that is my fate, perhaps you can change it," I suggested.

He lifted my hands in his own and looked at them keenly. "You have lost a lover." It started as a statement then somehow changed into a question when he looked at me. I knew he meant to confuse me, for love is one of the words used in the past to cover untruths of feeling. We, being more evolved, called this thing aruna, which was the connection of bodies, and much more truthful.

"I have heard talk of this," I replied. "I know what you mean. If aruna is love, then what you say is true. The har who touched me most went to Doon. I never saw him again."

"And what is this *Doon* you speak of?"

"The tower, as I told you. The one that made me walk. Those who seek death go there to find it, I suppose. I only went there to remember Ananke. I had no intention of seeking death, or at least I'm not conscious of doing so."

"There are no towers that bring death in this city."

"This is no longer a city, and how can you know about the towers? Many strange things can be found here. Anything is possible. This much I know for sure."

The palm-stroker raised his brows, but said nothing. He resumed his scrutiny of my destiny. I watched him wrinkle his nose and shake his head. After a while, this discomforted me so much that I snatched away my hands. "Clearly, you don't find much joy in what you see," I said.

"Nothing is permanent," he replied. "That's what I do – change the future."

"Then change it."

"First, I must have my silver – in this case the molten metal of your loins, the priceless currency of your breath. The future for you as I see it is this: very shortly we shall be part of each other, which I shall enjoy. Then we shall see about the rest."

He had about him the heady aroma of desire, which filled the dull night air with flowers. When he removed his robes, I could see the marks of old scars upon his chest and arms, the marks of deprivation which were the revelation of his ribs and hips. I lay down in the dust and ashes and he said, "You are far too passive." It was not a comment I felt the need to respond to. He gave me visions of crimson skies, a sweet smell of smoke that brought the dawn with it, and a single bird high in the light grey sky, dipping and soaring. We had taken aruna through the night, yet it had not seemed that long. I held out my hands. "You promised," I said.

The palm-stroker smiled. He rubbed my fingers with his thumbs and pushed hard against the skin of my palms.

"Little need," he said. "You will find what you seek in the Tower of Doon. Go back and climb it. Face the direction of what is hidden and – perhaps – something may be revealed."

I looked over my shoulder. To the west, I could see the crooked finger of Doon against the sky. Climb it? Clearly, this har was insane and I had wasted my essence on him. My palms tingled.

"You doubt my words," said the palm-stroker.

"Is death my only future, then? Did you do this to me?"

He shook his head. "A long time ago, your people were cursed into the wilderness. As time goes on, it may be that the curse fades and some of you may escape it."

"What curse? Why?"

The palm-stroker got to his feet and slung his bag over his shoulder. "It may be that your fate was to wander eastwards until some calamity befell you, or you were adopted into some other lost tribe. I changed your future for you, as I promised. Now I must go. Take my advice, do what I say." He bowed and expressed a sweeping farewell with his free arm. I watched him clamber over the rubble, robes flapping, towards another spire of smoke, where others might wait for his art.

For a while I felt quite alone and kicked at the ashes of his fire. There seemed little to do. Life was beginning to creep around me; the suggestion of hidden hara, furtive animals or curious spirits. I turned around and walked back the way I had come.

There was luck for me on the return journey. A small group of traders, attracted by my loose hair, which in their body language signalled an invitation of some kind, encouraged me to share their fire. I spent most of the day with them, listening to their tales of the city circuits. They spoke of places where hara had set themselves up as kings, like men, and gave orders in loud voices, clawing back the ruins into some kind of order. They told me of other places, where everybody lives alone, shunning all contact except on certain nights, when wild, orgiastic rituals take place for the conception of harlings. And there were places too, at the end of all tales, where life and death have become inseparable, and strange creatures of light and dark walk the shattered stone. I wasn't sure how much to believe of what the traders told me.

Halfway through the night, a pull from the west dragged me from under the blanket I was sharing and to my feet. The har whose arms had held me muttered in his sleep, no doubt feeling the cold, but I was already off into the night, shivering like prey, determined as a hunter.

In the grey predawn, I reached the steps of the listing spire that is the Tower of Doon. The cracked glass and crumbling, granular stone were close enough for me to touch, should I want to do so. I paused on the threshold and tried to peer through the dark glass. There was nothing to see. It was all too dim. Knowing I could only go forward, I took a great lungful of air and stepped through the door.

What I found was disappointing. I had expected arcane and terrible things, but all that faced me was merely rubbish; faded writing on the walls, old strips of cloth and paper hanging down from the walls and ceiling. Well, I thought, then I must go up. And up and up and up. There was no sound in the Tower of Doon, other than my own bare feet on the greasy stone. I could smell damp, though, and in places the walls were moist and rotten. It was almost completely dark in there. Had Ananke trodden these steps before me? What had been in his mind? It occurred to me, for the first time, that he could not have felt much true liking for me, to leave me so abruptly and so finally. If it had been me in his place, would he have wandered into the ruins in his grief? Would he now be climbing these steps? Somehow, I thought not. Questions filled my head, and just a faint whisper of anger. Was it really Ananke I was looking for? Was it he who'd dragged my feet to the east, or something else? I paused in the dim light and it was so far to go back down, so far to carry on up. I had no weapons with me. This was senseless. I kept on climbing.

I came to a floor with glass walls all around. Most of them were cracked, all of them were dirty, so it meant that a strange light came into the building there. The sun was beginning to rise. Tired of climbing, I decided to investigate the rooms. I must have been virtually at the summit of Doon, for the glass-walled place was really a sort of path that curled round the edge of the tower, with rooms leading off it. I walked along the path, around and around, peering into the rooms. They all seemed empty. Looking out through the glass, I could see for such a long way. I had never seen so far. It made the world look so small. In the distance, I could even see dark dots that I thought might be the tents of my tribe, and there was a glinting, sulky stripe that just had to be the Torrent. A heat haze to the South proclaimed the boundary to the realm of fire. And to the north... Nothing could have prepared me for what I saw in that direction.

There was a great tumble of stones, each one bigger than the sky itself; grey and black and brown. Paler ribbons threaded through them that looked like deep walkways through the rock, some of them coruscating slightly, as if water flowed there. Ragged birds hung over the sharp peaks of the stones, screaming in the new day. The north; of all the directions of the world, it was the most fascinating, because we knew so little about it. From the territory of the Obliviata, all that could be seen of it were black cliffs in the distance, but here... I was awed by the size and splendour of the bare rock. How many hara had stood as I stood now, gazing out through the glass, perhaps waiting for death, and unsure how to claim it for their own? Was Doon the shrine of self-destruction – the dark cup, the razor knife? I had seen no sign of life or death here. Doon was empty. I was sure of it.

And then the sun lifted himself from the bed of dawn, rising behind the Tower of Doon, up over the cracked and fallen city, up above the broken needles of other, lesser towers, to stretch out the sleepy limbs of his muted light over the mountains before me. It happened suddenly, as if there had been a crack in the enveloping clouds – which I knew was impossible – but the grey and the brown and the black of the hidden north absorbed the light and threw it back to me in a splash of colour; green and purple, dark

79

blue and yellow. I blinked against this unbelievable vision, this hallucination of exploding light and life. There before me, yet far away, I could see the sparkling foam of water falling, the placid gleam of a great lake, the moving black motes that became, as I stared, a slow-moving herd of beasts loping to the water. There were great forests that swept down onto lawns of flashing green, starred with acid-bright blooms. The Tower of Doon took the sun, impaled upon its crown, and showed me this: *this* that existed, unseen by the Forgotten hara, above the black cliffs, the gateways of impenetrable, vertical stone. This. If I'd known the word then, I'd have called it Paradise.

In those moments, as I blinked at the hills, I thought of my tribe scrubbing, banished, exiled in the wilderness and how they never questioned what might lie beyond the boundaries. All we needed was courage to investigate. We could follow the Torrent to its end. We could run across the plains of fire. There had to be another side to the ruined towns – they couldn't go on for ever – and above the black cliffs, there was life. Whatever we had done to be imprisoned within the wilderness, within the city, within ourselves, meant nothing. There were no real barriers to cross other than those erected by our own lassitude, our idle acceptance of the very least, because it required effort to attain the very most. Some hara must know the truth because they came from far away and yet they never told us. The palm-stroker had known - obviously. This was the secret of the Tower of Doon. Death, yes, maybe, but not extinction of the flesh. Ananke must have seen this. Did his bones still lie here or...?

I looked towards the north once more. I felt hot tears gather in my eyes. It was a strange experience and oddly cleansing. I wept aloud, as a harling might, as the harling I'd once been probably had, at the time his hostling had become cold for ever. I could not remember. To me, the release was the first of its kind. I had not wept for Ananke.

"You did not come back for me," I said, and punched the thick glass with my hand. "Why didn't you come back? Why?"

There was grief, hot and hard, around me on every side, that I could not escape. There was anger too, but it would not stop me following him. We might never meet again, but my future had been changed for me. I would follow. I would find a way through the black cliffs, and soon my feet would be trampling grass, not ash, and my vision self would have a face, and it would embrace me, and I would be whole.

There are no questions in the wilderness...

Beneath My Skin a Vein of You

You know why we came up with the word chesna? You think it was to elevate our passions above rank humanity? Not really. The word was pretty, yes; as were a lot of those we invented: aruna, althaia, harhune, feybraiha, Wraeththu itself. But beauty and ascension were not the only reasons this term of affection came about. Basically, we rebelled against the human idea of love and its consequent life-trap, nuptial contracts. We'd seen it all, what we considered the pettiness of it, the destructive nature of love, with its shadow selves of jealousy and fear, the numbing unlife of the decades' long marriages we'd witnessed around us in our human families and those of our friends. The prison walls of perpetuating the species, overseen by a jailer on an eighteen-year contract. We wanted none of that. We celebrated liberty, the freedom from what we considered outmoded human notions and customs, human states of being. We were *other* now.

But still, we loved.

And – once the orgy of inception had inevitably blackened to cold embers – we needed to reproduce.

So, we became chesna – chesnari, not lovers. We got with pearl and not with child. Our young were colts and calves, soon running at our sides, not helpless pups easily slaughtered or hampering our mobility. But beneath it all, always, were inescapable realities. Dress them up in ritual finery, so we might. Didn't change anything, not really. Chesna wears fantastic robes, but within its shimmering folds hide the mites of undoing.

I am Barley; this is my tale.

Passions were crater-hot in our incandescent early days; mine no less than any other's. Running with the Unneah out of Carmine City, newly-incepted and strong in my bones, I felt I ruled the world. I might no longer be wholly male, but I was more fierce, more brutal, more unforgiving. No concessions to soume, that terrifying female aspect of my being. And yet...

Wake up, become…

And yet...

I remember how easy it had been to be brazen and hungry with most other hara. How we laughed at our own debauchery, our wanton coupling. *This was life* and freedom, unconstrained. Nothing could hold us back and certainly not the lightless voids of human emotion. We had transcended such things. Until, inevitably, the unexpected happens. The unspeakable.

Shaska was not a regular at our fires. He simply appeared one early evening with two other hara. At that time, the phyle, which comprised about thirty of us, had taken over an old, half-dilapidated three-story dwelling, but we continued to build our evening fires outside, in the air. I didn't notice Shaska at once, like I'd done with so many others I'd then been immediately ravenous to sample. These newcomers were cautious hara, smelling us out, deciding whether it would benefit them to hang around. They were tall and oaken-skinned, from an Indian-Asian ethnic human group, with finely-drawn features and brooding yet piercing eyes. They wore their hair coiled in black ropes upon their heads and had painted sunburst stripes on their foreheads in red and yellow. Our phylarch made no secret of the fact he found them interesting, exotic perhaps. Phyles competed to have the best decorative elements, livestock being the most coveted. Sometimes, these hara became fixtures, other times they stole away without even being noticed that much. Shaska and his friends were destined to stay, at least for a while.

He noticed me before I noticed him, and when I felt that attention, I began to show off around him, for no particular reason other than to enjoy myself. I didn't at first realise how he lit me up from the inside out, made me more amusing, more flamboyant, more *glittering*. Then, when I *did* notice something, specifically how keenly I felt the absence of these qualities away from his presence, I accepted I had to have him. It was no different from any previous desire, I thought. Same hunger, same longing, same physical pull. Delicious craving that's almost painful, and the relief when it comes breaks the stars.

That night. As the phyle devoured their evening meal, Shaska and I gazed at one another across flames and through smoke. I could not put food to my lips, for he was the only sustenance I wanted. He had watched me with patience for months, perhaps extending tendrils of his light to touch mine. Now, our slow-burn desire was ignited to its full.

I stood up and left the group, knowing he would follow. The ruins of the city around us were as stark as black and white cartoons, each moment of our encounter like frames on a storyboard. The sky was deepest red at the horizon, fading to muggy black above us. No stars to be broken. Just the silhouettes of the past and the heat of the universe, our being. We had no need of words.

Far enough away from our hara, yet not so far as to put ourselves in danger, we crept into a derelict house and set about our business. Sounds uninvolved, doesn't it, mindless even? But that's how it was, how it was supposed to be, at least. I intended to have this animal itch within me scratched as deeply as possible, then I could move on. Perhaps he felt the same. We never spoke of that. But something happened to us that night that went beyond physical needs. This was no sky-shattering arunic explosion, simply a kind of recognition, a soft falling of feathers within that murmured, "Ah, I see now. I see."

Although we parted on cool terms, just the touch of Shaska's fingers on my face, I knew I was changed. Couldn't define it exactly. I went back to the fire and ate the cooked meat that had been left amid the tin plates and ashes. Nohar had noticed us sneak off, and by that time others had also left the gathering, no doubt to scratch itches of their own. Shaska did not come back to the fire. In its dying embers, I felt cold. The meat was burned and acrid.

After some minutes, I felt I had to move and slunk down to the slow-moving river two streets away from the phyle house. Sentries were posted among the riverfront ruins: I could see the occasional orange spark of their cigarettes, but nothing more. Cries drifted across the water, and once a convulsion of gunfire. I saw a gout of flame. Then all fell to silence, the rind of the red sky turning the water to burned lead: a huge molten metal snake sliding towards a distant ocean. I felt somehow sad, somehow stretched, yet at the same time joyous – these were alien sensations. Instinctively, I knew I must stay away from Shaska; he had infected me somehow. My mind kept replaying scenes of our intimacy. I wanted to deny them, but couldn't.

Dreams that night, of course, were plagues. I was searching for Shaska through the ruins of the city. I couldn't find him. I stumbled across corpses and every time thought – and dreaded – it would be him. I dreamed I walked up to him by the evening fire and spoke his name, and he looked at me as if he didn't know me. Then I dreamed of aruna and we had become one being with four arms, like a goddess of his human ancestors. There was no division between us.

The following day, I didn't wait, but sought him early, before groups of us set out to forage and scavenge. He was walking away from our phyle hideout with his two friends, and I ran up to him, put a hand upon his shoulder to halt him. The others glanced back once and, without expression, carried on without him. He looked down at me, taller by six inches or so.

"What is this?" I asked him. "You did something to me. What *is* it?"

He shrugged. "Don't you know, Barley?"

"You fucked with my mind," I said. "Make it stop."

He expelled a sigh that was partly a laugh. "Grow up," he said, and moved away from me.

Astonished, I watched him go after his friends, undecided whether to pursue him and strike him or walk away with dignity. Eventually, he was too far from me to follow.

He left me to digest and process what had occurred. I couldn't tell anyhar else, because I sensed what I felt was forbidden. I didn't think I could face Shaska again. I burned with humiliation at the thought of it. Perhaps I should go away for a week or so; hara did that sometimes, seeking spiritual ignitions. I told myself what Shaska had done was bad; he'd used mind-influencing magic on me while I'd been vulnerable. If I told our hienama, Shaska would no doubt be cast out. You simply didn't *do* things like that to hara of your own phyle.

But I said nothing. I waited for the night.

By sunfall, I'd convinced myself that if I took aruna with Shaska again, perhaps more than once, the inexplicable sensations would burn themselves out. This was obviously the action to take and the advice the hienama would have given me. But Shaska did not come to the fire that night. He did not come for two more days.

Unable to stem my anxiety, I asked others if they knew where he was. Nohar seemed to care and were baffled by my interest, its eagerness. Shaska and his companions had not cultivated close friendships within the group. Outsiders still, to a degree. I imagined him dead in a hundred terrible ways. The pain of his absence was almost unendurable, and I had to draw away from friends in order to conceal it. I searched for him in the parts of the city I was able to access without too much trouble, and was on the brink of exploring more perilous zones, when Shaska reappeared.

I was fishing at the river's edge in low afternoon light, and he simply walked up from behind and stood next to me. At first, I was so shocked to see him I couldn't speak, and he said nothing to me. The profile of his face was perfect, like that of an ancient god, surveying the waters. The surface of his skin was like copper pearl. Eventually I was able to utter, "I thought you were dead."

"I had business," he replied. "It's done."

I didn't ask what that business was then, and never did thereafter. There was no time for such things; we lived from moment to moment. Burnished with riverlight, he let down the rope of his hair, which fell into separate snakes to his thighs, somewhat oily but intoxicatingly fragrant. He cast off his clothes, led me into the water, away from the muddy banks, and there touched my pain, my longing.

"Don't ever vanish like that again," I said, drunk on relief and pleasure. "I felt like I was dying. What have you done to me?"

"I did nothing. You did nothing. It made itself," he said.

He enfolded me in his hair and the currents of the river coiled it around me, as if it were living arms. I was entangled, yet safe, so safe. This was the only time he allowed that, and I didn't realise its significance. Not for a long time.

Sated, we swam to the bank and there sat naked, smoking thinly-rolled cigarettes, gazing out across the water. "This city is dead," Shaska said, folding up his hair once more. "It's time to go. Only fools will stay."

As if in punctuation to his remark, a howl stretched across

the river, cut off abruptly.

"Madness," Shaska said, expelling smoke through his nose.

By that point, I had already decided I would follow him anywhere, merely to prevent him disappearing, so simply said, "When?"

He shrugged. "Later... maybe." He leaned over and kissed me, blew smoke into me along with his breath. "Neither of us have anything to leave behind, and the world is immense. So much emptier than before. We can't raise the thing we created here."

"What thing?" I snapped, momentarily cold with horror.

"Our love," he answered, smiling. "Don't be afraid, Barley. We've outgrown these primitive corners."

It's important you know how we began, Shaska and I. We left Carmine around a week later. Although Shaska never gave me the full details, I think he had some problem with his friends, who wanted to remain under the protection of a strong phyle and felt he should do the same. But ultimately, they didn't prevent us leaving. I said goodbye to nohar, didn't even thank my phylarch, his deputies or his hienama for the haven they had provided for me. Never shed a tear for friends I wouldn't see again. I walked away into a different life.

For some months we travelled, often taking temporary shelter with other nomad phyles, or even the unthrist, those who allied with no tribe at all. Shaska discouraged the making of friends for, he said, they could become burdens. "When you clasp a hand in friendship and look a har in the eye, so a contract is made," he said. "Thus made, it must be honoured, so it's best to be cautious in these matters."

He spoke often like a scholar, and hara liked to listen to him. He could have become a hienama if he'd wanted to. Disdainful of the hara he saw around him, he was impatient with what he saw as their pettiness, their inability to appreciate the measureless gifts they had been given. But he disguised this impatience and spoke from his heart. The message he conveyed, whether through parable or not, was "wake up, *become*." I dare say there are many hara around, met fleetingly on our journeys, who now admit there was a har who once had a great impact on them, changed them even. That would be Shaska.

During this time, I learned what it was to love, and recognised it was not wholly pleasant. I understood more keenly what the hienamas meant about love's shadow selves, for I was often jealous, more often paranoid, and occasionally terrified. I would think of Shaska dead, or taken from me in some other way, and my heart would begin to pound desperately, my breath come in caged-bird flutters. A black cloud of dread hovered over me. Eventually, I told Shaska about these attacks, and he said, "Do not compare this moment to the past you know or the unknown future. Live it for what it is, fresh and new and forever remade, then we are never apart."

What he meant of course is that the terror of separation sullied the beauty of love and its expression. Dark anticipation was a worm in the heart of love and should be cut out.

Shaska did not hold back when he looked at me. His gaze was direct and swollen with meaning; he made the contract of friendship with me and I was no burden to him. He taught me that the contact of eyes and breath, and even the lightest touch of fingers, was in some ways more profound than the physical union of aruna.

"Do you see the kiss in my eyes?" he once said to me, smiling.

I did.

Shaska was never possessive or afraid, always serene. Sometimes, I mistook that for indifference and would play up. He was patient and encouraged my fears to flap brokenly out of me. He told me I was growing, that I stood within a changing wind, and soon the tatters of humanity that still hung from me would be blown away entirely. My feelings for him consumed me: adoration, visceral desire, grovelling gratitude, the greatest respect. I still don't know exactly what it was he found so interesting in me. You can find beauty in a flower or a cloud in the sky. Neither of these objects could be exhausting, as I'm sure I often was.

"When I gaze at you, I am reading a poem," he once said, and stroked the air around me lovingly.

So perhaps I was an ideal, a picture even, of beauty. I heard him say another time that you can drink from beauty and be replenished in spirit. But whatever his true feelings were for me, he shaped me, and eventually I developed awareness. I grew up, as he'd once advised me to.

By this time, we'd settled in a small community, which was an ancient human village, reclaimed, carved into a hillside, surrounded by forest. The narrow lanes between the buildings were almost vertical, but we had a gathering place that was flat, where there were no buildings, and we could celebrate our rituals there. Below the village was a moody river, which was sometimes kind and placid but sometimes cruel, even in the summer time, when rains excited it. Occasionally, we were told, it took lives. The hara who'd formed this community had sought a degree of isolation, having broken away from various tribes, because they wanted to carve their own way. They called themselves the Oormareen, and were dedicated to attuning themselves with the natural world. Shaska liked them. He thought some of them were rather stupid, but they had honest hearts; a stupidity he found tolerable. The Oormareen didn't have a phylarch, but a council of hara to make decisions should they be needed. They had also a coven of seven hienamas, whose skins were black as starless night, and whose most senior member was Azool. Because of their human spiritual heritage, the hienamas had fashioned our local spirits to be somewhat more capricious and tricksy than most. I could taste their power; they were real to me. I felt protected by them.

Shaska and I lived together in Softblades, the Oormareen village, for nearly five years. The name of the village referred to grass, the achingly vivid shoots that pushed up between the trees in the spring. This was also how the Oormareen saw themselves. Shaska had been keener to join this community than I had been, but neither did I have any objection. I loved the forest, its sounds and silences, its stillness, its immensity. Here, more than anywhere I had visited, the world no longer breathed in tired relief at the passing of humanity, but had come to believe this bliss would last.

One day, in the early spring, Shaska and I went across the river to gather pine nuts. We might also hunt if the opportunity presented itself. The Oormas were not against the consumption of meat, but the act of killing must be attended by respectful ritual. Certain conditions had to be met, such as a stag bowing his antlers at your feet, offering his neck to the blade.

No, I make fun. It wasn't that ridiculous.

Mid-morning, we came to a glade we both loved, where there was a pool often used for spiritual ceremonies, and here sat down to refresh ourselves. We ate some of the pine nuts, because we had so many, and drank from the pool. We wanted to make an offering to the landscape, so took aruna together, sharing its energy with our environment. Afterwards, Shaska put on his clothes and said, "I have something I must do."

"What?" I asked, reaching for my own clothes.

He put out a hand to stop me. "No. Stay here, dream awhile." He leaned down to press his face against my hair. "I'll see you later."

"You mean... shall I not wait?"

He was already walking away, and blew a kiss to me. "Later, flower face, later."

He had never called me that before: flower face. A name to suit a cat or an owl, maybe. I wanted to question him but he was gone.

The question was never answered, because there was no 'later'.

The Oormareen sent out search parties. Crevasses and caves were examined, rivers followed, pools and lakes explored thoroughly. Questions were asked in neighbouring communities, some quite far afield. The hienamas scried in flame, crystal and clouds. I prayed to the sky, to the Aghama, to whom I'd never prayed before. Flower face. So quickly faded. Was this why he'd left me? I wasn't thinking straight, of course. Harish flowers hold their bloom for perhaps hundreds of years, but it's easy to say that so far from the moment.

There was no sign of Shaska, no blood, no indication of a fight, whether with an animal or another har, no evidence of an accident. It seemed he'd simply walked out of this world.

The first raw grief lasted around five years; one year for each we'd spent together with the Oormareen. I thought the pain would never fade, despite what my friends told me. Without them I doubt I'd have survived. Shaska was my life, my light, my reason for being. I felt estranged from the world, the space at my side where once he'd stood became a yawning void. I dreamed of him, of course, but they were not meaningful dreams, laden with messages. No, they were simply flickering recollections, old pictures. I walked in the forest alone, every day, hoping to feel him near, hear a whisper, catch a glimpse of him, his ghost, but found only silence and emptiness. I yearned for answers, scrabbling through all manner of divination techniques, but they were all without voice. Was he dead? I had to know. Was he? *Was he?* The hienamas were patient, told the truth, all saying: "We don't know, Barley."

I asked them to guess, but they wouldn't.

Azool I trusted the most, because I knew his sight was strong, although he always insisted he was "working on his wisdom". When I spoke to him about Shaska, he said, "I'll be honest with you, Barley. It's as if Shaska never existed. I can find no trace, however faint. I don't know what that means."

The other hienamas felt uncomfortable owning up to not knowing things, but not Azool. When he said these words to me, I knew hope would not be enough to bring Shaska back.

Had ever a har been abandoned so thoroughly? My mind couldn't even fabricate suggestions of his proximity. He was truly, irreplaceably, gone.

I never thought of leaving Softblades, because it was my cocoon. My heart bled so much I could barely move, and my friends, those burdens with whom I made contracts irrevocably, helped me through my darkest years. Also, I couldn't stray from the spot where Shaska had vanished. If he'd slipped into another world, as some hara suspected, there was the possibility that one day he might return. I had to hold onto that hope, however weak it was, but eventually even that faded to no more than a wisp invisible in sunlight.

Once the five years of mourning were over, I began to revive, take an interest more fully in the world around me. For five years, I'd been faking it, but one day, walking in the forest, I realised – with surprise – I felt quite content. The trees were putting forth their leaves, growth was stirring in the maturing year. Living softblades illuminated the earth. It was as if the universe told me, "You've had enough time now, Barley. Take up your life again."

At the spring festival we now call Feybraihatide, I took aruna with my friend Lixy, and after that our union became habitual. We were chesna, but it was not the same as what I'd shared with Shaska. I knew I'd never feel that again, whatever it had been, perhaps something other than love.

Six years after Shaska had vanished, Lixy bore our son. He suggested we name him Shaska, but I balked immediately at that: the name might be a curse. We called him Bird, because that was the first word he uttered. He was always reaching for the sky.

When Bird was around four years old, a visitor came to Softblades. The moment I laid eyes on him, as he walked up the hill path, the breath stilled in my throat. There was a sense of Shaska around him. He was tall, robed in russet cloth with one shoulder bare, his hair hanging in braids to his thighs. He carried a tall staff of rough wood, which was wound with ribbons of cloth and feathers. His face, like Shaska's had once been, was decorated with stripes of yellow and red pigment. From similar human stock, I thought, steadying myself. But I did not go to greet this stranger, only watched from the shadow of buildings as my friends welcomed him in, took him to the communal hall that served as an inn. I knew he was here to scathe me; that's the only way I can describe it. Old feelings, laid to rest in linen and fragrant herbs, locked away deep within me, were revealed again. I could smell the smokes of Carmine on the air.

Visitors were rare for the Oormareen, so when anyhar arrived, it was an excuse for celebration. We were hungry for stories of the outside world, for that place no longer seemed quite real to us and our only other contacts were small tribes like ourselves, who'd chosen a peaceful life in the wilderness and with whom we traded. We ached for fireside tales of the decaying cities, the wild, cruel hara who still lived in them.

Later that day, it being a warm summer evening, my kinshara built a fire in the gathering spot, and two wild boar were roasted upon coals nearby. There were salads and seeds, grown on our own tended land or else farmed from the forest.

There was rough wine and ale, roots cooked in the fat of the boar, dark, moist bread, and fish from our petulant river, stuffed with hot berries. A feast for us, of which the stranger partook politely.

There was a mountain lion who, over the past few years, had often come to watch our gatherings. Azool had said we must not fear him, but keep his favour for he was the eyes of the gods. Whenever we ate together, hara would take the lion a cut of the meat, leave it on a rock near the hiding place from which his eyes shone green. The lion always took these offerings. But that night, despite the intoxicating aroma of roasting boar, our catamount did not come. It wasn't that he was hiding, because I had no sense of him and usually his presence was palpable. I looked for him, and saw others doing so. I hoped he wasn't hurt or worse. But even then, deep within, I knew; he would not come while the stranger was with us. For, as creatures, they were enemies.

The stranger's name was Eniki, and he told us he was Colurastes, a tribe known also as the Serpent Hara. He was far from his home, I thought, but he explained that he was travelling, documenting the tribes of Wraeththu for the hienama of his phyle, who was interested in such things, the way our kind were developing. I wondered why the hienama couldn't come and see for himself. I wondered also how Eniki had been able to find us, hidden as we were in the high forests.

Eniki eyed our sloping village expressionlessly and said, "the Colurastes would rather live in caves than human dwellings, however scoured."

Azool replied rather stiffly that the entire place had been cleansed and blessed by him personally, along with several others of his calling.

"What is right for us is not necessarily right for everyhar," Eniki replied, inclining his head respectfully and thereby restoring accord.

I wasn't taken in; he was patronising us, a community he saw as backward woodshara, unenlightened and primitive.

I loved our village, its rain-polished wooden planks and tiles, its worn sinking dwellings, its mossy rooves, its brokenness that was beautiful. I didn't think the humans who'd once lived there had been bad, either; just unfortunate to have been alive at the time it had all ended for them. Others in my community felt the same; we laid nuts and fruits on the old graves of the previous tenants at the end of our year. But Eniki was modern, a sign pointing to the direction many hara were now taking.

Later in the evening, once the drums and fiddles had come out, and hara were dancing happily to their din, Eniki caught my eye. We were some distance from one another, but when he spoke, it was as if he sat next to me. "May we talk?" he asked.

I could hardly refuse, so sidled close to him. "What do you wish to say?" I couldn't keep a needle from my tone, but he ignored this.

"You have a shadow," he said. "Perhaps I could scry for you."

In our circle, such words were more personal than if he'd asked me to strip off my clothes and take aruna with him, right there in front of everyhar. Oormareen respected privacy as the hara of the cities did not. There were times for communal intimacy, but this was not one of them. "I don't think so," I said. "Thank you all the same."

He smiled a little. "You're wary of me, I understand that. Colurastes are *different*; we choose to be. But that doesn't make us enemies, Barley."

I wondered who had told him my name; he must've asked somehar. I didn't believe for an instant he'd intuited it himself. "If I have a shadow," I said, "then it follows me quietly. There is no need to scry."

"But I think you want to *know* what I might tell you," Eniki said.

I stared at him without speaking.

"You lie in a comfortable bed," Eniki murmured, drawing a long brown finger across the ground in front of him. "This community, this *idyll*, this dream humanity once might've had. The harish fruit of old races nestling alongside each other like colours in an artist's palette."

"That is not a dream," I said coldly, "but our reality. And the bed is not always without stones. The landscape is as harsh as it is loving. Some of us have fallen to our deaths in the winter snows, or drowned in the angry river. We are not foolish harlings, Colurastes, whatever you think." I made to stand up, but Eniki grabbed me with one hand that was like steel, pulling me down.

"I'm not insulting you," he said. "And believe me, after what I've seen in other places, Oormareen *is* an idyllic dream."

"What is the *point* of this conversation?"

"Lie with the snake and you take part of his skin."

I uttered a cold laugh. "I will *not* be lying with you, Colurastes."

"That isn't what I meant, and you know it to be so." He drew back from me a little, straight-backed and majestic in the firelight. Nohar was taking any notice of us, not even my chesnari and son. It was as if I'd been taken somewhere else, outside of my life, yet still attached to it. "Have you heard of us, Barley? Do you know what we are?"

"You call yourselves the Serpent Hara," I said. "Yes, I've heard of you. There are many Wraeththu entertainers out in the world, play-acting and dressing up. Do you want to *be* snakes or simply worship them?"

I knew I was being rude and perhaps only proving to this har that I *was* ignorant and backward, but I couldn't help myself. He didn't appear to take offence, just said gently, "Hold out your hand."

Despite the gentleness of the request, it was somehow impossible not to comply. I held out my right hand, and for a moment all was still, then suddenly something lithe and prehensile whipped out and grabbed my extended wrist, squeezed hard. A snake hidden in the folds of his robe? I uttered a short yelp, tried to pull away but was held fast. It took some moments for me to realise that what held me was a braid of his hair.

"Get off me!" I hissed.

"Struggle, and the grip grows stronger," Eniki said mildly, "so strong it could cut through your bones."

"I'm sorry," I said, hearing the note of panic in my voice. "Please let me go."

The grip relaxed a little but did not relinquish its hold. "There," Eniki said, "now you see I'm not posturing or acting. Are we clear on this point?"

I nodded vigorously. "Yes, yes."

The braid slithered away from me, looped itself back into its brothers. My wrist burned and itched where it had gripped me, but I resisted the urge to rub it.

"Some of our kind are seekers," Eniki said. "They leave their tribe and travel the world, looking for the source of our being. They bring knowledge back to our leaders, storing in their breath and bodies all they see and experience. In the dark hours after the moon has set, they may sing these secrets to the night, and our hienamas can fish for them with silver nets of thought. *You* are in those secrets, Barley. He saw a light in you."

"No," I said, instinctively. "You don't know me. You don't."

"I don't know what name he gave to you, Barley, but his true name is Ulupi, and he is a son of our *takshata*, our... phylarch." His eyes appeared entirely black, but with the smallest pin pricks of emerald light within them.

I felt as if I'd been beaten by rods of iron. "Where is he?" I managed to ask.

"I was hoping *you* would tell *me*."

A thread of strength came back to me then. "You're looking for him, for Shaska."

"If that is the name he gave you, yes. And you must tell me, Barley, for your own good and the good of your hara." He cast a meaningful glance towards Bird and Lixy, who were holding hands, dancing in the flickerlight of the fire.

"You can't threaten me, Colurastes, because I can't help you. Shaska vanished from our lives. Not even our hienamas know what happened to him. It was as if he never existed."

Eniki studied me for a few moments, obviously deciding whether or not I was lying.

"You can taste my breath to see the truth," I said coldly, "not that I'd relish the contact." I paused a moment when he did not respond. "And there is no shadow. I never feel him near. He left me fourteen years ago, without trace, and nohar has seen him since." Again, a pause, and then I said. "Is he hiding from you?"

Eniki appeared to come out of a partial trance and I suspected he'd been communicating by mind touch with hara elsewhere. "No, he has nothing to hide from."

I wasn't sure of that. "When did you start looking for him?"

"That's not your concern. Be silent now." He closed his eyes. After almost a minute, which was an unendurably long time to me, he opened his eyes again and said, "You must show me the place where last you saw him."

"It will make no difference. We searched thoroughly, there's no sign, not even an etheric trace. And now the evidence, if any remained, is old and cold."

"Don't be difficult, Barley," Eniki said. "You will show me because you want to know as much as I do."

"Tomorrow," I said. I didn't want to be alone with him in the night forest.

I didn't tell Lixy about my conversation with the Colurastes, mainly because I didn't want to worry him over what might be nothing. I felt that Eniki was lying, and that Shaska had run away from his tribe, perhaps from his father or hostling, whichever role in his life their leader had owned. Shaska had had two companions, about whom I knew nothing, not even their names. Shaska had never spoken of them, which in itself now seemed odd, because they'd clearly been tribe-mates of his. I wondered whether Eniki had found and questioned them, or even knew of them. But still the mystery remained: Shaska had vanished and nohar knew why, how or to where he might've gone.

In my bed, I found myself rubbing the wrist where Eniki's hair had gripped me; the skin still burned. I remembered Shaska taking aruna with me in the river of Carmine, so long ago, how his hair had caressed and embraced me, and how after that he'd never loosed it again in my presence. He'd braided and looped it into a prison. He'd hidden so much of himself from me.

The following morning, Eniki presented himself at our door. I took up my bow and quiver before we left, and then led the way to the river. Bird had wanted to come with us, but I'd not allowed it. There might be danger ahead; I couldn't risk it. I could sense Lixy was curious as to why I was taking the Colurastes into the forest, but he held his tongue; questions would come later and by then I might be able to answer them.

At the ford crossing, which was close to Softblades, Eniki balked.

"It's safe," I said, turning round to him, "the water's shallow here." The river was in fact playful that day, rushing and foaming around stones and rocks, but not deadly.

"This is hollow serpent water," Eniki said.

I had no idea what that meant but wasn't about to ask. "Can't you cross it?" I enquired instead, remembering how Shaska had done so easily.

Without words, Eniki followed me across the shallows.

We did not speak further until we reached the glade where Shaska and I had taken our rest. Here, Eniki prowled around, examining shadows and tree bark, patterns in the leaves overhead, the stillness of the pool. "He's never left here," he said at last.

I laughed, couldn't help it. "He's not here," I said. "I'd know, feel it."

"His skin is here. The one he shed."

"We searched. There's nothing."

Despite his glamour, his aloofness and the indisputably eerie properties of his hair, I felt Eniki was no stronger or wiser than me, just more practiced at appearing that way. He was uncertain now, I could sense it.

"He must've been taken in some way," I said. "He would never have left me voluntarily. I know this in my blood." And I did know it. "Perhaps there are things about your tribe you're not even aware of."

Eniki peered back towards the river, which we could no longer glimpse through the trees, although we could still hear it, faintly. "There are things about this landscape you're not aware of either," he said. "In the high places, where the clouds touch the earth, so things come back. This is the power you serve, which keeps you safe."

"We serve nothing," I said. "We respect the land, and it gives us its bounty. We take no more than we need. This is the way we're supposed to live upon this world."

Eniki fixed me with a stare, hard as emeralds, black and green. "You may lead me back to the river," he said.

I wanted to remain as aloof as he was, but curiosity was eating me from the inside out. "What do you think happened?" I asked. "You must think *something*, now."

Eniki would only say, "There is nothing I can do here. Forget I ever came. You have your life and it is good for you."

Once we'd crossed the river, Eniki bowed to me, and said, "From here, I go backwards on my path. There is no point in going on."

"Be safe," I said, half meaning it.

I did tell Lixy everything, also the tribe council and the hienamas, but what answers were there for us? None. Simply more mystery. Shaska had come into my life and changed me. We'd had good years together. Now he was gone, and I had a new life, the one I was meant to live. Shaska had brought me here. I realised that, at last.

Some weeks later, a harling of our community celebrated his feybraiha, so we once again raised a bonfire in the gathering spot. After ceremony and feasting, we danced in the flamelight, singing our songs of life to the night and to the forest, which was motionless, monumental and towering above and around our settlement. The river was a silver coil in the moonlight, and a white owl, with the face of a flower, flew over our gathering. Was that an omen? We left meat for the catamount, and somehar said they caught a glimpse of his shining eyes in the darkness. By morning, the meat would be gone.

We went back to our houses before dawn, but I could not sleep. I felt strangely alert while at the same time drowsily content. Lying in bed, with Lixy draped over me, snoring softly, I listened to the last sounds of the night. Then I heard a huff outside, and a noise like something thudding against our door. I eased myself from the loose clasp of my chesnari's limp arms and padded naked down the bare wooden stairs. Dawn was coming in grey light, so I needed no lamp. But when I opened the door, I saw two lamps across the yard, gleaming like green stones under water. Our lion. He crept forward on his belly a few feet towards me, and I stood frozen, unsure whether I was safe or not. The lion had something in his mouth, which he dropped in the space between us. Then, in a lithe movement, he turned and leapt away over the fence. I saw the tall silver grass of our meadow slope shivering as he passed through it. Then all was still.

I went to the object the lion had dropped, knelt down to examine it. I found a folded, shimmering garment of some kind. Very delicate. I began carefully to open out the papery, silvery pleats, and soon realised it was not cloth that I held. As it lay over my arms, the substance of it flaked away, falling like snow over my knees. By the time the birds sang to the morning, there was nothing left at all.

Battle Call of the Beast-King

In the tall tower that shadows the fallen statue,
Shattered and ivy-wreathed,
Dour as the pale snakes that crawl the ruins,
The Beast-King summons his lithe warriors
From the ravaged lands beyond the Plains of Sands.
His cry is fluting through the twilight,
Shaking the fragile aether with command.

"Come, silver-eyed hara of the forest,
And mottled spectres of liana haunts!
Hara of the waters, rise!
Liquid-speared, with trembling limbs,
Shaped from the life-blood of the crashing falls,
Plummet the lushness of the Northern Vales.
Slink to me, pantherine and silent,
Leopard-spotted, lithe and tawny hara of the plains!
Sheath your sharp and deadly claws in swiftness,
Rustling the skirts of pampas in your hidden flight.
Come to me in Darkness,
Sure-footed hara of the mountains:
Moss-haired, streaming svelteness,
Russet-maned fauns
and steaming mist-wraiths of the swamps!
Rise, oh founders of the new race from the Dead!
Rise! To take the threads of time, and weave new breath."

May 1977

Son of a Swan Wyrd

Clouds Like Hair

Long ago, when Wraeththu first came to walk upon the land, the world was a wild and unpredictable place. We had magic we didn't know what to do with, and other magic that we *did* know what to do with but maybe should not have touched. There are stories of those times, and they might sound like make believe, but they are true.

In those days, tribes were forming and changing, falling apart and rebuilding, like the spring rains coming down the mountain. Much froth and disturbed stones too! There was a phylarch named Moysante, who was Sulh before there were Sulh. He lived in the mountainous White Lands and fought hard to protect his phyle from fierce wild hara who had been raiding their farming land and stealing their livestock.

One day, after beating back a band of raiders with his *filiwyr*, the hara who fought with and protected him, Moysante became disoriented within the steep forest beyond the valley fields. The woods here were thick and vengeful, because they were still devouring the towns of men. Moysante, though, had known those woodlands all his life, and had never been lost before, and it seemed strange to him that the hara he'd thought he was pursuing into the dark trees – following their crashing flight and the snapping of branches – had fallen to silence. Strange too that his *filiwyr* had dropped so far behind that he'd become separated from them.

Now, you know as well as I do, my little pearl, that when a har finds himself unaccountably alone and bewildered in forestland he knows well, there is strong magic about. But one of the tricks of such magic is it makes you not think about it, or even consider how strange your situation is. Moysante rode further into the trees, half in a trance, and the twilight came down through the branches in the veil of night.

Worried he would be lost till dawn, Moysante decided he must dismount and make himself as comfortable as he was able in a nest of young bracken, but as he wound the ferny fronds around his hands, he saw a soft buttery light shining through the nighted tree trunks. This light moved, drew closer to him. He pulled out his knife, ready to defend himself if he must, but then saw the source of the light was a single har, dressed in a long, hooded cloak and carrying a lantern. The har stepped out from the trees before him.

"You are lost," this har announced in a silvery, whispery voice, "and you are a leader of hara, are you not?"

"Darkness made me lose my trail," Moysante replied. "Who are you?"

"A friend," replied the har and threw back his hood. Beneath was a small dark face, green-brown of colour, a little like a monkey's, but with startling silver eyes. Hanks of black hair fell forward over the har's breast. The har was not ugly but peculiar. "The name you may call me by is Creeken. Now, what can I do for you, leader of hara?"

Moysante had no wish to aggravate this individual, because he sensed a creature of wyrd, and of course they must always be appeased. You don't ask the wyrdkin how they know where to find you, how they know things about you, so Moysante merely said, "Can you show me the way from the forest, down to the Step Bridge of the river? I'll pay you in whatever currency you prefer."

Yes, you might well pull such a face, my pearl, for I agree with you – what a foolish thing to offer! But Moysante was an honest har and thought only of coins and goods to barter.

The strange har drew closer to him, raised his lantern. "I'll help you," he said, "and, as it happens, I do have a price. I live alone out here with my son, and I feel he should have a different life among others of his kind, rather than being kin only to the forest creatures and the trees. I would like him to have power among hara, for he is strong and wise and deserves it. You are alone in life, aren't you? Take my son with you, bond yourself to him, and he will bring great gifts to you, and your tribe will prosper. So... you'll have more *from* me than you'll *give* to me. What do you say?"

Moysante didn't want to bond himself to anyhar, not least because he'd lost the har he loved to a blade three years before, when their tribe had been fighting yet again over territory, and he was still grieving about it. His chesnari had been a very powerful witch har, a swan-wyrd named Alarch, who'd known he'd die young. He was so full of magic that before he was killed, and in the seven happy years they'd enjoyed together, he had given to his beloved four pearls, three of which Moysante had carried. They'd each had two harlings hidden inside them. The fourth pearl Alarch had carried himself and its fruit was a single harling. This amount of pearls was unusual, for most hara consider themselves lucky to have even one son. I know myself blessed to have you, my pearl. Seven is a magical number, and Alarch used his art to create so many offspring. Moysante felt sure he'd never get over his chesnari's death, and to take another as life partner seemed a slur on Alarch's memory.

However, it appeared the strange dark har divined Moysante's thoughts for he murmured, "Grief is noble, Tiahaar, but so is joy. The world turns, the seasons change, life goes on. You found yourself on this path and our meeting was destined to happen. Take heed of fate and accept my offer." He gestured with one hand, back towards the trees. "Come, follow me to my dwelling and you can meet Asphodyl, my son. Then decide."

So Moysante followed the swaying light of the strange har's lantern, which made spiky monsters of the trees. He and his companion came presently to a small cottage that was more mossy thatch than brick, and was very old, hunched close to the ground. But the golden glow from its small windows was cheerful, and white smoke plumed from its chimney in a silky coil. Moysante crossed the threshold and went inside. There was only one room within, containing two beds, and a table and a hungry fire. Before the hearth, a young har sat in a tattered brocade armchair; the sight of him made Moysante jump in shock. Not because he was hideous; he was not. The truth was that Moysante had never seen so beautiful a har, who was as slender as a young oak, dark as a beech nut, with black hair hanging almost to the floor in snaky locks, and eyes the same silver as his parent's.

"Are you his father or his hostling?" Moysante could not help but blurt out to his rescuer.

Creeken put down his lamp upon the table, while the har before the fire stared at Moysante in the manner a cat might gaze upon a stranger. "Asphodyl has no father," Creeken said. "Well, are you content to let him leave the forest with you?"

Moysante considered that most hara – any in fact – would be glad to give this young har a new life. There was no doubt he was magical and strange, and full of uncanny wisdom, and phyles always have need of such individuals. He was extraordinarily lovely, a creature of raw nature, yet even so, he made Moysante feel unnerved. The phylarch felt dizzy looking into that inscrutable face. Despite these misgivings, he knew that to refuse might bring a terrible destiny down on himself and his phyle. Fate had indeed led him into the wood and confused him there, whether for good or bad.

"As you wish," he said to Creeken, and thus the deal was made.

In the morning, Asphodyl – who had so far said little to this har who would give him a new life – put a rope bridle on his small black pony, mounted it, and led Moysante along the secret tracks to the river. These tracks Moysante had never seen before, nor would ever find again. Eventually, almost at noon, they reached High Water, his tribe's settlement, in a place where the swift mountain river made itself into a lake above a foaming waterfall that nourished the wide valley below. Hara came quickly to Moysante's side, saying they had sent out search parties the night before, and had found the savaged corpses of their attackers, but no sign of their phylarch. What had happened?

"I lost my path," Moysante said, "for the forest dazzled me. It led me to the home of this har who has led me out."

Asphodyl gazed at the faces around him with what appeared to be a peculiar mix of indifference and calculating curiosity. Hara were surprised by him, of course. Many commented on his radiance, and others on his wyrdness, and a few on the fact that this stranger had ridden ahead of their phylarch into the village, rather than behind him. Some see omens in such things. But whatever he was, or whatever he might prove to be, clearly this mysterious har was a prize. He was dressed in garments that looked as if they were made of leaves, but they were not, just artful weaving, soaked with the colours of the deep groves. Moysante explained to his hara that Asphodyl's hostling, a seer living alone in the forest, wished for his son to be part of tribal life. So here he was.

Asphodyl moved instinctively towards Moysante's tall, wooden house in the middle of the village. As he passed, so the black geese that strutted on the common green and swam in its central pool fled from him. Asphodyl paused on the steps to the house, put his hand upon the carved columns that supported the lintel, where stories of Moysante's slain parents were engraved. He appeared to be assessing his new home. Then he passed inside, scorching the shadows of the hall, and it was plain he did not intend ever to leave.

At first, Asphodyl incited only the curiosity of his new neighbours. He was polite, if distant, and on two occasions healed a small hurt, one of a horse that went lame, one of a har who had hammered his hand instead of a nail. His presence was gracious and, despite the fact he was quite dark – but for his eyes – he exuded a strange sense of ice and paleness. Nohar had heard of a lone seer living in the forest only a few hours' riding distance away, as Moysante claimed, but then some hara, shunning society, had taken themselves off many years before and hid themselves. Asphodyl's parent must be one of these.

As for Moysante's sons, they were divided in opinion. The youngest, Miyalkin, who was not a twin, was at once wary of Asphodyl. Those next oldest to him – Gwyder and Chreeyr – admired the new resident of their house in the way they'd cherished their lost father. The next eldest pair – Tilluan and Eoshay – being rather remote and magical themselves, were indifferent, and the eldest pair – well – they fell in love with the stranger; not in the way of familial love, like their younger brothers, but that deep, hot, hungry yearning, under whose spell a har can kill. These two were Eryar and Curyll. Each knowing the other's heart, these twins fell out, and pined separately to win Asphodyl's attention.

Despite this, all went well enough for some time, a season or so, but then it became clear that Asphodyl had his own views on how the phyle should be ruled. He would not tolerate anyhar who was opposed to his ideas, and skilfully – in his quiet, inexorable way – he began to sift out those hara who might be obstructive to his plans. "Your enemies mock you," he murmured in his low musical voice to Moysante, his body swaying slightly as he spoke. "Their raids are a drain on our resources. Hunt them down. Kill them all. Every one of them."

Moysante's most trusted *filiwyr* had lived through the Devastation and had witnessed many terrible events. They knew that offensive strikes come with a cost in blood and lives. The wild hara who stole from them were desperate and lost, barely organised enough to filch a cabbage, but in their own territory –

the forest – they were strong. Hadn't they led Moysante astray? Perhaps this strange har living among them now was one of them. Might he not be urging them to attack their foes simply to divide, disorientate and destroy them? So, the first seeds of doubt were sown, but Asphodyl worked at once to unearth them before they could fully sprout. He convinced Moysante that in speaking against him, his counsellors were in fact betraying their phylarch and should be over-ruled. "All I will bring is prosperity to your phyle," Asphodyl said, in little more than a murmur. "My hostling promised you this and his word is his bond. All who oppose this promise are surely unworthy of our community."

"I will not send hara to the dark groves to die," Moysante said, torn.

"I will deal with our enemies," Asphodyl said. "None of our hara need die."

"Dark magic," Moysante said, resigned.

"No," Asphodyl whispered. "Simply warnings. I know these lands."

Whether Moysante believed Asphodyl could accomplish this or not, we do not know. Warnings may come in many forms, as can wards. But the truth of it was the attacks receded, at least for High Water.

Moysante felt bound, as if in iron coils. He was powerless, torn by desire and revulsion, love and fear. For Asphodyl was mighty in the arts of magic and of aruna. He knew how to ensnare a har and did so. And yet, as he had prophesied, the phyle grew stronger and more prosperous. Weren't the crops growing more fruitfully now? Weren't more pearls being created among hara, which before, but for Asphodyl's sons, had been rare? Asphodyl was a fair ruler, who protected himself, and who could blame him for that? He kept his word, didn't he? Safety and prosperity are precious above jewels and come with a higher price. Some among the phyle loved Asphodyl, some feared him, others held darker opinions. But his influence was absolute. Nohar dared speak against him. Other phyles came to regard High Water as a place of power. Prosperity came and stayed.

But perhaps there was a cost for this, even if it was not to be paid by High Water. Rumours grew among the forest communities that monsters had come to dwell within the deepest groves. No hara of High Water were harmed, but others were.

Sometimes a cry might be heard in the night, a scream of such woe and despair it turned a har's legs to water. Animals were found dead occasionally, hanging in the trees, just their skeletons, devoid of flesh but strangely whole. The hara of High Water saw nothing unusual on their excursions into the green, and yet on the nights when the moon was dark they kept instinctively to their dwellings. Some said they felt something move through the village on these nights, nothing physical as such, but sinuous and flowing, like a great muscle of natural force.

While making his nest within the phyle in this way, Asphodyl also eyed keenly the sons of Moysante, who were of course not his own. He made sure he quickened with pearl himself. As the pearl grew within him, so his glances towards the sons of Moysante grew sharper. He knew that Alarch had woven strong protections about them, and bestowed upon them guardians of nature. The eldest, Eryar and Curyll, had been named for the eagle and the hawk and were hunters, eventually to be leaders of hara. Basking in their own light, these two did not represent that much of a threat to Asphodyl. They were in love with him, after all, and for this reason divided, therefore at half their strength. A glance or a smile could control them.

Tilluan and Eoshay, witch-hara like their father, were named for the owl and the nightingale, magical birds. Their heads were always in the skies and, as they were so wrapped up in each other's enigmatic minds and the mysteries of the landscape, they had little time for mundane concerns. Asphodyl dismissed them as dreamers, because they were half asleep, preferring the unseen world to the real.

Gwider and Chreeyr were creatures of water, named for the goose and the heron. Asphodyl knew they admired him, and had found in him something to replace their lost father. They were easy to manage, free of the jealousy and bitter pangs endured by the eldest twins, happy to do Asphodyl's bidding as he required.

But the last, the youngest, the little blackbird, Miyalkin; of this one Asphodyl was wary. As magical as the night birds, yet unaware of it, as loyal as the water birds, yet contained about it, as regal as the hunters of the air, yet modest, he was the sum of all his brothers' traits. He had also grown in the body of the witch-har, Alarch. Perhaps Alarch had created him this way on purpose, because he had glimpsed what the future would hold and had therefore made some guard against it. Miyalkin was immune to Asphodyl's wiles and clearly neither loved nor feared him. Neither was he indifferent. In some way, he *knew*. Asphodyl could see that in the har's eyes on the rare occasion their glances met. Untwinned, Miyalkin had no support, no ears into which he might whisper his doubts. He kept his opinions to himself, yet Asphodyl did not believe this made the young har any less dangerous.

Alarch the witch-har Asphodyl hated. Hara of his calibre and legend never truly die, and the past cannot be undone, at least not easily. However, Asphodyl was a patient creature, so resolved to bide his time, wait and observe, and only strike when success was assured.

As for Miyalkin, a harling not quite at feybraiha, far from the height of his powers, he knew he was observed continually by Asphodyl, but could not intuit quite what this might mean for his own future. He acknowledged that Asphodyl had brought gifts to High Water and worked evil only against those who opposed him. He had not resorted to poison, either of the art or the tongue, to destroy his enemies. He merely turned them into mist in the phylarch's eyes, so that they drifted away, not even cast out, just ignored to the point where they were driven to leave the village and seek some other phyle where they were seen and heard. No doubt they took their suspicions with them, and no doubt among other phyles nearby, Asphodyl's name was spoken in dread. Miyalkin was sure Asphodyl wished for this to be true, so that his power, fired by his reputation, was strengthened.

Miyalkin could not decide whether he was in danger or not. If he kept his eyes down and avoided Asphodyl, surely he would be left in peace, but some part of him could not help but rage about the reign of this creature. His father seemed like a chained ghost, still himself in most respects, but no longer a free spirit. His brothers were similarly charmed, except for Tilluan and Eoshay, but they barely lived in the real world anyway. Miyalkin knew that if he should speak to the night birds about Asphodyl they would merely say: "He does not matter. He is a faint breeze in the great skies of eternity". In fact, little mattered to these dreamy birds, and if the forest and mountains should collapse about them, they would hardly notice it. They were waiting for a time when they could transform truly into their name birds and fly away from the everyday world.

Miyalkin thought it strange that Asphodyl's hostling had never visited him, nor was this parent ever mentioned. Perhaps Asphodyl visited him in private, for although he was never conspicuously absent from the village for long periods, who knew what he might get up to at night, when doors were closed and the eye of the moon was shut? Miyalkin wasn't keen to try and find out, because he sensed that if he was caught, such action would be regarded as a declaration of war, and he knew he wasn't strong enough to fight that battle alone. Yet who could he go to? Potential allies had gone away. Moysante was a minion now, no longer a leader. And a pearl grew in the belly of Asphodyl, which was undoubtedly destined to bestow a har regarded as the *true* son of Moysante.

Two weeks before the pearl was due to leave the nourishing darkness of Asphodyl's body and harden in the air of the world, the moon was huge in the sky and full of potency. Miyalkin experienced a heightening sense of dread, and felt insecure in his own home. He was sure that the arrival of the pearl meant an ending of the old ways, and he, as his hostling's son, must be removed.

Knowing Alarch had been akin to the round moon, Miyalkin felt safe enough to leave the village alone at this time. He followed the path by the falls to the lowlands below, where a placid lake with sedge-skirted islands lay smooth and black as a mirror of ink, in which a har might scry. Miyalkin took off his clothes and swam to the nearest island. Here, swans made their nests among the rustling reeds, but they paid no attention to Miyalkin, who was of course the son of a swan-wyrd. He was allowed onto the island as long as he made no fuss or nuisance, but they would not draw near to him. Miyalkin could remember, vaguely, being on this island with his hostling. In shadows of memory, he could hear Alarch talking to the swans, see the great birds lifting their wings and laying their long necks flat on the ground at Alarch's feet, but whether this was while Miyalkin was still only a pearl or after his hatching, he could not tell.

Full of an aching wistfulness, Miyalkin lay on the ground and gazed up at the sky. The weather was changing; the moon grew dim behind a puffing veil of clouds. A cold breeze rattled the canes of the reeds, but the swans were still and silent. Miyalkin closed his eyes as his skin grew chill. He wondered whether he should resign himself to what was and simply leave his home, seek out others who'd left before him and would surely offer him sanctuary. He wondered if this was what Alarch would want him to do. But hadn't he been created different to his brothers? Was he meant to fight, to rid his community of this curse? But how? He was too young. He had no allies and Alarch had died before imparting his knowledge to his heir. He whispered, "Alarch, speak to me. Tell me what I should do."

There was no reply, but for the night wind in the reeds and the branches of squat willows that did not weep but hid the nests of the swans. Miyalkin became drowsy listening to these sounds and, for a moment, caught between the realms of sleep and waking, he imagined he was back in his bed, warm beneath blankets, and his hostling sat on a chair beside him, leaning over him. Miyalkin could not open his eyes, but felt that his hostling was sad. Two heavy tears fell upon his closed lids and he heard a sobbing intake of breath. This brought him back to reality in an instant, and he opened his eyes to the sky. Rain was falling in fat drops, but in a peculiar slow way. Blinking, he stared through the rain tears in his eyes and saw the clouds roiling, like the smoke of a ritual fire, beautiful and languid. The more he stared, the more the strands of rippling clouds looked like thick, tumbling hair, and the shadowed moon was a glowing eye among them. The wind was a song now, rising and falling, and Miyalkin heard words within them:

"The wise kind snakes are hatched from eggs, but poisonous snakes are born alive. And the most dangerous snakes kill with both coil and fang. Suck blood, crush a life, poison flesh."

Miyalkin lay still, eyes closed again, hardly daring to breathe, because the voice could so easily fade back into the whistle of the wind. He flung another thought into the sky. *How shall I protect myself?*

'The poisonous snake is fond of cow's milk, but afraid of a horse's hair. When the moon is dark, plait a circle of hair from mane and tail. Lay this on the floor and sit within it. Leave the salt in its cupboard, for it cannot help you now. Horse hair is your protection.'

What else? Miyalkin thought. *Can we be rid of him? Am I in danger? Alarch, I beg you…*

And then the voice came clearer. Miyalkin opened his eyes. A shadowy, willowy form with clouds for hair stood some six feet away from him. He could discern no further features but felt the gust of love that blew from it. Alarch.

"My blackbird," said the ghost. "Would I leave you so vulnerable? Listen carefully, for I say this only once. In the dark of the moon, take precautions. Place a bowl of creamy milk outside your circle and the snake will lap this rather than your blood. Strangle him with your hair, for it will be mine, but know that the last part of a snake to die is its tail. Be mindful of this, for when fangs are broken and poison is drained, and the tongue is pulled, the tail still crushes."

Miyalkin began to form more questions in his mind, but already he was staring at an empty space where once his hostling had stood. The wind had died down and the clouds were hurrying away from the moon, as if to other business. Miyalkin got to his feet, swam back across the lake and dressed his wet body. Then he went home to think.

Clearly, Asphodyl would deal with threats to his son once the pearl had dropped. Always, Miyalkin had instinctively connected Asphodyl with poison, even though he'd never noticeably used it, but for Alarch to appear as he had must mean Miyalkin's disquiet was merited and he was in dire peril. How clear it was now that Asphodyl was a serpent-wyrd, perhaps more than that. He flowed like unravelling silk, he watched in stillness, he struck precisely. But for now, he was heavy and languid with the latter stage of pearl-bearing, and this curtailed his agility and quickness. Miyalkin had a scant couple of weeks in which to prepare himself. Never had he felt so alone. Daily, he burned sweet herbs and resins on the small shrine he kept in his bedroom to honour the memory of Alarch. But his hostling did not, or could not, return.

Miyalkin pondered Alarch's words. *The wise kind snakes hatch from eggs but poisonous snakes are born alive.* All hara come from pearls, which are like eggs, but did these words mean that Asphodyl's parent had born him live? If that were so, he was no ordinary har, if a har at all. Miyalkin, of course, did not know what Creekin had said about Asphodyl having no father, but we do, so we might draw our own conclusions from that.

When the rind of the moon faded to dark, Miyalkin set about protecting himself. Over the two weeks, he'd plucked hairs from the tails and manes of his phyle's herd of horses and had woven these into a plait, which was big enough to curl around his seated body in a circle. From the moment of the first dark, Miyalkin sat within his circle, his hunting knife by his side. A bowl of fresh milk was set before him, outside the circle. He had a lit lamp, which he'd set to the side, and this he'd covered completely with a metal cowl to contain its radiance. He had plaited his long black hair into a thick rope, which hung over his shoulder to his belly. For hours, all was quiet, but for the soft creaking of the house timbers and the call of nocturnal creatures outside. The night itself held its breath; all was still and eerie.

At midnight, just as Miyalkin had almost fallen into a doze where he sat, a cry ripped through the darkness. Unearthly, ragged, but somehow a challenge. Miyalkin picked up his blade. He knew the hour of the pearl had come.

No further cries were heard. As before, the house was quiet, but now Miyalkin felt as if the bricks and timbers were alert and watchful. After about an hour, during which time his tense muscles had begun to ache, he heard a soft, heavy thump somewhere in the house, although from which direction it came was difficult to discern exactly. The darkness condensed. All Miyalkin could see was the cool glow of the milk before him. In his mind, he visualised scant light reflecting off the polished scales of a thick reptilian body as it moved through the sleeping corridors of the house. This, he felt sure, was slithering towards him, intent on his murder. He repeated beneath his breath: "A poisonous snake is fond of cow's milk but afraid of horse's hair". This was his mantra, his charm. Both of his hands gripped the knife as he chanted.

Miyalkin heard a shuffling sound beyond his door, and hushed his murmuring. He held his breath; every muscle, every nerve, every sense focused on what might come. After an interminable few seconds, the door creaked slightly; Miyalkin had left it ajar on purpose. As whatever lurked at the threshold pushed it wide, it creaked several more times, until its inner handle banged against the wall.

Again, silence and stillness.

Then, a sound as of paper drawn across the floor, but paper holding something heavy.

Alarch, beloved, be with me now, Miyalkin thought. He could still see the bowl of milk, glowing dully like a full moon behind cloud, and then the pale circle was broken up as something... *something...* loomed over it.

114

Miyalkin still could not see what was there, but he could hear it lapping at the milk. Now was the time; he must strike before he was struck. Uttering a caw like a crow, he lunged forward and plunged his knife into what he thought must be the head of the snake. In doing this, his upper body went over the edge of his protective circle. Something lashed out and smacked him hard in the chest. He was thrown onto his back and as he scrabbled to regain his feet he saw a black column, darker than the night, rear up before him. Its eyes glowed like pearls and it uttered a long, lilting hiss, almost like a song. It was far slimmer than Miyalkin had expected, for he'd visualised thick, tree trunk coils. This was a sapling in comparison to his imaginings. But snake it was, and it had taken the milk, which had made it pause and perhaps had lulled it somewhat. Still, this was no kindly creature. It swayed before him, evidently unable to cross the circle of horse hair. Miyalkin reached out with one hand and took up the rope of his hair. Putting the knife between his teeth, he pulled the rope taut in his hands, jumped forward and wrapped it around the neck of the snake. Then he pulled the ends hard, tighter and tighter. The creature thrashed and hissed, its tail whipping Miyalkin's legs. Holding the rope together with one hand, Miyalkin struck with his blade. He struck again and again, feeling hot liquid spatter over his hands, and did not stop striking until the thing in his hold fell limp.

For a moment, there was silence, then something small fell to the wooden floor with a soft thump. This must be the head. *Must be.*

Miyalkin, now shaking, fumbled to lift the cover from his lamp. He could barely breathe, for his breath was stuck in his chest. Tiny stars prickled before his eyes. Finally, the lid was off and warm light flooded the room. Miyalkin saw first the blood upon his hands and clothes, then dared to look further. He wasn't sure what it was he beheld, so edged closer to find out. Yes, there was a severed head. This lay in the milk, turning it from cream to pink. And there was a body, twitching on the floor beyond it. And yet... The head in the milk was not that of a snake at all. No, it was the head of a small creature that resembled a har. And the body? This was indeed that of a serpent, and was still moving; it appeared to be trying to reach the door. Barely able to think, Miyalkin went to the tail and chopped it off, throwing it away from him out into the corridor. Then he saw what was left and realised he'd murdered a child.

At once the house reverberated to a terrible scream and a sound of frenzied thrashing, as of a great coiled body throwing itself against walls. Something crashed – perhaps a door flung wide. Then silence, but only for a moment. At once the whole house seemed to shudder and groan. Miyalkin knew some monster careered along the corridors towards him, shrieking as it came. He had only scant moments to gather his thoughts and retreat into his circle. Some instinct made him pull the cord from his plait so that it began to unravel, seemingly of its own accord.

Once again gripping his knife with both hands he waited for what must come.

Asphodyl reared in the doorway; a har to the waist but his lower body was transformed into the black glistening coils Miyalkin had imagined so clearly. His face was barely recognisable, resembling now the snout of a serpent, with hardly a nose and slanting eyes and a forked black tongue flickering out of a slit of a mouth.

Poisonous snakes are born alive...

"You sent your son to do your business," Miyalkin said, although his voice faltered. "Come, finish it if you can."

"There are many more sons," Asphodyl hissed and lunged. His coils hit the horsehair circle with a smack, and Miyalkin smelled burning. Ignoring whatever pain the ward inflicted, Asphodyl moved quickly, ensnaring Miyalkin in his body, trapping his arms. His hair too seemed like a multitude of slim serpents, hissing and darting forward to bite and snare.

Alarch! Miyalkin screamed in his mind. But then his own hair flexed upon his head. He felt every follicle stir, and it was like being stung by nettles. But the substance that plumed from him and curled around the serpent wasn't hair. It roiled and spilled and frothed, like the clouds of an angry storm. Asphodyl hissed and screamed in one long terrible sound. The cloudy hair wrapped around him, smothering his face, filling his mouth. But still his coils held strong.

Miyalkin was sure he would be killed, but then, even as he thought that, Asphodyl's body went rigid. For a moment, he was utterly still. Miyalkin gazed into the face before him, still covered with nebulous pleats of hair, as if a wet cloth had been put over it. The mouth behind this cloudy shroud was open, the eyes staring, glowing. Hideous. Then Asphodyl uttered a sputtering sigh and fell to the floor, still wrapped around Miyalkin's feet. Miyalkin was jerked downwards also, because he was still entwined with his enemy. The bonds around Asphodyl's twitching body were no longer clouds, but bloody and tangled and strong as rope. Frantically, Miyalkin sawed at his own hair with his knife, sobbing and frantic to cut himself free.

Then he heard his own name: "Miyalkin, be still. It's all right."

Through spots of red light, the blood in his eyes, Miyalkin saw his father before him, a long blade in his hand, dripping with the snake's ichor.

"Cut off the tail," Miyalkin managed to gasp. "Quickly."

This Moysante did and while he was at his grisly business, Miyalkin freed himself. His hair lay on the floor at his feet, spilling over the motionless corpse: a har now, nothing more. Shorn in sacrifice, Miyalkin felt lighter, naked, colder.

After dealing with the tail, Moysante severed the head. His mind was free now and he knew they must take no chances. After this task was done, Moysante went to embrace his son. "From the moment you struck, I was free," he murmured. "I came at once."

"He meant the son to kill me," Miyalkin said in a gulping voice. "Born alive... a poisonous snake."

Moysante pushed the rags of Miyalkin's cropped hair back from his face, took his son's chin in his hands. "For a moment, I thought... I thought he'd *come back*. That's what I saw. For a moment, it wasn't you."

Miyalkin laid his head on his father's shoulder, expelled a shuddering breath from deep within. "I had his hair," he said.

Together, father and son took the remains outside, and there burned them. As they were doing this so other hara, who'd heard the terrifying noises, came from their dwellings to see what was happening. Miyalkin's brothers came bewildered from nightmares, held asleep while the snake conducted its business, but now that the spell had been broken, not one of them grieved the loss of Asphodyl or his offspring that had not been a har.

Shivering by the flames, in shock, Miyalkin gazed at the sky. The smoke went up, dark and roiling, absorbed by the clouds above that looked as red as fire.

There now, my pearl, the story is done. What's that? No, Miyalkin's hair never grew back completely. It hung only to his shoulders to the end of his life. No, fear not, there are no snake spirits here. Our wards are strong against such monsters. But be mindful of the lesson in this tale, my son. Old powers live in the land and they find strength again now the human race has gone. Take care upon the forest paths, and if you should become lost, and somehar strange should come to you with a bargain, run fast and don't look back. Better to let the forest take you than a curse.

Without Weakness

Dream, Nicholas. Dream of voices baying in the night, of hooves galloping over hard ground, of shimmering heat, the smell of musk and leather. Toss and turn in your narrow bed, Nicholas, for they are coming for you, in their thousands, gleaming skin beneath the hard sun, so many horses' nostrils flaring, manes flying, the grip of thighs on heaving flanks. Can you feel their breath upon you, hot and sweet, reeking of blood? Can you feel their clawed hands upon you, the caress of talons against your flesh, and the ripple of silent laughter in the air? Are you waiting for this, Nicholas? Is this your sin? In the dark, in the night, do you turn traitor to your kin, to your God? I can see everything, boy, and I see your heart. You are not without weakness.

1

The boy, Nicholas, awoke with a cough and sat upright in bed. Serene moonlight came in through the narrow window, falling across the coverlet like a white robe. Sheets so white they made the eyes ache. Shadows so blue they seemed to be painted on the room. Gasping, Nicholas peered around him, but the shadows were still, and so was the night outside his window. He heard the night watchman call. *All's well. All's clear.* Just for tonight. But still the voice of God rang in his head, and God did not lie. What could Nicholas do to control his rebel dreams? He didn't want them, didn't invite them. He was their victim, and it took all his energy to fight them.

The door opened, and he half expected to see an avenging angel standing at the threshold with raised sword, but it was only his mother, Hannah. She held a lantern, and wore her night-robe, her hair loose over her shoulders. "I heard you cry out, Nicky. Are you all right?"

"Dream again," he said, wiping his brow, finding it as wet as if he'd been swimming.

Hannah came to sit on the bed, stroked her son's face. "It's not your fault," she said softly. "You do know that, don't you?"

Nicholas closed his eyes briefly. "I know, I know. It's *them*, outside."

119

"You must believe it, son."

"I do." He was close to tears. "I need the ties again."

Hannah frowned. "Oh, Nicky... no..."

"I feel safer."

"But there's not been an attack for weeks. They're far away, they really are."

"No," Nicholas said. "You're wrong."

He lay down again, resigned and sorrowful, like a young saint about to be martyred. Hannah looked upon him and could have wept at the sight of him, his fineness, his honesty, his purity. He was in danger – they all knew it – because of how he was. As a child, he'd seen spirits, and had sometimes dreamed the future. He could *tell* things about people. Sometimes he had *changed* things too: a touch, a fever gone. And he was very beautiful.

Sometimes, the beasts came in their dozens and assaulted the walls of the enclave, using their strange voices to unsettle the defenders. But Hannah's people were wise to such tricks. They blocked their ears, sang their own songs that helped drown out the eerie cries. They had survived for decades, but no one really dared think about the distant future.

Other times, only a few of the beasts would come. They would circle the enclave on their snorting horses; not attacking, but just galloping round, kicking up dust and singing their siren song. At those times, Nicholas' family had tied him to his bed, and in the morning his wrists and ankles had been crusted with blood. They had tried to stop his ears with rags, but the song had lanced right through them. He was a good boy. He always fought hard. They wouldn't win. His father Hugh would kill him before that happened.

"I'll stay with you," Hannah said, "even while you sleep." She stroked his hair now, his fine brown hair like autumn silk. His dark eyes were closed, the lashes long against his sculpted cheeks.

"Don't tell Dad," Nicholas mumbled. "He has enough to worry about, but tell Scrap about my dream. It means something. Tell him to double the watch, be alert."

"I will," Hannah said.

Scrap was Nicholas' elder brother, whose real name was Jack. Only three years between them, but at twenty, Scrap seemed much older. He had fought many wars in his young life, and commanded the garrison of the enclave. Nicholas called him an old soul, and his family did not dispute it. Scrap kept them alive.

He kept hope alive in the hearts of the men and women who defended them. But they were so isolated out here – for all they knew the last humans alive on earth. There was no one to help them, and even though they had a vast stockpile of weapons and ammunition, there would come a day when supplies ran out, and other than from the foraging missions some of their people ran, they had no way of restocking their arsenal. The radio had been dead for years, even though Hugh cruised the airwaves every night, telling the world they were there. It wasn't dangerous to do that, because the beasts didn't have technology. They were just animals. Or so Hugh said. The wonder was how they kept going, because they had no women. How did they replenish their ranks? They always took their dead with them after an attack. Perhaps some of them were female, and had mutilated their breasts like Amazons. Hugh thought they must have breeding stock somewhere; it was a hideous, but horribly possible idea. Was the world over-run with them now?

Hannah was tired to her bones. She didn't want this life, but it was all she had ever known. She had been born in the enclave, in the very early days and was therefore far younger than her husband, who had known the world before. Her grandmother, who had been with them then, had told her tales of the old days, what it had been like, but it was no more real to Hannah than the stories she told to her children, stories of angels who would come to whisk them away to heaven, right from beneath the noses of the beasts.

Outside, a night bird called, and Hannah's body went tense. You could never be sure they were really birds. "Nicky," she said. "I'll go tell Scrap now, you hear. I'll be back. Don't worry."

"I heard it," Nicholas said. "I think it was only a bird."

"Still, it would be best."

"Yes."

The attack came just after dawn. In the grey twilight before the sun broke through, they came out of nowhere; no one saw them approach. Thanks to Nicholas, Scrap had the battlements bristling with defenders. They were ready, but this time, there were too many beasts, more than ever before. Hannah stood high on the barricaded walls, beside her eldest son, with the wind blowing her hair over her face like a girl's. She peered out at the wilderness, where dark horses moved restlessly, and rays of the rising sun glinted off weapons. They had just appeared, hadn't yet made a move. Scrap was tense as a wire, staring at the enemy as if he could wish them away through the force of his will.

"Sometimes," Hannah said, "I wonder why they come, don't you? We're no threat to them. We have nothing they need."

"We have things they *want*, maybe," Scrap said tersely. "That's different."

"Jack," Hannah said, and paused for a moment before continuing. She only called him Jack when matters were serious. "I've never said this anyone, but, do you think, is it possible, they keep coming *because of Nicky*?"

"Mom!" Scrap looked as if he might hit her, and she backed away from him. "Never say that. You know why? Because if folk hear it, the next thing you know they'll be ganging together to have Nick trussed up outside the gates. Never say that! *Never!*"

"I..." Hannah shrugged. "I just thought it, Jack, that's all. I never told anyone. I never will again."

"Good. It's not true, anyway. They just want to wipe us out, that's all. They don't know about Nicky."

"But the song... the dreams..."

Scrap sighed. "Nick's not the only one affected, you know that."

"You never are."

"No. I'm stronger."

Hannah said no more, but she didn't think it was simply that. She loved Nicky with all her heart, he was her treasure, but sometimes, when the beasts came and people died, and the enclave hung on to survival by a prayer, she wished... she wished... *No, don't think it.* Jack was right.

The beasts began to howl then, an eerie sound that frightened up all the birds hiding in the scrub. Jackals ran out, biting their own tails. The hair on Hannah's neck and arms stood up. She knew there was no point putting her hands over her ears. That wouldn't stop the racket, never did, never would.

"Get down, Mom," Scrap said. "Go into the house. You know what to do."

She nodded and left quickly, but not before she saw them pouring slowly like heavy smoke towards the enclave. They had the heads of beasts. They wore jackal skins, with snarling muzzles over their faces. This could be the last time, as every time could.

2

General Ashmael Aldebaran of the Wraeththu tribe of Gelaming was in discussion with his immediate staff in his camp pavilion. This was supposed to be a small job, hardly worth his attention really. The Hegemony were interested in a human named Hugh Ferniman, and wanted to make sure there were no mistakes in securing his co-operation. So, they sent the best.

Megalithica: Ashmael hated this country. In his opinion, it gave itself over to barbarism like a whore, and the worst misfits had been bred there. Violence in the blood, in the air, in the very earth. Fragments of tribes that hadn't progressed and should have died out decades ago.

"We come out from the east," he said, poking at a map on the table before him. "Straight from the sun, from behind. The Hegemony says be merciful, but do what you must. The Hegemony never sees battle, do they? I'll not be taking notes."

A ripple of laughter went around the pavilion. They understood him. Rehabilitation was not in Ashmael's lexicon. He won battles for the Gelaming, by whatever means. And his reports juggled numbers of the dead.

"Is everyhar ready?" he asked.

They were.

"Then rally the hara and mount up. Let's ride."

He strode out of the pavilion into the cold dawn air, eager to get this little problem sorted out. This should have been a simple job. Only now the Gelaming scouts had discovered that rogue hara appeared to have their own, rather more brutal, plans for the humans Ashmael wished to speak to. An unexpected nuisance, yet how the human settlement had survived this long in such a dangerous environment was a miracle in itself. Ashmael's armshar held his *sedu* ready for him; the creature pawing at the ground, shaking its white mane out of its wild black eyes. Ashmael's *sedu* matched his temperament; he liked that. Then his heart sank a little when he saw the Kamagrian representative, Katarin, riding towards him. *Best to keep her out of sight of the action. She is the Hegemony's creature.*

"As soon as you can, you must take me to Hugh Ferniman," she said.

"Just stay at the back, Kate, will you? Let me do my job, then you can do yours."

He had to admit she looked as ready for the job as any of his hara, her hair tied back severely, her compact frame swathed in close-fitting leather. "There must be no risk of harm coming to the human," she said.

"I know that." Ashmael grinned. "So trust me." The *sedu* jostled to the side a little as he swung into the saddle. It trod on the feet of its groom. Ashmael gathered up the reins. "How many otherlane journeys have you made, Kate?"

She looked away. "I'm quite capable."

"I hope so. Personally, I think you should wait here. I'll bring the man to you."

"No. I'm sticking with you. I have my orders."

Ashmael raised an eyebrow and sighed, swinging his *sedu* around. She didn't trust him to carry out her part of the job as well as she could. To be fair to her, she was right. Ashmael had no time for subtle negotiation. "Let's do it, then."

The troupe had assembled at the ether gate entry point, and their ranks parted to let Ashmael through. A hundred splendid white horses, which were really *sedim*, not horses at all, ridden by the cream of the Gelaming military. Ashmael rode to the front and halted. Without turning, he raised a hand. As one the *sedim* surged forward, and the air fractured with a sound like brittle thunder. Then they were gone, and the camp was empty of all but armshara, domestic staff, empty ether drays and tents. Pennants bearing the arms of the Aralisian dynasty flapped listlessly in the early morning breeze.

Thirty miles from camp, the *sedim* leapt through another spontaneously-opening ether gate as if jumping down a high bank. They poured back through into familiar reality, ice splintering from their harness, their flying manes and tails. Without pausing, they galloped forward, the red rays of the early sun rubying their pale coats.

Ashmael shook his head to clear it of otherlane scramble and assessed the situation before them. Must be nearly two hundred hara attacking the human enclave. Perhaps a merge of tribes or phyles. The humans must have fought them off for quite some time, Ashmael thought, so a union of forces had been required. This wasn't unheard of. Even the most degenerate hara understood the concept of strength in numbers. A large percentage of the attackers wore jackal hides, and all of them rode small, dark horses. Some carried crude flags that bore the sign of the jackal: a canine mask over a human or harish skull. For some hara, jackals had become a totem animal, because once humanity failed, these tough little canines had escaped the human zoos and parks that held them and had interbred successfully with the native coyotes. They were a symbol of cunning, resilience and liberty. But who were these hara? Uigenna? No. Ashmael didn't recognise the standard. Could be an offshoot, difficult to say. No one really kept track of what bred in the desert wilderness of Megalithica.

Whoever the rogue hara were, they had their war song, and it was strong, but then the Gelaming had their own. The rogues were taken by surprise. It was almost too easy. Arrows and bullets came from the enclave, which was a slight problem, but the harish enemy were no match for the Gelaming. When you sing to the soul and tell it to be terrified, that it has no chance, the hardiest warrior will lay down his weapons and weep. Ashmael indicated a few should be killed, however, just to make a point. Some had actually breached the human defences. Noticing this, Ashmael signalled to ten of his best hara and rode for the sagging walls. His *sedu* sailed over the rubble with sure feet, hardly seeming to touch the ground. Within, the spirits of slaughter howled and screamed. Some humans lay dead on the ground, or spiked on the defences. Hara were galloping about on their horses, shrieking and lashing out with blades and makeshift blunt weapons. Older humans and children were running in terror, presumably trying to defend themselves, hide.

Ashmael sighed. *Nuisance, nuisance.* He could be at home now, looking forward to a pleasant meal with friends, swapping gossip and admiring Immanion's fair evening. He urged his horse forward and took a certain amount of satisfaction in cutting down the jackals that still prowled. "That's for my lost dinner," he told the last one to die.

Kate's *sedu* trotted up to him almost at once. The Kamagrian's face was set in an expression designed to prick at his conscience, a ploy doomed to failure. "You call these hara animals," she said, "but I wonder..."

"Yes, yes, I know your sentiments," Ashmael said. "You want the human. Let's find him. I want to be home within an hour."

Kate would not respond in kind to Ashmael's wry smile. "That might not be possible. These people will be suspicious. We'll have to negotiate, placate them, convince them."

Giving up on trying to win her round, Ashmael reverted to abruptness. "*Your* job, I believe?"

"And you are here to protect me. *You*, Ashmael. No har else. Brave Ashmael, fearless warrior. I bet you were a real bully in the playground."

Ashmael ignored this remark and gazed around the compound. All was eerily quiet. The jackal survivors had been rounded up and taken back to the camp, where they would be assessed. Their fate did not interest Ashmael. He was content to let the mealy-mouthed therapists deal with them. The surviving humans, however, appeared to have gone to earth in the fortified buildings, no doubt wondering what the hell was happening. The hara who'd slaughtered the attackers might not be any better than those they'd killed. The largest house must be Ferniman's headquarters. The humans had guns, and would no doubt fire on anyhar who approached.

"We could do the white flag act," Kate suggested. "Look, they'll think I'm a woman. I'll go."

Ashmael cast her a sidelong glance. "I doubt they'll notice the distinction. You are with us, and they'll be blind to details at the moment." He sighed again, for perhaps the tenth time that morning, deep and heartfelt. "We wait," he said. "Let's see if they come out."

"They won't. Would *you*? Use the song."

Ashmael laughed. "I'm almost tempted to. Clearly, you have no idea what it can do to humans."

The parage coloured a little. "No. So *don't* use it. Wait, then."

The Gelaming assembled in the compound, waiting for orders. Ashmael assessed the house. They could storm it, but sniper fire could take out any of his hara and he cherished them all. No point wasting any on a job like this.

After an hour, he told one of his hara to sing a peace song, discover whether it would touch the human hearts, and instil calm. The clear voice rang around the silent compound, but did not inspire any humans to venture outside. Too much to hope for. They wouldn't be able to identify the nuances within the song.

After two hours, Ashmael gave vent to another deep sigh and signalled to Kate. "Come on," he said.

"Where?"

He started walking towards the house. "You coming or not?"

"Ash!" she said. "Ash, wait."

He was fed up with waiting and mustered all the art of his caste training to protect himself. A shield, an air of non-threat. This was all he could do. The house seemed to regard him with hostile sentience, but no bullets came.

Kate caught up with him as he reached the front door, which was made of steel. "Now what?" she asked.

He grinned at her, and knocked on the door.

Kate rolled her eyes. "This is ridiculous. Are you mad?"

"Hugh Ferniman!" Ashmael called. "If you're inside, please come out. We mean you and your people no harm."

Silence.

"They won't answer," Kate said. "They'll be terrified."

"Hugh Ferniman," Ashmael began again. "We have dealt with your enemies. *We* are not your enemy. We wish to talk. Please come out."

Silence.

"I have a woman with me, who would like to talk to you. She knows of you, Hugh Ferniman, and I have brought her to you."

After a few moments, they heard a heavy bolt being drawn, then about a dozen more. The door opened a crack, on several security chains. Ashmael saw a hostile eye, framed in bloody skin, gazing out. He bowed. "I am Ashmael Aldebaran of the tribe of Gelaming," he said. "I have been sent by my people to assist you in the matter of the individuals who were molesting you. This has been done. Now, we wish to talk on matters of mutual benefit."

"What do you want?" A gruff male voice snapped.

"To speak with Hugh Ferniman. Is he there?"

"What of? What do you want?"

"I wish to speak to Mr Ferniman in person, or rather my colleague here does. Look, we have healers among us. If you have wounded within, we can be of help."

"We don't want your help."

"Very well, but I would like to speak to Hugh Ferniman."

"Are you beast?"

"Occasionally, or so I'm told," Ashmael said, "but in general, I don't think so." He cast a glance at Kate, who grimaced and shrugged. "I'm an officer in the Gelaming army. But you won't have heard of the Gelaming, of course. We are... we are not like the jackal hara... *people*. We wish you no harm."

"Please let me speak to Hugh Ferniman," Kate said in her gentlest tone, and it seemed her more feminine voice did the trick. The chains rattled and the door opened about six inches. They saw a young man standing on the threshold. He had wounds – to a shoulder, a thigh – which had been hastily bound but were still bleeding. Ashmael knew the look in his eyes; it was that of someone who was holding on with the last of his strength, who could collapse at any moment.

"Hugh Ferniman is my father," he said.

"May we come in?" Kate asked, sweetly, harmlessly.

"Are you *beast*?" the young man asked again, his gaze flicking between them.

"He means," Kate said to Ashmael, "are you Wraeththu?"

"Not the kind you've met before," Ashmael said. "We are not your enemy."

"*All* beasts are our enemy."

"Yet you've opened the door and are now chatting to me on the step," Ashmael said. "Please stop being stupid and let us in. We are unarmed."

Another, older male voice boomed from inside. "Let them in."

The young man stood aside, clearly with the greatest reluctance. Ashmael entered first, Kate close on his heels. A tall, gaunt man stood in the doorway to what appeared to be a kitchen beyond. It had been a long time since Ashmael had seen anyone suffering from cellular decay. If this was Ferniman, he must only be around sixty years old – around the same age Ashmael was himself – yet the human's face was lined, his hair thinning, his body sagging. Why had Ferniman submitted to this gradual deterioration when at one time he could have been har? Ashmael inclined his head respectfully. "Thank you for seeing us."

"What do you want?"

Ashmael gestured flamboyantly at Kate. "Your stage, my lady."

Kate cast him a scornful glance and stepped forward. "Mr Ferniman, I am Katarin har Roselane. I represent the Hegemony – the leaders – of Immanion. I won't waste words: they have an offer to make to you concerning your particular talents."

Ferniman's gaze was steady on her. "I don't know these people or the place you mentioned. Is it a human enclave?"

Kate's pause was almost imperceptible. "No, but..."

"Then I have nothing to say to you."

"Mr Ferniman," Kate said, "I think you should face facts. We are aware of your situation, since you have been broadcasting it in detail. Wraeththu rule this world now, but..."

"*You* are not one of them. What are you? A traitor to your kind? What did they offer you?"

Kate took a breath, touched her breast with the tips of her fingers. "I am *not* human, Mr Ferniman, but this is not the time to split hairs over how Wraeththu I am. Succinctly, I am of a race called the Kamagrian, who have chosen to favour the feminine aspect of our being. But I am not a woman."

"Yet here before us to pretend to be one, to get into my house."

"Yes. It was all we could do, under the circumstances." She smiled. "Believe me, I do not lie to you. We wish you no harm, in fact quite the opposite. How you've survived out here, surrounded by rogue Wraeththu tribes, is astonishing and very rare. The world *has* changed, Mr Ferniman, and the majority of Wraeththu – and *all* of the Kamagrian – are against war, either with humans or the type of hara who attacked your home. It's not the wish of the Gelaming, one of the most advanced of Wraeththu tribes, to destroy what is left of the human race. Many are inclined to preserve it. You are a skilled geneticist, and the Hegemony would like to hire you to study harish – that is *Wraeththu* – origins. They want to know how they came to be, because they believe it derives from genetic *human* engineering in the past."

Ashmael could tell Kate's words had pricked Ferniman's interest.

"That's not beyond possibility," Ferniman said. "In fact, it's quite likely, given the state our world was in. I've often wondered about it myself."

Kate ducked her head once. "I am obliged to say that should it be your wish, you and your people may remain here, fending off barbaric tribes until the last of you is dead, or the rogues have been eradicated and rehabilitated by more enlightened hara. We cannot, nor want to, force you to do anything. However, if you co-operate and accept Gelaming protection, there will be many benefits. No harm will come to any of you, nor will any be incepted... that is... *changed* unless of their own free will. It's your choice, but I wonder how many of your people, given the opportunity, would opt for your refusal?"

A woman appeared at Ferniman's side. She appeared to be in her late thirties; an attractive woman despite the lines of worry etched into her face, the tiredness that weakened her body. She glanced rather coldly at Ferniman, and then gestured. "I'm Hannah Ferniman," she said. "Come into the kitchen. We will talk."

"Hannah!" Ferniman growled.

"Quiet, Hugh," the woman said. "We should hear more of this. We're at the end of our rope now."

"Thank you," Kate said.

She and Ashmael followed the woman into the kitchen. Around two dozen humans were clustered there, both male and female, some of them wounded. The younger ones stared at the newcomers with wary yet curious eyes, while the adults covered their fear with surly expressions.

"We *do* have healers," Kate said, "very accomplished ones. Are you sure you don't want to avail yourselves of their services?"

"None of that hoodoo!" Ferniman spat, shutting the kitchen door behind him. "We've seen enough of what your kind can do."

"So speaks the scientist," Ashmael remarked drily.

Ferniman turned to him. "I've seen enough to change my mind about a lot of things," he said. "I'd kill my boys myself before I let your kind have them."

"Hugh!" Hannah said. "That's quite enough." She turned to Kate. "How do you know of us?" She gestured for Kate and Ashmael to seat themselves at the broad kitchen table.

Ashmael remained standing, but Kate sat down, laced her hands on the table top. "We... picked up on your broadcasts a few weeks ago."

Hannah glanced at her husband. "So, you're saying that some of the people we call beasts have developed technology... a civilisation..."

Kate nodded. "Yes. As I said, a lot has changed, and in a relatively short time. The Gelaming peacekeeping force is dedicated to assisting people in your situation. So, we came to assist."

Hannah's eyes narrowed. "It isn't just that though, is it? You spoke of wanting to make use of Hugh's expertise."

Kate gestured with one hand. "Yes, we know about him. He earned quite a reputation during the Upheavals." She addressed Ferniman. "You tried to investigate Wraeththu back then, didn't you? You made records of your theories concerning genetics and how Wraeththu could have sprung from humanity."

"Whatever initially created them, in essence they sprang from hell," Ferniman said. "It might have been a hell *we* created, but hell all the same. I told you, I've changed my mind about a lot of things."

"We've suffered," Hannah said, by way of explanation.

"We understand that," Kate said. "And we don't expect an answer immediately."

"I don't see how I can help you," Hugh said gruffly. "I've never managed to get my hands on a whole corpse, let alone access to the instruments I need to explore such material."

"You will have willing test subjects in Immanion," Kate said. "I'm quite sure the equipment you need will be made available to you, or substitutes that will do the job."

Hugh expressed a suspicious grunt, clearly still not persuaded.

Kate dipped her head to one side and said softly, "You do know you can't continue to live here in this way indefinitely?"

"We've managed," Ferniman snapped.

"Admirably," Kate said, "but whatever happens out there, you can't remain as you are. You are, in essence, no longer isolated, no longer cut off from..."

"Look," Ashmael blundered in, "if I'd wanted to, I could have shattered the minds of every human in this enclave. But I didn't. We're here to talk, to make an offer. However, the fact is I'm not going to leave empty-handed. There are a hundred Gelaming outside. See reason, Mr Ferniman, and stop posturing."

Kate shot him a deadly glance, sniped at him in mind touch. *Thanks, Ash. That really helps.*

Ashmael made a dismissive gesture at her. *It's a fact. He knows it.*

A new voice sounded behind them. "What are you *really* here for?"

Both Ash and Kate turned. The young man who had let them in had come into the kitchen. He leaned against the door, his hand leaving a bloody print.

"You don't need my father," he said. "I only have to look at you to see that – well-fed, smug and so *civilised*. You mock us. What is this *really* about?" He gestured beyond the walls of the house. "Why did you kill your own kind out there? What have you come for?"

"Scrap," Hannah said softly. "Jack..."

The young man turned on her. "Mom, wake up! They bring a

woman to get into the house, or what *looks* like a woman. But we know they kill humans, they shun women." He turned his gaze on his father. "And now *you've* let them in, Dad."

Hugh glanced at his wife. "I did?" he said. "Ask her about it!"

"We were given an explanation," Hannah said patiently to her son. "Perhaps you didn't hear it properly."

The young man uttered a snort of derision and pointed at Kate, fixing his mother with a stare. "You don't know what's *really* sitting there. They're like evil spirits. Perhaps they can take on any form. And you *let them in*." He turned his gaze to Kate. "What's the true price? Won't you name it?"

"I am not a Wraeththu har masquerading as a woman, if that's what you think," Kate said. "And there is no price, only an offer."

Ashmael was silent for once. Let the parage deal with this. He was tired of it now.

The young man staggered further into the room and crumpled to his knees. Kate went immediately to assist him, but he pushed her off, falling instead against his mother, who had also hurried to his side. The effort made him pant. "You were right, Mom. I see it now. They've come for…"

"Scrap, shut up!" Hannah hissed, pulling his head against her breast as if to stifle his words.

"Nicky. They've come for Nicky."

There was a brief silence, then: "Who or what is Nicky?" Ashmael asked.

"He's delirious," Hannah said, still holding her son close.

"Then let me help," Kate said. The two women hauled him to a sagging old sofa against the far wall. "He's badly hurt, Hannah," Kate said. "Please let me summon one of our healers."

"Who's Nicky?" Ashmael asked again.

"Ash, forget that," Kate said. "Get somehar. Now!"

"I won't let you…" Hugh Ferniman began.

"For God's sake!" cried Hannah. "Let them!"

"You go," Ashmael said to Kate. He looked around the room and, acting on instinct, headed for a door that did not lead back to the hall. Ferniman sprang after him but Ashmael turned on him with a snarl. "Don't try, old man." The look in his eye made Ferniman back off.

Ashmael opened the door and went through it. What was this? A mystery, a secret. He smelled something interesting. Panic and fear had eclipsed the perfume, but he could sense it now. Strong, summoning. They were hiding something here. But what? They were only human. Ferniman had followed him, at a distance. "What is it you've hidden in here?" Ashmael said, his tone threatening now that he was away from Kate's hearing. "Tell me." They had reached a flight of stairs. Ferniman threw himself in front of Ashmael, virtually collapsing on the bottom step. "Don't," he said. "I'll do what you ask... Take *me*."

Ashmael uttered a sound of annoyance. "Get up. I'm not doing any *taking*. Stop being a fool. I don't have to pander to the parage now we're out of her hearing, so I'll tell you this: You'll do what we want, anyway. I want to see what you're hiding. Now, do you show me, or do I find it myself?"

"Don't take him," Ferniman said. "It will kill him."

Ashmael pushed the man aside and leapt up the stairs, three steps at a time. He could smell it more strongly now: terror and power. A sweet perfume of potential.

The door was at the end of a long corridor. A light that could not be seen by human eyes leaked thinly round its frame. Ashmael marched directly to it and turned the handle. Locked. No matter. He kicked it in effortlessly. There was a scuffle of activity within. He saw two women, one quite young, restraining someone, whose hands and feet were bound. A har. It was a har! What had they done? How?

"Release him!" Ashmael snarled. "At once!"

The women cringed away, hands held out as if to ward him off. Ashmael then saw his mistake. What lay before him was not a har but a human youth. Such a creature, though. It had been easy to misread the signs. Perhaps the people here had somehow taken this boy from one of the rogue tribes. A failed inception? Or stolen before inception had taken place? He could not yet tell.

Ashmael hunkered down and began to pull at the boy's bonds. "It's all right," he said. "I won't hurt you. I'll set you free."

The boy whined and writhed frantically on the floor like a frightened cat, making Ashmael's job almost impossible without harming him. Ashmael was not the kind of har who could soothe with a touch. He knew his limitations. He stood up and turned to the women. "Remove his bonds," he said. "Now."

Reluctantly, the younger woman stepped forward.

"No, Liza," cried the other, but the girl shook her head.

"It's the end of it," she said. She went to squat beside the boy, and began picking at the knots.

"Why is he bound?" Ashmael asked the older woman. "Locked in? What's going on here?"

"To keep him safe," the woman said, with dignity. "*From you.*"

Ashmael turned from her. The boy seemed mindless. And yet initially he had given off the *feeling* of a har. Clearly, he had *abilities*, but was too damaged, perhaps, to use them or even understand them properly. It was obvious what was behind this imprisonment now: the boy's family had bound and hidden him because of what he was. They had thought the Gelaming had come for him, and it was most likely the jackal tribe *had*. The burning smell of potent natural energy was so strong, it filled the room. It would reach beyond this ramshackle compound and haunt the night. It would have driven the jackal hara into a frenzy. One thing was certain; whatever happened, this boy had to be protected.

The girl had finished unbinding him and was coiling the narrow ropes around her right arm. She looked resigned, defeated, grief-stricken. The boy lay twitching on the bare floorboards. Ashmael tried to lift him to his feet, but the boy – suddenly alert and fleet – squirmed away with an animal cry. He fled across the room to a chest of drawers, where a glass pitcher rested. Before Ashmael realised what was happening, and amid the startled cries of his relatives, the boy had smashed the pitcher and hurtled towards Ashmael with sharp shard in his hand, blood already running from his lacerated palm. Ashmael had no choice but to knock him out. The body slumped limply at his feet. The women uttered cries of fear and clung to one another, hair over their faces, which were masks of horror.

"Who is this?" Ashmael snapped at the women. "Speak!"

He loomed over them, a tower of threat. "I said *speak!*"

"It's Nicholas," the younger one said with difficulty, "my brother."

3

Wake up, Nicholas, wake up. This is just another dream and you must resist it. Wake up!

It was not a dream. Nicholas knew where he was and how he'd got there. It was a camp of war and he was lying within a cocoon of soft, striped blankets in one of the tents. The beast had taken him. He had come into the room looking like an angel, but he had the devil's heart. Fallen one, father of lies. Unnaturally tall. Nicholas hadn't expected them to look like that. It was the worst lie. And now, his God was testing him further, because he was still alive. Horrors would come.

In the dim light of the tent, where thin draperies veiled the entrance, Nicholas saw a shape before him. As he stared, this resolved into a figure, sitting upon a cushion. This person sat upright, their hands clasped in their lap. The face... it was a strange girl, who looked most severe. Her skin was clean like air, her pale hair bound up on her head and pierced with ornate silver pins. Was she real? She didn't look real. Nicholas hadn't seen a girl like that even in the picture books he'd loved as a child.

"You're awake," said the girl in an odd voice. Odd because... it sounded almost like the voice of a boy, yet was not.

Nicholas could not move. His limbs felt bound, but they were free. His head was thick, as if stuffed with straw. An enchantment, a curse, or perhaps simply a drug. He was no doubt expected to say things like "Who are you?" and "Where am I?" but he didn't want to hear the answers. He would be able to tell if they were lies, and generally more information came to him by listening rather than by speaking.

"I'm awake," he said.

The figure shifted upon her cushions. "Good. I am Reydis the Seer, and I'm here to assess you."

No lies there. Nicholas said nothing. He only had to wait.

"I'm not a healer, although you may talk with one afterwards, if you like. I can tell you that your physical damage is slight, although hurts of a deeper, more intimate nature are not. I can see you are intelligent. You will have been aware of your differences most of your life, I expect."

Nicholas did not answer. *Aware I can hear thoughts? Yes. Aware of lies? Yes. Aware of being physically helpless at this moment? Yes.*

"That is precisely what I mean," said the girl, and she smiled, although it wasn't a genuine smile. Nicholas could tell the girl was thinking about something else as well as her 'assessment'. He could pry into her thoughts and find out what this was, then tell her. But that was what she wanted him to do, so he wouldn't.

"It's pointless to play games," said the girl. "We need to assess you, because from what our healers have ascertained, inception might be the best *treatment* for you. I don't know how much you've been told before being brought here, but that procedure is not mandatory for humans nowadays. However, under certain rare circumstances, it *is* advisable."

Nicholas didn't know what she meant, and found it hard to interpret the thoughts that went with the words. She was cloaking them now. "I would like to go home," he said.

The girl pursed her lips a little. "You know that your family is in danger," she said, "and, as well as that, they are not equipped to deal with a person such as yourself. You are safer here, and will be cared for appropriately."

Nicholas closed his eyes. He didn't want to hear any more. He knew he couldn't ask for his mother or his sisters, because they weren't here in the camp.

The girl changed her voice; it became softer. "I know you're afraid, and I know that you lack all the information you require to make wise choices. You can ask me anything and I'll do my best to answer clearly."

There were guards at the door, two of them. Nicholas could see them in his mind. He extended his senses, easier now as he forced himself to relax, and let himself drift like a wave over the camp outside. Many of them. Not like the jackals. Different in some ways, not in others. They were not cruel, he could sense that too. But...

A whirlwind of colour and noise suddenly erupted in his mind as someone marched into the tent. He opened his eyes.

A woman stood over the girl, hands on hips. "What are you doing here?" she demanded.

The girl twisted her head to the side. "My job. I'm here to assess the boy. As you know, this is the proper procedure in cases like this."

"There is no *case like this*," the woman snapped. "General Aldebaran gave express instructions Nicholas Ferniman was to be left alone, except for essential healing. Why was his mother not brought here?"

"That is not procedure."

The woman snorted, raked a hand through her thick hair. "Get out," she said mildly. "I'll speak to your supervisor shortly."

"I'm not sure what authority you have here..."

"Plenty. I'm here on behalf of the Hegemony concerning the matter of the Ferniman family. I think you'll find my credentials *proper*, if you care to check."

The girl stood up and without another word exited the tent.

The woman shook her head and sighed. Then she folded her arms and smiled at Nicholas. She was not a woman, he could tell that now. The colours around her weren't right. But she wasn't a beast either.

"I want to go home," he said.

"I know," the woman-thing replied, "and I'm sorry that can't happen just yet. I'm Katarin, Kate. I came to your house after the battle a few days ago. You've been unconscious since then, following some kind of seizure. My colleague, Ashmael, found you bound and locked in a room of your house. That was why you were brought here, because families do not generally keep their relatives tied up in a locked room."

"It has to be done," Nicholas said. "Do I have to tell you why? I don't think I do."

"No, you don't, but it's not a good way to live, is it?"

Nicholas shrugged. "I know it's over, in some ways, but I can see you're honest. I have simple requests. Let me go home or kill me. I don't want to be made like... not like you, because you're different, but like the others."

"Do you really understand the differences, Nicholas? What happens when a human is made har?"

He bared his teeth at her. "I saw much of it because *they* showed me. They corrupted my dreams. I saw what the demons of hell do when they are loosed on earth, what they do with each other and to their victims. My family don't know. How could I tell them? It's so much worse than they know."

"So... are you saying that *you* asked for the bonds rather than your family forcing them on you?"

The glance he gave her was filled with contempt. "Of course. You've jumped to conclusions about my people, haven't you? What I know inside, what I can't ever tell them, is abominable and that's why I make them bind me and lock my room. I don't *want* to live that way. Do you think I'm mad?"

"No," Kate replied. "I think you're afraid and more so because you don't have all the information you need. The hara around you now are as different from the creatures who violated your dreams as you are from a hornet."

"I don't care. If you really want to help me, stop the hornets coming for me."

Kate sat down on the end of his bed and regarded him for a few moments. "From what little I know of you already, I don't think they'll ever stop coming for you – well not until you're so old you won't be worth the bother. But as for the immediate future, should you elect to remain human, and your father agrees to work with the Gelaming, a safe haven will be provided for your people among other humans. In this place, you will be protected."

"Like in a reservation," Nicholas said. He knew the ancient history of his homeland. *"We* are the ousted natives here now, those of us who are human."

"There is some truth in that analogy," Kate said. "What you have to think about is that this is not a human world anymore. You can try to preserve the past, and many hara would agree with you – lost species, like lost languages, are gone forever if they're allowed to die out. But you also have opportunities. You look upon Wraeththu as an abomination, a curse, the enemy. And so they were, once upon a time. But while your family has tried to hide away in the wilderness, the world moved on, very quickly. The days of terror have gone, Nicky – if I may call you that. You were living in something like a little capsule, in a nightmare. You need to see the truth of the world now, before making decisions about your own future."

"What are you?"

"I am a parage of the Kamagrian, similar to Wraeththu yet also different in some ways. Like Wraeththu, I have no single gender. Like them I am blessed with abilities that humans did not have. And yet... *you* have some of those abilities. Isn't it interesting a human was born that way? You also appear androgynous to an outsider. Ash thought you were a har when he first saw you. And our healers have picked up... *anomalies* in your physical makeup, hidden to the eye but there all the same. You could say, Nicky, you're not quite human either."

He wanted her words to be lies, but they were not. He turned on his side, to face the wall of the tent. He didn't want to look at her, or *feel* her, but she wasn't ready to go away yet. "Please, if you have any decency at all, don't make me like *them*. I can't do it. I've seen."

"What exactly have you seen?"

Furiously, with a surge of energy he *showed* her. *Not just sight. Terrible screams that no living soul should hear. The smell of blood and other fluids of the body leaking out. The sight of mutilated bodies, those who writhe with the infection, those who do not survive and whose corpses lie in a pile to rot or for their dogs to eat. The way they touch each other. The anger inside. The lust to kill until there is nothing left to die.*

He felt Kate wince away from the blast of thought. "I've seen what they do, believe me," he said.

Kate looked shaken; how could any decent person not be? She scraped a hand through her hair, made an effort to speak in a level tone. "That must have been... terrible." She knew, of course, those words were inadequate, but she persisted in trying to win his trust. He almost felt sorry for her. "I understand completely your feelings on what you've experienced. All I can say is that what you've seen in your nightmares is not the way things are amongst civilised hara. The jackal people aren't what Wraeththu *are*, Nicky. They are... *remnants* from the early days, hara who are damaged and broken, who never rose up from the wreckage as better beings. They are full of hate and fear, yes. They know no better. You mustn't think that the Gelaming are anything like that – they're not."

"You're deluding yourself," Nicholas said. "Some are still like that but hide it." He turned back to her. "You're doing what that other girl did, only in a different way. You think you know what's best for me."

He could tell he'd hit a nerve with those words, for she said nothing.

"You want to do that terrible thing to me, because you think you can help me afterwards, show me your world. You can show me so many things. It's a beautiful picture and you are kind. But I don't want it. I can't be touched."

"Can't be touched?"

"I'm given to God."

Kate stood up. He could see she was thinking that there'd been no sign his family was religious. She was puzzled and didn't understand. But then neither did his family. He didn't speak of it to anyone. At least his family didn't try to change him. They didn't want to lose him. And now they had.

"Can I see my mother?"

"I'll do what I can."

"Your people won't listen. They want to change me."

"Ashmael, the one who found you, ordered that nothing was to be done with you before he returns, other than simple care.

He's had to go back to Immanion for a couple of days. He'll come back tomorrow to talk more with your father."

"I don't want to see him. You must keep him away. He's like the jackals. He has their thoughts."

At this, Kate laughed, although she smothered it quickly. "That's not... Ashmael is a soldier, of course, and has his *ways*, but he's a good har, and very powerful. He'll help you."

These words conjured a picture in his head of the one he'd encountered in his bedroom back home. Tall. Angel. The woman-thing's words felt like a wall of flame passing over the earth, devouring everything in its path. Nicholas cried out, attempted to shut down his mind. He must go inwards to a safe place, where the chanting was, and songs to God.

She was worried about him, this woman-thing. He could feel her concern pouring off her, but it was not enough to douse the flames. Already his body was stretched taut, tremors starting up in his limbs, his spine like a bow. "Go!" he cried. "Go! Go now!"

She went.

Kate walked through the camp, dazed. What she'd seen in the tent unnerved her. The boy had suddenly had some kind of psychic fit; destructive energy had blasted out of him like poison fireworks, filling the space with unhealthy sick-green ether. He was terrified, but the revulsion he felt was stronger, deeper. She supposed she must tell the therapists what had occurred, but didn't relish it; then she was roused from her thoughts by a stern voice.

"Katarin? A moment, if you please."

Merxis stood before her, Reydis's supervisor, here to assess the mental state of the humans in the compound. He was not tall, but gave the impression of being so. His fair hair was severely plaited. Kate had noticed most of the therapists adopted this tidy style, perhaps to instil the idea of order and routine in those they treated.

Kate inclined her head, "Tiahaar."

Merxis wrinkled his straight, narrow nose briefly. "Reydis tells me you dismissed him from Nicholas Ferniman."

"Yes, because that is what General Aldebaran instructed."

"The boy has to be assessed. He's a vortex. Even you must see that."

Even you. Some hara were somewhat prejudiced against

Kamagrian. In fact, it was more likely Kate would *see* more than Merxis. "We have our orders. There is no benefit in bullying the humans, as I can't see how this will help General Aldebaran's mission, which is, of course, to bring Hugh Ferniman to Immanion. In essence, fascinating though he is, Nicholas is none of our business." She smiled sweetly.

Merxis grimaced. "You're not suggesting he should be returned to his people?"

"Why not? Yes, he's a human enigma, but he's not why we're here. Interfering could jeopardise the Hegemony's plans."

Merxis folded his arms and assumed a slightly belligerent posture. "Hugh Ferniman is only a man. I fail to see how he can be so important. His son, however, could be."

Kate deliberately mirrored Merxis' stance. "Then we should protect him. Hopefully, Ferniman will take up the offer and his people can be moved to a safer area."

"Tiahaar, the boy has *fits*. I know you've seen one. I imagine these will only get worse in proximity to hara, as he now is. I believe he is destined to be har and this should be attended to."

"At the risk of his sanity?"

Merxis laughed softly. "My dear parage, the hara of my department are more than qualified to deal with any psychological fallout. The physical change is important and whatever happens afterwards will be managed."

"General Aldebaran gave specific instructions that no major decisions concerning Nicholas Ferniman should be made until he returns. I believe his orders outrank yours on this occasion."

Merxis inclined his head. "I'm responsible for health and well-being. Sometimes my decisions are beyond rank. You should know that."

"Give the boy treatment for the fits. Surely you can do that?"

"He doesn't allow hara to touch him. He gets violent, even while fitting."

Kate widened her eyes. "Then do it from a distance! *You* should know *that*." Unable to bear any more, she walked away from Merxis. If she remained, all they'd do was argue in circles. The only thing she could think of to help Nicholas was to replace the guards at his door with two of Ashmael's trusted hara. Surely that would keep Merxis and his meddlers out, at least until Ashmael returned.

Of all the Fernimans, Hannah - Kate felt - was most likely to be willing to discuss her son's condition. But it was all too soon. The Fernimans were distrustful - understandably so - and Kate did not feel comfortable with suggesting Nicholas should be incepted. This would surely only reinforce the family's negative thoughts about the Gelaming's motives. If such a step were ever to take place, it should be after the Fernimans had been taken to Immanion and learned for themselves there were no ulterior motives. But perhaps there were. Merxis was keen to incept Nicholas because he was curious and wanted to see what came out of it. He would never admit to that, of course.

With great misgivings, and after she'd instructed two of Ashmael's hara to guard the boy, Kate rode her *sedu* down to the enclave where the Fernimans had been left alone to discuss their future among themselves. Here, harish healers were still attending to the injured. The dead had been cleared away. When Kate presented herself at the Ferniman household, she was not greeted warmly. A girl she'd not met before led her into the kitchen, where a dozen people were gathered around the table. She felt that discussions were not going well and that the family was divided. This was not the atmosphere in which to talk about what was on her mind. Instead, and rather lamely, she said, "I'm here to see if you need anything."

"Our son?" Hugh snapped coldly from the head of the table.

"May I speak with you about him?" Kate asked, all the time clenched up inside with foreboding.

"Can we stop you?" one of the women replied.

Kate ignored this remark. She stood uncomfortably before the seated company and braced herself for a fight. "How long has he been having fits? Have you noticed them getting worse recently?"

"He'll be fine back with his family," Hannah said, from the other end of the table. "It's you who's making it worse. You have no idea how he feels about..." She shook her head, pressed a hand against her eyes. A woman next to her took her free hand and squeezed it.

"I do have an idea about it," Kate said, "because he's told me. His religious convictions seem very strong."

"It's how he copes," Hannah said, looking up once more.

Kate nodded. "I understand. You do realise he has certain abilities not normally found in humans?"

The family glanced at one another but it was only Hannah who said, "Yes, we know that. But such things have always been found in special people. It doesn't make him like you."

Kate sighed inwardly. "I will be honest with you. Nicky's condition, and the fact it appears to be worsening, has resulted in some of our therapists believing he should be incepted, made har. You know what this means?"

The family stared at her stonily, not speaking, as if they were a single entity. She felt one might leap up at any moment and attack her. "Personally, I disagree with this stance, as does General Aldebaran, but it's difficult for me to argue against what's regarded as the safest procedure in these circumstances. Hara don't wish to harm Nicholas. I can't emphasise that enough. They think they know what's best for him and want to end his suffering. They might be right, and Nicholas would rise from althaia – that is, the changing – with relief and gratitude. But I believe the decision should be his, not anyhar else's. I'm here because..." Again, just the angry silence. Why *was* she here? For their blessing? That wouldn't happen.

"You mean well," Hannah said, offering a weak smile.

"They have always come for him," said one of the men, who Kate recognised after a moment as a cleaned-up Jack, the brother. "It was Nicky who asked to be bound, because he would rather die than be changed in that way. If you have no power among your own people, perhaps the kindest thing you could do is to kill him."

"Jack!" Hannah snapped, and a ripple of murmuring started up around the table.

Kate took a deep breath. "I wouldn't kill your brother even if he asked me to himself. Life is precious." She held out her hands to them, trying to convince them of her honesty. "I want you to see Immanion, to see the world of civilised Wraeththu as it is *now*. You must understand that a great change has come, like a planet-wide earthquake that has shaken everything up. It will take time, perhaps centuries, for things to settle, for equilibrium to be found. But there are pockets of it already, and that is what gives us hope."

For another few moments there was only silence, then Hugh Ferniman said, "Then tell us about it. Tell us what you are, how some of you look like women and some like men, yet we are told you are neither. Tell us how your city came to be built, how the beasts there evolved, found peace, found education, found a future. All we've ever seen is the face of the jackal out there." He pointed at the wall of the house, out beyond the enclave, to where dull fires might still burn in secret caves and savage eyes gleam with their light. "Convince me what you are is meant to be."

Kate sighed, raked her hands through her hair. "May I have a seat? This will take some time."

It was past ten o'clock at night when Kate left the Ferniman house. By this time, she had talked with them, eaten with them, and if not exactly made friends, had perhaps reassured them a little. She had suggested that Hugh and Hannah visit Immanion, although she needed to talk with Ashmael as to how feasible it was for a human to be transported by *sedu*. This might be impossible, or at least too dangerous to try. Travelling by sea would take a long time, perhaps too long under the circumstances. Kate felt sure, though, that once the Fernimans saw the city and had spoken with hara and parazha, even other humans, their minds might be eased somewhat. She knew through experience these things could take time and needed careful, gradual handling.

She also acknowledged, however grudgingly, that Merxis and his hara might be right, even if their motives weren't. Nicholas had been exposed to hara, and his differences had somehow caused a gate to open within him. She realised he was already part har, in some strange way, yet he resisted so strongly. The implications of what he was were immense. The general belief among Wraeththu was that hara had been created by humankind, perhaps not deliberately, but as part of an operation to save their people from extinction. If this was not so, and individuals who displayed harish traits were being born to women, perhaps the creation of Wraeththu was more natural than anyone – or anyhar – thought. Yet Nicholas was young, the early days were long past. It might be that hara were somehow affecting humans now from afar. She had no idea; it was a puzzle.

Her thoughts were abruptly interrupted by a harsh and desperate cry, like that of an animal in pain.

4

Why are you running, Nicholas? Don't you know it's too late for that? Better to end it now. Jump from a cliff. Throw yourself into a river. What are you waiting for?

He ran, stumbling, arms flailing, his skin on fire. Sometimes he was blind. Other times what he saw before him couldn't possibly be real. And yet at other moments he could see with intense clarity, perceiving the details of each tiny pebble on the rough ground ahead of him. Sounds, like the passage of a vast wing, plunged through his mind; this was not just overhead, but around and *through* him. Sounds that blotted out the stars, that had colours. Shards of light pierced his inner ear. He should listen to the voice in his head, find a high place. End it. But within him the desire to end his life warred with another desire to survive. Two beings battling in his mind. One of them wasn't himself.

5

"He's gone, Ash! He's gone!"

Kate looked wild with worry, waiting for Ashmael at the ether gate point. He knew at once to whom she referred. "How?" he snapped, dismounting from his *sedu*.

Kate rubbed at her face. "The fools incepted him! I told them not to, Ash, to wait. They just did it while I was out of the camp."

"Is he dead?" Ash said. "Is this what you're telling me?"

She shook her head. "No. As soon as he came round, he ran. He beat down his guards and ran."

Ashmael made a wordless angry sound. "Then that's as good as dead, isn't it, unless he's found? Have they sent hara out?"

Kate nodded. "Of course. I sent *your* hara. Merxis sent others. Nicky's left no trace... I think his abilities, even at this stage, have strengthened."

For a moment Ashmael rested his forehead against his *sedu's* neck. "Stupid fucking idiots," he said. Then he sighed and remounted the *sedu*. "Kate, come with me. Perhaps you'll be able to pick up some sign."

She didn't question him. "Just give me a minute to get to the stable."

You feel that cracking within, Nicholas? That's your body breaking down. It's liquefying, changing. Perhaps you don't need a cliff or deep water. Perhaps simply running will do it, until you're reduced to a pulp, crawling along the ground, until you crawl no more.

Nicholas fell to his knees, sobbing. Bloody slime trailed from his mouth to the stones beneath him. His skin burned, his insides were aflame. His skin had become scaly, like a sick lizard's that was about to moult. Strips of it hung from him in papery ribbons that smelled musty, rotten. His arm, where they had sliced him, was three times its normal size, looking as if it was about to burst. He knew instinctively that if he kept moving he would literally fall apart. Here was the choice: stop or carry on. He was afraid: of the pain, of disintegration. This did not seem a noble death. Waves of sound continued to pulse over him, sound that was energy, of the planet itself. He could sense the soul of the world and it was curious about him. He had never sensed that before.

He rolled onto his back, stared at the stars, panting. They alone were clear in his sight. He sensed enormous beings striding between them made of ether and starlight. He could almost see them; the gods of humankind throughout the ages. Perhaps they sensed him too but they were impartial, inexorable, fixed upon incomprehensible tasks. They would not help him. Nicholas did not want to die, yet neither did he want to become the *other thing*. Where was *his* God? The voice had gone silent, perhaps because he'd stopped moving, given in.

Then he perceived activity behind him, from the direction he'd come himself. Painfully lifting his head, he saw a cloud of blue radiance studded with stars hurtling towards him. Was this annihilation or a fragment of the distant gods? He could no more move out of its way than shift the planet from its course in the heavens.

"Ash, stop!"

Ashmael commanded his *sedu* to halt and it did so, skidding along the ground because it had been galloping so fast, half in this reality, half in the otherlanes. Ice crystals showered from its flanks.

"There!" Kate cried, pointing.

Ashmael could see the body on the ground ahead. He hoped they weren't too late.

Kate was the first at Nicholas's side, gently examining him. He was clothed in a stained nightshirt, now torn, presumably by his hectic passage through the rough desert. Other than that, it was difficult to discern details from a short distance, and there was a gut-deep reluctance within Ashmael to draw closer. The trail they'd followed had indicated the boy had travelled fast, yet virtually on all fours like an animal, through spiky brush and over splintery stones. He'd run until he could run no more, perhaps was already dead.

Ashmael knew Kate had worked on Hegemony missions to rescue isolated settlements of humans who were in dire condition. Inceptions had taken place on those missions and she'd assisted with them. Ashmael didn't think she'd had to cope with an inceptee who'd fled before, though. Generally, they were incapable of fleeing. She'd had the presence of mind to bring drugs with her. Now she was pawing through the satchel she'd taken from her shoulder, taking out a flask of water and various packets of dried herbs.

"We could do with shelter," Kate said. Both she and Ashmael gazed dispiritedly at the flat desert landscape; the mountains were too far away.

"Can we move him, take him back to camp?"

"I wouldn't advise it," Kate said. "These herbs could really do with proper heating but we don't have the time. I need to get at least some of the medicine inside him really fast."

"What can I do?"

She was mixing the herbs in a small ceramic bowl she'd set on the ground. "Put your hands around this, help me warm it."

Ashmael placed his hands over hers around the bowl, tried to concentrate on summoning Agmara energy, but it wasn't easy. This wasn't his province, and he found it hard to make his mind slow down enough to channel the energy. He wasn't some floaty, ethereal type, such as those found in therapy centres, a kind of har he secretly despised. He was a creature of swift action. Apart from skills useful to his job, Ashmael hadn't particularly bothered with honing his natural abilities. If he needed heat, he'd usually order some other har to do it.

"Can't I go and find some tinder or something?" he said. "I'm not much use to you here."

"You're har, aren't you?" Kate snapped. "Too ouana-focused, of course, but still har. Dredge that half-dead soume part to the surface for a minute, will you?"

"My soume-part is not half dead," Ashmael said indignantly. "It's just... well an *uncompromising* sort of soume."

"I knew girls like that once," Kate said dryly.

"I'll make her co-operate," Ashmael said and renewed his effort. Kate was right. Focusing on his soume aspect did help, although it wasn't that comfortable for him. *We continue to learn about ourselves*, he thought, *when we think we know it all.*

They will poison you further, these demons. Resist! There is little time left, Nicholas. Your suffering will end.

Nicholas could still only perceive the stars clearly; everything closer to him was indistinct, although he was aware of moving forms, hands upon him. He sensed their hot concern, the need for haste. If he should die, his suffering would not end. He could read this inescapable fact pouring from one of the entities beside him. The feeling was raw, without artifice, because it did not know he could read it. He learned that even if he left this body, there would be pain, confusion, an inability to move on. He glimpsed a dark and arid realm, where the souls of those who did not survive the change were lost and wandering. There would be no release, no escape. Did this mean the voice lied to him, and perhaps had always lied?

Icy fluid poured into his mouth, which he could barely open now. This fluid was like the stars to him, blue and radiant, suffusing him with cold light, feeling its way through blood and bone, quenching the fire within him.

"Kate, you'll burn him," Ash said. "It's too hot."

"No." Kate continued to dribble the heated liquid through the tiny gap in Nicholas's locked jaw, steam rising in a hissing cloud around them. Ashmael held the boy's head steady, aware that the flesh was parting from the scalp. The body before them no longer resembled the boy he'd taken from the human compound; it was like a rotting corpse. He felt nauseated, wanted to let go, but hadn't he been like this once? Some har had remained by his side and seen him through althaia, the changing. There was no time to feel sickened, only particular tasks to attend to.

Once most of the liquid had been administered, Kate took a pot of unguent from her satchel. "Help me," she said. "Cover his body with this." She was already removing what was left of the nightshirt. Parts of it were glued to the boy's body. She had to tear it, taking skin along with it.

Ashmael swallowed with difficulty. He had no desire to touch that disintegrating flesh. He had never attended inceptions or helped with them. He had only been called upon afterwards to bring new inceptees into the family with the seal of aruna. In the past, that must have been almost as traumatic for new hara as the althaia itself. Kate would know this, of course. Now, some part of Ashmael wanted her approval, to show her he was more than she judged him to be. This must be the consequence of dragging forth that soume half; it always brought problems with it. Sighing, he dipped his fingers into the thick ointment and applied it to Nicholas's head and face, which seemed the least unpleasant to touch. He was not a squeamish har; there was no room for that in what he had to do in life, for his leaders, for his hara. Yet here he was, squirming like a harling in revulsion, his heart beating fast.

"That's it," Kate said. "Quicker, Ash. Don't fumble about."

"What do we do after this?" Ashmael asked. "We can't leave him out here in the open."

"We have no choice," Kate said. She shook her head. "It's weird – he's so far into the change. Can't possibly be moved now, and yet it's too soon for althaia to be this advanced." She fixed Ashmael with a stare. "Once we've coated him with the ointment, you must return to camp, bring supplies, shelter, hara to protect us so the process isn't disturbed. Much as I hate the idea, Merxis must come too. I've never seen anything like this."

"Of course." Ashmael half rose to his feet.

"Not yet, Ash," Kate commanded. "This job is far from finished."

The cold blue fire lifted Nicholas from his body as if with hands of ether. He could look down now, see those who were trying to help him. The woman-thing – Kate – felt out of her depth. The other... he didn't care for this and yet he cared a lot. Part of his caring involved anger at being disobeyed, that this had happened. He also felt responsible, because of course – he *was*. Nicholas felt no resentment about that now. Everything had changed, not just what was happening to his body. This thing they called inception was not a pretty process and it was dangerous. So many had died; he could sense that, as if a legion of the dead hovered behind him.

The alternative had been extinction for everyone. This he could also see.

You do have a purpose, Nicholas. Do you understand this?

The voice in his mind was different now, a lower, softer tone to it.
"Are you my god?" he asked.
You choose your gods, Nicholas, as does every living thing.
"Then what is my purpose?"
You know...
Nicholas turned his perception around to face what lay behind him. He saw them: rank upon endless rank of indistinct forms, revealed only by the dim light of a dark sun. These were not the dead; they were something worse. They were half-creatures, failed inceptions, discards. They had waited for a long time for someone to hear them. So many whispery voices. Some were trapped in seemingly lifeless bodies in hidden corners of the earth. Others were separated from flesh and had been drawn to the dark realm he had perceived a few minutes before. Yet more were functional – barely – as living beings, yet unfinished. They hid, they scavenged, they yearned for completion.

His consciousness was drawn back in time. He saw nascent Wraeththu tribes pouring like ink over the landscape. Wild howling in the night. Atrocities of every description, perpetrated *by* Wraeththu and *upon* them. He saw humankind, what they'd been doing to each other and the planet, their home. Violence without thought or reason moved like a canker over the world, bringing death and destruction. The good had been annihilated along with the bad, on both sides of the conflict, until all that was left was burned and blackened battlefields that smelled of carrion. But then... shining reeds of light appearing in the darkness, creatures of thought, of opinion, of compassion. Without form, souls seeking homes in the bodies of the new.

Nicholas knew that what he had seen was like a compressed snapshot of history, a metaphor for what had come to pass. Not all Wraeththu were evil, as not all humans were good. His father was an honourable man; he had been spared. He too still had purpose, even in this changed world.

All this, Nicholas could have seen at any time, yet he'd been afraid and had clung to outworn idols to protect himself. This was so clear now. The voices in his head were his own.

He was drawn back into his body with a sickening rush, gasped, sat upright. Light flared from him in spiralling rays. He could barely breathe, and yet when his lungs finally did take air, it was like the essence of spring, of a season he'd never truly witnessed.

Kate was knocked over onto her back by the energy that flared from Nicholas's body. His skin looked burned through the coating of ointment, black and red, yet his eyes were a sheer and frosty blue.

Ashmael leapt to his feet and jumped backwards, landing in a fighter's crouch, ready to defend himself.

Nicholas got slowly to his feet between them, held out his arms, examined them, turning his hands palms up, palms down. Then he began to pick the black papery stuff from his flesh, exposing clean skin beneath.

"No!" Kate exclaimed. "This is impossible."

"What?" Ash yelled. "What the fuck is going on?"

"It's over," Kate said. "I think... Nicholas?" She stood up tentatively. "Nicholas, do you hear me?"

He turned to her. "Yes. Is it done, this thing?"

"I think so... It should take three days, even more, but... this was *hours*. I don't know." She shook her head. "I really don't know."

They took Nicholas back to the Gelaming camp, directly to Merxis's pavilion, where they found the har awake, awaiting news from the scouts. He wasn't as abrasive as he usually tended to be, which Kate assumed was because he found Ashmael intimidating and was also aware his actions could have precipitated Nicholas's death. He could be disciplined for this and was subdued by that knowledge. Even Ashmael, shaken by what he'd experienced, did not appear to be in the mood for arguments. In his arms he held Nicholas, who had lapsed once more into a semi-conscious state. Clear, pale skin showed through from the cracks in the blackened, bloody carapace that covered him.

"This is astonishing," Merxis said rather feebly. "How has he survived?"

"It appears he underwent althaia in a couple of hours," Kate said. "One minute he was virtually dead at our feet, the next he sat bolt upright."

At that moment, Nicholas raised his head and said, "Please, give me water."

Merxis hurried to comply and allowed Nicholas to drink. He sipped slowly, as if aware hasty gulping would harm him.

"Let's get you bathed," Merxis said. "Get that mess off you."

Nicholas sighed and relaxed back against Ashmael's chest. He shuddered jerkily once or twice, then lay still.

Merxis called for one of his hara to prepare Nicholas a bath. They took him back to the pavilion where he'd first rested, and from where he had escaped. The paraphernalia of inception still lay around the room, and there was evidence of a scuffle, furniture turned over, the bed streaked with blood. Merxis's assistant, Reydis, set to clearing away this discomforting evidence. Kate recognised him as the har she'd shouted at when she'd found him 'assessing' Nicholas the day before. Now, he avoided her gaze.

Nicholas was passive and appeared dazed, still only half conscious. He did not protest or fight against them. His eyes, however, remained open wide, strangely *fiery* in a cold, wintry way.

"Do you think the inception really is complete?" Kate asked Merxis, once Nicholas had been laid on the bed and Reydis had departed to organise hot water for the bath.

"Superficially, it would appear so," Merxis replied. "I'll need to do a more thorough examination, of course. This is unprecedented in my experience, and I've seen some fairly odd inceptions over the years."

"Well, we knew he was different," Kate said.

Merxis nodded, his expression unusually distracted. "To be perfectly honest with you, I'm not sure what we're dealing with here. Was he ever in fact human?"

"We've questioned that too," Kate said.

Ashmael stood up from where he'd been crouched beside Nicholas. "He doesn't seem that angry about what happened," he said. "We might not be able to say the same about his family, which could impede my mission. Should I go and speak to them?"

Kate shook her head. "No. Wait until morning. We need to know more about Nicholas's althaia, whether it is in fact over."

"If it is, what about the rest?" Ashmael said. "He'll need aruna, won't he?"

"Are you volunteering?" Kate asked archly.

"No. But surely the question must be addressed. In my opinion, althaia takes place over several days for a reason – to help a har come to terms with what he's becoming. This is sudden. Should normal procedures be followed now or not?"

"Your opinion is valid," Merxis said. "I want to examine our new har as soon as possible. But for now, let's give him privacy while he takes his bath. That too is one of the rituals of inception, the washing away of the old. Come to my pavilion; let's take a drink together while we wait."

Nicholas lay in the scented water, allowing the har who attended him to bathe him. He felt detached from his body somehow, whereas before he'd been furiously private about it. There was so much to assimilate, to examine and understand. He was aware his change had been different to what was considered normal. He didn't yet know what this meant for himself. And yet he didn't feel different at all, simply overwhelmed, as if he'd come face to face with a ghost, incontrovertible evidence of the unseen, and now his version of reality had been shattered. The pieces were too numerous and too tiny ever to be reassembled into what they'd been before. He needed to rest, yet his mind was so active, working on several different levels simultaneously.

"Can you make me sleep?" he asked the har who knelt beside the bathtub, whose warm hands gently cleaned his skin. He hummed a soft and wistful tune, and Nicholas could see the har was remembering his own inception, the ritual bath, the kind hara who had once sung to him too.

However, Nicholas's voice alarmed the har, because he hadn't expected the new inceptee to speak. He looked almost frightened and his song ceased abruptly. "Why do you want to sleep?"

"To quieten my mind, so I can look at things one at a time. It's like I'm full of voices."

The har nodded sympathetically. "I'll speak to Tiahaar Merxis. He'll want to examine you, to make sure you are well."

"Nothing went wrong. He needn't fear that."

"Well..." The har straightened up, stiff-backed beside the tub. "It's best you're checked over."

"Let this be done, then. I need to sleep."

The har brought Merxis, a creature of order and routine, who liked things to be done precisely, who didn't like alterations to familiar processes. Nicholas found he could perceive many things about this har, the fears he hid behind the mask he wore. Everybody wore these masks. Would it be uncomfortable to see through them like this, with everyone – every*har* – he met?

Merxis inclined his head to Nicholas in greeting. "You are agreeable to me examining you? This will have to be quite... thorough."

"Do what you must," Nicholas said. He rose from the water, noticed it was full of drab, floating debris. He held out his arms so that the har who'd attended him could dress him in a towelling robe. His skin seemed to glow.

"Reydis, will you remain with us, please?" Merxis said.

The har bowed his head. "Of course, Tiahaar."

Merxis gestured for Nicholas to lie down on the bed nearby. "Reydis will be your care-har."

Nicholas recognised dimly this was the tent in which he'd first awoken. He remembered now the prim little har who'd spoken to him there, before Kate had ordered him out. Was this Reydis the same person? He seemed completely unknown and yet the face was the same. Only he wasn't so stiff and formal, because he'd been woken in the middle of the night for this duty, his hair drawn into a hasty, loose knot at his neck. Had he been at the inception? Nicholas couldn't remember a thing about it now, other than coming to his senses and fighting his way free of the pavilion. They had drugged him, of course, but not enough.

"Reydis will answer any questions you might have," Merxis said, "although you may speak to me too."

Nicholas stretched out on the striped blanket. "Can I see my family?"

"In time," Merxis answered smoothly. "Please just try to relax. I'll be as gentle as I can." He smiled. "From a superficial inspection, all appears to be in order, but I want to be sure." Merxis seated himself cross-legged beside the bed.

Nicholas closed his eyes. He didn't like what had to be done but knew it was important to Merxis. He winced as the therapist's fingers probed him internally. *Don't think about that. Not yet.*

"Are you in pain?" Merxis asked softly.

"No. The sensation is strange, that's all."

"All seems fine down there," Merxis said. Reydis brought him a bowl of water and he rinsed his hands. Then he probed Nicholas's body externally, asking if any points were uncomfortable.

"No, there is no pain," Nicholas said.

Merxis got to his feet. "Then I think I can safely pronounce you har, although you have undergone the fastest inception I have ever seen. You must surely understand our caution."

"Yes."

"Perhaps this acceleration is natural, due to evolution within us all." Merxis paused. "Nicholas, there is something you must accept, and I hope this will not be difficult for you."

"That I am no longer male? Yes, I know that. It doesn't matter." To him, that part of the change was irrelevant; it was the rest that awed him, the way his already supernatural senses had become so strong, so intense. He knew there was so much to explore. He was not afraid, simply eager, but also bone-tired.

"Not just that," Merxis said. "Part of the process of inception is that it must be sealed... cemented. The way this is done is through aruna, physical intimacy between hara. Do you understand what I'm saying?"

Nicholas closed his eyes briefly. "Yes." He could get through that like he'd got through the examination. They'd leave him alone once their routines were complete, and then he could sleep, dream of his new being.

"Is there anyhar you would prefer for this?"

"No."

Merxis hesitated. "Hmm. You seem... unresponsive. I think perhaps we can wait on this part of althaia."

"I don't care. Just do it."

Merxis smiled warmly. He was a kind har at heart, no matter how officious he might seem. "That's not the way it works, Nicholas."

"Then let me sleep."

6

Ashmael and Kate visited Nicholas in the morning. They found him awake, sitting up in his bed, supported by several thick pillows, eating the breakfast Reydis had brought to him. Nicholas could sense how he appeared to them: healthy and serene, despite having lost a lot of his hair, perhaps because of the accelerated inception. What was left of it was tied at his neck. This loss didn't bother him; he knew it would grow back thick and strong. He was amused Ashmael found it remarkable he seemed so unfazed by what had happened, given how he'd been before. He lashed out a thought into Ashmael's mind. *It's because of what I saw.*

You have much to learn, Ashmael lashed back. *First, it's rude to pry. Be mindful of your inner sight.*

"I apologise," Nicholas said aloud.

"How are you feeling, Nicky?" Kate asked, glancing at Ashmael curiously.

"Well enough," he answered. "Nicky is dead, though, Tiahaar. Reydis has told me about inception names. I will be Fernici, from my family name and a remnant of who I was."

Kate smiled uncertainly. "I see. May I call you Fern?"

"As you wish." He could see Kate found him confusing and was unsure how to relate to him. Perhaps they would be friends. Or perhaps soon she'd go somewhere else and he'd never see her again. He liked her and hoped their future was that of friendship. As for the other: he could not look at Ashmael.

"We thought perhaps you could come with us to visit your family, if you feel up to it," Kate said.

Nicholas, now Fernici, considered her words. "I'm not sure I can talk to them yet, although I appreciate they'll want to be reassured. I don't want my mother to worry."

Kate nodded. "OK. Then perhaps you could write them a note."

Fernici was aware of Ashmael looming tall behind him. He could feel the har's awkwardness, the defensive folding of his arms. "If you want me to, if it'll make things easier."

"I think it might." Kate glanced around her. "I'd better find something for you to write on and with, hadn't I? Won't be long." She glanced at Ashmael, smiled secretively. "Well, perhaps it will take some time." She left the pavilion.

Fernici was left with the silent Ashmael, listening to the sounds outside. He knew what Kate had been thinking and that Ashmael was thinking of it too, albeit in rather a confused way. Fernici knew he would have to deal with this before anything else. Reydis would be returning soon. Fernici could sense him in a pavilion nearby, engaged in various tasks to do with his work, writing up a few hurried notes, grabbing some food hastily himself, wondering what he might bring to Fernici to help him, what questions should be asked, what statements made. He worried too much. To Fernici, it was all very simple.

Ashmael cleared his throat and moved into Fernici's line of sight. "Nicholas... Fern... I realise I've brought this upon you. I would've acted differently if I'd known."

"Always impulsive," Fernici said. "Isn't that so?"

Ashmael pulled a quizzical expression. "Are you prying still?"

"No, that was an observation based on evidence."

"I think you see too much."

"I wanted to be blind, but I can't be. I would simply have gone mad, or the jackals would have taken me. I should thank you, I suppose. Don't feel bad about it." Fernici put aside the remains of his breakfast.

Ashmael hunkered down beside the bed. "If there's anything I can do for you... I think you know what I mean."

Fernici looked into Ashmael's eyes. He was honest, sometimes thoughtless, brave, witty, a har of power. Many fine qualities. And beautiful. Ashmael had watched over him as he'd lain unconscious during that first couple of days of being in the Gelaming camp. He remembered this now as if it were a dream. He had a dim memory of hearing Ashmael say to Merxis, just outside the pavilion, "Don't touch him!" And then he'd gone, and Nicholas's fits had started, the opening of a gate, the blindness slipping from his eyes.

When they'd come to him, dressed in their fine ceremonial robes, with a blade and blood, he'd accepted what must be, because in a way inception had already started. He knew now that afterwards, when he'd been driven to escape, it was because an inner part of him – perhaps the part that had already been har – had sought to endure the change alone, like a wounded animal. They'd not understood that. Neither had he.

Now, he reached out and put the fingers of one hand gently against Ashmael's lips. "No. It can't be you," he said.

Ashmael looked baffled, but then he was rarely turned down. "I hope one day you'll forgive me," he said.

"That's not relevant. It's just not the time. I've not *become* yet, Ashmael. I want to be what I am to be. It's hard to explain. You've done much for me. I like you, and for this reason, strange though it sounds, it can't be you."

Ashmael stood up, rubbed the back of his head. "I feel like I've lived through several months in a few days. It's very odd. That boy I saw bound on the floor of his house lived aeons ago. Now we have Fernici, *very* sure of himself." He smiled. "When you come to Immanion, my house is always open to you and your family. I hope you'll visit, when you have *become*." He inclined his head. "Be good to yourself."

Fernici watched Ashmael duck out of the pavilion entrance. *I think part of me actually did go mad*, he thought.

Reydis came back into the pavilion, glancing behind at the retreating Ashmael. He too was intimated by that har, but Fernici wasn't surprised about it. "He offered himself," Fernici said.

Reydis uttered an irrepressible snort of laughter, and it was as if they were friends already, had known each other a long time. "From the look on his face just then, I take it you declined. That was brave!"

Fernici sighed. "There are new feelings inside me. I don't know them yet. But if I ever take that step with him, I want to know myself, be in control."

"That's wise of you." Reydis held out his hand. "Here, I brought this for you. It's a custom." It was a bangle of plaited leather, wound with lapis lazuli beads and chips of white crystal. "An inception gift."

Fernici took the bangle. "Thank you." He knew Reydis wanted his experience to be as uplifting as his own had been: the bath, the song, the gift. He opened the blankets of his bed. "Sing the rest of the song to me."

"You're sure?"

"I'm sure."

7

Three days later, five members of the Ferniman family were taken to Immanion, the humans drugged into an induced sleep so they could withstand the otherlanes journey. The Fernimans had been offered the choice of who would be in the party, and had elected for Hugh and Hannah to go, and also their eldest children, Jack and Liza. Fernici was the fifth. He wasn't sure if his parents and siblings still regarded him as family, because there was now an inescapable gulf between them, but he did what he could to be like how they'd known him, hiding his blossoming talents, dressing as he'd always dressed, in his old clothes, a bandana over his head to cover his hair. But he knew he looked so different to them now. Their feelings were confused, because they couldn't deny he was serene and accepting of his new state, but at the same time they mourned the boy they'd known, and couldn't entirely dispel the resentment they felt towards the Gelaming who'd changed him. But the world moves inexorably on, and only a fool would not appreciate the benefits that were on offer for the Ferniman clan and their dependents.

Kate, Merxis and Reydis accompanied them, along with hara who carried the humans through the otherlanes. As he made that unimaginable first journey, Fernici was already wondering how he could get his own *sedu*, or access to one regularly, to explore this intriguing otherworld. While he and Reydis had been discussing his future over the past few days, Reydis had told him some hara were employed as Listeners, who were like the organs of communication between hara who were physically far apart. He had also told of hara who roamed the otherlanes, working with their *sedim* to ensure safety for travellers, even to explore new worlds. So many possibilities. If it hadn't been for his father's desperate attempts to communicate with others, none of this would have happened.

And now Fernici stood with Reydis upon a high balcony at the villa that had been allocated for the Fernimans' use while they were in the city. Reydis alone had remained with the visitors. Later, officials would come to welcome them to the city, to answer their questions, make plans for where they would live, what they would do.

Kate and Merxis had departed to see to various arrangements and appointments, to make reports. Hugh and the others were still groggy from the journey and were resting. Fernici knew that many painful conversations were in store. His family were not wholly trusting and were wary of what he'd become. If acceptance should truly come, perhaps other younger members of his family might choose to be incepted, either to Wraeththu or Kamagrian. But for now, he didn't have to worry about the future. He could bask for a few hours in what was simply before his eyes. Immanion too was another world, like a dream from an idealised past. It took your breath with its beauty, with its strange sentience like that of a living creature.

"Immanion *is* alive," Reydis murmured to Fernici, their arms touching as they leaned on the balcony rail. "It was built by magic, you know."

Fernici laughed, shaded his eyes, to gaze down at the distant harbour, the flock of sleek ships idling there, their sails folded like white wings. "Magic!" he said.

"It's true. You'll see. I shall be very surprised if Thiede doesn't want to meet you, given your talents."

"Thiede?"

"He was the first," Reydis said and made an expansive gesture before him, taking in the whole of the landscape before them. "He *made* this, Fern. Immanion is his creation, as are we."

"And he used magic..." Fernici said, unable to keep a note of humour from his voice.

"Well, perhaps forces we don't yet fully understand," Reydis replied. "But trust me, it might as well be magic."

"In that case, I look forward to talking with this har. It seems incredible Wraeththu all came from one individual, though."

"It does," Reydis said. "But don't think about that now. Enjoy your new being. There will be plenty of time for education." He pointed out to the north. "You see all those villas with the big gardens over on those hills? That's the district where Ashmael lives."

"He's probably already forgotten me," Fernici said.

"You know that's not true."

"Shush, I've got so many other things to think about, and lots of things to see."

"You're not just an extraordinary mind, Fernici. Don't put aside *any* of what you are now. And be mindful of signs and omens."

"You're in the wrong job," Fernici said. "You'll be asking to read my palm next."

Reydis sighed, smiling, and squeezed Fernici's shoulder. "You are so lucky. I remember what it was like. So much to learn. So much to be astounded by."

A flock of iridescent birds clattered up from the garden below, wheeling around the balcony, uttering sweet cries, as if they had been summoned by Reydis's words. A single perfect feather drifted down and alighted upon the back of Fernici's left hand. He picked it up, held it to his nose. "It smells of life," he murmured.

Reydis grinned. "You see?" he said.

Dream, Fernici. Dream of voices singing in the night, of hooves galloping across untrodden worlds, of unthinkable vistas. You are riding with them; gleaming skins beneath alien suns, opening the horizons of your kind. You are waiting for this, Fernici; it is your destiny. You can see everything, even your own heart. You are without weakness.

A Social Incident

Fernici stood at the edge of the gathering, not wanting to feel intimidated but unable to help himself. His companion, Reydis, had momentarily left him alone, and this was his first big social event in Immanion since he'd arrived. It was being held in a salon of the palace Phaonica, and Fernici didn't know anyhar there. It wasn't too grand a gathering, because no Aralisians were there, but it was still overwhelming to Fernici. He had half hidden himself amid immense obsidian pillars at the edge of the room and hoped Reydis wouldn't be long.

As if this nervous thought conjured a har into being, an apparition dressed in matte peacock-blue silk manifested before Fernici. He'd glided up from the side. "You're the newly-incepted little har, who Ash found in the wilderness, aren't you?" this being drawled. His eyes were a cruel green.

"That would be me," Fernici said, scanning the crowd, desperate to find Reydis's face among them.

"How are you finding Immanion?" asked the apparition, and by that question, Fernici knew the har was really asking "How are you finding civilisation?"

"Very big. It will keep me occupied for a time simply exploring it."

The har laughed. "Yes, you could say it is very big." He put his head to one side. "You're something of an enigma, aren't you?"

"Am I? I'm not sure what you mean." Fernici braced himself for some slicing remark about a human being incepted so late upon the Wraeththu timeline.

"I wonder what's so interesting about you, that's all." The har grimaced, but in a sly way. "Whenever any of us ask Ash for the story of what happened out there, he won't speak. Was it all so terrible?"

"I... no. I don't know what you mean."

"Well, you must be somehar of note, something *interesting*, to be here now. We wonder what the story is."

"There's no story other than that I was incepted and brought here."

"Oh, I think you hide your light, Tiahaar. I can *smell* a story."

Fernici realised he was at the point where the only way he could extricate himself from this uncomfortable conversation was to say something rude. He looked at the har, this elegant and confident creation. Did he mean to be insulting or was it simply the way socialising was in Immanion? Fernici had no idea, but he did sense that it might not be advisable to offend this har.

"Well, if it *is* a story, and I don't think it is – much – when they tested my abilities after althaia, the results for one of them were good. They thought there could be work for me here."

"Which ability?" asked the har, both his eyebrows raised in amusement.

"Psychic ability. They thought perhaps the Listeners…"

"Oh, how dull." The har grinned. "Never mind." He glanced around, perhaps looking for somehar else to bother, then clearly noticed the opportunity for sport. "Oh look, there is Ashmael." Before Fernici could do or say anything, the har had raised a hand and in a voice like a bell called, "Ash, over here."

Fernici saw Ashmael raise his head, the blankness that came over his features. Ashmael hesitated, then crossed the few feet of floor between them. Fernici was shocked again at how tall he was, almost alien. "Good evening, Tiahaar," he said and then nodded his head at Fernici. "Hello, Fernici, you have settled in well?"

"Yes. Thank you."

"I was just talking with your little protégé…" said the peacock har.

Ashmael laughed politely. "No protégé of mine, I assure you." He smiled stiffly at Fernici. "No offence, Tiahaar, but I consider you are your own creation, not mine."

Fernici, for a moment, was flooded with the remorse of lost opportunities. He realised that Ashmael's pride would never forgive him for what he'd done, and yet, it had been entirely the right thing to do at the time. Fernici had said no when Ashmael had offered himself after the althaia, and Ashmael

Aldebaran Har Gelaming was not used to being refused. But what could Fernici say to mend this affront, especially in front of this gossipy other har, who would no doubt report any conversation across the entire gathering?

"Well, thank you for your part in it," he said eventually, inclining his head, but wincing inside.

The peacock har laughed. "Oh, two corpses in a badly-written play," he declared. "And you say there is no story."

There was a silence, and perhaps having decided he'd got enough gossiping meat to be going on with, the peacock har drifted away.

And now we are alone together, Fernici thought, *with a bottomless gulf between us.*

"They found you useful employment?" Ashmael asked, but Fernici could tell he didn't care.

"I'm training for the Listeners," he said. "They said I could take it further one day."

"Makes sense." Ashmael looked around himself, perhaps hoping to spot an escape route, somehar he *must* go and speak to.

Fernici thought he might mention the invitation Ashmael had extended for Fernici to visit him, the last time they'd been together, but was afraid Ashmael would only look at him blankly and pretend he didn't remember. If Ashmael wanted to see him, he could make that invitation again now, but Fernici knew it wouldn't come.

"Don't stay on my account," he said, offering – rather mercifully, he felt – the escape route. "Reydis is here with me. He'll be back shortly. I expect you've got lots of hara you need to talk to."

"Well, yes, that's true." Ashmael smiled unconvincingly. "You look well, Fernici. I'm glad things have worked out for you. Until later, then…" He inclined his head and walked away.

Fernici steadied his breathing. This encounter had had to come. He'd known he'd have to face it, yet knowing that hadn't made it any easier. The reason he'd refused Ashmael was because he'd liked him too much. He'd wanted to be fully har, to understand his new self, before any meaningful closeness with another could even be considered. But clearly Ashmael could not see past the word 'no'. Now it was too late, yet perhaps for the best. Fernici could always tell himself it was for the best.

Reydis wandered up, carrying two drinks. "Sorry that took so long," he said, "but hara kept waylaying me! Were you all right on your own?"

"Yes," Fernici said, taking the drink. "I'm all right on my own."

Painted Skin

The stage lights were ablaze in their strange, unworldly manner; a deep acid green, with beams of almost lightless cobalt firing through it. I walked onto the stage dressed in white, soon dyed by the inky radiance. My skin was green and blue, my eyes, with their reflective lenses, some alien glow; not harish.

I wanted *him* to be there; took it for granted that he would be. He came always for the first three nights of any new performance. Thereafter, his presence could not be guaranteed, although my skin could always tell when he was there, even before I took the stage and saw him. He sat on the front row, each time swathed in a concealing robe with a hood that revealed only the pale lower half of his face. No cosmetics on those finely sculpted lips. I found it difficult to discern the colour of his robe because of the lights in the auditorium. All I knew was that it was of very dark fabric that had a dull, silky sheen. And his hands were long and thin, clasped somewhat tensely in his lap. He always sat on the edge of his seat, a little hunched, certainly not relaxed. He reminded me of a picture I'd once seen, of the Shadetide dehar, Lachrymide, sitting stiffly at a crossroads in the dark end of the season.

My curiosity – I wouldn't call it desire – was no secret among my fellow performers, because at first I made a joke of it. "Even the dehara come to hear me sing," I said, laughing, after that first night I'd seen him. "Did you not see him on the first row? Lachrymide?"

The musicians hadn't taken notice of the audience and my choir were similarly uninterested as to who sat below them. But on the next night, he was there again, and I made a signal to Shiran, the flautist and my closest friend, so that he could see. (Did some part of me fear the strange figure below was *not* real and only I could see him?) But Shiran saw and afterwards told me so. "He's either weak in the head, an eccentric, or the son of a prominent house wishing not to be recognised. Or maybe even a celebrity, like you, Dimici. Perhaps a rival!" He grinned, clearly hoping for the last of his suggestions to be true. There was some merit in that idea, though. The dark one always did appear at the start of every run, perhaps making notes, comparing, or perhaps just acting as my greatest admirer. I had no idea. But he fascinated me, because he was so different, because he stood out and because there was something undeniably – deliciously – sinister about him.

After two years, he became almost like my personal dehar, my luck, if you like. One of the musicians once said to me, "I hope you never get to meet your idol properly. Then he will be revealed for something less than your imagination supposes. I don't think I could bear your heartbreak. Please promise me you will never try to talk to him."

Strangely, I had not considered trying to engineer that. Some inner part of me must have agreed with that har's assumptions.

And here I was again, about to open my mouth, my throat, my lungs, my heart and soul, to the new witcheries dreamed and written by Tiahaar Margolin Har Prest, the best of the city's composers. And there *he* was again, my intriguing Haunt, poised like a mantis on the front row, his paws intertwined, stiff. It had become my habit to sing to him alone on these nights, even though I could not tell if he was looking at me or not.

There was some kerfuffle during the interval that night. "*He's* here!" somehar hissed at me.

"Who is?" I demanded.

"The Phyle's Pride, Vana, that's who!"

"Halfway through the show...?" I was nettled. Vana was the chesnari – well, consort – of the city's phylarch, Metrice. For Vana to arrive only at the interval was mildly insulting, perhaps worse than if he had not come at all. Previously, he had attended my performances only twice over the five years I'd been performing in Trisque, and he'd never requested to meet me. This slight had been noticed by others; it vexed me.

The stage manager of the venue, a building known grandly as The Orchestrium, stamped through us, as we milled about drinking the wild-flower cordial they'd laid out for us. "There's to be a reception after the performance, up in the observatory." He stared at me in a birdlike way. "Don't get changed afterwards, Dimici, but perhaps refresh the cosmetics." And off he stamped.

So here it was: my invitation at last.

Consorts of high-ranking hara *have* to be beautiful; there is no choice in the matter. They are part of the sumptuous appointments of the post, creatures to be admired. They have a certain way with them, and are of a certain breed; hara who become the consorts of the rich and powerful. After the performance, as I reapplied pale unguent to my face, I wondered if in fact these hara were actually *bred* somewhere, and trained like the famous concubines of history, both harish and human. Famous and *soul-deep* beauties become steeped in mystery, and they know how to maintain it. Not for them anything cheap, tawdry or embarrassing. Every movement, every glance, every low-pitched word is a work of art. Yes, they are performers too, like me.

When I entered the observatory – a glass dome at the top of The Orchestrium – purposely twenty minutes after everyone else, my eyes were immediately drawn to Vana. He was holding court at the brink of the balcony that overlooked the High Nayati, which that night was a blaze of candlelight below us, owing to the feybraiha of some rich hara's son. Vana was dressed in a costume of tight-fitting black trousers and tunic, which were covered in small coruscating beads of jet and white crystal. His platinum white hair was wound in a single artful coil behind his head, speared with a harpoon of jet, from which dangled three strings of tiny onyx beads. One cat's tail of hair looped down over his breast. His face was quite square and angular, like a sculpture, his mouth wide and pale, yet the smile upon it like the kiss of life. He was indeed perfect, in appearance and manner, even bowing his head to me in a gesture of respect when he saw me approach. I had to speak to him before I did anything else in that room; it would be noticed if I didn't.

"You make me weep and soar rapturously in equal measure," Vana said, extending a hand. I lowered my head and pressed my forehead to his cool fingers.

"I am glad the performance pleased you," I murmured. Little else was expected of me.

Vana gave a tiny frown. "Not as much as it *could* have." He laughed then, touched my face swiftly, because a frown of my own had started. "Oh, don't take me wrongly. I meant I missed the first half tonight." He paused for a second. "I have a gathering in two weeks' time. Would Tiahaar Dimici har Dusklight be free to come and perform for me then?"

This was patronage that hara would kill for. They would

probably kill any impediments in their diaries also to make room for it. I did not make a show of hesitating or pretending. I simply inclined my head. "That would be a great honour."

"Good, that's settled, then. My hara will speak to your agent."

He did not dismiss me exactly, but now his business was done with me, and he turned the beam of his smile upon another. I was grateful for his request. I knew this was a covert apology for turning up late, and the message this might have implied to the audience. He would know my invitation to perform for him was long overdue, but he was a busy har, and there were thousands he had to appease, woo and charm on his own behalf, never mind on behalf of his consort, the city, or his tribe in general. And he did so gloriously. The most beautiful hara do not have to be cruel or mean or jealous. It is in them to be courteous and kind. Why be otherwise when the world has been so kind to *them*?

The room was full of hara of note who had attended the performance that night, their ranks augmented with presentable hara of lesser note. Of course, I looked for *him*, my haunt, but I also sensed he would not be there. He would have risen from his seat and quietly taken his leave, while everyhar else was whispering together, having heard the rumour of the reception near to the sky, and concerned they might not be invited. From the size of the crowd up there, I don't think the house manager had left many out; it was a good party and continued till dawn. Vana left at half past one. But by that time hara didn't seem to notice he was no longer among them.

The Ley House of the Phylarch was set upon a hill to the north of Trisque. In the twilight, I could see its high domed roofs against the sky; it looked to me like a city of toadstools, a fairy ring upon the hill. The front door stood wide open and at the threshold a househar took my gloves and coat. He offered me a cherry encased in peppered sugar; a little warmth against the night and the encroaching season. Autumn leaves blew in across the dark tiles of the hallway, yet the door was left open, presumably to welcome guests.

An assistant of Vana, who clearly had been waiting for me, stepped forward with a bow. After introducing himself, he said he would conduct me to a room where I might prepare myself. He asked what refreshment I would like before, during and after the performance.

"White tea before," I replied, "a glass of iced water for during, and the most robust berry wine you have for afterwards."
The assistant smiled and inclined his head. "I shall see to it."
The room was in fact a guest suite, comprising a sitting room, a bedroom and a bathroom. There was a balcony but the window doors to it were locked now. Curling leaves were piling against the glass. Dim lamps were lit, but there was a brighter one I might use by the mirror, should I wish to. I had attended to my appearance before leaving my abode. Now I found I would be rather bored waiting to be summoned to sing.
Vana's assistant appeared, accompanied by a lesser minion bearing a tray. On it was a porcelain pot of white tea, a small jug of cold milk, a crystal tray of sugar, and an enormous cup and saucer fashioned of the most delicate china and decorated with blue and gold birds. There was a plate also of cat's tongues, those delicious Trisquish delicacies of the thinnest, crispest biscuits; I could smell their almondy spice even from across the room, and that delicious newly-baked warmth in them.
"Do you require anything else?" the assistant asked.
"Well... forgive me for asking, but how long will it be until Tiahaar Vana requires my presence?"
The assistant glanced at a wonderfully ornate silver timepiece, set into a bangle of tangled, beaded serpents on his wrist. "Eleven minutes," he said. "Tiahaar Vana thought you could grace us with your gift before dinner, so that you might enjoy the food afterwards and mingle with the guests."
"That is thoughtful of him," I said. I had already received a note asking me to sing for twenty-five minutes. Exactly. Vana was precise about time if nothing else.

I sat in the room, in a chair facing the mantelpiece, staring at the clock that stood there, which was unusual: a slim white tower of Classical lines with a crystal or glass clock face at the summit. But behind this transparent pane there was a small shadowy figure. Occasionally, it moved forward to press its pale face against the glass, stare out. I could tell it was a clockwork figure, but even so, it was quite eerie, and absolutely compelling to watch.
At the appointed time, the attendant came for me, led me to Vana's salon and here ushered me to stand upon a dais, surrounded by towering vases of white flowers. A bank of golden floor lights shone softly in my face, but their sundown radiance

was enough to eclipse all but silhouettes of the audience ahead of me. All I could see was the occasional wet gleam of an eye or the shiver of hair ornaments.

I began my recitation with a historical ballad, which while perhaps sombre in content contained several tunes that were popular and widely sung, albeit most likely with different words of a more salacious nature. I heard hara humming along with me, which signified an initially good response. This I followed with a wordless angelison, its phrases soaring and flying around the heads of the audience, raising the hair on their heads and bodies. I could sense their quivering delight. Bringing them back down to earth I sang two arcadians of benevolent and mischievous mythological beings, which teased the citizens of Immanion who might venture into the hills above the city. Poking gentle fun at Immanion and the Gelaming was acceptable at such gatherings, and I heard the odd chuckle from the audience. And then finally, sensing my minutes were drawing to a close, I sang an amoris, the archetypal ache of unrequited love. As few hara escape this condition in life, whether it be at feybraiha or long afterwards, the amoris always aims for the heart and strikes it cleanly. Such songs are almost hallucinogenic in their effects and as usual I felt my voice was beyond my control, soaring and gliding, then drawing the string of the fatal bow.

The applause was loud and long. I bowed. And the lights came up. Vana, who had been seated on a chair right in front of me, stood up and came to take my hands. "You are splendid, Tiahaar," he said. And I saw his eyes were glittery with unshed tears. Some memory of lost love had haunted him for those minutes.

"It is my pleasure and my privilege," I replied, inclining my head.

He released my hands. "You will sing for me again some time."

"It would be my dearest wish."

He nodded and made a quick, imperious gesture. A har glided to his side, most likely one of his highest-ranking attendants. "Keep company with Tiahaar Dimici." Within these words lay the order to introduce me to others, keep me entertained, without a bored moment. His duty to the entertainer thus fulfilled, Vana drifted off to mingle with his guests.

The har smiled at me. "We will be dining soon. May I show

you around the salons while we wait?" He extended a hand to direct me. "There are some exceptional portraits on the walls that might interest you, and various artefacts from ancient times to examine." Another har materialised at his side with a tray of drinks, and he took two turquoise flutes for us. I wasn't sure what drink was in them; it tasted of orchids and fire.

As we walked into the second salon, I froze. My guide sensed this and cast me a questioning glance. I'd seen the robe, that silky, sulky fluid of fabric, gliding between the hara that thronged the room. "Please excuse me a moment, I've seen somehar I know," I said and moved forward as quickly and discreetly as possible, which wasn't very polite under the circumstances, but my companion did not follow or attempt to stop me. My Haunt was here! I had not – perhaps for the first time since he'd been present at a performance – noticed him in the audience that night. Still, this proved he was no ghost. I could see him ahead, appearing momentarily between the clustered bodies, as if he walked through a summer forest and the sunlight touched him sometimes. Moving, he was as graceful as he'd appeared in his seat at my recitals all these years, and now neither tense nor stiff. His hood was up, as usual, but there was no mistaking him, even though I could see clearly only his head and the top of his shoulders. I longed to turn him around, see his face properly for the first time. That he was here at the reception indicated he must be a har of rank.

I followed this mysterious creature through three galleries devoted solely to paintings, observing him more than intending to make contact. He paused before many of the pictures, enabling me to glimpse his profile from the nose down, the rest of his face still obscured by his hood. The nose was straight and elegant, his chin firm. He held a turquoise flute of liquor and sipped from it. Nohar spoke to him and, although it might have been my over-stimulated imagination at work, it seemed to me that others tended to move away when he drew near to them.

In the fourth gallery, we were alone. He could not possibly be oblivious of my presence by now. The room was huge, dominated by gargantuan portraits; famous beauties and herohara, politicians and phylarchs and a couple of actors. These fragments of history stared down upon us; I found their gazes oppressive. I stood in the doorway, observing my Haunt, who was staring up at a monstrous portrait of some locally significant har, whom I did not recognise. For a moment, I visualised all the colossal images coming alive and stepping down from their frames. We would be like ants to them. I shuddered. At that moment my Haunt turned, as if the shudder had been a sound. He was looking at me. I could not lose this moment. I inclined my head and moved forward swiftly. "Good evening, Tiahaar. I was just thinking these portraits are rather too large, and if they should come alive we would be crushed beneath their feet."

The har glanced back at the portrait. "That is a fearsome thought. Now I will never be able to walk through this hall again without thinking it."

"You are a regular visitor here?"

He shrugged. "Now and again. This is your first time, of course."

"As you attend so many of my performances, you must already know that."

He smiled a little. "Now you make me sound rather sinister and unpleasant."

"Not at all. I can hardly insult one of my most regular patrons."

"True." He then threw back his hood, in a somewhat challenging manner, to reveal a face I hadn't expected. He wasn't ugly, but the eyes were not as large as I'd imagined, nor as luminous. They were a rather flat hazel colour, and his brow was also lower than I'd visualised. I thought, uncharitably, *No wonder he favours the hood.* At the same time, I was strangely glad he was not one of those unearthly, vat-grown beauties like Vana.

"You must know all about me," I said, somewhat coquettishly. "Perhaps I can learn something about you?"

"Why?" His face still held that faint smile.

"Well... because you're such a regular member of my audience you feel like a friend, yet a friend I do not know. Will you tell me your name at least?"

"Cherrah har Freyhella."

This information did not give much away, other than he hailed from a northern tribe. The identifying part of his name was general. Hara used their tribal titles only when they wished not to reveal community or family details. This made it easy to obfuscate and confuse. Any har can of course have several names, used for different purposes. His accent did not sound northern, though.

"Do you travel a lot, or live here in the south?"

"Both, really." His smile widened. "There isn't much mystery to me, if that's what you're looking for. Not much of interest at all. I'm simply an admirer of music."

"Every har has something interesting about him," I said. "Thoughts, beliefs, habits, knowledge – all the things that comprise a being."

"Do you seek to flatter me?"

"Probably. Does it offend you?"

Cherrah har Freyhella twirled his glass in his hands for a moment. "No. It's just that I keep to myself most of the time. I'm unused to this kind of conversation."

I folded my arms, head to one side, still coquettish. "What do you do to occupy your time?"

"You mean how do I earn my money?" He laughed softly. "You can tell I have some, of course, otherwise I wouldn't be here. I'm not obliged to *tell* you."

"Of course not. I was making conversation, that's all. And I'm more curious about your interests than your income."

He nodded slowly. "Very well. I make clocks to..." He grinned. "...to pass the time."

We both laughed.

"Clocks?" I said.

"Yes. As my parents did, and my hurakin. A family tradition. My father made the fountain clock that stands in the hall of Metrice's private apartments. I made the feather clock that Vana keeps by his bed. That is why I'm here."

"And the clock in the guest suite? The white tower with the ghostly face behind the glass?"

He nodded. "Yes, that's mine too. Would you like me to make *you* a clock? I could put your voice in it."

A shiver ran through me, like the opening of a canal lock gate and cold water pouring down. "I'll keep my voice to myself, if you don't mind." I softened the remark with another smile. "But maybe I *would* like a clock. Do you have a show room?"

"No. I have some pieces in my apartment, though." He delved into a small flat purse he took from a pocket of his garment. "This is what you want, isn't it?" He withdrew a tiny card and handed it to me.

I looked at it. The card was deep purple and the writing upon it penned in thick gold ink: "Cherrah, clock-maker, Apartment 6, House of the Red Stairs, Fern Hill, Trisque." A respectable address.

175

"Thank you. Might I make an appointment?"

"Tomorrow, or 'Calasday. Afternoons are best for me."

"Tomorrow will be fine."

"Good. Shall we say around two?"

"Yes, that is also fine."

Cherrah inclined his head. "Now I must be going. I've exhausted the paintings and have finished my drink."

"You're not staying for the dinner?"

He grimaced. "No, the fare is too rich and the conversation too loud. As I said, I keep to myself most of the time. Thank you for another faultless performance. Goodnight, Tiahaar."

He walked past me swiftly, and I turned to watch him leave. I could see the back of his garment was paned with carefully patterned lace of green, gold and deep blue. Then I realised it was not lace at all, but what appeared to be body art or a tattoo. The robe was backless. But before I could take in more than this, he had disappeared from view.

I knew I must now go back and seek my guide, make my apologies for running off. "*Not* interesting!" I said aloud, and shook my head, my smile wide. Then I put the card into my pocket.

The following day, I'd arranged to meet Shiran for an early lunch, since he wanted to know everything that had happened at Vana's reception. We both arrived at the cafe at the same time, and took seats in the conservatory, which overlooked a square where Zigane musicians played, and a harling tumbled and danced, while passersby threw the ensemble coins. Red and gold leaves swooped through the air, decorating the performance.

"Well, I hope your evening went well, and will be the beginning of wonderful things," said Shiran as he sat down and arranged his jacket on the back of a chair beside us.

"I think it went well," I said, and began to examine the menu.

"Oh, don't be all coy and smug! Come on, details, har, details."

I explained meticulously for him all that had occurred from the moment I'd entered the manse. Only I left a hole where Cherrah should have been, passing over him to the other hara I'd met, the list of engagements I'd secured.

"Marvellous!" said Shiran. "I hope that to some of these events you will take your personal flautist and best friend." He pantomimed a bow.

"We could certainly work on a couple of pieces just for the two of us," I said. Generally, at such events I had no accompaniment, but I wasn't so mean as not to include Shiran in my good fortune.

"Seriously? I was half joking."

"Of course you were!"

He reached over the dark green tablecloth for one of my hands and laughed. "Nohar could begrudge you this. It should have come sooner, if you ask me." Then he narrowed his eyes at me. "I seem to find myself more excited than you. How can you be so dispassionate about it? Vana's patronage will open many doors."

He was right. I didn't feel that excited about it. If anything, my meeting with Cherrah had cast a strange lightless shroud over the whole experience. I felt as if he was the only important thing that had happened to me. I shrugged. "I suppose it hardly seems real to me, not yet."

"Well, it *is* real," Shiran declared. He paused. "Did... something *else* happen?"

"What do you mean?"

"Oh, I don't know, but I do know *you*. You're distracted today, as when you've met somehar you like. I recognise the general air of not being quite with me."

"I'm merely dazed from the whole experience, Shir. I *do* know what a big thing it is."

He continued to eye me suspiciously. "If you say so."

Lies and silenced truths create walls, which help create assumptions designed to break the walls, which in turn help create divisions or even injury. I sighed. "Well, there was something else..."

"My ears are tuned to no other song but yours."

I grinned, then let the smile fall from my face, aware I was not wholly comfortable revealing my encounter with Cherrah to Shiran. "The har from the audience, the har who always watches me..."

"Your greatest admirer! *He* was there?"

"Yes. I spoke to him. He's a speciality clock-maker, from a family of them. The phylarch has one of his father's creations, and Vana has one of Cherrah's. I believe there must be quite a few of these clocks in the Ley House. I saw one in the guest rooms also."

Shiran rested his chin in his hand. "Hmm, well-connected, then. Almost a shame. I'd really wanted to believe he was some kind of ghost."

"Despite being proved a living thing, he is still somewhat mysterious."

"Beautiful, of course. Are you now truly smitten?"

I shook my head. "No, not beautiful, and no, not smitten. He's not unsightly, but not what I'd expected. He's rather too arid to adore, I think."

"But? And there is a 'but', isn't there?"

"I'm visiting him today, to look at his clocks, perhaps to buy one, or commission one."

"Good move," Shiran said, "Vana will no doubt hear of it, as will everyhar else who's a patron of the clockmaker. What's his full name? I'll do some digging."

"Cherrah har Freyhella."

Shiran pulled a face. "That's all? *Here in Trisque?*" He sniffed and leaned back in his chair. "Family or home town can't be up to much, then."

"Don't be a snob, Shiran," I snapped. "Cherrah said clock-making is a tradition of his family. Perhaps he doesn't care about 'connections' as much as you do."

"Or maybe he doesn't care about connections in the same way Metrice and Vana don't care about affluence; if he has privileges, a polite har will pretend not to notice them. Yet such hara are still aware that fame, fortune and good connections are a bunch of gold keys in their fists. Did you ask to view his wares or were you invited?"

"Something of both."

"Sounds positive. Might we dine together tonight so you can tell me more of your adventures?"

"Possibly. I can't promise." I grinned. "After all, I might get a better offer."

Shiran laughed loudly, causing those dining around us to glare in our direction. "In that case, breakfast together tomorrow is a *must!*"

Fern Hill is a picturesque area of Trisque, a desired address for those who can afford it and who do not seek liveliness and activity. The large old houses, interspersed with newer buildings constructed in antique style, stand in fair-sized gardens dominated by mature trees. Narrow cultivated areas, comprised mainly of long-fronded ferns, run along the centres of the few winding, steeply sloping streets of the hill. Favoured mainly by successful yet creative hara, who have drifted into the life of producing harlings with a chesnari, the area exudes a tranquil air. This is a perfect place for an artisan har, preferring privacy, to dwell. The houses are big enough to accommodate workshops and storage areas, and the occupation of clock-maker could not possibly produce irritating noise – or so I thought – that might bother neighbours.

I was having a short break from work now, before Shadetide, when the troupe would appear at various festival events, both public and private. Then there would be two weeks of intense work and moving about. Festivals were always a busy time for us. Often, we didn't get a moment to eat properly between appointments, and uninterrupted sleep of more than four hours was a luxury. As well as appearing in the city and nearby towns, we'd have to travel to the wilder places beyond, where old harish families kept the ancient traditions alive, which were wound like ivy around and through newer beliefs.

I walked slowly up Fern Hill, absorbing my surroundings. When walking, I am always working, in the same way a writer does. Ideas for songs come to me by what I might glimpse at a curtained window or in a windswept garden. I decided I wouldn't want to live in such a place, but it would be pleasant to have a friend who lived there I could visit. The lives beyond those tall windows might be mundane in the extreme, but the artist in me wanted to imagine secrets, mysteries, tragic romances, even horrors. Hara are entertained by such things. Compositions about normal lives with nothing happening, other than quiet good fortune, would have to have catchy tunes indeed to become popular.

Was there, then, a song to be created about Cherrah Har Freyhella?

The House of the Red Stairs was an enormous old mansion, very near the top of the hill. The building had been divided into a number of apartments, including the stables and other outhouses. Cherrah's apartment was in the old stable block, or rather *was* the old stable block, no smaller than any of the elegant town-houses I had passed on the way, and of two storeys. The doorbell, perhaps fashioned by Cherrah himself, allowed visitors to give warning of their arrival via an ornate iron ring-pull, with merhara and hippogryphs, wound with seaweed and shells, writhing up its shaft. As I pulled the bell, I wondered why I had not heard of

Cherrah before, and why he'd been a stranger also to my colleagues. He lived in this upmarket house, he roamed the circle of the phylarch. No stranger to Trisquish society, but yet a stranger to me. I had based myself in Trisque for five years, and for around two of those years Cherrah had been a regular attendee of my performances. What I found I couldn't remember now was whether he'd attended events beyond the city. My troupe travelled wide in the summer, working through the white-stone towns along the coast. I really couldn't remember if Cherrah had followed me to these places.

Before I could ponder further, the door opened and there was Cherrah, not a member of his staff as I'd expected. He was dressed in simple tunic and trousers, his pale hair plaited and falling over one shoulder. I experienced a strange moment of utter disappointment at his ordinariness but this was mixed uncomfortably with a dart of interest and attraction. Such opposing poles.

"Hello again," he said, smiling. "Come in, please."

I muttered a greeting and sidled past him into a dim hallway. The windows here were small and few, although the floor was of beautiful amber-coloured wood, polished to a silky sheen. There was a table near the door where lay a pair of cream leather gloves, resting against the base of what at first I took be some kind of model or dolls' house. I was drawn to this immediately, once I heard the soft ticking that emanated from it.

"You like that?" Cherrah asked, as he took my coat and placed it carefully on a hook by the door. "It's a copy of the coach-house you'll find round the back of this place. The clock in the centre of the eaves there is the same as what's outside, only considerably smaller of course. I got that old clock working again when I moved here, and then had the idea for this model. On the hour, a coach comes out of that left-hand door there, and the horses rear and neigh to call the hour."

I peered through the tiny windows in the doors, could just make out shadows of a dull-gleaming coach, maybe even the horses. I fancied some creature was shuffling about in there. Had to be clockwork, but I'd never seen har-skill like it. "It's incredibly ornate and detailed, almost like a dolls' house." I touched the tiles of the roof, found them made of wood and painted to look like mossy slate.

Cherrah stood with folded arms beside me. "I'm rather proud

of it. I like creating buildings and making the clocks part of them, but there's not a great call for this type of piece. They take up a lot of room."

"Yes, I can imagine. In many houses, they'd just get damaged by hara lumbering by – my own, for example!"

Cherrah laughed. "And what kind of clock do you like?" I did not answer at first. He indicated for me to follow him into a room on the left, which was revealed to be a comfortable yet sparsely furnished sitting room. A fire was burning in an immense marble hearth. On the mantelpiece, around the inevitable timepiece – this time a replica of a narrow, crooked house whose attic window was a misshapen clock face – a group of mechanical kittens were frolicking.

I went to the clock, examined it. "Don't tell me, on the hour the mother cat comes out and pounces on the kits, one for each hour."

Cherrah laughed. "No, on the hour they leap onto the roof and yowl, once for each hour." He pointed at a pale-cushioned sofa before the fire, which looked virtually brand new. "Please sit down. Would you like refreshment?"

I always feel the offering and acceptance of drinks is the initial part of any social call, which establishes rapport and ease between host and visitor. To refuse always seems somehow cold or rude to me – I hate it when visitors to my house say "no" and I sit there drinking tea alone, because I always insist on having it, even if the guests won't partake, meanwhile thinking what impolite creatures they are, how they're not really participating in the visit. Or perhaps they have harsh news to relate, which teas, coffees or tisanes are too frivolous to attend. Anyway, I accepted Cherrah's offer at once.

"I'll go and see to it," he said. "Think about your dream clock while I'm gone."

My *dream* clock...

Weirdly, an image came to me at once, which I think was partly influenced by the piece I'd seen in Vana's guest suite. I visualised a tall, circular, temple-like building with a domed roof, which would be enveloped in ivy. The clock face itself would be a sundial before the temple. On the hour, a figure would emerge from the temple, a har or perhaps a dehar, swathed in Classical drapery. They would have to emit a sound of course, but not my voice, not my song.

Cherrah returned with a tray, holding a pot of green tea

covered with a cloth and two mugs decorated with – hardly to my surprise – clocks. He must have had hot water ready, waiting for my visit. I had the feeling now the house contained no staff. "Hope you like this brew," Cherrah said. "Have you thought about your clock?"

"I think *it* thought about *me*," I said, smiling. "An image came to me almost the moment you left the room, but whether it's possible to create or not, only you'll be able to say."

Cherrah sat down next to me on the sofa, began pouring the tea, which he'd set on a low table before us. "Describe it to me, then."

I did so.

Cherrah nodded, handed me a mug of tea. "I see your vision, but will do a couple of sketches for you, before I begin work."

At this point I realised I had unwittingly entered into a contract. "I don't wish to be indelicate, but before we go any further I'll need to know what this piece will cost."

Without pause or apparent embarrassment, Cherrah named a price, which was not beyond my means, but certainly far more than I'd ever have considered spending on a clock. "That will be fine," I said.

"Good. Shall I drop the sketches over to you tomorrow? I can whip up a few ideas while I'm eating my dinner later."

"Yes. That's good of you, very swift."

He raised a hand, as if to stem the compliment. "I just love my work. It's no problem. The origin of a new clock is always an exciting time."

"Perhaps we can meet for lunch tomorrow," I suggested. "This is one of those rare times in the year when I'm free to do what I like."

Cherrah frowned slightly. "Oh, oh, that would be... I'd like to, but you see, I'll have a lot of work to do on your clock. I just need your approval to begin, that's all. I'd like to start tomorrow, as soon as you've seen the drawings."

I was rather taken aback by his urgency. "But what about all your other commissions?"

He made a dismissive gesture. "I work very quickly when the mood takes me. I'm intrigued by your idea and want to do that first."

"Well, all right, if you're sure. Perhaps lunch once the work is done?"

He smiled tightly. "Perhaps, yes."

I finished my tea quickly and put down my mug on the table. "Do you require an advance, Tiahaar?"

He shook his head. "No, that won't be necessary."

I got to my feet and realised he didn't intend to see me to the door. "I'll let myself out," I said.

Cherrah was staring at the fire, apparently hardly aware of me. I placed my calling card on the table by the tray. "Until tomorrow, then. May I expect you around mid-day?"

He nodded but said nothing, and I went unescorted to the door.

I didn't wait for dinnertime, but went directly to Shiran's apartment, which was very near my own, close to the Orchestrium. He was surprised to see me, but clearly delighted I was there, because it must mean gossip was imminent. "Give me coffee," I demanded, before waiting for his invitation.

"Let's sit in the kitchen," Shiran said.

His househar was in there and Shiran instructed him to prepare coffee in the largest receptacle available. We sat at the table while the househar bustled about – he was one of those rare finds, being both attractive and efficient. I knew Shiran paid higher wages than was necessary to keep him. The har was also very discreet, so I began to relate what had happened on Fern Hill.

"Hmm," Shiran murmured, after I'd finished my tale and we were drinking the coffee. "You didn't get to see his collection or his workshop?"

"I've told you everything," I said. "There isn't any more. All I saw was two clocks, albeit amazing ones." I frowned. "Strange there was only one clock in each room, though. You'd expect a clock-maker to have them all over the place."

"Not if he cares enough about his art to show them off to best effect," Shiran remarked. "No point us trying to put mystery where there is none. There's more than enough of it without that."

"What do you think?"

Shiran pulled a face. "At face value? He's a fan of yours, perhaps fanatic in the true sense, and couldn't believe he'd got you in his house. He'd been pacing up and down for over an hour before you got there. The tea was waiting – he might've poured away two pots that had gone cold."

"Hey, I was on time!"

"Hush, you're spoiling my drama. I don't think he cares about the money, but he *does* care about you, what you think. He's put all his other commissions aside to work on yours, and I don't believe for a second it's just because your clock intrigues him. Personally, I think your idea's a bit trite."

"Thanks."

"You're welcome." He grimaced. "I don't know, Mici, maybe you should be careful. Fans can be, well... you don't need me to tell you."

We looked at one another and shared a few silent seconds of agonised memories.

"Do you really think it's just that?" I asked.

Shiran shrugged. "What do *you* think?"

"I'm not sure. He's sort of... otherworldly, I suppose. I don't think he was lying about the work, but perhaps he does want to impress me as quickly as possible, and that's why he's shoved my clock to first in the queue. He said no to lunch, remember. Perhaps he's not as much of a fan as you think. If he was that interested in me, he'd have leapt at the chance, surely?"

"Depends how devious he is. A clever har would not jump at the first opportunity." Shiran rested his chin in one hand, drawing circles in spilled coffee with the other. "It does seem odd that we've never heard of him before. He was just a face in the crowd, if a regular face. Why wasn't he at Vana's reception at the Orchestrium? He must surely have been invited. Why is he suddenly available to you? Was he waiting for your credentials to become more respectable, as in Vana offering his patronage?"

"He doesn't strike me as the social climbing sort," I said. "I don't think he even has house-hara, not even one. I don't suppose you've had chance to do any digging yet, have you?"

Shiran shook his head. "No, but I intend to start immediately. Shall we meet at *The Swan's Neck* for dinner?"

"Yes. I'll see you at the usual time."

At home, I felt jumpy and nervous, which to me indicated the well-known symptoms of developing an interest in a har, but at the same time this didn't feel like that. I couldn't concentrate on anything, so went out for a long walk in Thornbloom Park to the east of Trisque. The closing year shuttered the day early. A chill breeze shuffled the falling leaves. Autumn's gaudiness would not leave the land until after Shadetide, but its festival dress was beginning to look rather worn.

I arrived at *The Swan's Neck* early, and consumed two flutes of russet wine before Shiran came to my table.

"You look calmer," he said, removing his coat and sitting down.

I raised my glass to him.

"I see. Well, not a lot to report, I'm afraid. Tiahaar Cherrah is *known*, but only in the most tedious fashion. There is no gossip or mystery. He is a har who makes clocks. He moved to Trisque around two years ago, and letters from his family helped him secure work and connections. Hara like his pieces, but don't have much to say about the har who makes them. Quietly, his devices have gradually come to measure time in most of the homes of Trisque, or so it seems. He doesn't only work for rich hara. He sells a few cheaper pieces to shops for anyhar to buy."

I grimaced. "I'm just surprised we haven't heard of him before."

Shiran nodded shortly. "You know, I think hara only hear of him when he wants to be known. He slips beneath notice, and the hara I spoke to were almost weirdly surprised to remember him. A ghost who is not a ghost. Intriguing. I think I want to meet this enigma."

"He's coming to my house tomorrow. Don't expect to be impressed."

Shiran arrived for breakfast at 10 and we spent some time discussing ideas for the events for which I'd secured bookings. Most would be for over the Natalia period, so we had time to prepare. That morning, a note had arrived from Vana's secretary, requesting my presence at the Natalia Extravaganza at the Ley House. Shiran said he would murder me if he were not to be included in my performance there. I told him I'd have to make enquiries to see if it was acceptable for me to take him. The phylarch and his consort might not want a spare flautist floating about, no matter how well he played.

We were so wrapped up in playfully sniping at each other, and marking events on my calendar, that the time zipped by. Mid-day came, and with it a knock at my door. I was on my feet in an instant, yelling to Furze, my househar, that I'd answer the knock myself. I skidded into the hall, then collected myself and walked sedately to the door. Opened it.

Cherrah stood on the threshold, wearing a hooded cloak that covered the upper part of his face. One pale hand clutched the fabric at his neck. Over his shoulder hung a battered, wide leather satchel.

"Good morning, Tiahaar, come in, come in," I said.

Cherrah stood motionless, silent.

"Is anything wrong, Tiahaar?" I asked.

At that moment, Shiran rushed past me and out through the door. I called his name.

He turned and ran backwards for a few steps so he could shout at me. "Sorry, Mici, have to dash. I forgot. I forgot!" Then he turned and was gone, sprinting up the street.

Neatly, Cherrah came into my house and carefully peeled back his hood. He looked about himself, but still did not speak.

"I... er... apologise about that," I said. "That was my friend... er... well, never mind. May I take your cloak?"

Cherrah shook his head. "I won't be staying long." He took the bag from his shoulder. "Do you have a table where I might lay out my drawings?"

"Of course." I ushered him into the dining room.

Carefully, Cherrah removed a sheaf of parchments from the satchel and laid them out slowly in two lines on the table. A couple of drawings? This was more like over a dozen.

There was only one design, shown from various angles, several barely different from others. A couple of drawings revealed some of the interior workings of the device. Yet even though there was no choice in the design, the one Cherrah had realised for me was perfect, reflecting entirely the image that had been in my mind at his house.

"Is this to your liking, Tiahaar?" Cherrah asked.

"Of course it is. It's exactly what I imagined. Are you a mind-reader?"

He did not smile at my joke. On one of the frontal view drawings, he pointed at the sundial, before which stood a noble, draped har. "To have the dial work as in reality, I would have to create a facsimile sun. I feel this might be too bright and intrusive for your hallway."

I raised my brows. "My hallway? Is that where you think I should place the clock?"

He nodded.

"But you haven't seen the rest of the house..."

"I saw the hallway, which seems right for the piece."

"Very well, if that's your opinion." I considered privately I didn't have to concur with that once the piece was safely in my possession.

"So," Cherrah continued, "if it's acceptable to you, the clock in the sundial will be of the normal kind. Of course, you won't be able to see the time until you stand over it. The hands of the clock can of course be shadows. Again, I must ask if this is acceptable. If not, we can modify the design."

"Well, looking at it, the piece is more of an ornament than a clock, beautiful as it is. The time piece will be a surprise for anyhar looking at it."

Again, Cherrah nodded, but not, I felt, in agreement with me. He simply nodded so we could conclude our business. "If you're happy with the design, I'll leave a drawing with you and go to start work. Would you like to choose one?"

"I'll take one of the frontal views – you choose. Keep the ones you need."

Cherrah removed a drawing and handed it to me. "I don't need any of them now, but this shows the full clock from the front, with the hour figure revealed. I want you to keep it to compare with the finished piece."

"Well, thank you, but I'm sure that won't be necessary."

Cherrah smiled at last. "No, it won't, but please take it as a gift."

I had a feeling then that his sketches for customers might well command a decent price themselves. I looked down at the drawing. The figure, the temple, the foliage, the sundial; all looked so realistic. Cherrah was an artist, a sculptor, as well as a clock-maker. "I'll feel privileged to share my home with this art," I said. "Truly."

"When it is finished, I'll contact you about installation."

I felt it would be coarse and somehow inappropriate to mention his fee again, but would make sure this was ready for him once the piece was delivered. He began to lift his hood over his head once more, but before his eyes were covered he stared at me deeply. There were messages in that stare that normally I would consider it easy to interpret. Perhaps not so much with this one. I saw desire, yearning, yes, but what else? Subtle emanations. I wasn't sure.

I felt absurdly sad. That stare should have streamed from lovely eyes, full of stars and reflections. Cherrah's eyes were small and unremarkable. He had been given such gifts but perhaps at a price.

I shook myself mentally to disperse these bizarre thoughts. "How long do you anticipate the work will take, Tiahaar?"

"Not long. There will be plenty of time." He gathered up his remaining drawings and replaced them in his satchel.

I laughed, a little nervously. "For what?"

The satchel went over his shoulder. "For your clock to be installed before you begin your work again."

I could no longer see his eyes, his brow, his forehead, only his perfect nose, his exquisite mouth and chin. A shiver ran through me. "I see. Thank you. That will be very quick for such a big job!"

He inclined his head, positioned his hood carefully. "This is my occupation. I'm adept at it."

Then he glided from my house, without waiting for me to accompany him to the door.

Shiran reappeared about two hours later. "What was all that about?" I demanded as he came into my sitting room. "Rushing off like that?"

He flopped down in a chair opposite me. "I really don't know, Mici." He frowned. "I was simply sitting in your kitchen, anticipating the meeting with your clock-maker when I... remembered something, a really important appointment I had entirely forgotten. I was compelled to grab my coat and just run from the house, as if the Mahallatu were on my tail."

"What appointment was it?"

Shiran turned bewildered eyes to me. "That's just it: I don't know. I ran around town for maybe twenty minutes, panicking, terrified I was missing something life-saving, or vital in some other way, but I wasn't going anywhere. I couldn't remember where I was supposed to be. The fear was terrible. Eventually, like a drug wearing off or something, I came to my senses and staggered into a cafe. Here I fortified myself with liqueur coffee until I could face the journey home. Thank dehara, there was a carriage rank right outside the place. My limbs were like those of a newly-hatched harling; I could barely stand."

"That is most... *strange*," I said inadequately. "Like a nightmare." Shiran was not a har given to nervous fits. An idea came to me at once, but I shrank from voicing it. Not so Shiran.

"I think I was driven out of this house, Mici, and you know by whom. I wasn't wanted here. He wanted you to himself or he didn't want me to see him."

"What *did* you see, as you ran past him?"

"Very little, I was in such a panic. A har draped in a dark cloak, that was all. When I ran past you, it was like you were only a blur, but he wasn't. He was clear to the eye and perfectly still, but... hidden."

I rubbed my arms as if cold, sure my teeth were chattering, though the room was warm. I got to my feet and went to the fire, held out my unaccountably chilled hands to it. "Perhaps... perhaps I should cancel the order for the clock. Even if he's begun work on it, he'll surely be able to sell it elsewhere."

"No, I wouldn't do that!" Shiran said hurriedly. "No, Mici, don't antagonise him further."

"Further?" I froze on the spot before the hearth where I'd begun to pace up and down.

"Me being here was antagonism. Go through with it, pay your money. Then you don't have to speak to him again if you don't want to. There's something weird about that har, and my instincts are hissing at me: don't anger him."

I pressed my icy fingers to my eyes, at that moment utterly frightened. Was Shiran simply over-reacting and feeding my fears? I couldn't tell. All I could focus on was Cherrah's great beauty when half his face was hidden, and the reflex of virtual repugnance and disgust it inspired when he revealed his eyes and brow. No, he was far from normal, and had perhaps compensated in unusual ways for his differences. I lowered my hands from my face and said, "I should seek protection from the Nayati."

Shiran reached out to touch my waist. "No. He will be aware of that. I just *feel* this. Every atom of my being cries out for you to go along with him, then once the job is done, back off."

"What if he doesn't want me to back off? Am I allowed to seek protection then?" I was beginning to think Shiran was over-dramatising the situation. Cherrah *was* strange, and it wasn't unheard of for powerfully psychic hara to influence others in the way Shiran had perhaps been influenced. Cherrah had wanted me alone; this much I believe was true. Also, that he hadn't wanted to be seen by my friend. So, he'd taken action, but I didn't want to think this had been malicious, merely necessary to him: the quickest way to rid himself of Shiran's presence without too much fuss. "Perhaps he's the one who's frightened," I said. "He's not that social a creature. Perhaps he wanted to avoid you inspecting him. Is that unreasonable?"

Shiran made a placatory gesture. "No, but let me just say this. You're not a native of this land, Mici, nor have you ever visited the northern realms. Magics linger in the clouds, the forests. Hara who formed there... well... perhaps they have more of ancient mysteries in them than we know."

I laughed. "Oh, for Aru's sake, Shir, what are you saying? That Cherrah is some kind of sorcerer?" I pantomimed a scary creature with hungry claws. "He's come down from the mystic north to make me a clock and then devour me!"

Shiran was staring at me. "Why do you scoff in that way? Do you think we know everything about the way our race has developed?"

"No, but dreaming up wild ideas is hardly helpful in this situation."

"Why does Cherrah conceal so much about himself, then?"

"Maybe he just doesn't *care*!"

Shiran took in a deep breath through his nose. How had this become an argument between us? "So, you don't believe me, fair enough. But I have your welfare at heart, Mici. All I'm saying is fanaticism mixed with some kind of *difference* might be dangerous."

"I appreciate your concern," I said, feeling I must defuse this situation. "And I didn't mean to mock. I'll do as you suggest and simply finish my business with him – it seems wise. But afterwards, if there's any kind of trouble, I'll take action. Hopefully this won't be necessary. Let's simply wait and see."

"Be careful, Mici," Shiran said.

I didn't hear from Cherrah for nearly three weeks and began to wonder whether my clock would indeed be finished by Shadetide. Our troupe was due to begin performing three days before the festival, and for over a week thereafter. Then we had a steady calendar of work up to Natalia. We started rehearsals at the Orchestrium, and because I was so busy, not least with writing two new pieces Shiran and I were to perform at the Ley House, the thought of the clock slipped from my mind – more or less. Sometimes, a shadowy figure I felt was Cherrah haunted the rim of my dreams, though.

Then on a Lo'itsday evening, when I returned home, Furze told me a har had called and had left a message. Something in his expression, a mix of puzzlement and distaste, advised me the visitor had been Cherrah. The message confirmed this; my clock was ready.

I wouldn't be able to have him deliver it during the day until the weekend, but my evenings were clear for the next two nights. I asked Furze to deliver this information to Fern Hill and to secure a reply.

When Furze returned, there was no written message, simply a verbal one. He again looked somewhat bewildered. "Tiahaar Cherrah said to tell you it will be tomorrow evening. He said that owing to your work preventing lunches for the time being, maybe dinner tomorrow would be a possibility. He asked if that might be here, in the house. He said if he didn't hear from you, he'd consider arrangements for tomorrow were acceptable."

I stared at Furze for some moments and he stared back. I could tell he didn't know what to think about the somewhat presumptuous tone of the message, but he *did* feel uncomfortable about something.

"Have his money ready for him, would you, Furze?" I wrote on a note slip the amount due to Cherrah; Furze had permission to withdraw funds from my bank.

Furze glanced at the note, made no comment other than, "Of course, Tiahaar."

Cherrah had banished my friend from the house to avoid meeting him - *apparently* - yet seemed at ease relating personal messages through my housthat. Asking to dine at a har's house rather than out at a restaurant construed an unambiguous message, and only somehar utterly naive and stupid wouldn't realise that. None of this added up to what I had presumed to be the character of Cherrah Har Freyhella.

At the Orchestrium the following day, I didn't tell Shiran I'd be seeing Cherrah later that night. Mainly, I told myself, this was because I didn't want him to worry, but I also wished to avoid any lectures on my safety and so on. Nohar was more aware than I that Cherrah was no ordinary har, and might be dangerous, although I found that difficult to believe. Cherrah seemed timid and self-conscious, more than anything else. The episode with Shiran could not be denied, and had definitely been peculiar, but I still believed this must have been down to a weird kind of self-defence on Cherrah's part.

At seven o'clock, Cherrah delivered my clock. He arrived in a carriage, and two hara he'd hired for the purpose transported the piece to my hallway, where I'd already cleared a table for it. When Cherrah removed the packing cloth from the piece, it was much larger than I'd anticipated, and perhaps wouldn't look quite right on the delicate table I'd chosen to be its plinth. But Cherrah arranged it there, removing wadding of soft cloth he'd placed between its most fragile parts and, when he stood back, the clock appeared to be perfectly at home.

The piece was maybe three feet high, and even though it included no facsimile sun – or moon for that matter – as Cherrah had briefly mentioned, it gave off the impression of standing in evening light. Well, I told myself, why would it not? It *is* evening, after all. But the light around the clock spoke of summertime, the soft fall of daylight into mystic moonshine, foliage heavy upon the trees, yet motionless and breathless before the true advent of night. Two oaks stood behind my clock, the leaves so beautifully and realistically carved they seemed to rustle. How had Cherrah completed this piece in so short a time? The carving alone must have had him up till dawn every night. The temple was of smooth white marble. When I touched the domed roof, there was a faint grittiness to it, but the columns at its entrance were like glass. Ivy fashioned from silk and wire drooped over it, twining also about the trunks of the oaks. Its interior was a dark blue shadow.

"Would you allow me time to check the clock and see to its correct working?" Cherrah asked, and it took some moments for me to realise he meant: would I give him privacy to do it.

"Of course. I'll see how dinner's progressing." With a polite bow, I took my leave.

I gave him ten minutes before I returned to the hall. He was still arranging ivy leaves over the temple roof, standing back to observe the effect, before making more minor adjustments. "It looks marvellous," I said. "Thank you so much, Cherrah." I held out an envelope. "This is for you."

He took the money, inclining his head respectfully. "Thank you." The envelope was secreted into his satchel, which I saw he again wore over one shoulder.

"May I take your cloak?" I asked.

He glanced at me. "All right." As always, he revealed his eyes and brow in that slow somewhat challenging manner, before unclasping the cloak at his neck. And as before, I started a little inside when those features were revealed. Would it ever not be a shock to behold them? It was not as if he were deformed or ugly. Just... something strange.

I stood with the limpid fabric of the cloak lolling in my arms, while Cherrah turned his back on me to fiddle once more with the clock. As at Vana's reception, he wore a backless robe, this time of matte black linen, exquisitely cut. Colours flamed across his back and shoulders. I couldn't help but approach him to look more closely.

He must have felt me studying him, because I became aware of a slight tension in his body, yet he did not turn around. The design of the tattoo, because I could see clearly this was no temporary illustration, seemed to be of the trunk of a tree, wound about with flowering vines and ivy. I say *seemed to be*, because it was more of an abstract impression rather than a literal replica of a tree. There were creatures on the bark, birds like miniature peacocks with spreading tails, long-haired mice, or mice with manes like lions. I even saw a pair of yellow eyes peering out from what appeared to be a deep, dark hole in the trunk.

"That is the most amazing tattoo you have," I said. "I feel I could look at it for hours and see more in it as every minute passed."

Cherrah straightened up and turned round. "Thank you."

"What a pity you can't admire it yourself very easily."

He smiled. "I know what's there."

"So, you were a canvas once," I said.

"I wondered whether a mask of feathers across my face would be interesting," he said, standing very close to me, and in his words an unspoken challenge. "Do you think so, Tiahaar?" He touched the collar of my shirt provocatively.

There was no helping it; I took him in my arms so we might share breath. But he merely kissed me in a shallow manner, then drew away, keeping his secrets to himself.

I remembered him saying, when he handed me his calling card in the Ley House, "that's what you want, isn't it?" and was tempted to say the same now, because surely seduction was his purpose, beneath all other considerations? But I kept silent, staring at him for long moments, saying at last, "My househar,

Furze, is ready to serve us dinner."

Cherrah nodded. "Very well."

Before, I would have taken his arm to lead him to the dining room but now, feeling rebuffed, I simply walked ahead of him, indicating the way.

Furze was already placing the soup. I noticed he gave Cherrah a sharp glance as we entered the room, and was very quick to escape. Cherrah sat down where I pulled out a chair for him. I was suffused with a bewildering mix of strong desire, unspecific fear and giddiness.

As Cherrah consumed his soup, neither greedily nor sparingly, I noticed he wore a sort of gauntlet over his right forearm; it was a watch, of course. A watch made of silver armour and encrusted with black pearls. His thin hair was drawn back into a severe plait. There was little conversation during the soup.

Once the first course was consumed, Furze materialised in the startling way he sometimes has, and whisked away the plates. Even Cherrah seemed a little surprised by his abrupt appearance and disappearance.

"He's very efficient," I said, lamely.

Presently, the meat course was brought to us; lamb and berries accompanied by vegetables of the season.

"Efficient and an excellent cook," Cherrah said, tucking enthusiastically into the pink-centred slices of lamb on his plate.

I nodded. "Do you have househara, Cherrah? When I visited you, the place seemed empty, I could not sense others. Do you prefer to live alone?"

"I have few needs to be seen to," he said, "and those I do have I can manage to satisfy by myself."

Was there an implied criticism there, of those who could afford to hire hara to attend to the most basic of daily tasks, so as not to be bothered with them?

"I like the company," I said, aware it sounded a little defensive.

"Like the ticking of a clock," Cherrah said.

"Is that all you need for company?" I asked.

He looked up at me. "Most of the time, yes. A clock has a beating heart." He glanced at his right forearm. "Talking of which, we must not miss the hour. I want you to see him."

I glanced at the ordinary, straightforward clock that hung

upon the wall, opposite my seat. "Well, let's take a break before dessert. That should time it neatly."

We continued to consume the main course in silence.

Glancing at Cherrah occasionally, I was flushed with moments of desire, followed by chills of disquiet. This har woke such contradictions within me. My revulsion for him was not caused solely by the unkind arrangement of his facial features; it went deeper than that. Part of him was beautiful, a creative, sensitive soul. But there was another part, a part perhaps hinted at, which I had not yet truly seen.

At two minutes before the hour, we went out into the hallway. The room was in blue starlight, with only the dimmest autumnal gleam from the wall lamps, which Furze had turned down very low. The temple of the clock gleamed upon its table. Standing close to it, I saw the shadow of the marker upon the dial, which stood on a slim column, slightly to the left of the temple entrance. How had Cherrah achieved that and would it work so effectively in daylight when the sun was falling directly upon it through the tall, east-facing windows by my door? The temple and dial were surrounded by soft grass that seemed to breathe.

Cherrah came close to me and took my right arm in his hold. "Watch," he murmured.

As the shadow moved over the dial to mark the hour, a figure emerged from the temple. Its thick, blue-black hair cascaded over its chest, which was partly revealed by carefully arranged drapery. Its arms were by its sides, but now it raised them, and uttered a low, melodious tone. This was not repeated; it was a single sound. But I swear the lips had opened to release it. "Cherrah," I whispered, for I dare not raise my voice, "is that me?"

The figure had lowered its arms now, and bowed its head, before retreating into the temple.

"A little like you," he said softly. "Are you pleased with the clock?"

"It's exquisite," I said, and now it felt acceptable to talk at normal volume.

"I'm glad you like it."

"Shall we return to the dining-room?" I asked.

"I do not want dessert there," he answered. "The hour has spoken, it is time." And now he wrapped his arms around me and put his lips against mine. This time, he let me see forests, and smell the heady scent of sun-baked pine. I saw high mountains, and eagles swimming in the clear air. His home.

I took him to my bedroom, consumed by the need for aruna, but also aware this was perhaps the culmination of Cherrah's plans from when he'd first started to haunt my performances. Did it really matter? In the darkness of my room, I could barely see him, but starlight fell in through the window in a bar across his mouth and chin; the rest of his face was in shadow. I put my arms around him, pulled him close, and it seemed to me that my hands upon his back traced textures, as if his body art was more than mere paint injected into the skin. Leaves, rough bark, and even the skitter of a soft-footed creature across the back of my hand. This aroused me even more.

After that, events are hazy in my memory, although with crystal sharp exceptions. He was soume for me, taking me into a hallucinatory realm of fabulous visions, of countries in the clouds that I could not have imagined. We rolled in the bed as if we were rolling in the sky, eagles mating on the wing. I was beneath him, cushioned only by air, and for a moment panicked. I dug my fingers into his back.

What I found there...

A fallen, hollow tree, aged and buried beneath wet leaves. Its hidden side turned to the air, it was as putrid as wet, decaying fungus, alive with devouring beetles and grubs. Spongy and smelling of over-ripe mushrooms. My hands were consumed by this wriggling, rotting mass. I think I screamed. I hear the echo of it.

Hollow. He was a dead, hollow tree.

I cried his name, pulled away, my hands before my face, covered in dark streaks. He gazed back at me through those small eyes, yet devoid of expression.

"What *are* you?" I asked, afraid that at any moment he might fall upon me with suddenly long claws and fangs.

"As you are," he murmured. "Fragments of the past brought into the present, refashioned. I didn't think you'd see... caught in this mundane world as you are." He uttered a sigh. "It is not to be."

He lashed out with one arm and I remember flinching away, but there was no blow, only a descent into darkness.

As might be expected in such a tale as this, I didn't come to my senses until the dawn, and of course Cherrah had gone. As I lay on my back in the bed – I had checked for remnants of decaying wood and had found none – I wondered how much of what I'd felt beneath my hands – which had been as much physical as visual – had been pure hallucination, brought on by the loosened ecstasies of aruna. This can do very strange things to a har's mind, as any har can tell you, not to mention the wine I'd drunk at dinner – rather too much of it because of my nerves. I'd concocted for Cherrah a strangeness, and perhaps his tattoo had somehow influenced me. What I'd felt could not possibly have been real, could it? And yet I remembered what he'd said to me, *fragments of the past refashioned...*

Later, when Shiran came to call, I told him everything. I expected him to scoff and joke at the climax of my story, but he did not.

He stared at me, as I stood before the fire in my living room. "As I said to you before," he said, "who knows how hara have... *developed* in corners of the world?"

I shook my head. "Shir, this was not some tribal deviation..."

"Listen," he said, "because I've lived here all my life, whereas you have not. There are old stories about the Elle folk, who weren't human and who lived beneath the land. Humans were afraid of them, and appeased them at all costs. The female Elle, though beautiful, were said to be hollow, lovely only from the front, illusions of beauty. The males were ugly all over, and were said to breathe pestilence."

I considered. "So, you're saying a harish Elle, if such could exist, being androgynous would contain elements of both genders – the hollow back, aspects of ugliness, yet aspects of beauty also."

Shiran nodded quickly. "Exactly. It does make sense, doesn't it? I knew there was something about him..."

"In a strange kind of way, it does make sense," I replied. "But could it possibly be true?"

Shiran shrugged. "I wouldn't try to find out if I were you. Returning to the Elle folk, despite their power over humans who lived near them, they were ashamed of their ugliness and their hollow backs, and were dangerous because of this. No human would provoke an Elle. If they came across one, male or female, they would never laugh at an ugly face, and would certainly not show fear. That would be the greatest insult, and an insulted Elle, apparently, was a violent thing. "

I laughed uneasily. "It *is* a great story, but can we really believe that Cherrah is some kind of harish Elle, that he's from a *tribe* of them?"

Shiran raised his hands expressively. "I'm saying that Wraeththu brought many changes to the world and awoke old magics as much as fashioned new ones. Who is to say that tribes developing in the far north of these lands weren't influenced by emanations from the earth itself? Think of the endless cloud-crowned forests, the space... anything could come into being there. Think of the Colurastes, who are perhaps the only tribe to mingle freely with others, and who have certain... *aberrations* of being. There must be many more, hidden away. I've always thought so. And perhaps some *do* want, like the Colurastes, to be accepted by mainstream harish culture. Who knows? But who can deny it as nonsense, eh?"

I sighed. "And now I expect Cherrah has vanished mysteriously from Trisque, leaving only an empty house, and we shall never know."

But he had not disappeared. Although he made no move to contact me again, nor I to contact him, when I sang my Lachrymide hymn before all of the city on the first night of the Orchestrium's Shadetide events, there he was, on the front row as usual, his hood over his eyes, his cloak covering his back. Shiran's ideas were ludicrous, and yet... As I sang to him, as I always had, I felt saddened – appropriate for a Lachrymide lament. If there were any truth at all in Shiran's suppositions, how tragic to be such an outsider, half fairy, half har, yet also neither.

Cherrah left the Orchestrium at the end of the performance, and I made no move to contact him or detain him. That is how it has remained. I've found I don't even look for him now, as if the enchantment drained away from the moment I took him to my room.

As far as I know, he still makes his clocks on Fern Hill. Mine is neither enchanted nor haunted, but it keeps excellent time.

The Elle Har

There was once a harling named Cherrah, who lived in the far north, where the mountains meet the sky. He knew, because his hostling had told him, that his tribe was not like other hara. They were creatures far older, who had lived hidden for a very long time, when humans had ruled the world. But when humanity had fallen, they had crept from the cracks in the earth and found other cracks to creep into; the minds of hara, their flesh.

One night, Cherrah was woken by the cries of an owl outside his window, and went to follow its ghost shadow on the soft snow. At length, he came to a precipice over a chasm so deep there were stars trapped in its depths, which had fallen and could not get out. The owl spread its white wings on the night and said, for it was rather more than an owl and could speak, "Here is the pit where your heart will lie."

Cherrah grew up, and on the night before his feybraiha, the owl came again and, as before, the harling followed it out into the darkness of the high murmuring pines and the endless sky. The owl led him to the biggest pine in the forest and then swooped down upon him and opened up his back to the spine with its claws. "This is where your beauty lies," said the owl. Cherrah fell back against bark of the tallest pine, his body aflame with pain. And it seemed the tree pitied him, for Cherrah could feel it filling his empty back with parts of itself, so that from the front he looked like a har, but from the back was a hollow tree.

The harling went home to his tribe, where everyhar was gathered waiting to celebrate his feybraiha. They stood around a fire, all in clothes of russet and green. His father came over and put a cloak of dark green wool about his shoulders that hung all the way to the ground, and his hostling came forward and pulled the hood of the cloak so that it covered the top of Cherrah's face. He could peer out beneath the edge of it, and as he did so, he saw his whole tribe turn their backs on him, as if he must be forgotten. But it was not this. It was merely to show him they were all like he was, kindred to the pine.

"It is not always," said Cherrah's hostling, "that you will show your true nature. As we crept from the earth so we brought its secrets with us. You will learn how to seal your flesh, and your face is enough like a har to fool any who might look, not of our tribe."

"But can't I stay with the tribe, so nohar else might ever see or have to be fooled?" said Cherrah.

"No," said his hostling. "You will go out into the world and be part of it. Your father will take you to the cities of hara, and you will learn his trade of clockmaker, and bring our arts to these cities, for we have a way with time. This is your duty to your tribe, to bring us riches." His hostling kissed him upon the brow. "But for tonight, you need think of nothing but he who waits for you. There he is, beyond the fire. Do you see?"

And then the har came to Cherrah, who would lead him to adulthood, and he went into a moss-roofed house a harling and came out in the morning a har.

On the night before he was to leave for the cities of hara, the owl came again to Cherrah. "I won't follow you," he said. "You bring only bad to me."

And the owl replied, "Truth is never bad. My task was to take you to the forest, which I did."

"But you opened my back with your claws, and now I will never be truly har but half tree, because of the pine's pity."

"Rather my claws than any other kind," said the owl, "for what I did was with love, not fear or cruelty. And you were *always* half tree. Come, follow me now. This is the final thing I can teach you."

So Cherrah followed the owl, expecting something he would not enjoy or that would make him sad. The owl led him high into the mountains, where breath turns to frost upon the air and the sky fractures with cold like glass.

"Do you feel the cold?" asked the owl.

Cherrah drew his green wool cloak about him. "Of course. It's always there."

"Does it pain you?"

"What do you mean?"

"Does the cold bring pain to your body, discomfort?"

"Of course not." Cherrah took off his cloak, folded it, and set it

200

upon the ground so he could sit on it. He gazed out across the jagged peaks with their green cloaks of pines. Tomorrow, he would be gone from this land and didn't know when he would be back.

"You are more than har," said the owl, perching on a fallen tree nearby, "for as the cold does not blight your flesh, neither can water drown you, nor fire consume you. You cannot be crushed. You can walk inside the mountains and listen to them speak. Ordinary hara can die by the elements, but you cannot, because you are their creature. And that is a reason to be happy not sad."

"But I will be lonely," Cherrah said, "I can already feel it, looking at this landscape to which I belong, and which I must leave. Loneliness might crush, or burn or drown me. As could love, because you've already told me my heart lies in a pit from which it can't get out."

The owl lifted its wings wide upon the night. "Ah, but you are a creature that came from the secrets of the earth," it said. "Your hara do not obey the ordinary laws. You came from a fairy tale and everyhar knows that such tales can end in miracles. You must never give up hope, because a miracle might always be around the next corner."

"I suppose I must be content with that," Cherrah said, "and thank you for words that did not make me sad and no experiences with claws that hurt me."

"Goodbye, Cherrah," said the owl.

Cherrah returned to his tribe and the owl stayed behind in the white mountains. In the morning, as he readied himself to leave, Cherrah put into his bags a sprig of pine, an owl feather and a small cold rock to remind him of home. Then he followed his father out into the world, hoping to come upon a corner in a city that had something wondrous round it.

Beyond a Veil of Stars

In those days, there was a village called Long Marn near to the edge of the wilderness where no-one went by choice. Those who lived there were defiant remnants of human civilisation, scratching an existence from the wild earth and the angry river that rushed past the edge of their fields. The world belonged to Wraeththu, and had done for a long time. It was said that Wraeththu had brought back to the world an ancient knowledge, that they were neither men nor women but something of both; either a new form for human life or a reversion to a very old one. The people of Long Marn were aware that Wraeththu were able to breed among themselves, but had originally derived from human stock. Occasionally, but with increasing rarity, they might still seek to call the youths of human settlements to join them.

In Long Marn were young men who had not heeded the call and older men to whom the call had never come. There were women and children too, although not many. In the past, young men had sometimes heard whispers in the night that whistled out from the wilderness. In the morning, one of them might have disappeared, and tracks, like those of big cats, had marked the dirt around the skirts of the village walls. But, despite this, the community had survived.

They lived uneasily near to shrouded Caracanti, a city of the Wraeththu: believed in, but never truly seen. Sometimes, on a clear day, a ghost that might be the city could be glimpsed rising tall and splendid far away, winking like quartz in the pale sun, but on another day it could not be perceived at all. The people believed that sorcerous fogs eclipsed it from view. There were tales of how, long ago, in the vibrating night air, distant voices had sometimes been heard, raised in strange ululations. The sensual scent of incense had crept in tendrils down the narrow village streets.

There were stories too of how, when the city had been built, Wraeththu had come out of the wilderness to the village and told the people where they might walk, and where they might not; where they might plant their crops and graze their herds. There were boundaries that must be respected, and if this was done, the people would not suffer harm.

The Wraeththu had spoken softly of conservation and co-operation, but they had been – and were – remote like gods. They had never offered assistance. The people of Long Marn feared them, because they were not human, because they had stolen the world.

The leader of Long Marn was a man named Jacob, who had a wife, Mara, and two sons: Ahtau and Attjan. One of the reasons Jacob led the community was because he and Mara had had children; it was a rare thing nowadays and regarded as a gift from the Land Mother. People so blessed were above all others, and there were, in all, only eight young people in the village of Long Marn and two of them were 'not whole' in the mind. There were other small communities huddled around the plains and forests, but Long Marn was the largest; it boasted youngsters. Most of the other small settlements were inhabited only by the elderly and frail, and had been dying for a generation. Yet more settlements were now no more than the abode of ghosts, where lonely winds blew memories before them down the empty streets.

But not so Long Marn the Prosperous.

The sons of Jacob and Mara were long-limbed and hardy youths, and faithful to their people. Wraeththu would never steal them away. Each night, they burned certain herbs before their doors to repel the Whisperers in the Dark, those particular spirits believed to work with Those From Beyond the Wilderness. The boys had been raised strictly, and Jacob believed he had shaped their inner morals to repel all subtle forms of attack or seduction. Mara had taught them special words, which she said made a person immune to the magic of Those Beyond. If Caracanti had ever sought to woo these boys, it had long since given up trying.

Then, one day, Ahtau fell ill.

The villagers had never encountered a sickness like it. The boy simply dropped in his tracks as he walked in the long fields by the river. Very soon, all colour left his flesh and the temperature of his body fell to an unnatural cold. The people carried him to his home, wary of his iciness: it was a chill that spoke of death, but still Ahtau breathed. Ahtau and Attjan were not just boys to the people of Long Marn; they were sacred symbols. For ill to befall one of them was a dire omen indeed.

For thirteen days, Ahtau wasted before his family's eyes. It seemed impossible he could still live. His flesh seemed to fall from his bones; his ribs were a visible cage, and his closed eyes had sunk into pits above the blades of his cheekbones. He could not eat, and the only fluid Mara could force inside him was what she was able to dribble into his dry mouth with a sponge. Anything more than that made him choke and splutter.

She sought to revive the boy with herbs and poultices, and when this made no difference, she called for a healer man who lived in a cave in the forested hills across the river. He laid his hands on Ahtau's gaunt frame and sought to restore him through faith. When this also failed, Mara called for a woman known to be wise, who lived among the trees of Grey Crow Woods. She burned acrid resins in Ahtau's bedroom and invoked his totemic animal spirit. This did not help either. Nobody could tell Jacob or Mara what ailed their son. But some had their suspicions.

One evening, a new healer came to the village, a travelling woman who lived among the skirts of the wilderness, and who was always moving. She had heard of the trouble, she said, and had come to offer her services. She wrapped Ahtau in damp cloths, imbued with eye-stinging resins, placed hot stones upon his chest, and burned bitter herbs in a dish. Then she knelt upon the floor beside his bed and fell silent for some time. Jacob, Mara and Attjan stood by the bedroom door, watching anxiously. Presently, the healer sighed and placed one of the damp cloths over her burning herbs to extinguish them. She removed the stones from Ahtau's chest.

"What have you learned?" Jacob asked.

The woman would not look at him. She shrugged. "It is no ordinary sickness, but this you already know. I am tempted to say it is not a sickness at all, but something else."

"An enchantment," said Mara.

"Evil from beyond us," Jacob murmured softly. He closed his eyes.

Mara and Attjan watched helplessly as Jacob walked out of the house and went to stand in the dying sunlight. Quietly, they followed him, and saw that the other villagers, seemingly attracted by his distress, had all come out of their dwellings and in from the fields, to stand around him. All were silent. Then Jacob uttered a terrible, hoarse cry and banged his bunched hands against his eyes. The villagers flinched at the unexpected outburst: Jacob was normally a calm and measured man.

To Attjan, his father's cry was the most hideous sound he'd ever heard; it was the quintessence of despair and grief.

At sixteen, Attjan was Ahtau's junior by nearly two years. Like his brother, he was a striking youth; tall, with long black hair, which he wore tied back at the nape of his neck. For some days, he'd been unable to face visiting his brother, despite the urging of his mother, who felt that Attjan's voice might somehow soothe Ahtau's troubled soul. But the emaciated creature who rasped and trembled beneath the blankets hardly even looked like Ahtau anymore, and Attjan found the sight both repellent and frightening. He wanted to remember his brother as the vibrant and humorous person he'd once been.

They had been inseparable. Together, as young children, they had trembled beneath their blankets in the dark of moonless nights while eerie sounds had whispered in to them from outside. Then they had whispered of terrible monsters with blades for hands and fire for eyes, and when the wind sang its wild song on the night, Ahtau would always say in a low, sombre voice, "They walk tonight." And Attjan's skin would freeze momentarily with a delicious horror, to be savoured because he believed their parents' house was so safe. Then he and Ahtau would laugh together, fearing nothing in the warm darkness of their beds.

As time went on, the childish games had ceased, but sometimes, when the wind called in a hollow voice above the fields, they would talk of Those From Beyond. It was almost impossible to resist, even though it went against the laws of their people. The Wraeththu had not been seen for three generations by any of the people of Long Marn. What proof did they really have that these beings still existed? And yet here

Ahtau lay, a husk amid his damp blankets, barely able to draw breath, the flesh visibly melting from his bones.

How could this happen now? Attjan wondered. He knew from his father's veiled words that Jacob believed the Wraeththu had exhaled a toxic breath from Caracanti to ensorcel Ahtau. But did Attjan believe this himself? He knew it was forbidden even to think of the Wraeththu, and perhaps he and Ahtau had provoked this situation by doing so. They had felt so secure and strong, sneering at the folklore that spoke of how a simple thought of Those From Beyond gave them power over you.

The healer came out of Jacob's dwelling and Attjan was moved to speak to her. His voice sounded absurdly loud. "Is there nothing you can do?"

The woman looked at him in silence, tying a cord around her ritual cloths.

This unsatisfactory reaction brought Attjan's helpless anger to the surface and he spoke without thinking. "It *is* Wraeththu work, then! Why not admit it? When do we cut his throat before they come for him?"

He was unaware of a swift movement behind him, and only realised his father was there when he'd been swung around. For a second, he looked into his father's eyes – his savage, despairing gaze – then Jacob's open hand smacked him hard across the jaw. Attjan was knocked backwards against the wall of the house, where he slumped, dazed.

After a few moments, he picked himself up and ran away to the edge of the wilderness, his eyes streaming silent tears. Here, at the very place where the verdant green of the West Pasture gave way to the rocky stubble of the wilderness rim, Attjan flopped onto his stomach on the bristly ground. His jaw throbbed with pain and his vision was occluded by boiling spots of light. He thought he could see eternal Caracanti shining in the distance, but it was only a cloud, towering in the sky.

The evening meal in Jacob's dwelling was consumed in uneasy silence. Four of the other village elders were present; two couples, Bethy and Orin Wheathook and Sharn and Mirkis Rakehollow. It was clear that they expected an announcement of some kind from their leader. Attjan had come creeping home at sundown, and now sat in a corner of the room, being ignored by his father. His mother had given him a plate of food, which he picked at without appetite, his jaw still painful. Jacob sat at the table, eating slowly and carefully, a thoughtful expression on his face. When he had finished, he drank deeply from a cup of ale set beside his plate. Six pairs of eyes glittered at him fearfully.

Jacob drew in his breath. "There is no hope for Ahtau," he said.

At once, the tension in the room was broken. Mara uttered a choked, sobbing sound, her fingers pressed to her lips. The four elders mumbled in response, without words. In such a situation, words were difficult.

Jacob raised his hand for silence. "I have decided that *something from the wilderness* is responsible for my son's condition," he said. "However, I might be wrong."

Silence fell. It appeared that no-one felt capable of agreeing or disagreeing with his conclusions, although Attjan knew Jacob had merely voiced aloud what others had been whispering behind his back.

"Even if I am wrong," Jacob continued, "it seems to me there is only one way to save Ahtau's life. We do not have the knowledge ourselves, but *others* do."

Mara uttered a shocked sound. She was the first who dared to speak. "What are you suggesting?

Jacob stared above the heads of all present. "Tonight, I will go to the wilderness and beg *them* for aid."

There was a further moment's silence and then – pandemonium. Everyone spoke at once – except for Bethy Wheathook, who remained silent, her arms crossed across her chest. Mara was clearly horrified. Attjan's mouth hung open in mute shock. Jacob seemed to lean away from the onslaught of words, then smashed his fists against the table-top for silence. "I know you think I should go to Ahtau now and end his misery with a knife. I cannot!"

"But Jacob, are you really suggesting we surrender your first-born to... to *them*?" Mirkis Rakehollow enquired, in the most reasonable voice he could muster. "It is unthinkable."

"Our community has survived," his wife Sharn added, "as

many have not. This act would be seen as submission by our people, Jake. You cannot do it. It will crush their spirit."

Jacob shook his head. "No! We will still survive. Do you not understand? I love my boy more than life itself, and I would rather he lived with *them*, than died, than suffered."

Mara put a hand upon his arm. "I love Ahtau too, but I can't bear to think what might happen to him with them. Death would be preferable. You don't know what you're saying. It is grief. It is..."

Orin Wheathook interrupted her. "Jake, the boy might suffer more with them than he does now. You, as much as any of us, know the stories of grotesque mutations and slavery. Is that really a better fate than death? You are clutching at nothing!"

Mirkis nodded vigorously. "Our way has always been death rather than submission," he said. "*They* have stolen our future generations. *They* have slaughtered most of those who escaped humanity's fate. They are *not* our friends, nor our helpers. And we once made a pact between us they would have no more of us. Jake, see sense. Don't be lost in the marsh of emotions. You mustn't give Ahtau to them. You must save him from that fate in the only way we know how. Of course, we understand you might not be able act yourself, but one of us would perform this sacrifice, with honour and humility."

Jacob stared Mirkis in the eye for long uncomfortable seconds. It was clear he was considering what he'd heard. He did not look like a person lost in the marsh of emotions. Eventually, he dropped his gaze, sighed and stood up. His eyes were fixed upon the back wall of the room. "This involves our son, and it is our decision." He glanced at Mara. "Will you hear me out?"

She nodded.

Jacob sighed heavily. "*They* are all the things you said. I don't deny that. But what has befallen Ahtau is not their way. In the past, when they took people, it was simply a siren call that lured our sons from their homes. There was never sickness, never... *this*. Those Beyond the Wilderness either steal or kill quickly, and it has been many years since they have done either of those things. We are nothing to them now, no more than wild sheep grazing on the fields alongside their homes. We are no threat and no attraction. I don't believe that what has befallen Ahtau is their doing. But if any living creature has the power to heal our boy, it is them."

Mara uttered a sad moan and pressed one hand across her eyes.

Jacob laid a hand upon her shoulder. He spoke softly now. "I promise you all that no ill shall come to any of you, or our people. If sacrifice is to be made, I shall make it, not you."

The silence was broken only by the hunger of the flames burning in the home hearth. Then Orin shook his head. "Jake, you are insane. We should bind you with cords to prevent this thing."

"Perhaps he *is* insane," agreed Orin's wife Bethy softly, "but I think that we've been lucky and that sometimes sacrifices *have* to be made. Perhaps, in this instance, the sacrifice is something other than the death of a beloved son."

She addressed Jacob. "I have trusted you for many years, and if your heart speaks to you now, I know it speaks in truth."

She fixed each of her companions with her deep brown stare. "Change is the nature of the world and we resist it at our peril. Although comfort and safety lie in what is known, sometimes situations arise that require the courage to walk into the unknown. I think we have little to lose, for as Jake has rightly said, we are nothing to *them*, tolerated simply because we are not even a nuisance. But perhaps we have something to gain."

She turned her stare upon Jacob. "There is another dreadful thing we must consider. What if others among us should also become afflicted like Ahtau has? Is it not better to seek aid or advice before that happens? We do not know what caused this ailment, but something did. It might be that Those From Beyond would thank us for informing them of what has happened and could prevent further tragedy. We have no way of knowing, not truly, but in my opinion – Jake must follow his heart."

Jacob held Bethy's steady stare, while the other elders considered this for a while. Of all of them, Bethy was the quiet oracle who did not speak much, but when she did it was usually with wisdom. After a minute or so, they grudgingly nodded their heads.

Mirkis sighed and addressed Jacob. "Bethy has voiced a

truth. I still think what you propose is madness, Jake, but if you are determined, I will not stand against you."

"Nor I," said Sharn.

"I trust Bethy's feelings," Orin said, although he did not look too happy about it.

Mara curled a hand around her husband's clenched fists. "They might kill you," she said miserably.

Jacob shook his head and looked down at her. "They never kill us," he said. "Not now. I shall simply go the Western Crossroads and speak aloud, as was the way in the days of our ancestors when the ancient contracts were devised. I shall ask for their aid. They might comply, they might not. They might take Ahtau, they might not. It is a risk we shall have to take. In my heart, I feel the worst outcome is that they will ignore me."

While Mara served hot drinks to her guests, Jacob rose from the table and went out to the porch. It was his custom to smoke his pipe out here in the evenings. Attjan was moved to follow him. "Father," he said. His voice was low but carried easily on the still night air.

Jacob turned. He held out an arm and drew his son towards him as if in apology for what had happened earlier. They stood for a while in silence. Their house faced the village green, where seasonal festivities were held. In its centre was the well that was the heart of their community. It was named Deepest Life. Attjan knew that his great-great-grandfather had sunk that well and that it was a symbol of his people's will to survive. Sometimes at night, it gave off an almost imperceptible blue glow, and it was said that spirits dwelled within it and made the water sweet.

"I'm puzzled," Attjan said. "All my life I've been told that Those Beyond are to be shunned at all costs. Now you say you must go to them. Wouldn't their aid, if they were prepared to give it, be an abomination in the eyes of Mother Land?"

Jacob squeezed his son's shoulder. "Listen to me," he said. "When your great-great-grandfather was very young, people made the world like this. Thoughtlessness, greed and cruelty made the Wraeththu happen." He paused. It was not often that word was spoken aloud. "Humanity flayed their Mother, tore Her skin, infected Her body with disease. No one cared, and something came seeping from the Mother's wounds. A great many somethings, like rats from the cellars of a great burnt out house. Perhaps She made them on purpose, to punish us, to remind us for eternity of all we'd done to Her. Who are we to call Those from Beyond evil or wrong?"

"Does She hate us that much?" Attjan asked, appalled.

"She is our Mother," Jacob replied. "I believe She is mostly sad for us."

"Let me come with you tonight," Attjan said hurriedly. "I can throw a spear. I'll protect you."

Jacob laughed softly and patted Attjan's shoulder. "Throw a spear, eh? Those From Beyond throw spears with their eyes, spears of fire. You must remember that once they coveted the sons of humans. They might not have taken anyone for many years, but that's only because there are few to take nowadays. I can't risk losing you as well, so I won't take you anywhere near them. If Ahtau is taken from us, you must and *will* be the next leader of our people."

Attjan went cold inside. "It sounds as if you don't think they *will* be able to help Ahtau. If so, why bother going to them?"

Jacob rubbed his eyes wearily with one hand. "Even if Ahtau survives, in a way we *will* lose him. I'm sure that if he is cured, Caracanti will have him, if only because the cure itself will reveal too much of them. I didn't speak of this at the table back there, but let me trust you with these words, Attjan. The Wraeththu will ask a price, and that will be Ahtau himself. I have a strong feeling that will be so, but, strange as it might sound, not through ill will, but to protect their secrets."

"Then why...?"

Jacob put a hand over Attjan's mouth. "Hush now. Humanity's day is done, my son. We will never rise to reclaim all that was once ours, and perhaps that is the right way. We will continue here, as we always have, and it is not a bad life, but through Those from Beyond, Ahtau might still have a life too, whatever happens to him."

Attjan stared silently; his father's hand was still over his mouth.

Jacob seemed to remember he'd put it there, and took it away, patted Attjan's shoulder again. "My thoughts are strange to you. They are strange to me too, yet something speaks to me...it feels deep and ancient. I cannot let him die."

Hours later, after the twilight hour, Attjan watched his father walk away from Long Marn, until his figure became a silhouette in the dusk, then not there at all.

In the morning, Jacob came back to the village. His face was set into a weirdly blank expression, but his steps were sure. People saw him come, saw him walk down the main street to the green and the well; many had been watching for him all night. Perhaps watching also for something worse. They came out of their houses and, following Jacob, congregated on the green outside his dwelling, clearly anxious to hear what had transpired in the cold wilderness night. Before entering his house, Jacob paused with his back to them. The people saw his shoulders slump, then rise. He turned to them and said, "They will come." And then he went inside.

The Wraeththu took two days to comply with Jacob's request. On this day, not long after noon, Attjan was squatting on the porch to his home. The day was hot but brooding. Although the sky was clear, it was haunted by the impression of thunder clouds. Long Marn was mostly empty, since the people were at work in the fields. Jacob would not speak of what he'd seen and heard when he'd met with Those From Beyond, and perhaps had been forbidden to. He was anxious, haunted; he renewed all the wards about the house every day. And every day Attjan wondered whether whatever price they must pay would be worth it.

Musing glumly on this matter, Attjan saw two girls run past the house: Merri Wheathook and Janna Fairfly. He became alert at once. The girls' white dresses blew out behind them, along with their hair – auburn and blonde. They kept looking behind themselves, holding on to each other's hands. Jacob wasn't sure whether they were laughing or crying. He stood up.

Tension filled the humid air, which shimmered at ground level and glowed almost blue. A few old people came out of their dwellings, gazed up the street in the direction the girls had come from. Something was coming. The people could feel it. They were drawn in from the fields, perhaps against their will. As they gathered in the centre of Long Marn, three proud, high-stepping horses came towards them from the wilderness road.

Attjan did not want to stare but could not stop himself. His skin prickled, as if he was cold, and his heart beat quickly. The leading horse, a beautiful white creature with a dark nose and black eyes, bore a figure swathed in black cloth. All that could be seen of this individual was his eyes and his booted feet. His two companions were not so disguised. They were tawny-skinned and their hair was white like the coat of the leading horse. They wore silvery-grey cloaks that were draped over their horses' hind quarters. Their eyes seemed to flash in the hot air like amethysts and they were armed. They looked superficially like humans, but there was an ambience about them that suggested otherwise: it might be a smell too subtle to detect with the physical senses. They looked like faery folk, creatures of legend from a distant romantic past that had never existed. They looked like beings from a dream.

Jacob emerged from his house just as the riders were dismounting from their horses. The Wraeththu had come to a halt by Deepest Life, and now the horses stood patiently, shaking their fine heads. Jacob went to the well. Attjan could not hear his father's words, but could read the movements of his body, which seemed at once both accommodating and anxious. The air smelled electric. The figure clothed in black appeared to be paying close attention to what Jacob was saying. He was a leader, certainly; he had an air of command. But why did he hide himself? What did he hide?

Now, the group approached Jacob's home, villagers moving slowly behind them, keeping their distance. Those From Beyond might be seen as the enemy, but their presence conjured curiosity as much as fear. No one had actually seen one of these creatures for generations. Two worlds had overlapped, and somehow it seemed too ordinary, as if it happened every day.

Attjan braced himself against the door of the house. He could flee if he wanted to, but instead he moved carefully to the side, to hide behind the chair where Jacob liked to sit in the evenings. They were passing by him now, so close, and he couldn't smell anything, couldn't hear anything different. What comprised their difference went beyond superficial senses. Two

of them had approached the house; another remained with the
horses upon the green. The Wraeththu swathed in black
mounted the three steps to Jacob and Mara's house. He paused
at the threshold, and then directed one glance at Attjan
crouching behind the old chair. His eyes were dark, his
expression remote, but they were eyes like any seen in a human
face and perhaps more terrible for it. He did not pause long.

After the Wraeththu had gone inside, Attjan covered his face
with his hands. He was filled with a dread compulsion to see
the face beneath those human yet not human eyes. He wanted
to see what lay beneath the cloth. To kill it. No. No. That was
the call of Caracanti. Suddenly afraid of the dark in his mind,
he opened his eyes.

The Wraeththu who had remained outside stood before
him, staring down. His mouth was smiling, but his eyes were
hard, or perhaps it was the other way around. "There is no
need to fear," he said in a low voice.

Attjan could not respond. It was forbidden, wasn't it?
Around him, his neighbours had turned to watch. For a
moment, he was the condensed essence of his community. "I
fear for my brother," Attjan managed to say. "He is very sick."

The Wraeththu nodded. "I would like a drink from your
well" he said. "I feel the water is very good. May I?"

Attjan still wasn't sure if he was doing the right thing by
communicating with this creature, and he could feel keenly the
eyes of his neighbours still upon him. But since childhood he
had been reared to offer hospitality to those in need, and to
share the bounty of his family's hearth. Without speaking, he
got to his feet and went to Deepest Life, where he drew up
clear, cold water. This he poured into a clay cup that was
attached to the well with a chain and offered to the Wraeththu,
who drank freely. His flawlessness was marred only by a white
scare on his long neck, where it showed very prominently
against his tawny skin as he threw back his head to drink. Had
blood once come from that wound? Was it red as human blood,
or like light or fire?

The Wraeththu handed the cup back to Attjan. "Thank you
for your kindness." He inclined his head and strolled back to
the horses.

Attjan felt quite empty. After a few minutes, he walked back to the family home. Here, he went to his room, which was next to Ahtau's. There were many cracks in the wood-panelled walls. Attjan knelt down, his face against the wall, and turned his eyes to spying.

Ahtau's room was filled with an unfamiliar smoke; its scent could have come from another world. Jacob and Mara were not in the room; the Wraeththu had been left alone with Ahtau. The leader began to remove the concealing cloth from his face and body, but moved out of Attjan's line of sight before all was revealed to him.

The leader spoke. "They think we did this," he told the other. "They think us capable of killing flesh like this. And so we were... once." Attjan saw a shadowy dark hand touch his brother's brow. "Fortunately, we are not too late. Asneis, come here to me."

The other paused. "Tiahaar, forgive me... should you be doing this? Send healers... somehar else. It should not be you."

"Why not me?" the leader replied. "I remember we all come from humble beginnings, even if you do not. It was no coincidence it was me who heard when the plea for aid came. I am interested to see where the omen of that leads."

"As you wish, Tiahaar Tashmit." The guard bowed his head and came forward. "I meant no disrespect. Only that generally dedicated healers would be called for such tasks."

The leader had a smile in his voice. "I know that. Sometimes we *have* to intervene, Asneis, and quickly. I know many hara believe the humans should be left unmolested, but to be *humane* sometimes you cannot turn your back."

"You will incept this boy?"

"No. He is in no condition for it. I am puzzled as to what's caused this."

The one called Asneis pursed his lips. "As you said, we were once very capable of killing. Things happened around here, a long time ago, and the taint of it still haunts the land in places. Such taints lie in wait and are triggered when the unwary walk over them."

"It has waited a long time, then. How selective. What intelligence drives such a taint?"

The other shrugged. "I only offer an explanation."

"Well, we shall see. First we should dispel this blight."

"As you wish."

There was a soft crackle, and then more smoke came into the room. The one named Tashmit began to chant in a soft hissing voice. It seemed the smoke danced to the tune of his words, which were of no language that Attjan knew. Those musical yet alien sounds attached to him like an invisible chain. They wound around him, spiralling like a helix, holding him in their grip. He heard voices, his brother's among them. Ahtau was shouting for aid, as if he was lost. Another voice; "Follow the sound, Ahtau. It is the light in your darkness."

Attjan came to his senses suddenly and found himself sitting against the wall of Deepest Life. For a moment, he was disorientated. Surely he had gone inside the house and spied through a hole in the wall? He couldn't remember coming back outside. The entire population of the village appeared to be waiting on the green. Jacob came outside first, followed by the two Wraeththu. For a moment, the Wraeththu leader leaned against the wall of the house. It seemed that whatever he had done had drained him.

Attjan could not remember how, but suddenly he was in front of the creature and a strange voice spoke from his body. "What sort of monster are you? What lies beneath the cloth?" He was aware of his father's hands on his arms and a worried, frantic voice without words in his ear. But he was free. Free, and his rebellious hand tore the cloth from the Wraeththu's face. He gripped the creature's shoulders, feeling its warmth for a moment, before he *saw* what he held.

Within a week, the whole incident was practically forgotten. The people of Long Marn appeared to push it from their minds and got on with the business of living. But subtly, they avoided Attjan and his dark, haunted eyes. They dropped their gaze when they came upon the revived Ahtau walking among them. It was a wonder to Jacob, to them all, that Ahtau was still with them, but maybe Jacob was the only one who was not sorry.

Ahtau had tasted Wraeththu sorcery. Attjan and his family had heard the whispers: one day, *they* would come again, and

Ahtau would walk the streets no more. Was it not better he went now, this living ghost among them? He *had* changed. No one could say how, and perhaps even, in some strange way, they *wanted* the change to be there and therefore made it be, but Ahtau was not quite one of them anymore.

Attjan knew his brother was different, but this did not drive him away. They became closer, avoiding everyone else. Ahtau did not speak of what had happened, and Attjan did not press him. If a time came when Ahtau needed to speak, he would have an ear there waiting for him. Attjan shared the communal feeling that one day his brother would be gone, lost forever to ephemeral Caracanti, the city of mists and dreams. The ache within he felt about that could not be quelled by this newfound, silent closeness.

Neither did Attjan speak of what he had seen when he'd ripped the cloth from the Wraeththu leader's face. But surely others must have seen it too?

One evening, Ahtau and Attjan went out to hunt. Long Marn had no pressing need for meat or furs, since their domestic animals provided well enough, but it was Ahtau's suggestion. Attjan sensed his brother wished to escape the village for a while and was happy to provide company. They went up into the forested foothills of The Lean Guardians, where bears or mountain cats might lurk. But the night was silent, strangely so. Ahtau made them pause on a rocky platform that looked out over the diminishing forest to the east, from whence they'd come. "Build a fire," he told his brother.

Attjan, unquestioning, set about finding branches. A dead thornwrake jutted out from the rock; its white-crusted limbs would do well enough. They cracked like bullets firing as Attjan broke them from the trunk. The night was too quiet, the air humid and heavy on the skin.

Ahtau looked round and made a sound of irritation. Behind him a noiseless trident of lightning broke from the sky and speared the forest. Attjan saw a flare of flame. "A storm comes," he said. "We should find shelter."

"More comes than that," Ahtau said.

Attjan looked up at his brother and for the first time wondered whether in fact the person who stood in front of him was Ahtau at all.

"What comes?" he asked, but he could feel the air stirring around his body; a wind that came from the ground, from the wilderness. But they were far from the wilderness road here; Caracanti lay a long way to the West. This was mountain territory, the home of ancestral spirits and other less clement presences.

"Can't you feel it approaching?" Ahtau murmured. He glanced beyond Attjan, at the stony path that rose up behind them.

Perhaps it was only Ahtau's uncanny words and tone that made the shivery feeling slither up Attjan's spine. They were not alone. "Is it Wraeththu?" Attjan asked, daring to speak the word aloud. "Are they coming for you again?"

"They never came for me. What are you talking about?" Ahtau snapped. "I knew where it lived when it touched me. I knew it rolled down the mountain to lie in the ground."

"What was it?" Attjan asked breathlessly.

Ahtau shook his head, frowning. "Hatred," he answered, "like a hole in the ground that leads out of this world into somewhere dark and cold and utterly without life. Tashmit brought me back. It scarred him, I think. I smelled his blood."

Attjan shuddered at the sound of the Wraeththu's name. "I saw him," he said abruptly. "I tore the cloth from his face. His skin was scaled like a snake. I thought it was a woman. I still wonder that, but the voice..."

Ahtau stared at his brother. "They are not like us," he said. "Don't imagine that they should be."

"What is coming?" Attjan asked. "This hatred you spoke of?"

Ahtau peered over the lip of rock. "You can see," he murmured. "Look."

Attjan went to stand beside him, glanced down. There was an eerie light to the land, which made it easy to see the rocks, the trees, the glint of water between ancient trunks. But there was also a ring of darkness about the hill, darkness that was simply a hungry *absence* of life and light. "It's all around us," Attjan said, "We must leave, do something..."

Ahtau did not seem to be afraid, which in itself added to Attjan's fear. Again, he felt it was not his brother standing beside him. "It is like graves opening," said Ahtau, "the past spilling out." He raised his arms, holding them out to the side, his head thrown back. It seemed almost like a gesture of welcome.

"Ahtau, what must we *do*?" Attjan cried. "We can't stay here. Should we try to run through it?"

Ahtau expelled a snort, but did not lower his arms. "You've seen what happens if we try that."

"Then...?"

"I'm sorry, Yan," Ahtau said, "perhaps it was wrong of me to bring you, but I didn't want to be alone."

"What?" Attjan shrieked. "What?"

The darkness was covering the hillside like a sleeve, creeping ever closer. Attjan had no doubt that once it touched them, they'd be lost.

"I had to pull it out of the earth," Ahtau said. "I'm sorry." Now he threw back his head and closed his eyes. His jaw dropped open and from it came a sound that should not derive from a human body.

Attjan dropped to his knees on the rock, shut his eyes, pressed his hands over his ears. This was madness, a dream. Surely, it could not be real. The echo of Ahtau's cry rang around the mountains like a bell; weirdly beautiful now it was not attached to his body.

"This has to be done," Ahtau said in a chillingly calm voice, "otherwise it will kill everyone, not just our community but everyone else who is left."

"You mean... we let it kill us so others might live?" Attjan asked.

"No," Ahtau said. He turned to his brother, a ghost of a smile across his lips. "I was simply the lure." He raised his head to the sky once more and Attjan could see the planes of his face illuminated by a silky starlight that did not derive from stars, at least not those in the sky above them.

Attjan looked up also and saw a strange whirling shape above him comprised of light, of stars, of mist, perhaps even water. He'd never seen anything like it and lacked the words to describe it, even to himself. This bizarre maelstrom grew larger as he gazed at it, until it burst asunder and something, or a pack of somethings, spewed out of it in a burst of blinding radiance. Attjan smelled ozone, and bizarrely the scent of hyacinth. He crouched down and covered his head with his arms, as what seemed to be immense shapes comprised entirely of stars leapt over him, down into the encroaching shadow.

Ahtau pulled roughly at his brother's arms. "Don't hide your face," he snapped. "Look!"

Attjan did so.

The darkness was like the sea, throwing up black waves, with droplets of black flying off them. Amid this whirled the shapes of white horses, but they were glowing with icy fire, constellations within their semi-transparent bodies. Only one of these creatures bore a rider, a near-naked form with skin like that of a serpent. He wore a veil of shimmering cloth around his hips, nothing more. His black hair was filled with sparks of light and he sang to the creatures he'd brought with him; a high, eerie mantra that made Attjan's skin prickle over his entire body. The star-horses appeared to be devouring the black sea; snapping at it, *eating* it.

"I don't know what I'm seeing," Attjan murmured, clinging to his brother's legs. "What are we seeing?"

"I had to call it out, only me," Ahtau replied. "Then Tashmit can destroy it." Now, he lowered his arms and hunkered down beside his brother, took Attjan's body in his arms.

"You'll leave with him now, won't you?" Attjan murmured, still aware of the ringing cries of the star horses around them, a strange almost mechanical thumping sound, the high clear voice of the Wraeththu who rode the brightest star.

Ahtau laughed. "What makes you think that? I'll be the leader of our people one day. My place is here. Even if I wanted to leave, I couldn't."

"But..."

Ahtau hushed Attjan's words with his hand. "Be silent," he said. "It is over."

Tashmit and his eerie host stood now at the base of the hill. Around them the night was clear. Attjan could see in the trees nearby the fire of animal eyes, creatures drawn to see. They had no fear of the Wraeththu nor of the strange beasts he had brought with him. Now the horses looked more real – perhaps had always been that way – although their startling coats glowed in the starlight, so that it seemed the light came from inside them.

Tashmit turned his horse and waved to Attjan and Ahtau, then he was riding towards them up the precarious trail.

"Thank you, Ahtau," Tashmit called. "That was well done. Not that I had any doubt." Once he reached them, he jumped lightly from his horse's back.

"My brother fears you will steal me away," Ahtau said, his grin so wide Attjan found it insulting.

The Wraeththu laughed. "Well, I understand this fear." He looked Attjan in the eye. "The time has come for change," he said. "But first I must explain something. Come, let's sit."

The three of them arranged themselves around the fire Attjan had made, which he now fed with more wood. Ahtau produced an earthenware jar of his mother's berry wine, which he passed to Tashmit. Inclining his head in thanks, Tashmit uncorked it and took a swig. "Now that is a taste of early autumn," he said. "Very fine."

"Last year's batch," Ahtau said.

Tashmit handed the jar to Attjan. "You know, of course, there has never been commerce between our people and yours," he said.

Attjan nodded. "You used to steal and kill." As soon as he'd said those words, he wished he hadn't.

"That was a long, long time ago," Tashmit said. "Those times live in the memory of your people more than they should."

"Perhaps because we were the ones who lost most by it," Attjan couldn't help saying.

Tashmit nodded thoughtfully. "Not all hara – Wraeththu – wanted to destroy humanity entirely. We knew their time was done, and that was not our doing, but what was meant to be. The next step. Evolution of the world. But my race was birthed in blood and screams as much as any human child. The transition was not... easy." He fixed Attjan with a stare. "You might want to take a swig of that wine before I continue."

Attjan grimaced and did so. The autumn fire of it warmed his flesh.

"Some of us became guardians," Tashmit said. "All that you see around you, to the invisible perimeters of your territory, is

the world we gave to you, that we created for you. This place...
it was never upon the Earth. That's not where we are."

Attjan stared at Tashmit in silence, then said inadequately,
"What?"

"It is... another realm, another world, if you like. We created
this copy of Earth for you, untouched, untainted, but perhaps
we were not careful enough. We took from Earth some
lingering parasites perhaps, parasites of consciousness. That is
what Ahtau unwittingly ran into. It was an evil that had lain
dormant for many generations."

Attjan shook his head. "But this is real, this is home..."

"Of course it is," Tashmit said gently. "The only thing you
didn't know about it was that it was not quite *where* you
thought it to be." He reached out and briefly touched Attjan's
arm. "We were never your enemies here, Attjan, although we
believed it was in your people's best interest to believe us so.
We wanted you to continue as you were, and if we'd shared the
new world with you, that would not have been possible."

Attjan blinked. "Like animals in a farmyard or in the zoos
humans once had," he said.

Tashmit nodded once. "Yes, it might be seen like that.
Preserved, a rare species. This is the nature reserve in which
you live safely." He paused. "Your people have been here a lot
longer than you think."

Tashmit's words were shocking, and yet Attjan was aware
that in some ways he felt relief, as if a burden had been lifted. It
was as if he'd suddenly been given proof of the existence of
benevolent gods; they'd been cared for all along. He shook his
head, laughed shakily, then glanced at his brother. "How long
have you known this? Since you were sick?"

Ahtau nodded. "Tashmit told me everything then."

"It was because I could not conceal it, given how I had to
pull him back," Tashmit said. "There's another thing I'd like
you know. I've been involved in the maintenance of your
community for around fifty years, and almost since the
beginning I've had doubts about the way things have been run.
Luckily, it was me who heard your father's call when Ahtau fell
ill. It might have gone differently if certain other of my
colleagues had received it." Tashmit grimaced. "But that is not
your concern. I heard it, and here I am."

"Are you not ruler of your people?" Attjan asked.

Tashmit laughed. "By the dehara, no! I am ruler of my own small office, I suppose." He shook his head, still smiling. "Anyway, I have since spoken at length with those who *do* govern our city, and have persuaded them that your people should no longer be kept in ignorance. It might be that now we can help you repopulate. The danger always was that if our species should mingle, share our means of travel between worlds, your young would leave home and seek to become Wraeththu. Sometimes it is not just the whims of nature that can destroy a community but the lure of what is beyond it. That is why we instilled within you the belief that we were... evil... that inception to Wraeththu was a terrible thing."

"Why would any child born of our people not want it?" Ahtau asked. "Humans are frail vessels as you've show me so plainly. You can't force people to remain that way if there is an alternative, an evolution, as you call it."

"I know," Tashmit said. "That is the dilemma."

"I will stay," Ahtau said. "I've already told you this, but I can't speak for everyone, nor those who might be born to us."

"We can only let events unfold," Tashmit said. "It might be the preservation of your species is at an end, being a conceit on our part, or a misguided delusion."

"We will go back to our people," Ahtau said. "We shall come down the mountain with the knowledge, as was the way in so many old stories."

Tashmit smiled. "There is a sweet mythic quality to it, I agree," he said. "But first, you might remember from other old tales how those who met angels on the mountainside were often given glimpses of the cities of angels, sights they could not adequately describe with the words available to them. Would you like to see my city?"

"Yes!" Attjan said at once, although part of him was aghast he so readily accepted as truth all that this inhuman creature had said to him.

Ahtau laughed. "I might've known. My brother has always been headstrong and rash."

"Would you like to see it, Ahtau?" Tashmit asked.

Ahtau paused for a few seconds, then shook his head. "No. I'm to stay here. I would love to see it, but... no."

Tashmit nodded. "There will be a time, have no fear." He stood up. "Come Attjan, choose a *sedu* and climb onto his back."

"A... *sedu*? The horses?"

"Yes, but not quite horses as you know them. Come." Tashmit remounted and turned his beast with a light touch of his hand upon its neck.

Attjan felt as if his feet weren't truly on the ground. Perhaps he would soon wake from this strange fever dream. But then the dark eyes of a *sedu* were upon him and he swore he heard a whisper inside his head saying: *Come ride the stars with me...*

He went to the creature, plunged the fingers of his left hand into its thick mane and vaulted onto its back. At once a ripple of energy coursed through him; he felt... *connected.* There was no other word.

Hold tight... whispered the voice in his head. *Hold tight and I will not let you fall.*

The air around them was swirling, fracturing, creating patterns that could be felt rather than seen. The scent of hyacinth and ozone was building up again.

Attjan saw his brother's face: serene, contemplative. He raised his hand in farewell, and a wave of love passed between them. Ahtau had paid the ultimate sacrifice for being healed, but it was the opposite of what his people thought. Staying with them was the sacrifice.

And then the stars began to sing and far galaxies were pulsing against Attjan's inner eye. Reality opened to him, to countless new realities, and he was on his way to a city of fiery rivers and radiant thrones, to the unimaginable dream of all dreams.

A Tour of the House

The house had not been lived in for over a decade, yet somehow, even as a museum or a place of learning, it still retained an ambience of homeliness. *We Dwell in Forever.* But the hara who had so named the house were long gone.

Gred stood in the doorway, shaking the rain from his umbrella, water dripping from the tendrils of his long dark hair that hung over, or were stuck to, his face. A har standing beside the reception desk indicated his umbrella should be placed in a stand with several others. Water pooled on the cream marble floor. Outside the sky was blue-grey with summer storm, while the foliage of the soaring ancient trees was acid green against it. Within the house, the double-doors of highly-polished oak stood open to the day, but the hallway was dark, smelling of rain and trodden grass.

"May we take your bag, Tiahaar," the employee asked, and Gred handed over his modest luggage. "We'll be happy to hold this for you until your visit is over."

"Thank you."

The har glided off and secreted the bag in a store room behind the reception area.

Relieved of this minor burden, Gred looked around himself. Other visitors were clustered around the desk, looking at informational guideleafs. A soft-voiced guide, dressed in a uniform of moss green tunic and loose trousers, was gathering a group of hara together, ready for the next tour of the house. Gred decided grudgingly to join them. He had travelled far on this pilgrimage. He had wanted to visit for so long. Part of him resented having to share the experience with so many others. But he was just a tourist, like them. There would be no special privileges.

The tour would begin in five minutes. Gred closed his eyes briefly, a ghost at the edge of the crowd. He thought about the feet that had walked these marble tiles, that had descended the sweeping stairs ahead. He thought of the tragedies and romances of history, wrapped up in legend.

"We shall start with the lower west wing," the guide said.

The group turned as one towards a corridor that led off to the left and followed the guide, who moved slowly, allowing everyhar to absorb the surroundings, examine the fittings, the pictures on the walls, the atmosphere itself.

"The house was built in the style of the type of country mansion found in ancient Alba Sulh," said the guide. "During the human era, this estate was undoubtedly occupied by a moneyed family attempting to emulate the lives of Sulhian gentry."

A soft ripple of laughter spread through the group.

The guide smiled indulgently at the follies of the past. He paused before a painting. "The hara who came to inhabit this house during the Upheaval were susceptible to the same impulses. Here, for example, is a portrait of our tribe founder, Terzian, with his horse and dogs. In style, it resembles the antique paintings of high-ranking humans that would have been found in all the large houses of ancient times, especially in Alba Sulh. There are many pictures within the house in this style. Useful for us, because they tell us much about the hara who lived here."

The artist had captured a day very similar to today, Gred thought. Early summer, searing green foliage, a purple sky gravid with storms. And Terzian, young and proud, his yellow hair a shock of corn against the bark of an old oak. His horse; the whites of its eyes showing, yet standing calm. At Terzian's feet lay the hounds, looking up at him, tongues lolling. This was a har who had built a tribe, slaughtered thousands, human and hara alike. Long dead, but living in a picture. Gred wondered if the portrait had hung in the house following Terzian's death or whether it had been very recently brought out from storage, unwrapped from dusty cloth, simply for the benefit of tourists.

"Do any of the family still occupy any of the rooms?" somehar asked.

The guide shook his head. "No. Although the family have only recently donated this property to the Megalithican Heritage Trust, no Parasilians have occupied it for at least eighty years. Until about ten years ago, it was used as a centre for the Galhean Arts Brotherhood, who lacked the funds or resources – or indeed inclination – for proper upkeep. The family did little to maintain their ancestral home. We still have much restoration work to do."

"Why did they leave?" Gred asked.

"Marlet har Parasiel had a new house built for the family following his chesna-bond to Ambel har Unneah. Some say he was plagued by ghosts..."

Again, a ripple of laughter.

The guide made a languid gesture with one hand. "In fact, he thought it time for the family to move away from the past and the looming shadows of those who had come before. Megalithica had changed, as had Galhea. History, especially of the volatile kind associated with the early Parasilians, should remain in a museum. This is what the house has become."

Madness, Gred thought. *How could anyhar leave this place, its ghosts, its histories? Somehar having no imagination or no heart.*

The guide was gazing at Gred speculatively. "It is rather like reading a novel," he said. "The stories are romances, probably less than half true. Nohar wants to live in a story. The new house is very beautiful. Parts of it are open to viewing twice a year." His smile had become somewhat tighter. "Now, shall we continue? To our left is the family sitting room."

Most of it was roped off to protect the elderly carpets and furniture. A small area was provided for everyhar to crowd into. There was a smell of ancient dust, perhaps caught in the heavy drapes at the windows, which were tall and with wide sills, where hara might once have sat to gaze out at the gardens, the long driveway, lined by poplars, which wound towards the town. There was also a green smell; a whiff of pine. In the fireplace, long unused, was a vase, filled with a glorious display of evergreens: several species of ivy twined around sprays of fir branches and sprigs of holly. The guide indicated this. "The foliage display you see was a tradition upheld by the family in remembrance of Tiahaar Cobweb, who was Terzian's consort in the early days of the house and subsequently lived here for nearly three centuries. We have reinstated this tradition."

"Why is it in the fireplace?" somehar asked. "Did they burn it as a tradition too?"

Yet more laughter.

The guide was grinning now. "No, it originally stood upon a side table between two of the windows. When we took over the place, there was still a fragmenting old display there that had perhaps remained from the days of family occupation."

"Did you keep it?" Gred asked.

"The display is replaced regularly," the guide replied. He sniffed dismissively. "Members of the family who were in residence would meet here in the evenings. It was sometimes used to entertain guests known well to the Parasilians. An informal room."

Two large unyielding sofas, several stiff padded chairs; all looked uncomfortable and far from informal to Gred. "Are these the original furnishings?" he asked.

The guide shook his head. "Unfortunately, the original furnishings that remained were beyond repair. The items you see here are our attempt to recreate the room as it once was. They came from another house we care for." He rubbed his hands together. "Come, we have the dining-room and the main reception salon further along this corridor."

As the group moved on, Gred lingered a moment, gazing back into the room. Here, Cobweb had sat upon the floor before the fire, perhaps sketching in one of his notebooks. Many of those remained. One was on display in the museum in Immanion, held open at a page, under glass. You couldn't touch it. Gred held out his hand to the air of the room. It was all still here, just a little.

"Tiahaar?" The guide was calling him.

"Excuse me," Gred said. He caught up with the rest.

In fact, there was very little left of the original appointments. Megalithican Heritage had filled the rooms with furniture that belonged elsewhere, to other lives. What was the point of trying to emulate the past when the pieces were merely mismatched impositions? Empty rooms would have been better or even the rotting remains of what the Trust had found when the house had opened its doors to them and let them in. Cobweb might have approved of the Galhean Arts Brotherhood. No doubt they had made a mess, not cared at all about maintaining an image of the past. They had just lived here.

The original mahogany dining table remained, although the guide complained it had to be covered with a cloth, since the GAB had used it as a cutting table for various projects and had ruined the surface irreparably. The guide talked about what a magnificent piece it had once been. Gred wondered why the Trust hadn't replaced it. He nearly said so, but held his tongue. Places were set for diners as the Trust assumed they would have been. Multiple sets of cutlery, several different glasses for several different wines. Delicate, gilt-edged crockery.

Gred could only think of gloves left on the table, and books, some pencils, a few feathers and stones from the garden that harlings had brought in to show the family. Crumbs on the table cloth, knives smeared with butter laid across plain white plates. Cold cups of coffee, half drunk. This was what he'd always imagined when he'd heard stories of the past; he had always felt he'd 'seen' beyond the dry facts into these colourful lost lives. He was quite sure the Parasilians would never have eaten off the polished table, except when distinguished visitors were present. Most of the time, it would have been swathed in rough white linen. Gred thought of shoes kicked off beneath the chairs. Mud traipsed in from the stable yard. He thought of laughter. Sullen silences. An argument. A reunion. Simmering lust. A sharp-tined fork plunged into a hand. He knew that story, how Tigron Calanthe, long before he became Tigron, when he was still mad, had stabbed Terzian with a fork in this room. The Varrs had sheltered Cal when he'd needed sanctuary. In their way, they had helped save him. News had come to this room also, as the family had sat to eat breakfast or dinner. Gred could visualise the door flying open, somehar rushing in with something to say. Sometimes something bad.

In the reception room, with its views of the terrace where urns still stood, resplendent with ferns, the guide talked about how the Parasilians had entertained there. "Terzian initiated the custom for all the seasonal festivals to be celebrated here at the house. Hara from Galhea were invited, and festivities were held outdoors so that everyhar from the local community could be accommodated. Within the house, high-ranking hara, their friends and family, plus members of Terzian's militia, would gather in this room. The family maintained this tradition until they moved to their new residence. The Galhean Arts

Brotherhood, of course, did not continue it."

"Do the family still hold these festivities in their new home?" somehar asked.

"The house is open twice a year for viewing," the guide replied. "Those times coincide with a couple of festivals and there is some entertainment provided in the grounds during the evening. I believe there is a guideleaf about it in the entrance hall."

"I suppose all the famous hara of the early days of Wraeththu came here at some point," somehar else said. "Would Tigron Pellaz have been in this room?"

The guide nodded. "Undoubtedly. He visited the family before he became Tigron, and thereafter remained a constant friend, especially to Tiahaar Cobweb, who was often an advisor to him."

Gred smiled to himself. So few words to describe such a huge history. *"Visited the family before he was Tigron..."* This idiot had no idea. Gred gazed about the room from beyond the tasselled ropes that kept everyhar away from where events had actually happened. He closed his eyes and inhaled. This room would always be redolent of Natalia, the winter festival. The flames would have been ferocious in the imposing fireplace. The sideboard to the left of the room would have been heaped with traditional, seasonal fare. The air would have been heavy with the scents of mulled wine and sheh. And among the guests, a thousand embers of feeling.

It was true that the Aralisians, the ruling dynasty of Immanion, had often spent Natalia here, especially so in the later years of Pellaz's reign. Galhea had become the capital of Megalithica eventually, the small agricultural town expanding into the metropolis it was today. In those days, the house had been on the edge of the town. Now its hill was surrounded by roads and parks and suburbs. The Parasilians and the Aralisians, separated by an ocean, remained close allies if not close friends. Yet the magic had somehow seeped away from that famous alliance. The characters who played the stage today were not the towering, vibrant creatures of history, who had shaped early Wraeththu, who had bled for it.

The guide broke into Gred's thoughts. "You are a student of history?" he asked, somewhat archly. He must have noticed

Gred's absorption in the house.

"In an amateur fashion," Gred replied.

"You are from Almagabra?" Was that a slight note of accusation? Gred's accent coupled with his olive skin must have given him away.

Gred smiled, inclined his head. "Yes, I am. As you can imagine, Galhea holds great interest for my harakin. It is a large part of our heritage, or shall I say our *combined* heritage, since for Parsics, this area is also of great significance." That sounded too pompous.

The guide had narrowed his eyes. "You are Gelaming, then."

Gred was tempted to lie. "That is my tribe, yes."

"Then naturally this area holds racial memories for you," the guide said dryly. "The Gelaming concentrated their efforts in Galhea, especially after the death of Terzian."

"I thought that Imbrilim was their centre, to the south," Gred said. "The Varrs, then later the Parasilians, always maintained control of Galhea." So far, the term Varr had not been mentioned in the tour speech.

"Superficially, yes," the guide replied. He perhaps became aware how the tour group was starting to feel uncomfortable and smiled brightly, raised his voice. "The history of this area is colourful, but again much of the detail has been embellished over time. Shall we move on?"

The group visited Terzian's private office, a small room, now empty but for a desk and chair. The guide did not speak about how some of the greatest decisions of Megalithican history had been made in this room, nor that it had been Terzian's son Swift's office for a great deal longer than it had been his father's. The guide did mention that the desk and chair were original, though.

From there, the group moved on to the domestic quarters, the kitchens and laundry. These had been reconstructed and filled with copper pans and other antique-looking artefacts. Wax vegetables and fruit were placed neatly on the table.

While the guide spoke about the day to day running of the house and what tasks the staff had engaged in, Gred stared at the table. It too was original. He tried to think of festival times, when the kitchens had been busy and fragrant with cooking, but all he could see in his mind's eye was a time of panic and fear. The attack on Galhea by the Teraghast tribe was fairly well-documented, and Gred had read all he could find on the subject. Now, he could only visualise the body of Ithiel Penhariel har Varr laid out this table, his throat cut. He'd been killed in the town when the Teraghasts had attacked it, all those centuries ago. Hara had brought him here, the house's defender. It had been a time when grim decisions had been made. Swift had been absent then, dealing with the aggressors further afield. Gred visualised Cobweb, Swift's hostling, alone and frightened, having to rally his hara round him in the face of limitless threat. This house had died for a while after those times, when the Teraghasts had sacked it, and the family had been forced to flee into temporary exile.

Some of the Parasilians had remained Varrs at heart, Gred had no doubt. He could not think of a figure like Ithiel, such a prime if quiet mover in the early days, Terzian's right-hand har, becoming Parsic in anything but name. They could call their tribe something else to hide the past, but it had never left them, not really. Perhaps that was another reason why Marlet had built his new domain, on the other side of the town, far beyond the river, surrounded by trees. This hill could not be seen from there.

There were no roped-off areas in the kitchens and the tour group was free to walk through the rooms and touch things. Two hara brought refreshments on a tray – the traditional local sheh liqueur and hot tea for those who preferred it. Gred took a glass of sheh. He smelled it but didn't drink it. He wandered from room to room. Part of him wanted to weep, another part simply wanted to sneak off like a harling and explore the rest of the house on his own. The guide, no doubt, would notice.

Once the refreshments had been consumed, the tour continued. Now the group was taken upstairs to view the bedrooms. To Gred this seemed slightly voyeuristic. However, the reality of what he saw banished that feeling. The rooms looked twee, too tidy, and again furnished with items from other houses. Cobweb's chamber held no feeling of him, and neither did Terzian's. The group was shown the bedroom used by Swift before he came of age, and the quarters of Tyson and Azriel, other sons of the house. Strange how so many hara had lived in these rooms since those times, yet they were still referred to as belonging to their original occupants. Gred thought of later Parasilian harlings lying awake at night, besieged by history. It must have lived on here. It must have haunted the place. In many ways.

"The attics were only opened up and refurbished following the siege of Galhea," the guide said, as he led the group towards the narrow staircase that led to the upper story. "When the family returned to Galhea, they found the house had been badly damaged. Tiahaar Cobweb had parts of the attic converted into a studio, as he was something of an artist. He also commissioned a new apartment for himself up here."

Is it going to be mentioned he made a chesna-bond with an Aralisian, Snake har Aralis, Pellaz's own brother in fact?

"Tiahaar Swift, who was by then Archon of Galhea, took over the east wing on the first floor with his immediate family."

No, didn't think so...

Gred felt cheated of the experience he'd wanted to have, but for that he'd have had to be alone. Two great Wraeththu dynasties had combined in this house. Battles of many kinds had been fought and won, or fought and lost. But the years had not nurtured the alliance of the two houses. Now they were only the most distant of relatives, and there was an undeniable distaste of the Gelaming branch on this side of the ocean. It was reflected within the entire tribe, hence the guide's frostiness upon discovering Gred's origins. No mention was made of the Aralisians who had once called *Forever* home: most importantly Cal, then Snake and his son Moon, who had formed a chesna-bond with Tyson har Parasiel. To Gred, it felt like these hara had been erased from the house's history, undoubtedly because of being Aralisian. In part, perhaps the Gelaming's reputation as relentless conquerors was deserved. But that had been only the start. If it hadn't been for that great alliance, perhaps the world would be a different place now, and not a better one. The guide had alluded many times to history being rewritten with a romantic slant, but it seemed clear that in Galhea it had been rewritten in more than one way.

The guide led the group back downstairs; the tour was over. He told everyhar about the restaurant in the converted stables, and where maps could be found for those who wished to explore the gardens.

But there was one final sight to be shown before the group left the house. This was a reception room off the entrance hall, somewhat unprepossessing and allegedly used rarely by the family at any time in its history. The guide said that Terzian and Swift might have met lesser dignitaries in this room or received messengers. But it was famous now for only one reason and that was because a portrait of Cobweb hung over the fireplace. Why it had been placed here, in this unloved corner, Gred couldn't guess. Perhaps once it had lived in another room.

The tour group expressed an audible gasp when they saw it, perhaps even those who'd seen it before.

"Yes, it is magnificent, and strangely bewitching," said the guide. "It was commissioned by Tiahaar Swift when his hostling was one hundred years old."

The portrait was of a willowy har with pale luminous skin and abundant black hair, dressed in flowing garments of pale green. He was depicted sitting upon a stone wall in a dark and secluded corner of the gardens. He seemed to shine from the picture, his deep brown gaze at once melancholy and whimsical.

"Is it... embellished, do you think?" somehar asked. "I mean, was he really that... arresting?"

"There are other pictures," the guide replied. "I think we can safely say that Tiahaar Cobweb was indeed as beautiful as the legends say."

Gred went to the restaurant and ate a late lunch of very good cold roast chicken and salad. He drank one large glass of the local sparkling wine, made from 'flowers of the field' as the menu said. He sat alone, his mind strangely empty. Outside, the sky had cleared a little, and the wet stones of the courtyard beyond the window of the restaurant gleamed and sparkled in sunlight. Gred had picked up a map of the gardens. He was savouring the moment before he began the last part of his tour, this time thankfully without company.

First, he visited the lake with its blanket of water lily pads and cuffs of yellow orris. A mass of huge orange and silver fish haunted the banks, expectant of food from the tourists. To Gred they looked like entrails, squirming and tangled as they were.

He had nothing to throw to them. The sun was hot now, although dark clouds still roamed the distant sky. A shimmer of steam rose from the lawn as Gred walked barefoot across it, his sandals dangling from one hand. The umbrella was a nuisance, awkward and damp beneath an arm. He walked around the lake towards a folly of tumbled stones. Here, evergreens scented the air. Gred put his sandals back on. The stones were rough beneath his feet, sometimes sharp. He was surrounded by 'presence'; he could put no word to it other than that. If he concentrated hard enough, could he summon the past to him like moving pictures? He wanted to know everything about the hara who had lived here in the distant past, but most of the details were lost. He felt Wraeththu had a tendency to tidy away their history, embarrassed by their early heritage, tainted as it had been by the humanity that had lingered in the harish psyche.

He saw the summerhouse as shards of whiteness through the trees. No other tourists had come to this spot as yet, perhaps most were still engrossed in leisurely meals at the restaurant. The summerhouse was round, its wood painted ivory. Within was a central pool with a fountain. Water spattered onto the stone bench that surrounded it. Gred sat down and closed his eyes, listening to the music of the water. His heart felt swollen with love. *I was born into the wrong time,* he thought. He yearned for the passions of the past. At thirty-five years old, very young by harish standards, he felt momentarily ancient, displaced in time. He sighed, opened his eyes, and found that somehar was sitting next to him. He physically jumped and uttered a smothered cry.

"Excuse me, I startled you," said the har beside him. This har was dressed in clothes of dark green, perhaps an employee of the Trust, since his garb resembled their uniform. He had very long black hair, covering him like a shawl. He did not turn to face Gred, which seemed a little odd.

"It's fine," Gred said. "I was lost in my thoughts, didn't hear anyhar come in here."

"It has always been a place for meditation – of one kind or another." The har laughed softly.

"I've been on the tour," Gred said. "I was hoping for more history."

Now the har turned to face him and Gred's chest contracted. For a moment, he could not draw breath. That face. Those eyes. "You are... you are Parasilian?"

The har nodded. "Yes. I expect the family resemblance is obvious. As is yours, of course."

"Er... mine?"

"Aralisian, yes?" Again, the har laughed. He reached out and touched Gred's arm briefly. "Don't worry. I won't tell a living soul."

Gred risked a smile, although he was feeling light-headed now, disorientated. "That is probably for the best. Do you work here?"

"No, I just watch them."

The har must be quite old, Gred decided. He had a translucent quality to him, which was often seen in older hara: the slow fading to spirit. But the resemblance to hara like Cobweb and Swift was shocking. Gred hadn't expected that. His mind was a maelstrom. He should use this moment to ask for information and stories, but his tongue was a stone in his mouth. He felt shaken in a peculiar way.

"I'm glad you came back," said the har.

"I... this is the first time I've been here."

"That's not what I meant. You should visit the family. I can tell you haven't."

"They moved from here," Gred said. He felt that was reason enough to explain why he hadn't visited them.

"*Forever* is a leaky old place," said the har. "Don't think too badly of Marlet. I try not to. Anyway, the Meglets probably look after the place far better than we ever did."

"Meglets!" Gred laughed. His unease was fading. "It's such a pity they've rammed the rooms full of things that don't belong here, though. I would have preferred emptiness to that."

"Well, they have to earn enough funds to maintain the place. Most visitors want a theme park, not reality. Marlet and Ambel took most of the furniture with them to Murmur Heights. You'll see more to your taste there, I'm sure. And they *will* talk to you, if that's what you want." The har touched Gred's arm briefly again. "Perhaps it's time for old alliances to be rekindled."

"I wonder why they ever faded. I sometimes think it might

be because hara are embarrassed about the past, don't want to be reminded of it."

"It's not just that," said the har. "Things happened over the years. Petty arguments. Differences of opinion. The Parasilians didn't want Immanion to have its fingers in the Megalithican pie. And by that time, all the original players were gone. Emotional attachments were gone. But I do think Marlet would be open to patching things up a little. Times change."

"Yes. Thank you." Gred paused. "Perhaps I could go to the Heights with *you*?" He wondered if that was too presumptuous.

The har studied him for a second. "I stay here mostly," he said. "You don't need me to guide you. Just say I sent you."

"Who... sent me?" Gred asked.

"They'll know." The har stood up. "It will rain soon. You'd better set off." These words were clearly a dismissal.

Gred also got to his feet. "I will. Thank you. It was... very interesting to meet you."

The har inclined his head. "Pleasure to meet you too." He walked to the door and out into the green light.

Gred couldn't follow. He was rooted to the spot. Then the rain came and he was released. Outside, he opened his umbrella and fled back to the house to retrieve his luggage.

Gred took a float car to Murmur Heights. He wasn't sure if this was really the right thing to do or what kind of welcome he might expect. But the strange har in the summer house had affected him deeply. He kept trying to dismiss the thought he'd met a ghost, but it nagged at him seductively.

There were guards at the gates to the Heights, to whom Gred presented his identification. The guards appraised him warily. Aralisians on Galhean soil again? They did not obstruct him unnecessarily, however. It seemed there was little fear in this land of hara who might wish the family ill.

The front door to the Heights was opened by a har in a green uniform of flowing garments, much like the uniform of the Trust employees and the har he'd met in the summerhouse. Rather stiffly, Gred told this har who he was and that he hoped that the family would not mind that he'd come to visit.

"Come in," said the har. "This is a surprise. I'll tell Tiahaar

Ambel at once. Tiahaar Marlet is not at home." He gestured for Gred to come into the hall. It was indeed a beautiful house, full of light. "Allow me to take your coat, bag and umbrella."

Gred shrugged off his coat and handed the items over.

"Thank you. Please sit here. I won't keep you waiting long."

Gred sat down on the chair indicated to him. He felt slightly breathless.

Presently, a tall mature har, with a plait of chestnut hair hanging heavily over one shoulder, and an open, good-natured face, came into the hall. He was dressed in loose tunic and trousers of a colour to match his hair. "Hello. I'm Ambel har Parasiel. I believe you are a relative, if somewhat distant!"

Gred stood up, bowed his head. "Yes, Tiahaar. Thank you for receiving me. I am Gred har Aralis."

The har waved an arm at Gred. "Hush. No need for formalities. What brings you to our home?"

He gestured for Gred to follow him, and Gred noticed how similar this house was in layout to Forever. They would turn left and presently come to the family sitting room, and they did.

"I've always been interested in the history of our two families," Gred explained. "And then I had the time for a protracted holiday and thought I'd come over here. I went to *Forever* today."

"Fascinating place, isn't it?" Ambel said. He indicated Gred should sit down on one of the sagging old sofas, which embraced him like loving arms. "I've ordered tea for us. It won't be long."

"*Forever* is a wonderful house," Gred said. "But then, so is this one."

Ambel looked around him. "Yes... In some ways, we were sad to leave *Forever*, but it is a... *heavy* place. We both thought it was better for the younger generations to have a new home, somewhere lighter and not so damn haunted." He laughed.

"Really haunted?"

"But of course. What can you expect? It was never *our* house, Gred. Not really. It belonged, and still belongs, to the hara who created our tribe and who shaped early Wraeththu. It's right that the house is now for everyhar. It's their history."

"I felt there wasn't enough of it there."

"Well, there's so *much* of it, and the Trust don't like to dwell on the melodrama, as they see it. We have plenty of old pieces here that we brought from the house, if you want to see them. Marlet will be back soon. He can show you his collections. But I warn you; it can be boring after a couple of hours!"

"Thanks. I'd like that, and I *won't* be bored."

"You must stay here, of course. Have you booked into a hotel in town?"

"Not yet, no. That's kind of you."

"Kind?" Again, Ambel laughed. "Don't be ridiculous! We'll want the gossip from Immanion too. There's a lot to talk about." He paused. "Marlet was only recently thinking of contacting Sahaan, you know. We wondered if overtures would be welcome."

Gred grimaced. "If you contact anyhar, make it Tulsel. Sahaan is not the most affable of hara. Tulsel is. He's my high-father."

"Well now we've contacted you, so we're halfway there," Ambel said. "What a fortunate coincidence!"

"Somehar... somehar told me to come here. He told me to say he'd sent me. One of your relatives. I met him at *Forever*."

Ambel frowned slightly. "Oh, who was that? I can't think of anyhar who'd be over there today."

"He didn't give me his name, but he was an older har. He looked very Parasilian, if you know what I mean. It sounds mad, but I did wonder if he was a ghost, to be honest."

Ambel drew in his breath, rolled his eyes. "I see. Why am I not surprised?" He shook his head. "He's a stubborn old beast. He won't leave, you know. His rooms here are barely touched."

"You mean it's somehar who still lives at *Forever*? The tour guide said all the family had left."

Ambel paused a moment. "Technically, we did. The har you met is not a ghost, but he might as well be. It was Cobweb."

Gred couldn't speak for a moment, and yet he had known all along really. "That's impossible. Surely?"

"He won't leave this world, Gred. He should, but he won't. Don't ask me why. Everyhar else has gone to wherever they go. He's not like us. He's not wholly *here*. He doesn't really have to 'live' anywhere."

"But nohar lives that long. Do they?"

Ambel shrugged. "Like I said, he's not quite *with* us. It's not something we talk about with outsiders. As far as everyhar else is concerned, Cobweb faded nearly a century ago. He keeps himself to himself most of the time. But he would have seen Pellaz in you, no doubt, so decided to communicate."

"Does the Trust know he's still... *haunting* the place?"

"Not officially, no. Marlet has told him he shouldn't hang around there during the tourist season, but I suspect that the Trust secretly likes the idea of ghosts. The visitors would no doubt relish it. I expect Cobweb does manifest from time to time when the mischief takes him."

"Does he ever come here?"

"Sometimes, usually just to make me jump. I'll be in the house or the gardens then suddenly he's there beside me, criticising whatever I'm doing, or complaining about the Trust, or demanding I make him a meal. He doesn't have to eat much, but occasionally enjoys the experience of good food. I sometimes think he's still around because he's just too stubborn and awkward to move on. He's not sad, though, and that's the important thing. If he's happy, he can do as he likes, in my opinion."

"This is hard to take in," Gred said.

"Understandable," Ambel said airily. "We're just used to him. I realise it must be rather a shock. Which is no doubt what Cobweb intended. I'd be grateful if you didn't talk about this too much. We don't want to attract attention to Cobweb. He's persistent but in some ways fragile."

"Of course. I'll be discreet." Gred smiled. "I'd give anything to be able to talk to him properly, though."

"Who knows? He might comply. He might not. I can't predict. Ah, here is Zaya with our tea. You've met our housekeeper, of course."

The har who'd let Gred into the house had appeared with a tray.

"Do join us, Zaya," Ambel said. "Gred has had a Cobweb experience over at Forever."

Zaya pulled a humorous face. "Oh dear. Nothing too alarming, I hope."

"Not at all," Gred replied. "I want to say... without sounding too sentimental... that I'm really glad I've been welcomed here. I wasn't sure what to expect."

"I suspect this wariness has maintained the distance between our kin long after any stupid arguments in the past were long forgotten," Ambel said. "I'm also glad you came, or that Cobweb interfered enough to send you to us."

When Marlet came home, he was not alone, and suddenly the Heights was filled with noise. Hara and dogs spilled into the room where Gred still sat with Ambel. Introductions were made; a list of names and a sea of faces Gred could not remember. Hounds jumped up at him, eager to lick his face. He felt slightly overwhelmed, but he'd never been good with crowds. Marlet was something of a throwback to the Terzian strain, as he lacked the fey dark appearance of Cobweb's type, being fair of hair, tanned of skin; a har of the outdoors. While he was ostensibly Archon of Galhea, the post was mainly ceremonial; day to day government of the Megalithican tribes was the domain of the Hundred Fires, the name for the ruling council of the country. Marlet was a land custodian, more at home in the fields than in any chamber of government. That was clear.

Marlet was more restrained than Ambel had been in his greeting of Gred. He wasn't hostile, or even impolite, but the reticence was plain to see. Gred didn't feel he should make too much effort to break that down. This might appear artificial. Marlet must take him as he was.

"Is it your duty as envoy of Immanion to meet with us?" Marlet asked.

"No," Gred replied. "Nohar knows I'm here. I didn't want to be burdened with any diplomatic tasks. I just wanted to be here in Galhea, see for myself."

"You are discontent," Marlet decided. "You seek solace in the past."

Gred uttered a wordless protest, but Marlet held up a hand.

"No matter. You're welcome here. I hope you find what you're looking for."

Dinner was a raucous affair, with multiple family members, and their harlings and pets, stuffed into the dining-room. The food was excellent but the din soon made Gred's head ache.

Everyhar had to shout to make himself heard, cats jumped on the table, and were only occasionally brushed off it when they became too unashamed about stealing food, harlings squabbled and eventually ended up running around the room, yelling at one another. To Gred, it was like a madhouse. His own family were restrained and courteous. Harlings sat quietly at the occasional big family gathering. Animals would not be allowed in the room. Now, Gred faced a barrage of questions from the Parasilians, some of them quite presumptuous, who apparently found the Aralisians pompous and easy to mock. His own questions, the ones he ached to ask, lodged in his throat. He couldn't bring himself to ask them.

Eventually, Gred pleaded exhaustion and asked permission to retire. It occurred to him that the Parasilians were in actual fact very like how he'd imagined their ancestors to be; informal and numerous. He recalled the fantasies he'd had earlier in the dining-room at *Forever*. Reality was something different.

Ambel escorted Gred to the room that had been made ready for him. "I can see the family have tired you out," he said. "They mean well, but they are rather draining, I know."

Gred smiled. "A little, although I envy you as well. I have nothing like that. I live alone mostly, keep away from the family. They're not as intimate with one another as yours are."

Ambel eyed him speculatively. "Don't feel you have to join in with all family gatherings while you're here. You're free to come and go as you please. Zaya will see to your meals if you prefer to be alone. Just let him know."

"Then I would be a poor guest. Forgive me, I'm simply not used to this kind of life."

Ambel put a hand on his arm. "Sleep well and sleep long. I usually take my breakfast late, in the orchid house. You are welcome to join me there. Around 10. Just ask a member of staff where to find me."

Gred inclined his head. "Thank you." He opened to door to his room, was about to step inside.

"This room..." Ambel said, rather suddenly.

Gred paused. "Yes?"

"As you'll no doubt have noticed the Heights was constructed to the same design as Forever. You will be sleeping in Cobweb's room, the one he originally had. Well... its copy."

Gred nodded. "Thanks... Perhaps I can dream more here than if I stayed in that travesty of a room back at Forever."

"Indeed you might," Ambel said. "Goodnight, harakin."

Alone inside the room, Gred sighed and leaned back against the door. A lamp glowed dimly on a table beside the low bed, which was spread with a beautiful embroidered coverlet of dark green and cream that depicted a tangle of birds and trees. An oil burner on a chest beneath the window released a gentle scent of jasmine. Fresh fruit had been left for him in a green glass bowl, along with cordials and a pitcher of water. Gred mixed himself a drink from an essence of 'flowers of the field', most likely the same that were used to make the wine he'd drunk earlier. He gazed out of the window at the gardens. A wind had come up, making the trees dance. Everything was utterly dark close to; in the distance were the dim lights of the town like snakes of fire.

His drink consumed, Gred took off his sandals and went to lie on the bed fully-clothed. He knew Ambel had put him in this room for a specific reason.

How do you tell when a ghost enters your space? Does the air go cold, condense, and an unreasonable feeling of terror shingle the skin? Or is it more subtle than that, a simple awareness you are not alone, and that the presence with you is 'other'?

After maybe twenty minutes of staring at the wall, thinking of not much at all – perhaps in readiness his mind was clear – Gred saw a shadow by the door, which resolved itself into a shape that walked towards him. He sat upright on the bed, hands braced against the coverlet. Was he afraid now? He didn't know.

"They will have told you, of course," Cobweb said. "May I sit down?" He didn't wait for a reply, but seated himself graciously at the end of the bed. He seemed to waver like a mist, more like a ghost now that Gred was sure he was not.

Cobweb folded his arms and regarded the speechless Gred. "Such a sad soul," he said. "What are you searching for here?"

"Meaning," Gred replied awkwardly.

"Ah, I can't give you that. Life is such a strange, cruel thing, isn't it? I look back on mine and it's as if it happened to another har, or it was a book I read. I don't know when it changed and I found myself in the other half of life. I can't remember it happening. When I was in the first one, I thought nothing would ever change, and then I would die, but it's not like that. The life of youth is another world to the one I live in now. It dies, but you are not dead, you're just this older har and the past has gone, many of the hara you loved with it, even though they might still live. You wake up one day and realise most things you took for granted have disappeared or been done with. You are somehar else. But you can remember so well..." He sighed, then smiled with great warmth. "I should not be here to heap you with melancholia. In truth, I feel no grief, only an astounded wistfulness. But that is not how you feel, is it?"

I have been given a chance, Gred thought, *so rare and brief; I must make the most of it. Every second will count.* "No... I feel... lost." He shook his head. Couldn't he put it better than that? Words eluded him.

Cobweb waited patiently. Gred felt the har trusted the words would come. And so they did. "When I look at the world, in Immanion, it all seems so... *bleached*. It doesn't feel real to me. I don't think any other har feels the way I do. We live in a prosperous country, we have peace, we have art, we have exploration, we have learning. If there is darkness in the world, it is far from our door."

"That is what we worked for all those generations ago," Cobweb said softly. "It didn't come easily, I assure you. There were dark ages."

"I know and that's why I yearn for those days, those hara," Gred said. "In peace have we become somehow less? Is it only conflict that drives a har to passion and greatness?"

"Perhaps so," Cobweb said, "but perhaps also you are an anachronism. All those hara in Immanion – and indeed around us here now – are content in the world that was made for them. They do the things they were supposed to do – the pioneering frontier is within. Or they explore the Otherlanes and beyond, seeking the mysteries of the multiverse. That's not so bad a life, free from war."

"No, most hara would say it is the perfect life."

Cobweb reached out and squeezed one of Gred's feet. "But not for you, poor harling. I would be a liar if I said those early days weren't cauldrons of great passion, daring and courage, even though we lived in blood and terror many times. Love was an anvil on which our hearts were forged. All that was human within us was a bonfire, raging always. And that is perhaps what is lost to me now." He frowned. "What a quandary. I wonder why I'm still here, but there is no call for me to the ancient graveyard and beyond. Even though my loved ones wait for me there, and will wait for me forever, this world is still my home. I would not say I am here by choice, but then I have no great yearning to leave it either. And it is your home also, Gred har Aralis. So, what is to be done with you?"

Gred laughed weakly. "I would not presume for you to sort *that* quandary out!"

Cobweb pursed his lips, thought for a moment. "The hara who are not already in bed will still be sitting round the dining table. It won't be hard for us to sneak out unseen. Well... for *you* to do so. I go where I please, seen or not. I'll clear a space for us. Come." He stood up.

"Where?"

"Where do you think? Silly harling. We'll go to the house."

Cobweb took Gred to the stable yard, again a copy of *Forever's*. True to his word he had 'cleared a space' for they ran into no family or members of staff. "This is so typical of us now," Cobweb said, as he led the way. "These float car things stabled alongside our horses. We still use horses, although some hara with the gift can fold through an Otherlane in the blink of an eye. I regard these inconsistencies with affection."

"Car or horse?" Gred asked. "Or will you fold us there?"

"I was never a great lanes traveller," Cobweb replied, "despite being the grateful recipient of many other gifts. I *think* myself to where I want to go most of the time, but could never take anyhar with me. And I do appreciate speed and comfort. We'll take a car tonight."

It seemed incongruous to Gred, if not utterly bizarre, for Cobweb, this being of myth, to take the driving seat and competently pilot one of the Parasilians' sleek grey float cars out into the night. He steered it above the trees, where the stars were watchful sparks. He left the lamps unlit and the roof open, so they wafted through the darkness as if on a magical carpet.

"This seems absurd to me," Gred said. "I would never have imagined you driving a float car."

"Why ever not? The energy that vitalises them is the pure source, made from hara themselves. That to me is magic. Also, a car is less likely to have a funny turn and throw you into a ditch. Ah, here we are."

Cobweb landed the car softly on one of the lawns at the back of *Forever*. There appeared to be no security at the house. There were no lights to be seen.

"They just lock up at night and leave this place unguarded?" Gred asked.

Cobweb chuckled. "Galhea, for all its pretensions to grandeur, is still a country village at heart. Everything is safe here." He sighed, gazed up at the house, which glowed pale in the starlight. "I am still deeply in love with the old place. Perhaps it is the house more than anything that tethers me to this world."

Gred ducked a formal bow. "Then, Tiahaar, it would please me greatly if you would conduct a tour of the house – this time a proper one."

Cobweb inclined his head. "Of course." He offered his elbow for Gred to link with. "Come."

They entered the house through a window-door that led into the old family sitting-room. It was ostensibly locked, but the mechanism was so old a gentle shove made it give way. Now Gred was on the other side of the ropes that earlier had fenced the room from him. It made him feel spectral, somehow.

Cobweb lit a candle, and Shadetide shadows danced across the walls.

"I don't know how you can bear it," Gred blurted, "coming here now, it not being your home."

"I had to get used to many things or go entirely mad," Cobweb replied. "The time for tears is done. At least I have the choice over which memories to revisit, and I choose to remember all that is good. *Forever* deserves no less."

"Are there ghosts here other than you?"

Cobweb laughed. "Me, a ghost? Ha!" He patted Gred's shoulder. "Well, there are quite a few. They are simply memories, the house dreaming, or thinking aloud, as it were.

There are no chained souls here, Gred, only thoughts."

"You must miss everyhar, though. It seems cruel you're left alone."

Cobweb said nothing. He was prowling round the room, examining the appointments and ornaments, few of which could have once belonged to him.

"I mean," Gred continued awkwardly, "I know you have family – lots of it – but it can't be the same, surely? I don't wish to pry but..."

"These are the things that eat at you, I know," Cobweb said. "You want more than ghosts, don't you? You want to be able to slip through a chink of time and find yourself back here, hundreds of years ago."

"Yes. If I am honest, yes." Gred paused. "If you are honest, isn't that what you would want too?"

Cobweb considered. "My hara call to me," he said. "Quite often. Snake, Swift, Tyson, all of them. But it is as if I say back to them, 'wait a minute, I'm not quite done'. I don't feel any urgency to join them, because they are always there, and at the same time, always with me. Time means nothing in the realm they call home now. Perhaps they are sitting waiting for me to join them for dinner, and then, when I do join them they'll have waited only five minutes, even though centuries have passed in this world. I'm not alone, Gred. I don't feel that way. All I lack is physical closeness, and after all this time that is not something I crave or need in order to survive. Not in this world at least." He smiled wistfully, perhaps thinking of his chesnari who waited for him somewhere 'other'. "But would I go back?" He was silent for a moment. "No. Because now I can relive all that is good, and there was much that was bad. There are certain things I would never want to live through again, nor would I want those I love to relive them."

Gred frowned, nodded. "Yes, I can understand that."

"You would not enjoy them either," Cobweb said. "Early Wraeththu were savage, Gred. You would be shocked, terrified even. When Cal, your ancestor, lived here, he was ravaged, ruined – in his mind. He came back to us, some time after his first visit with Pell, believing that Pell was dead. Cal had killed the har he thought partly responsible on the way to us, in the most gruesome way imaginable. He murdered one of the

249

greatest hienamas our kind has ever known, the har who was one of the first of all incepted Wraeththu."

Cobweb stared at Gred, who felt his shock must show plainly on his face.

Then Cobweb nodded, as if satisfied by what he saw. "Cal was a husk for a long time, and suffered greatly to overcome all that he was. Many early hara were tormented like that. They had seen, and lived through, so much that was terrible, unspeakable. And the ruin wasn't always confined to the mind or spirit. When I first met Snake, he was horribly disfigured, one half of his body crippled."

Now Cobweb paused, perhaps reflecting on that time, and Gred found he was able to speak, somewhat inadequately, he felt. "I'm sorry... I didn't know. It was wrong of me to assume..."

Cobweb shook his head. "Some things you will not have been told or read. To you, I expect Pellaz's famous consort Calanthe is remembered only as a wise and mighty ruler."

Gred grimaced. "Not entirely, although obviously there is a lot I don't know."

"Much," Cobweb agreed. "This room..." He turned in a slow circle, hands on hips. "Here I loved. Here I saw harlings grow. Here I spent priceless moments with friends and those I loved. It is a good room. Here I remember Snake, whole again, cured by what we found in the deepest mysteries of aruna together. That is a beautiful memory. But if we were to go Terzian's office, you would feel death sentences hanging over you. If I showed it to you as it really was, you would smell blood... carrion... You might even see it, some of it."

"Did you... did you love Terzian?" Gred asked.

Cobweb appeared to pull himself in, become somewhat more reserved. "Of course. He was a great and powerful har. Whether I would have loved him if he'd been only a farmer or something is another matter. I am not blind to realities. I was drawn to powerful hara, as many are."

"But you were one of them too."

"Not initially. Those around me contributed greatly to who I became, not least your ancestor, Pellaz. We were alike in some ways. He too came from humble beginnings, but it was right he became all he was. Anything else would have been a waste."

"I never met him," Gred said, somewhat bitterly.

"Yes, well, he was impatient to get away," Cobweb said. "This world and the hara in it often annoyed him, and it got worse over time. This world *does* age you, Gred. It makes your physical being grow thin; it's just part of what this realm is, even if you're a har who can live for centuries, perhaps even millennia. But what's inside us never fades or grows feeble. Some choose to fade away over time until they are blown like gauze into another life. Pellaz wouldn't wait for that. He wanted somewhere else, so off into the Otherlanes he went. Others close to him chose to join him at the time. They were done here, so they sought a new world. Perhaps that was his way of 'going back', only it was starting anew."

"I was never told that," Gred said. "They never tell us that. They say that Pellaz and his kin faded. They went to a mountain and were taken to what is beyond."

Cobweb snorted derisively. "How biblical! I suppose they don't really know what happened, or it's what they want to believe. Perhaps Pellaz did go to a mountain to open a gate. I can't remember. All I'll say is this: if he was standing here now, he'd call you insane for the things you desire. He'd say, 'get out of this realm, young har. If it bores you, there are limitless exciting places to discover'."

"Is that it? I'm just bored of my life?"

Cobweb shrugged. "Only you can answer that. I'm not sure if you're capable of withstanding true danger and excitement, but if you are, the Otherlanes and its realms is where they lie. But if you go there, and I mean truly go deep and explore, you might not be able to return. And then you might regret your decision, lost in an alien environment, where you would never feel at home. Pellaz had outgrown his home; it was different for him. You are young, full of fancies and desires and yearnings. You have a lot of living yet to do in this world."

"Perhaps... perhaps I should look for Pellaz," Gred suggested.

"Not yet," Cobweb answered shortly. "If a harling leaves the nursery before it's ready, reality will rapidly cause its demise."

"I don't feel that young," Gred said. "In fact, quite the opposite. I suppose every har is young in comparison to you, though. I understand your impatience with us."

"It's not impatience," Cobweb said. "Anyway, did we come here to have this conversation or to explore?"

"Both, I think."

"Then let's explore now."

Cobweb led Gred through every room in the house. The stories he told were not of conflict, courageous deeds, terror or destruction. He spoke of small amusing things, such as silly words Swift had spoken as a harling, various awkward romantic affairs that had taken place, arguments that had ended in humiliation or farce. They had come to one of the bathrooms on the second floor. "Tyson was terrible as a young har," Cobweb said. "He would push the harish body to its limit. I remember once a distinguished Gelaming visitor found him unconscious on this bathroom floor with his trousers round his ankles. It took some time for the har to push open the door since Tyson was lying behind it. Tyson's excuse was that he'd been meditating and had gone on some strange travel vision. In reality, he was just blind drunk and had fallen off the toilet."

Gred laughed. "You're not doing a very good job of persuading me the past is not a good place to visit. I wish I'd known all those hara."

"They're just stories," Cobweb said. "Make your own."

"In Immanion?" Gred asked incredulously.

"Even in Immanion there must be hara you'd want to know. It's just finding them."

"With my face, that's difficult. I carry the baggage of the Aralisian dynasty. Few hara beyond Phaonica's Mount are at ease with me."

"Then go somewhere else. Be somehar else. The world isn't exactly small." Cobweb sighed. "You've only looked at a very small part of it, haven't you?" He shook his head. "By all the dehara, this takes me back! I might as well be lecturing Pellaz again when he was having one of his *episodes*."

"Perhaps that was why I was drawn here."

"I'm beginning to think that was likely," Cobweb said dryly.

They had come to the threshold of Terzian's bedroom. Cobweb had left it until last. Even all the rooms on higher stories of the house had been explored first. "So much drama lingers in here," Cobweb said. "Really, most of it is embarrassing now. We were so self-obsessed."

"Tell me a drama."

Cobweb rubbed a hand over his face. "Oh, I'd rather not. Not one of my personal ones, at least. But Terzian died here, in that bed. It's the original."

Gred approached it.

"Lie on it," Cobweb said. "Pearls were delivered there, a har died, many loved."

Gred laughed shakily. "Now history frightens me a little."

"You see? You know your skin will crawl if you lie on that bed. My skin crawls in this room too. It's one of the bad places. Swift tried to live in it for a while. He soon saw sense."

There was a silence. Then Gred said, "Thank you for all this, Cobweb. I really appreciate it."

"My pleasure. I sometimes like to indulge myself and tell the old stories. The family have heard them a hundred times, so are a poor audience nowadays. There are a couple of the harlings I quite like. They seek me out all the time, and now and again I'll let them find me. It doesn't pay to lose my mystery and be too available. They love it, anyway."

"I wish I was one of those harlings."

Cobweb stepped forward and embraced Gred. "But my dear thing, you are!"

The tour was over. Cobweb and Gred went back to the sitting-room, where Cobweb extinguished the candle, now burned to a stub (a ghostly story for tomorrow's visitors?), and they went outside. Cobweb pressed the window door shut and the tired old mechanism clicked back into place.

"I'll never forget this night," Gred said.

Cobweb took hold of Gred's arm again. "But it's not over," he said. "How about we return to the Heights and assault Marlet's collection of rare sheh vintages? I have many more stories to tell and now, quite frankly, they are bursting to be let out."

"I'd like nothing better," Gred said.

They talked until morning, when the staff began to appear in the kitchen to prepare breakfast. Cobweb and Gred were still seated at the kitchen table, with two empty bottles of sheh before them. Gred felt happily, woozily drunk. But not tired. The staff did not seem surprised to see Cobweb there but had perhaps been trained by Ambel not to register surprise in such circumstances. This was still Cobweb's home, if only his 'other' home. A har discreetly made coffee and placed it before them.

"You should sleep," Cobweb said.

"But then you'll be gone, and it will be over," Gred replied.

"Never that," Cobweb said. "Have your adventures, Gred. Find hara you like. Fall in love. Take aruna with a har who makes you feel as if the act was created solely for you and him. Go into wildernesses. Find mysteries. Then come here to tell me of them."

"You'll let me find you?"

"You'll have to wait and see, won't you?"

Gred slept for three hours and then sought out Ambel in the orchid house. Beyond the arched windows, the day was clear.

"I heard you had a sleepless night," Ambel said, indicating Gred should take a seat beside him at the wrought iron table. "It isn't often the staff come across Cobweb in the house."

"You knew he would come to me," Gred said.

Ambel shrugged. "Strongly suspected. He *is* difficult to predict. But I can see that in some ways he has inspired you. You feel a lot lighter to me today."

Gred nodded, grinned. "It was an unforgettable experience."

"And did he help you choose a path?"

"I think it was more like he told me to make my own map. I'll have to think about it."

"Cobweb once told me that he and Pellaz would argue fiercely sometimes. Pellaz didn't always like the advice Cobweb gave him. But invariably, he took it." Ambel handed Gred a glass of tea. "Well, enough of the past. I hope you'll stay here for a while with us, and then when you return to Immanion we can initiate greater contact between our families. That, I personally believe, is one of the paths to go on your map."

Gred paused. "I think..." he said eventually, "that the hara in my country have changed far more than those I've found here. I don't mean it to sound rude, but in some ways being here *is* like stepping back in time. You might be disappointed by my harakin. They seem to me to be dour and dull in comparison."

Ambel laughed delightedly. "Perhaps they need some shaking up! Pellaz and his kin were never dour or dull, I *do* know that." He reached out to take one of Gred's hands. "And also, young har, bear in mind that the hara of Phaonica's Mount are not the entire population of Almagabra. I think you've been locked in your rooms for too long! Never mind braving the daylight enough to come here. Perhaps there are places for you to explore closer to home."

Gred pressed Ambel's fingers, held onto his hand; an intimate gesture he could not remember doing even with his own hostling. "Cobweb said the same."

"You see?" Ambel released Gred's hand. "Now, breakfast. Then you can delve into Marlet's collections. I'm afraid it's been mentioned we should have a dinner gathering while you are here, so hara from Galhea can meet you. Is that acceptable?"

"Yes, it's the first step, I suppose."

"Good. You never know what might come of it."

As Ambel set about preparing a plate of food for Gred from the various dishes available, Gred stared out of the window at the sky. Overnight, his life had changed completely. It was like shedding a skin or perhaps even emerging from a pearl. He felt, for perhaps the first time in his life, a sense of excitement, as if events and experiences – and hara – were gathering unseen amid clouds around him. They were not dark clouds, merely a shifting mist that concealed what was to come. He would walk into that gladly.

Wraeththu Juvenilia and Curios

The First Inception

The last twisted scraps of the grey and blasted city fell behind them and opened out into a grim mausoleum of sere dust. The sun hung sanguine in a clotted haze above the sliding dunes of ground glass. Rusted balls, which looked like tumbleweed but wasn't, crawled and rolled among the remains of human civilisation. This was the zenith of mankind's fear, its remaining shred of fear; the desert, an arid cruelty, scorched on the face of the earth like the hoof-print of a titan. It was death and dead, and the unlife that lurked among the ruins there was not as the people of the city knew life. The landscape was a shifting mirage of rainbow hues, and the shadows that flitted over its dry, choking sand were liquid and malevolent in their movement.

For a while, Jarad and Lianvis poised at the lip of the waiting void that sloped downward from their horses' feet in undulations of deceiving firmness. Faced with the wideness and emptiness that seemed to stretch forever before him, Jarad could no longer clutch at the certainty he had felt before. Even with the strange alien power of the creature Lianvis, was there really any hope of escape from this place? Wouldn't their steps ever end back here, this filthy, barely fertile spot of fading light and power, a remnant of the past, rotting on the edge of eternity. On one side, the poison depths of the sea, and forever westwards the desolation and contracted calm of the barren void.

As if in reply to Jarad's unspoken thought, Lianvis said, "There is life on the other side, beyond the dunes."

"The West was destroyed," Jarad said, dully, his interest and hope ever falling.

"You will follow me, then." Lianvis spurred the horse that carried him, and it faltered forward and downward, Jarad's mount moving behind it without command.

Over the lip and the heat engulfed them in a fleering wind. Jarad coughed on the dry heat, and his horse balked and shook its head vainly, a thin snickering falling from its mouth. Ahead of them, Lianvis's proud white mount held its head to the sun, stepping with the ancestral majesty that some horses have. Lianvis was straight-backed and fearless, his hair waving in inhuman coils in the hot breeze and his naked legs were the colour of the dead sand, like a lizard.

"How long will it take us to die?" Jarad asked him.

Lianvis laughed. "If I thought you would die, I wouldn't have brought you. If you will wait until we reach the floor of the desert..." His voice trailed off on the wind that played in his glistering hair, turning it to billows of fair smoke. Now that he had freed himself, his strangeness gathered in a wild aura about his body. He seemed to be molten, or fire and flames that licked the horse's back.

On the sighing sand of the desert proper, Lianvis halted his horse and leapt from its back. The wind was stinging now, with a fierceness Jarad had never experienced before. He was not a strong youth, having had no chance to seek strength, and the cruel wind bit his bones. He was lost in hopelessness, rebuking himself for being lulled into this perilous expedition by Lianvis' enchanting words and deep hypnotic eyes. The creature had brought him here to watch him die in searing agony, or else, his mind had faded into insanity, so he actually believed the void could be crossed. Jarad watched him striding indistinct through the wildly swirling motes of sand carried on the heated air, and it seemed he was taller than before, and filled with a greater power than the elements themselves. Jarad feared Lianvis for his strangeness and the unrevealed hints of something too great to be imagined that lived inside him. Yet Jarad felt that strength soften in the sculptured limbs that lifted him from his horse and set him upon the shifting sands. Lianvis's eyes glowed pale in the eerie light and Jarad was afraid to be alone with him in this vast emptiness. Now that the city was lost, the wilderness stretched forever all around them. But Jarad was hypnotised by the placid gaze and allowed himself to be drawn onwards into the dust-choked wind by fingers that were cold as ice against his flesh.

"Take this, Jarad," Lianvis said. "It is time." He forced a slim-necked bottle to Jarad's mouth, driving his head back so that the thin liquid within ran down his throat in an endless, searing torrent. Jarad wasn't sure whether it was an experience of heat or cold, but the bitter draught numbed his body. He was helpless in the grip of this monster, this half-human, who gazed at him with eyes of cold blue flame.

Eventually, the numbness passed and Jarad became conscious of Lianvis' cool touch again, and the wildness of the air, but it no longer discomforted him. He felt like a colossus above the wind, and its striking heat was a gentle caress against his skin.

"What was that?" he asked Lianvis in his new strength.

The creature smiled and unfurled his arms. "The only thing that could give you strength, make you almost as I am. It was a philtre of my own blood."

Jarad felt as if the gory potion would rise in his stomach, but the feeling passed and they went back to their horses.

The Ruins Walker

Now, as I sit here in the somnolent afterglow of the day, I am at peace. The curling paper lies on the onyx table before me, and I am ready to write. There is a beginning yet no end. The horizon beyond the staring mountains across the valley is hazy – its ethereal shimmer mutters of eternity – and there lies the ending. But the story burns within me, and I want to set it free. I want to set down this history in the confinement of words, and maybe someday, far ahead, when we are all forgotten, and have vanished forever behind the azure veil that dances over the hills, someone, some new creature, might find my testament and read it, finding pity or envy in their hearts, as they will.

I am tired and the air chills my bare shoulders, but I know that if I don't start writing now, the story will never be written and it *must* be done. I feel my attendant watching me from the corner of his eye. He senses the images inside me that convulse the air with power and the longing to be free. I could confess to him the need I have to tell my tale, but the words will mean nothing to him. Why should they? To him, my history is a commonplace thing, no awe-inspiring narrative. But enough. Soon the light will wane once more from the amethyst hills. The only sound is the scratch of my pen against the paper. I will tell it as it was.

I was young then, when the concept of ageing existed for me. The Devastation, which was more and less than war, had taken the lives of both my parents and my kin; even more, my friends, my town, my home. I'd lost everything and that was only the beginning. The Devastation was slow in its rising, but once its beastly climax came, the world was quickly taken, for those of us who survived were without hope, saddened and grieving. It was an easy thing for *them* to kill who was left. In the end, most of my kind welcomed it, I think. Life was uncomfortable and terrifying, consisting of Them and Us, and we forever running from Them. The world, our Mother, didn't help us. Why should she? We'd violated her for centuries. She wanted us gone, too.

I came to be alone, the ruins of civilisation ashes at my feet, depending only on the pity of those other lost and bitter souls who still shared my fate. We, who were all that was left of the Old Race, crouched like vermin among the twisted remains. We flinched at the cries that rang through the red-tainted nights, and cowered from the scampering sounds that whispered through the darkness. We hid from the vicious flares of flame; the leaping illumination for *their* lust and cruelty. I squeezed myself small into the rubble of makeshift sanctuaries with the others. We learned how to hide ourselves well.

How my spirit was not completely broken by all I saw and heard and knew to be so, I don't know. Perhaps it was indignation that held me together, the raw anger at *their* audacity. It made me want to scream sometimes, but that would have been an unforgivable invitation to the grisly agents of death. Also, a waste of precious energy and attention. All that mattered and *could* matter was keeping safe. There was no time for self-pity.

For the most part, those early years are a blur in my memory. I can remember only impressions, few actual incidents or faces. It was a time of fire and blood, raw and reeking. A time of nothing *whole*. Pain and terror reigned, and eventually it became too dangerous for us in the ruins. *They* began to hunt us out for sport, but their guard became lax on the perimeter, and several of us managed to escape, unharmed, into the wilderness. This was a big step for us; we were scavengers not hunters. We'd have to learn a different way to survive.

Before the Devastation, I was a child, but standing on the first green grass miles beyond the City I knew that my childhood had fallen from me. I was a woman, too young, yet wizened before my time. Leaving the others, I went alone into the green, trusting my instincts. I knew how to make a fire and how to kill things smaller than myself. There were old farms, where straggly vegetables and fruit still grew and, yes, there were places to scavenge among the dead. Eventually, I came across a farm that was inhabited – far from the City now – and the people there were willing to take me in. They called themselves refugees, but that implied there was a refuge, somewhere else to go and be safe, and of course there wasn't. Survivors, *remnants.* I knew that all we could do was wait for death, be that the following day or years into the future. People tried to fool themselves that something would change. But all you had to do was open your eyes and ears, really look and listen, and the world was quite willing to tell you humanity's time was done. We'd been replaced by a different model.

These people never became my friends, certainly not family, although they liked to think of themselves as one great, related support network. They meant well, and believed themselves safe. Poor fools. One night, we heard *their* unmistakeable cries, towards the east, by the river. In the morning, the elders went down and found one of *them* dead there. I heard it was deformed, but deformities were common among our own kind, never mind theirs, so that wasn't unusual to me. The body was burned in the field beyond the barn, and the sharp reek of it reached me and burned my tongue. After that, we took our water from further up the river and none went near the shallows where the body had been found.

The people who had taken me in might have told themselves they wanted to love me, but in fact they didn't even like me that much, however they might kid themselves about it. They had prayer meetings and asked me to attend. I couldn't even respond to such a request, thinking them mad. They hadn't come from the City, of course, so they didn't understand my strangeness, nor could they identify my aloofness as my armour of defence. They had travelled up from the ravaged sierras of the south, that we in the city had called The Place of Lethe, without really knowing what we meant by it. My benefactors never talked about the past, how bad it had been for them in their old homes, and I didn't have the energy to care. They were sadly wary of me, because of the distance I kept from them. To eat among them seemed a parody of dining, like animals aping what humans used to do, but perhaps it's just a reflex to cling to old customs when the world dies around you. If I should fail to take my place at the table, my neighbours would have been upset, even though my sombre presence must always have been a heavy weight on their digestion. They wanted to be good people, but I knew the truth behind their soulful eyes. I was important to them because I was female. Women were valuable and becoming rare. They hoped I might breed and sustain the moribund tribe. I saw the way the men looked at me, half afraid, respectful of whatever tragedies they thought I'd lived through, waiting for the time when they might make their approach to me. I didn't tell them I never bled, was barren before I'd even been fertile. If they knew about me, I'd be no more than another belly to fill with food rather than seed. I'm not sure whether they would have cast me out or not, but secretly they might have wanted to drive me away like a curse.

I didn't want to live in the big house with the others, but found an old disused barn some distance away from the other buildings. There was a ladder to a hay loft, where there were holes in the ceiling. I could watch the sky through them. There were bales of musty old hay, perhaps harvested in a better time. I loved the feeling of lost happiness that haunted the place, and was comforted there.

The pace of my life had slowed almost to a standstill. I inhabited increasingly a kind of waking slumber, living inside myself, sure that a large part of me had died back in the City. Outside realities impinged only vaguely on my mind: I could look at the splendour of the sun, bloody and potent, ruby-stippling the hills, and notice the dilapidated buildings had been lent a rosy glory as they creaked to their rest. Birds threw themselves like black rags against the sky that rang with colours so intense it was like a world-spanning clarion I could hear physically. All this I registered with my senses, but not its beauty. I could only imagine that the sunset-stained flanks of the hills were striped with blood, that the lazy cropping dots of sheep were threatening shadows among the red hues. The world was one exuberant cry of self-love, but I couldn't hear it. All I saw around me were potential hiding places and directions from which danger might come. The splendid horizon, where black peaks pierced the lowering sun, was a hinterland that harboured only death. Other people couldn't shield me from myself.

At first, young women around my own age used to try and

befriend me, coming to my sanctuary with little gifts. I didn't repel them, because for the time being this community was useful to me, but neither did I encourage them. I didn't know how to be friends. What was the point? We were living in a fragile bubble of glass, and I felt only *I* knew just how delicate it was. I couldn't tell if I was tired, and wanted to lie down and die, or was itching to burst free and run shrieking into the world. Talking to the indifferent stars about it made me realise that everyone and everything had a fate. I could search for mine through the crystal pane and hope it wasn't a painful death at *their* hands. I was pretty sure the end would come from them. True, in a way. One day, something happened that cracked the glass.

It was evening then too. Tasks over for the day, I was walking from my barn into the vanishing day, stretching my limbs, breathing deeply the cool-tainted warmth. I had taken a cat-lick wash and dressed myself cleanly to face the evening meal. I walked towards the orchard, which would ultimately deliver me to the steps of the main house. Birdsong seeped down from the lattice branches above my head, and crazy clusters of gnats danced in patches of gold light. Odd that these creatures will live on, unknowing, long after the Old Race, true humanity, has perished. Life had become a meaningless ritual, and there were around thirty of us there on the farm, senselessly prolonging it.

At first, I thought the strange sound came from an animal. It was halfway between a cough and a low, despairing howl. I stopped walking, listening, and in a while turned my head to the source of it. Then, reactions leapt up and bruised each other. I actually heard glass shattering, felt these imaginary fragments slice my skin. I'd felt little for so long, but now I was boiling with stark terror, then panic. I dropped into a crouch, searched frantically for something to use as a weapon, if only to use on myself.

Half in, half out of the drinking pool at the orchard's heart, lay one of the monsters, one of *them*. I knew at once it wasn't human, because my hair was crawling on my scalp, and there was a peculiar scent in my nose that I'd never smelled before – part burning, part musty, yet partly of flowers. I could not tell if the creature was still alive, or how badly harmed and where.

How had it got past the perimeter guards? This was right in the homestead, not down by the river. I had never seen one this close before, not a single entity. I had seen *them* only as an undulating wave of collective hate and destruction, and never close up, for I was not stupid. I must have stood there for less than a minute, but it was if those moments were an eternity and the seasons changed around me. Once the realisation I was not in immediate danger settled in, fear turned to mist and went away.

I picked up a rake that was lying in the grass and stalked forward. I don't know what drew me, why I didn't simply run to the house, yelling for the others, but I knelt beside the motionless form on the damp grass and laid the rake against a stone at the edge of the pool. At this moment, I began thinking of the intruder as he rather than it. He lay very still and made no further sound, not then. His back was perfect, not a mark on it, dark in colour, the flanks heaving slightly. I thought he might be poisoned, but I knew the pool to be pure. His arms were plunged into the water, and I saw the long russet ribbons that still unwound from them. I turned the body over and found the flesh warm. This being lived beneath my hands – something *other*. I can't describe the alienness of it – eldritch almost. His injuries were not extensive, but concentrated and bad. The chest was ripped and lacerated, as if a maddened thing had attacked him. His flesh hung off in bloody lumps in places, but I'd seen far worse in my time and did not wince.

Swearing beneath my breath, I stared at the gore-stippled grass, wondering what I should do. In one version of reality, I would run to the house and tell the others. They would come racing out and drag the creature to the stable yard. Then he would be burned alive, if he still lived by then, as punishment for crimes he might have committed, or mainly just for being what he was. Alternatively, I could give him a chance, and carry on to the house to take my evening meal. If he did not find the strength to move, some other would find him, and his death would not be my fault. These things I could do, yes, and neither choice would be a betrayal of my people.

But then… could I not drag him to my barn and help him? The idea both chilled and excited me. I couldn't bear the thought of this weird perfection being burned. It was like coming across a dangerous predator, a tiger or a bear, who was wounded and helpless. Such a beautiful thing, a crime to destroy it, no matter what it might do were it not weak. The feeling was uncontrollable, and there were words in my head: "he is not the one who killed your family". Senseless. He must've murdered thousands of others, and they were all *somebody's* loved ones. Yet still, I grabbed the wasted body under the arms, surprised by its lightness. It wasn't difficult to haul him away from the water and up the red sandy bank. At the top, the grass was green and dusk-cool. I squatted at his side, wiped smears of blood from his face. He was classically beautiful, but then it was said they all were. Animal camouflage to hide the monster within. He twitched once and opened his eyes; shocking, as if they had opened with a great crash. I looked into eternity; black pools, filled with experiences I couldn't understand nor interpret. For a moment, he stared at me in relief. Then he clearly realised what I was. Desperation twisted his features, and he attempted to crawl away from me, but was too weak to do so.

I thought at him, as hard as I could, *don't fear me. Let me help you,* because we all believed they could speak in thoughts. But the pain was obviously too much, for he had lost consciousness again.

I lifted him in my arms, though he was somewhat taller than me, but so starved he weighed hardly anything. Dirty rags were tied about his loins, a knife tucked into their folds, blotched with what I first took to be rust. Yet it didn't seem he'd used it to defend himself.

In the barn, I laid him in the hay and fetched water in a tin bowl from the cranky tap I had in the corner under the byre. I had to hurry, in case my absence from the dinner table aroused suspicion in the house. The creature moaned in pain as I washed his wounds, and I realised it would take too long this way, so I followed a strange instinct within me and laid both my hands, palm downwards, on the bleeding mass of his chest, summoning a new form of concentration, of which I had had no former knowledge. I seemed to draw power from the very air around me. I could feel the current flowing into the body beneath my hands, and he fed upon it. Once the power ebbed, I stood up, swaying in the half-light, drained and sickened. He turned his head in the hay and looked straight at me. He *knew* things, as if I'd told him. *Go now, you must go... they're waiting...* He repelled me from the barn with the slow beating force of his thoughts, until reality came back to me, and I was standing at the front of the house, with bloody hands it would be awkward to explain. But there was time to go to the kitchen, wash myself. A cut, I said, when someone asked.

After the meal, I stole food for him and a jug of thick milk, hurrying back to the barn under cover of darkness. For the first time in years, I actually felt the night around me, its cool, ebony wetness, and I could hear the chirruping of nocturnal insects. In the distance, the mountains reared, blacker than black, sleeping, wing-furled demons against the star-speckled sky.

I was only partly surprised to find him sitting up in the hay, gazing around himself. He saw me and flinched back into the shadows, shrinking against the wall with his limbs drawn up, rather like a frightened spider. We looked at each other warily. Then he sighed through his nose resignedly and relaxed. I pressed "*don't be afraid*" at his mind and he nodded, glanced at me strangely, as if amused.

He had helped himself to my washing cloths to clean his wounds; the water in the tin bowl was soiled and bloody. He reminded me of an ancient god, not a wholly benevolent one, lithe and tawny as the pumas that lived in the hills. As I gazed upon him, I was filled with a strangely sorrowful ache, because his beauty was tragic somehow. He always made me feel that way. When his body was at its most vibrant, I wanted to crawl off into a corner and cry bitterly, rather than yearn for his arms. Yet he never seemed aware of his appearance.

I stood there silent, unsure now what to say or do. If a being from another world had materialised before me, with extra limbs and eyes, or leathery wings, it might have felt more ordinary. I can't explain it properly; I could only *sense* the gulf between us. Me at the door, hanging up my lantern of yellow light, and he crouched in his bloodied bed, more animal than human, and something so much more than animal.

"Why do this, woman?" he asked me softly, and the shock of his voice unnerved me.

I shook my head and offered him the food I had brought.

"I can't eat in the presence of a human," he told me simply. I stared at him for a moment, then left the barn. Outside, the night was cool. I leaned against the barn's creaking wall. How did I feel? Was this sadness or joy? Was I excited or numb? What I did know was that for the first time in years my mind was stimulated to buzzing awareness.

I wondered why the creature was alone and how he had come here. Deserted, maybe? But I knew enough for that to be unlikely. He had accepted my help without suspicion, as if he had looked into my heart and read what lay there. But surely that in itself was suspicious? Yet I was not afraid of him and couldn't hate him. Had he controlled my mind somehow? Had he sensed me approach, and had crawled to the water hole, knowing.

Eventually, thinking he'd had enough time to feed, I went back inside. He'd climbed the ladder to the loft and had lit my oil lamp, which threw a vague topaz light over the old wood. When he heard me open the barn door, he looked down at me.

"It's safe here," I said.

He nodded.

I climbed the ladder and squatted in front of him in the dusty darkness, wondering if he'd tell me how he'd come to be there, alone and injured by the pool. But before I could say anything, he spoke.

"We must talk together," he said. "What's your name?"

I remembered and told him, although I hated the sound. "Bonnie."

He blinked at me, almost smiled, but contained it. "Among my kind, the first thing we are given, beyond the first gift, is a name. I give you Cereia in return for your help."

"A name from the mouth of my enemy," I said. "Inhuman." I tried to sound disgusted, yet already preferred it to the ridiculously inappropriate name I'd been given.

"You've taken it from me, so it must fit. I think it does."

"Call me what you like. How did you get here?"

"I was travelling and crossed the territory of the Uigenna – a tribe hostile to others of my kind… I took a risk because it was a quicker route, and I knew there was food and water along the way. Scouts found me. They thought I was a spy, and they don't welcome outsiders at the best of times. I was near to death when they'd finished with me. They wouldn't kill me, though, but brought me here as a warning to others like me, believing the humans would burn me alive. Instead *you* found me. Cereia, I realise you're the one I've been waiting to find. Human, yes, but different."

"Yet you cannot eat in my presence..." I could not help but say.

He closed his eyes, shook his head abruptly. "I was wrong. I see that now. You are more than human."

"I'm not," I said. "If anything, I'm less than human."

"It doesn't matter what you think," he said. "We're more alike than you know."

I thought he must be deranged. We weren't alike at all. "Where did you come from – originally?"

His eyes went dark. "South of the border – first." He stood up and stretched, and I noticed the wounds had already scabbed over on his chest. He looked at me keenly, touching my mind with his eyes. "We are destined to be... *conspirators.*"

"How?" I stared at him, and those marvellous eyes looked back; serious, timeless and scarred.

"The world is changing," he said.

"Yes, I noticed... Tell me what you are."

"I am what you see."

"Wraeththu." It hurt to say that word. We're not supposed to say it, because words are invocations.

He nodded. "Yes, that."

"We found a body some time back. It was... deformed."

"That's a rare find. Usually, the dead are taken away so the humans don't see what we are. Did you *see*?"

I ducked my head. "We all did."

"It's not a deformity," he said.

Was he the same? If so, he wasn't male at all, at least not what was accepted as male.

"My blood is unthrist," he said, perhaps to change the subject. "That means I have no tribe now. I was called away from my kin to walk alone."

"Why?"

He shrugged. "There's something I have to discover, but I don't what yet. I've been away from my tribe so long. I went into the wilderness. Lost touch. When I left, there was killing and killing and many faces."

He looked wistful, and I saw him scan the past with pain. The affinity deepened and I could say, "Some of them might still live."

He smiled and shrugged, as if it did not matter. "When I'm strong again, I'll continue my journey. The Uigenna want to stop me. They are mad and bitter. But there's a city I must seek across the desert. If they have built it yet."

"And you want me to come with you?" I asked, frowning. It seemed so unlikely.

He nodded, smiling his white grin at me. "Yes. You've no great yearning to stay here. You were waiting for me too."

"No, I wasn't, but neither do I want to stay here particularly. Why do you want me with you?"

"Because when I opened my eyes and saw your face, I knew you were kin. I couldn't believe it at first, because you are human, but now I accept it. You reached into death and took my hand, pulled me out. You knew what to do. I didn't tell you. And more than that, you *could* do it."

"That's true," I said. "It was instinctive. Strange, because any sensible human would have bashed out your brains with the nearest heavy object."

"Humans haven't been sensible for centuries, if ever."

I fixed him with a stare. "We know you take boys and make them like you, and that you kill everyone else. What exactly do you have planned for me?"

"I don't have any plans, just a feeling. We'll find out. Don't you feel it too, something waiting?"

I shrugged. "I'm not sure what I feel. This is all too surreal."

"You're a survivor," he said. "Strong..." He narrowed his eyes. "Somehow apart, disengaged. There are others like you, I've heard, though I've never met one. They are called Ruins Walkers, because they can pass through the dead places unscathed, perhaps not even seeing, just wandering, searching..." He shook his head. "Stories, maybe, but..."

"Yes, I *am* a Ruins Walker," I said. "I've walked through many, and at every boundary I cast off a part of myself."

"You can say that without bitterness."

"Apparently."

He blinked at me. "Can you get us horses? I smell there are some here."

I nodded, putting aside the vague sense of guilt that I'd be stealing from people who had little to start with. The few horses they had were precious. But then, what did it matter? It would be over for them soon enough, I was sure of it. "When do you want to leave?"

"Give me a day to rest..." He glanced at me sharply. "Think about it, Cereia. I can't force you to come with me, and I want you to do so with full awareness. You might be more alone with me than you've ever been, as if you've never felt loneliness before. I can offer you little more than a name. I can't promise anything, except the unexpected."

I knew it wouldn't be easy, but since when had my life been easy? I'd been coasting here, waiting, without knowing it. I knew I couldn't watch him leave alone. He offered me more than a name. He offered me life. My beautiful enemy. I hesitated at the top of the ladder, with a raging thought I had to voice. "You would have lived without me, I'm sure. You healed yourself."

He leaned forward, wisps of black hair curling round his shoulders. "No, not *all* by myself, Cereia. You have healing in you, but there is something else in you as well. I can sense it. We have a long journey ahead, though. I think there's much for both of us to learn."

I realised he was much older than he looked, then. It showed in his eyes. He was ageless, a supernatural creature in this old decaying world, and there was a whole race of his kind.

"Can you tell me your name?" I asked.

He seemed to think that was funny. "You don't know what you ask," he said. "For a har's name can be used against him. That's why not many use their true name. Only old and trusted friends are granted the knowledge of that. You can call me Kiya."

I was not sure whether that was his true name or not, but I accepted it anyway, and crawled down the ladder to seek my rest.

We left the farm in the dampness of an early morning that was like red milk spilled into the grass, which we crushed beneath our feet, reflecting light from the sun we could not yet see. From the paddock, the farm's glowing stallion came to Kiya's hand like a lamb, on light hooves, and I watched from the outside their communion of souls in the half light. I could see the great arch of the red neck, a black silhouette against the hazy eastern sky; the first bird rustled its feathers and twitched the leaves of the orchard trees. I urged Kiya to hurry, before the people rose from the bleak farmhouse and discovered our leaving. (Would I ever be missed? Would it ever be noticed I had gone?)

He leapt onto the stallion's back, bare legs scarred and skinny against the bright quivering flank. It came to me that I had always liked the horse without really noticing it. I opened the gate for them to come out onto the road.

He had constructed two makeshift bridles of hemp rope I had given him, and now put one over the head of the red stallion. It looked incongruously shabby next to the gleaming cheek, yet I doubt if Kiya really needed its discipline. Nervous and sensitive to his commands, the great beast tentatively ventured onto the earthy road, ears pricked forward and the whiskered chin held in against the broad chest.

I went to one of the mares, a dappled grey, and put the other bridle on her. She let me clamber onto her back and we went after Kiya. I had wrapped my meagre possessions in a blanket, which I now carried on my back, along with the food I had managed to steal from the farm that would sustain us for a while.

For what must have been only a few weeks, but that stretched like months, we travelled southwards, away from the farm and the ravaged cities of death and decay, to discover what had become of the hotter lands that lay below. Although the travelling was hard and mostly unpleasant, I came to be at peace with myself. Often, in the ruby light of our camp fires in the evenings, I pondered deeply upon the way of things, watching the stealthy shapes that slithered beyond the flames' hurled light. I tried to remember a world without fear, a world that flowed along oblivious, on well-oiled tracks, but sadly its memory was lost to me.

Kiya once asked me of my time in the City, but I felt uncomfortable recounting the gruesome tale to him. I didn't want to tell him the horrors his people had committed against my people, but he encouraged me until I felt I had no choice but to speak. As I did so, I fancied terrible phantoms leapt in the flames of the campfire.

Memories came back to me that I had buried. I remembered the horrific clamour of my brother's screams as they had dragged him from the ruins of our home. He'd been bleeding, filthy, his eyes rolling in his head, calling for our mother. My father had held her against his body in the rough shelter we had made behind the house. How they never found us crouching there in terror, I do not know. My mother's mind died that day, but her body survived for a while. Her suffering was too great, because of what happened to her son. She wanted to go to him, die *for* him and *with* him, but my father and I had sense enough by then to know it would constitute a pointless gesture. They would have cut her down long before she reached him, long before she could have sunk her own blade into his chest to spare him.

I'd wished never to think of these things again. It was useless self-torture, but at the end of my tale Kiya said the worst spectres have to be exorcised again and again, until their horror is lost in familiarity, and they are just like the leaves of dead newspapers, blowing along the ground.

He listened to me pulling out my demons, mostly in silence, not even wincing as I reviled and cursed his people in the names of as many gods as I could think of. One time, I blurted out, "Where were you, then, in all this carnage? Which city did you help destroy?"

He looked so serious, I immediately regretted it.

"Do I look like a murderer?" he asked. His voice had tightened, and I sensed his deep pain. "Is that what you really believe me to be?"

I stared at him for a moment. "No, Kiya, I don't. I'm sorry."

He sighed. "I wouldn't blame you if you did think that. How could I? But please try to understand. You've turned from your people by choosing my company. Wraeththu has sprung from the ruins of human civilisation. In a way, we're primordial. We're *meant* to be. This is our world now. Humans couldn't accept they'd had their chance and had ruined it. They tried to kill us all, take it back. They failed."

"You attach some great meaning to it all," I said. "But I believe your kind were simply an accident, some genetic fault. I don't know... But it *was* an accident. All I saw were mindless monsters."

Kiya was inscrutable. "You don't know anything." It wasn't an accusation, just a fact. He leaned towards me. "I *know* the truth, the reality. Perhaps we *were* an accident, yes, but perhaps evolution is always a series of fortunate accidents. I know you're curious about where I've been, during the Devastation. Well, if I told you I had been away from this world, what would you say?"

I shrugged. "I'd listen to you. I'd believe that you believe." I risked a smile. "I think secretly you see yourself as a Messiah to these... Wraeththu."

He laughed, fiddling with twigs at his feet and throwing them into the fire. "Cereia, you're harsh on me. I'm no Messiah come to unite the tribes of Wraeththu, but those I met on the other side bid me seek Immanion, the city of the Gelaming, built on ancient blood that is older than the earth."

"Immanion," I said. "What a beautiful name. But how have these *creatures* organised themselves into building cities? I thought they were nomadic, fighting and slaughtering where it pleased them."

"There's an endless desert," Kiya murmured, and his eyes clouded over with far images. "It has come back from the past when the world was young. Beyond its silence and its illusions lies Immanion, quiet and hidden as the strange little foxes that burrow under the sand. But it's difficult to enter. You can walk towards it forever and keep coming back to the place you started from. It's guarded by spirits that can warp time and space to their needs..."

"Kiya!" I interrupted harshly. "That doesn't answer my question. Did Wraeththu build it?"

"From the rabble that first ran naked in the streets, butchering people as they haggled at the markets, will rise the greatest race since before the time of humanity. How it shall come about, I do not know. But it has begun beyond the desert and we must go there."

"All right," I said, exasperated. I stood up and shook the tiny stones from my flesh that had affectionately buried themselves there. "Keep your secrets, but now I must sleep and you are occupying the only comfortable space. Let me share it so I can rest?"

"Ok," he said and moved to make a space. We slept close to one another, but far far apart.

He never answered my questions directly, always changing the subject subtly with every reply, or rambling on like some deranged prophet. At first it made me want to scream in frustration, but gradually, I became used to his meandering speeches, that were mostly like foretellings or accounts of dreams. At least it was entertaining.

But of course, you want to know more of the tribes of Wraeththu, as I did myself. Kiya was very eloquent concerning the folk lore and constitution of his kind, thus equipping me with a considerable store of knowledge that was often to prove useful to me.

Once he said to me, as we settled down to sleep, "You must have patience, but don't take me wrongly. Certain things must never be. The gulf you sense between us is more than you can imagine. It's an abyss no human woman has yet crossed. That would be death to whoever tried it. Yet here we are in the night, and we know each other."

He was not of this world, not as I know it. He was a beautiful monster that had risen up from a dissolute society of fools and murderers, destroyers and thieves: humanity. In my heart, I couldn't blame him for what he was. Idiocy had allowed his kind to thrive, and complacence had crowned his leaders. He told me many stories, but not about himself. In the dark, beneath the eyes of the stars, I wondered what he must have seen and done, and wanted to know, so badly. But even so, I was aware that come morning I'd shy away from the history in his gaze.

The Lion of Oomar

Watchful was a sure shaman. That is, he could clip you to a tree with his rap; his wordings were saga-speak.

"What's the stiffest thing you ever done, roon? Take the blood, burn a gun, skip coals, kill? Nah, stiffest thing you ever done was wordings. Yes, kid. Git scribin'."

He was wrong. Hardest thing I ever did was live. I was never slashed out to be a Wise.

Time beginning. Time beginning at break of day. This day: any day. My Ma found Jesus beneath the hen-house. A light, she said. A light that spoke to her.

So, what did it say, this light?

Sez: lead you out of here mammy, onto the golden hills and far away, skipping children at your feet. Glory be. And such like.

Took a gun to the last hired hand next day, she did.

Goodrun and I watched from the house roof, eating cherries, spitting out the stones onto the wiry lawn. Saw Ma's dress clinging to her legs as she strode down past the high barn. The gun was ridiculous; too big.

"Looks like trouble, cuz," Goodrun said.

She was right.

No, didn't happen that way. Nothing happened but sunlight on the roofs, between the leaves of the red-apple trees, sunlight on bare, kids' legs. We thought nothing would ever change.

We played house behind the barn, Cousin Goodrun and me.

"See, you have to kiss me, like this," she said.

I remember now her squishy soft lips, the giggle behind them, the warmth of summer on the back of my neck; all this. I remember too as we stomped in the dust behind the barn being man and woman, we heard the silence come down over the buildings, and the blue in the sky turn electric.

"Is it a storm coming?" Goodrun asked.

It was.

You tell stories.
Yes.
Tell mine.

So, I drag sticks through the desert dust, making pictures. I paint legends in blood. How much of it is true? Tue that Manticker the Seventy rose up out of the north and whipped his pretties down the eastern coast, gathering souls like dew in a cup as he came. True that in the rite of Neoma, of higher magic, hara drank blood; small stuff. I know because I did that myself. True, we were all dying before he came and sniffed us out, and Jesus beneath the hen-house was just one symptom of the death. But I did not know that then.

Not true that the path was paved in glory and that the sons of humankind bowed before him. Not true he was invincible. My family killed scores of his kind before they were overwhelmed. That made Manticker's tribe pretty angry. They shaved the heads of all male kids and then broke their ankles. This was done partly to stop them trying to escape until the althaia was done, and partly because they had to learn the hard way. I know this because it happened to me. The perfume of vomit and fear are as familiar as the corndust smell of the old high barn, and the stink it gave off as it burned.

Manticker the Seventy clothed himself in the skin of my Da and danced in the flame-light of the farm as it died. As we died. All of us.

What lives on in this skin is not the kid born in that place. Easier to describe than live it.

When it comes and grabs you, can't believe it. Ain't happening, cuz. Ain't happening.

Crippled and in fear. Background noise of laughter, pleadings, the gulpy breath of others lying near. Brothers, cousins; all lost that day. Just noises of agony, feebly moving, like pups taken too soon from the bitch and left to die.

Happened so quickly. The taste of Goodrun's kiss still on my tongue when the fleet shapes come slinking down the orchard, and the rosy day goes matt black. Still with me, the taste of girl and apple spit, as they push me back against the barn.

Who are they? Like ghosts or demons, dressed up in feathers, daub and blood. Faces painted like skulls. Hair stuck up in spikes. But they smelled of flowers.

So quick, no time to think. They lift me, break my bones, sling me over shoulders, carry me past upside-down world of smoke and screams to the place where the burning begins. My home burning down. A heap of bodies on fire, slow smouldering.

Goodrun, I never saw again. Never heard, even, her last scream.

Lying in the dust, they took us one by one. Used glass to cut. Blood running out. Blood pressed to blood. No time wasted. Soon time to move on. The smell of flowers covering everything – the stink of shit, burning meat, blood and fear.

Did you see the dew on the grass, the plump flesh hanging on the trees, the sunlight through green, did you? The peace of it, oh, the holy peace of it. Gone.

I was taken third from the pile of dying man-pups. Like the others, I squealed and pissed myself and begged for mercy. Like the others, the last skin of being not-har was falling away, like a thin dried leaf twisting on the wind, the thinnest of tissues burning. Even now, wish I'd had dignity, silence, eyes above the tree-tops, waiting. *You ain't touchin' my heart.* Memory's never faded. What I saw after filled in the gaps. Lion-head, golden mane. Bare, blood-streaked legs scrabblin' in the dirt. Cruel hands, white teeth. It was said they raped the ones they took. That was another untruth. Some things were always sacred to them.

Never hoped for a rescue. Most hume settlements kept to themselves, kept their heads down, but some were said to trade with the wraiths. Me, can't believe that. Saw no evidence of that on the march. Always conquest – hasty, fearful, lest the humes rise up, find some guts, fight back. Them hara were always afraid, no matter how much they thought themselves invincible.

As a little 'un, I'd thought 'bout dying, facing Mother Death. Even then, with dim, earthy wisiness, could sense the giving in you'd have to feel. Taking in the blood was like that. When they cut me, fear just went away. Pointless fear. Soon, I'd be in what came next. Nothing to be done about that. Nothing. The pain wasn't much.

The ones who took me were a hefty phyle of the Uigenna, Manticker their leader. It wasn't the way for them to forage so far south, but the swell of numbers in the north made life uneasy. Each tribe shouted they were the true Wraeththu and the others just runts. Uigenna no different in this respect. Had a strong creed, though, which gave them power. Loyalty to the tribe was fierce. And to make this grow in the hearts of the taken, they treated us like holy relics. Brutal to start with, brutal, but Paradise after.

Manticker divided the taken up between his shine hara. I was handed to some har of Wraxilan's, Manticker's biggest shine, along with a boy who was the son of one of my Da's farm-hands. Never knew him well before and never did afterwards. He didn't make it through the blood. Wraxilan wept in front of his hara when this happened, and ordered everyone to shed blood over the body. It was burned like at a proper funeral. Only half-made, I shivered and watched the flames from one of the wagons, knowing I'd never end up that way. I'd never be a Wise but I was – still am – a strong psych. If I'd been a friend of that boy before, he wouldn't have died. I shunned him because the psych in me saw that weakness.

For a long while, my world was the wagon, its jarring movement, the sounds just outside it, the view when the canvas came up, and the people sharing its space. There were two skinny hume girls (another myth stamped out) and four hara. Eight to a wagon was the usual way, so we had more space than most. Every evening they yapped on about Wraxilan. Manticker, they didn't mention much. All hara in the phyle hankered to share Wraxilan's blanket and, as there were thirty-eight or so of them, Wraxilan was never short of company. Pecking order was decided by sex. Manticker lay down for distant beings in the north and was submissive to them, in all ways. Beneath him, the troupe leaders bent their necks to his word and were submissive to him. Wraxilan went when Manticker sent a call; prettied himself up for that. He and hara like him had their own favourites, and hara like me knew our place with them. Strict order, but simple. Survival code more than anything.

Spitz and Shishi saw me through the althaia. It was like having a bad fever. Cold turkey from being hume. The girls were patient – good kids. After the other boy died, a tattooed har used to come and see how I was doing. Girls said he was called Fire Dog, a shine-har of Wraxilan's.

So quick, my old life faded away, until less than a memory. New life to begin with was the hurting, discomfort, and then the prayer of magical hands on sore, flaking skin, a swallow offered from a bowl that made me numb all over, the time they doused the lantern to help my stinging eyes.

Althaia lasted short days, but felt longer, like weeks, or a whole fucking life. At the end of it, I crawled to the light at the back of the wagon and saw there was still a world out there. But it was new too. No-one ever talks about the time before taking the blood and one day you just stop thinking 'bout it. The change takes away the past, so you can't live in it.

The phyle was heading south. We joined with a host of souls, other phyles, maybe three thousand in number. Couldn't travel together close, 'cause of needing to forage and hunt, but came together sometimes, like when we found hume strongholds. Until althaia was done, I travelled in the wagon, so could look out on the hara, women and animals walking together. We had horses, cattle, camels, huge fighting dogs, cats and birds.

The day althaia stopped, and I woke up proper har, I was welcomed into the phyle. That end of day, the girls washed me, while hara danced around the fire. I was told to choose some har and picked the prettiest. We went into the wagon together, and he showed me the mysteries of aruna, stuck me deep with a flower.

Next day, I walked outside with the others, and became a sand-runner. We had no clear destination, although the talk was that Wraxilan wanted to stop over someplace for a while. Manticker, even then, was skittish 'bout the Lion, and summoned him whenever there was time or space, trying to keep him loyal with the bond of flesh.

Wraxilan was lush beautiful. As a sand-runner, I watched him ride that golden, froth-maned mare he had then, his hair the same colour as her bright flanks. He often had murder in him, took offence easily, killed members of his own phyle if they pissed him off. Dazzled by his own splendour, he was. I wasn't into him, wouldn't see myself worshipping that ground he walked on. You can never feel safe with people like that. No firm foundation to base your opinions on.

One end of day, Fire Dog came to our fire and told us Wraxilan had asked for me. My heart turned into a rope and tied itself hard. Although he often did this with new bloodings, probably just to see if any of us were any good, I wasn't happy 'bout it. Maybe he'd see through a smile to what I thought of him. I'd have to play act. Wasn't natural in me to do that. My companions were easy-goes and I'd fitted in well with them. Wouldn't be like that with the Lion.

"He's heard 'bout you," Fire Dog said as we walked between the camp fires to the awning where Wraxilan held court.

"Heard what?" I asked.

"Things, that's all."

"So, what do I do?"

"Just do what he asks."

I thought then there might be shine in it for me. Do good and I'd not be sharing a wagon with six others.

There was no one at the awning. It flapped, torn. Fire Dog went ahead of me to the Lion's wagon, and then went away, flicking his fingers against his brow at me, grinning.

I was afire, mumbling sorceries, making up a mask and hoping it'd fit. Saw omens in the sky; clouds like faces, birds like a tattoo against them. Didn't realise, at first, there were others waiting with me. Didn't get picked, did I. *He* didn't pick anyone. Sent another to do that.

I wondered what he'd heard about me. Wondered why Fire Dog said that.

Half through the night, I gave up waiting and sat down against the wheels of the Lion's wagon. Got drunk with the others. Ended up in a hot tangle. Others were led beneath the canvas, but we couldn't hear anything. Didn't care. Had picked each other anyway.

In the morning, we moved on, into a blood-red sky. For a moment, in the night, I might've been a light, a har above others. Someone with a history that one day people would sing about. But the light had gone out in the dark, not been seen. That's what I felt, moving into the morning. The Lion rode his horse ahead of us, dyed pink and red in the rising day.

That's when Watchful found me. Caught me staring with a look on my face. "Don't peer long at the sun, roon. Har go blind that way."

"Sun, is it?" I said to him. "More like a fire, and fires burn out."

Watchful smacked me round the head. "Hush it, roon. You wanna burn out?" He gripped my face in his claws. Ugly fucker. Hardly a har at all, withered and bad-made, but gifted with a sight so strong he could see through stars in the sky. Every har I knew feared him and wanted to hear his words. He could make a new life for a har, they said, if he liked you good.

"You're gonna be mine," he said. "Gonna teach you, stupid little shit. Got that?"

I got it. Maybe the light hadn't gone out of me after all.

A Raven Bound with Lilies

From the Diary of Tyson-har-Parasiel

I am sixteen years old. They tell me I am adult and, and have been doing so for years. In some ways, I feel grownup, but sometimes it's as if time has passed too quickly and I'm still a harling. I envy all those lost human children, who could be young for so much longer than we can. There's something missing, some part of me. I'm not ready to function in the world beyond childhood.

Who am I? I am the High Priest, who shall be reviled and held in awe.

I am the son of Terzian the Varr, Phylarch of Galhea, whose body was burned by his hara in the fields beyond the town. His ashes touched me, borne on the cleansing wind. My hostling was the divine whore, who was worshipped behind locked doors. Prayers to him must involve lonely sobbing. Sacred gestures include the rending of flesh by desperate fingernails.

In his empty bedroom, rarely entered, the inner sanctum of the temple, I can still find his yellow-white hairs among the pillows. If I listen hard enough I can still hear the echo of his breath.

Here in this house, they never speak his name, afraid their voices will betray them. His name was Cal. Calanthe. Beauty and poison. This house will forever be his, for as long as we dwell in it.

I often feel like I'm hanging on a meat-hook, which has pierced my skin, the vertebra, the very nerves at the back of my neck.

Occasionally, this feeling will be accompanied by a hollow sickness, as if my body has been thoroughly gutted. This is not an hallucination, but merely a legacy. It's the consequence of being the son of gods. Dead gods.

I can't escape the lethal inheritance, which their holy, tainted blood left in my veins. In other hara's eyes, I'm a reincarnation of events that should have long been forgotten. I'm an open grave. I'm a hearse drawn by six black horses, standing in the rain. And with each smothered recognition of somehar I am not, the hook slices my flesh and I'm drawn upwards, on an invisible, bloodied chain, to hang there helpless, dangling, twisting.

I am the victim of possession, although I do not know the alien personalities seen so often peering from my face. Sometimes, I catch hara wincing as they watch me. Perhaps I've just uttered something in a certain way that brings back their memories. Perhaps I've simply smiled, and a dead god has mocked them with my face.

There was a time before I realised what was happening, a time when the child-me struggled – bewildered – with the strange, furtive glances of my family, their friends. I was growing up, and the dead gods bloomed within me like dusky, velvet-petalled flowers that grow poisonously in dark places. They took my form, my words, my laughter, my secrets.

I can remember the day when, for the first time, my half-brother Swift looked at me in that closed, pensive way, which later became so familiar. That was the first hook. I felt its cruel point score my spine, but remained outwardly untouched.

I said: "What is it?"

And Swift furrowed his brow, shaking his head. He didn't want to say, afraid to tell me the truth. "A look on your face," he said at last.

"What look?"

"It's gone now."

"You're weird!" I laughed and looked in the mirror, there in the room. My own face looked back. There was nothing different. Whatever had been in me had gone.

I can't remember them. My father. My hostling. Their faces are denied to me. There are no pictures of them displayed in the house. Unless you count me. I am their portrait, the sum of their profane union. The shadows of their legend stretched over my childhood, denied me innocence. But the truth was – and is – I can't live up to their reputation. As hara wince, I'm also conscious of a bizarre disappointment that follows in the wake of pain. My parents might look from my face but I am not them. I am not *them*.

Hara might want to shun me, yet at the same time are irresistibly drawn to the ghosts in my blood. They come to be flayed, but what pain I can give them lacks sweetness. It's empty of the divine breath. My hands are clumsy because theirs were so adept.

Although my parents' wickedness has been impressed upon me since the moment I could understand it, part of their sorcery is that hara still love them. I can smell it. I know because, on the anniversary of my father's death, hara build a bonfire in the same field where he was burned. There are no effigies, no prayers, only offerings tossed on the fire. I know because, on the same day every year, Cobweb lays a bunch of wild-flowers on the edge of the dry fountain in the summerhouse, by the yew-shrouded lake in the gardens. I'm not sure what anniversary this marks, but am certain it's connected with Cal. A birth, a death, a kiss? Something significant happened at the lake. It's impossible to walk there and not feel it.

It is night-time. By the haunted lake, I find myself awake and searching. The house looms in darkness behind me, glimpsed through the trees, and I am here, outside in the damp night. This is the very heart of the shrine. The omphalos of power. Here lie the holy artefacts: the tumbled rocks, the rain, the moss, where once a sacred footprint was pressed into the earth. Here, I am convinced, my hostling performed hallowed acts that became part of history, became a mummer's play. I'm sure my father's ghost stands here often, staring into the weed-choked depths, which are haunted by ancient fish of bronze and black, some the size of a new-born calf. This night, he called me from my sleep and I kneel beside the rain-dappled water.

"Take me, father," I say. "Take me to the place where there are no memories."

There is no answer, only the echo of sorrowful, mocking laughter in the highest branches of the evergreens.

Wet soil seeps through the knees of my trousers, into my pores. A smell of earth enshrouds me. A long-dead passion fills the sky with boiling, fevered emotion. Then it is only clouds, passing away, and there are no spirits. The moon shows its face.

We Dwell in Forever. This haven. This temple to dead gods.

Despite all this, I know that somewhere in the past were hara who started off ordinary, and for most of their lives must have been ordinary too. They ate, they slept, they spoke the same words everyhar else spoke. Not every sentence they uttered could have been an invocation, or a skein of poetry. Not every act toppled nations and houses, or was a murder.

And so... My brother and I walk out into the summer night. We tramp across the moon-drenched fields, drinking sheh. It's my birthday. I'm allowed this privilege.

I know there is little of Terzian in Swift. He looks like Cobweb, his hostling, yet the beauty is tempered with steel. He's eight years older than me. We're not far from the spot where Terzian was burned, but my hostling's ghost can't wander this far, because he didn't do anything significant in this place. He never came back to watch my father die, be burned. It's my birthday. I'm sixteen years old. This night, surely, I can ask a question and be answered.

"Tell me what he was really like," I say.

We stop walking. Swift glances at me, takes a swig of sheh. "Who?"

I don't say anything, just stare at him, point at my face. How could he pretend to be so stupid?

Swift sighs. "One day, long ago, our father fell in love, was tortured and abandoned. But curses can come back and this one did. If he hadn't, I wonder what our lives would have been like."

"I wouldn't have had one," I say.

Swift smiles. "True. Some good, then..." He takes a breath and his gaze becomes distant, fixed on the horizon. "The day he came back... The rooks had left the gardens some days before. We tried to protect ourselves..." He shakes his head. "I tried to bind him with iron. Didn't work."

"You're making no sense. And it doesn't answer the question."

"On the day he came back, I found a dead bird in the snow. Bigger than those who had left us. A raven. It *looked* dead, but I wonder now if it was. I brought your hostling back, I think, because I broke the ward that kept him away, and the ones I tried to build afterwards were useless."

"How did you bring him back?"

"I was still a small harling. I spoke his name aloud."

"And now you still fear to."

Swift nods. "He'd come back again. We can't risk that."

I thought he was joking. The dead can't come back, especially if they never went away. "Why not? You and Cobweb both adore him."

Swift smiles, a little crookedly. "It's still too soon, Ty, to talk about him."

"How many decades will it take?"

He shrugs.

"Just give me something, one detail of what he was like."

"A raven bound with lilies," Swift says.

"What?" I laugh at him, to smother the cold shiver that eels through my flesh.

"Part of him is a ruined carrion bird, with its eyes eaten away, its feathers moving with insects and grubs. A memory of splendour. Yet the remains are bound with white flowers that hold it all together. The flowers are love and memory."

"He's dead."

There is a pause. Then: "He's not, Ty."

I look into my brother's eyes. What is this I feel: shock, joy, horror? "How do you know?"

"I just do. Everyhar does."

"If he's alive, it's worse. It means he's forgotten me."

"Never that. One day he'll come back. He simply can't *now*."

I carry on walking and Swift follows. I shake my head. "Religion is for the mentally ill," I say. "Blind faith." Then I say. "I will never love. Shoot me if I do."

Swift laughs.

We walk in the moonlight, with the world spreading out forever around us. Swift puts an arm about my shoulders. We sing drunken songs to the night. I am the son of a raven bound with lilies. Within the bindings, the eyes aren't eaten away but bright and alive. The feathers aren't dull dead black but white gold.

Glossary of Terms

Aghama – (*ag*-am-ah) the first of all Wraeththu, regarded as a dehar.

Agmara – (ag-*mah*-rah) natural energy, equating to chi or ki, used for healing and manipulated to affect reality.

Ai Cara – a calendar era in the history of Wraeththu, which began when Pellaz har Aralis became the first Tigron of Immanion. Generally regarded as the hypothetical moment when Wraeththu began to realise their potential.

Alba Sulh – what was formerly the British Isles.

Althaia – (al-*thay*-uh) the process and period of change from human to har following inception.

Almagabra – lands corresponding roughly to what was once Mediterranean Europe.

Archon – the overall leader of a tribe.

Arojhahn – (ah-roh-*zharn*) a season festival, the ritual to celebrate it.

Arotohar – (A-*rot*-oh-hah) the name given to the Wheel of the Year, the annual cycle of eight seasonal festivals.

Aruna – (ah-*roo*-nah) sexual union between hara that is both spiritual and physical.

Arunic – pertaining to aruna.

Astale – (ass-*tar*-lay) a ritual word of invitation and welcome, also a term of respect, most often used to greet invoked dehara.

Chesna – (*chez*-nah) a close relationship, a chesna-bond can be equated to marriage.

Chesnari – (chez-*nah*-ree) a partner in a chesna-bond.

Colurastes – (Col-ur-*ast*-eez) a tribe also known as the Serpent Hara, who have a particular affinity with snakes, and are famous for their hair, imbued with magical properties.

Dehar – (*day*-hah) a Wraeththu deity (pl. Dehara).

Devastation, the – one of many terms used to describe the final days of humanity, when the world was in turmoil, and there was catastrophic conflict between hara and humans. The days of change.

Ferelithia – (feh-ruh-*lith*-ee-ah) a town in Almagabra.

Feybraiha – (fay-*bray*-ah) a period of time equating to puberty in humans when a har matures sexually. The term also refers to a day of celebration for this. At the end of his feybraiha, when he is physically ready, a har will take aruna with another for the first time. This is regarded as an important rite of passage.

First Generation – hara who were became Wraeththu by being incepted as humans.

Gelaming – (*jel*-ah-ming) the most influential tribe of Wraeththu, whose tribal home is Almagabra.

Har – a Wraeththu individual (pl. hara).

Harakin – a term used by a har to describe members of his family, or within small phyles, other phyle members. Also *kinshara*.

Harhune – (hah-*hoon*) a ceremony during which inception takes place, the transfusion of blood that turns a human to har.

Harling – a young har not yet at feybraiha.

Herohara – hara of note or myth.

Hienama – (high-en-*ah*-mah) equivalent of a priest/teacher/ healer.

Housebar – a member of the household staff.

Hurakin – relatives.

Immanion – principle city of Almagabra, founded by the Gelaming tribe, regarded as a centre of culture and learning.

Inception – the process by which a human becomes har, involving a transfusion of blood.

Kanene – (ka-*nee*-nee) hara more than usually adept in the arts of aruna, especially of a darker nature, who sell their services to other hara. Kanene are regarded with contempt by the majority of hara, since aruna is viewed as a sacred act, and the practices of kanene as profane or sacrilegious.

Keephar – an innkeeper/landlord.

Kinshara – members of a phyle, sometimes bloody family

Mahallatu – a group of capricious spirits.

Majhahn – (mazh-*arn*) a ritual.

Megalithica – the landmass once known as North America.

Nayati – (Nigh-*ah*-tee) a temple or sacred space for spiritual work.

Ouana – (oo-*ah*-nah) the masculine aspect of Wraeththu.

Pearl – the egg or sac within which a harling forms. Hara carry pearls within their bodies, which are expelled or 'born' some weeks before the harling reaches to state to emerge. Pearl is also a term of affection used by harish parents for their offspring. (*With pearl* – a har who is carrying a pearl.)

Phylarch – leader of a phyle.

Phyle – a distinct community within a tribe, a sub tribe.

Pureborn – a har who has been born to harish parents rather than inception from human. A second-generation har and beyond.

Nahir Nuri – (na-*heer noo*-ree) a har of high spiritual rank, who has undergone all caste training.

Soume – (*soo*-mee) the feminine aspect of Wraeththu.

Sulh – a tribe of Alba Sulh, know for their magical abilities.

Swan-Wyrd – a har who has shamanic attunement with the swan.

Tiahaar – (*tee*-ah-hah) a polite form of address (as in Sir, Madam).

Tigrina – (tig-*ree*-nah) a ruler of Wraeththu, of the Gelaming tribe, in the city of Immanion.

Tigron – (*tee*-gron) a ruler of Wraeththu, of the Gelaming tribe, in the city of Immanion.

Uigenna – (*ew*-ee-*genn*-ah) one of the first Wraeththu tribes, renowned for their ferocity.

Unneah – (oo-*nay*-uh) a Wraeththu tribe of Megalithica.

Unthrist – hara who belong to no tribe.

Woodshara – small tribes who choose to live in wild, forest areas rather than in larger towns, or be part of a greater community.

Wraeththu – (*ray*-thoo) androgynous race that came to replace humanity.

About the Author

Storm is the creator of the Wraeththu Mythos, the first trilogy of which was published in the 1980s. However, the influences and inspirations for the Wraeththu world go much further back than that, and continue into the future as she plans more stories for it.

Her other full length works cross genres from science fiction, to dark fantasy, to epic fantasy, to slipstream. She has written over thirty books, including full length novels, novellas, short story collections and non-fiction titles. Her short stories, which she continues to write prolifically, appear in diverse magazines and anthologies.

Storm is the founder of Immanion Press, created initially to publish her out-of-print back catalogue, but which evolved into the thriving venture it is today. Her interests include magic and spirituality, movies, music and MMOs. Among her many occupations, most of which are unpaid, she runs a guild called Equilibrium on the EU servers of World of Warcraft. She lives in the Midlands of the UK with her husband and four cats.

IMMANION PRESS
Purveyors of Speculative Fiction

The Lightbearer by Alan Richardson

Michael Horsett parachutes into Occupied France before the D-Day Invasion. He is dropped in the wrong place, miles from the action, badly injured, and totally alone. He falls prey to two Thelemist women who have awaited the Hawk God's coming, attracts a group of First World War veterans who rally to what they imagine is his cause, is hunted by a troop of German Field Police who are desperate to find him, and has a climactic encounter with a mutilated priest who believes that Lucifer Incarnate has arrived...

The Lightbearer is a unique gnostic thriller, dealing with the themes of Light and Darkness, Good and Evil, Matter and Spirit.

"The Lightbearer is another shining example of Alan Richardson's talent as a story-teller. He uses his wide esoteric knowledge to produce a story that thrills, chills and startles the reader as it radiates pure magical energy. An unusual and gripping war story with more facets than a star sapphire." – Mélusine Draco, author of "Aubry's Dog" and "Black Horse, White Horse". ISBN: 978-1-907737-63-3 £11.99 $18.99

Dark in the Day, Ed. by Storm Constantine & Paul Houghton

Weirdness lurks beyond the margins of the mundane, emerging to dismantle our assumptions of reality. Dark in the Day is an anthology of weird fiction, penned by established writers and also those new to the genre – the latter being authors who are, or were, students of Creative Writing at Staffordshire University, where editor Storm Constantine occasionally delivers guest lectures. Her co-editor, Paul Houghton, is the senior lecturer in Creative Writing at the university.

Contributors include: Martina Bellovičová, J. E. Bryant, Glynis Charlton, Storm Constantine, Louise Coquio, Elizabeth Counihan, Krishan Coupland, Elizabeth Davidson, Siân Davies, Paul Finch, Rosie Garland, Rhys Hughes, Kerry Fender, Andrew Hook, Paul Houghton, Tanith Lee, Tim Pratt, Nicholas Royle, Michael Marshall Smith, Paula Wakefield, Ian Whates and Liz Williams.
ISBN: 978-1-907737-74-9 £11.99, $18.99

Blood, the Phoenix and a Rose by Storm Constantine

Wraeththu, a race of androgynous beings, have arisen from the ashes of human civilisation. Like the mythical rebis, the divine hermaphrodite, they represent the pinnacle of human evolution. But Wraeththu – or hara – were forged in the crucible of destruction and emerged from a new Dark Age. They have yet to realise their full potential and come to terms with the most blighted aspects of their past. Blood, the Phoenix and a Rose begins with an enigma: Gavensel, a har who appears unearthly and has a shrouded history. He has been hidden away in the house of Sallow Gandaloi by Melisander, an alchemist, but is this seclusion to protect Gavensel from the world or the world from him? As his story unfolds, the shadow of the dark fortress Fulminir falls over him, and memories of his past slowly return. The only way to find the truth is to go back through the layers of time, to when the blood was fresh. ISBN: 978-1-907737-75-6 £11.99, $18.99

The Weird Tales of Tanith Lee

"A story by Tanith Lee unveils a voice alone, a true Scheherazade, someone with a distinctive vision of the world and who explored that world, or those worlds to be accurate, with a highly perceptive and mindful set of eyes."

From the introduction, by Mike Ashley

This anthology of twenty-eight tales comprises all the short stories by Tanith Lee that were published in the seminal magazine *Weird Tales* during her lifetime. Some of them are previously uncollected, and appeared in print only in the magazine, so will be new to many of Tanith's fans. Her highly-respected and influential work spanned every genre, and this sumptuous collection demonstrates the range of her versatility. From the dark high fantasy of 'The Sombrus Tower', through the Arthurian-influenced 'The Kingdoms of the Air', the achingly beautiful 'Stars Above, Stars Below' of a science-fantasy Mars, the sinister retelling of a fairy tale in 'When the Clock Strikes', and the almost whimsical steampunk of 'The Persecution Machine', *The Weird Tales of Tanith Lee* showcases the myriad styles of the writer rightly known as the High Priestess of Fantasy.
ISBN: 978-1-907737-73-2, £11.99 $18.99

Immanion Press
http://www.immanion-press.com
info@immanion-press.com

NEWCON PRESS

http://newconpress.co.uk/

The very best in fantasy, science fiction, and horror

The Ion Raider by Ian Whates

As Corbin Drake receives his most unusual assignment for First Solar yet – one which he suspects is a trap but knows he can't refuse – his former crew, the notorious brigands known as the Dark Angels, are being hunted down one by one and murdered. Determined to find those responsible before they find her, Leesa teams up with Jen, another former Dark Angel, and together they set out to thwart the mysterious organization known as Saflik, little dreaming where that path will lead them.

ISBN: 978-1-910935-38-5 £12.99 paperback (Also in signed limited edition hardback)

The Best of British SF, 2016 edited by Donna Scott

Editor Donna Scott has selected the very best short fiction by British authors published during 2016. Twenty-four stories, from established names and rising stars, including Joanne Hall, Peter F. Hamilton, Eric Brown & Keith Brooke, Gwyneth Jones, Nick Wood, Robert Bagnall, Neil Davies, Liam Hogan, Jaine Fenn, Sarah Byrne, Ian Watson, Una McCormack, Den Patrick, Paul Graham Raven, Adam Roberts, Natalia Theodoridou, Sylvia Spruck Wrigley, Tricia Sullivan, Tade Thompson, Ian Whates, Neil Williamson, Michael Brookes, Adam Connors and E. J. Swift.

Available as a numbered limited edition hardback, each copy signed by the editor, and an A5 paperback.

ISBN: 978-1-910935-40-8 (hardback) £24.99, 978-1-910935-41-5 £12.99 (softback)

CPSIA information can be obtained
at www.ICGtesting.com
Printed in the USA
BVHW082308151020
591039BV00003B/149